WUTHERING NIGHTS

WUTHERING NIGHTS

An Erotic Retelling of
Wuthering Heights

EMILY BRONTË
and I. J. MILLER

GRAND CENTRAL
PUBLISHING

NEW YORK   BOSTON

Copyright © 2013 by Ira Miller

Grand Central Publishing
Hachette Book Group
237 Park Avenue
New York, NY 10017

www.HachetteBookGroup.com

Printed in the United States of America

RRD-C

First Edition: April 2013
10 9 8 7 6 5 4 3 2 1

Grand Central Publishing is a division of Hachette Book Group, Inc.
The Grand Central Publishing name and logo is a trademark of Hachette Book Group, Inc.

The Hachette Speakers Bureau provides a wide range of authors for speaking events. To find out more, go to www.hachettespeakersbureau.com or call (866) 376-6591.

The publisher is not responsible for websites (or their content) that are not owned by the publisher.

Library of Congress Cataloging-in-Publication Data

LCCN: 2012956205
ISBN 978-1-4555-7302-8

For my father, in appreciation of his ongoing love, support, and inspiration

WUTHERING NIGHTS

PROLOGUE

You venture to the northern part of England to a county called Yorkshire to visit its unspoiled, beautiful countryside and picturesque villages. You make it to the moors, an isolated area often victim to the atmospheric tumult of stormy winds. You come to a rough stone pillar where the road divides. The cut letters T.G. point to the north, toward Thrushcross Grange, an eighteenth-century estate completely modernized as a hotel with square, drywalled rooms, central air, cable television, and free Wi-Fi. You choose to follow the arrow labeled W.H., walking the two miles southwest—passing stunted firs bowed by the wind—until you come upon the strong, sturdy entrance of a fine bed-and-breakfast. Pass through the gates and witness a quantity of exquisite carvings depicting fiery griffins and dancing children along its wood frame. In sight of the main building, it is clear the architect had the foresight to build it strong, the narrow windows deeply set in the wall, and the corners defended with large jutting stones. A sign greets all who pass: WELCOME TO WUTHERING HEIGHTS.

Good fortune be with you and a warm, friendly greeting shall be made by one of the proprietors, either Mr. or Mrs. Earnshaw, a comely couple, the seventh generation of Earnshaws to call the Heights their home. There is a hearty meal of roast lamb finished off with the appropriate pudding, and the most delightful conversation around the main floor fireplace, cavernous and open, its ventilation ideal for roaring flames. After extracting a promise of fried eggs with bangers and mash for breakfast, you retire to your room.

As fate would have it, you are shown to the HeathCath suite, a chamber so quaint one half expects to be led there by candlelight. The space is bare, with a wood chair, a small table, a reading lamp, and a large four-poster bed headed by two enormous pillows. The bathroom is down the hall and shared by all on the floor, although on this night only HeathCath is occupied.

There is no telly, no Internet, no room phone, and no cell service. After a rousing windswept hike, a splendid meal, a warm fire, amicable company, and a promise of a rich breakfast, what else is there to do but turn in? Stripped to underwear, hand above the light switch, you notice—carved deeply into the wooden wall in a childish, crooked scrawl—a small clue to the unusual name of the suite:

HEATHCLIFF & CATHERINE.

Room dark, nearly naked, you hurry to climb under the thick, colored quilt, to rest head on pillow, to escape the cold rush of noisy air seeping through the nooks and crannies of the walls, to find some welcome warmth. Resting peacefully, finally, there still remains a rush from this glorious day. But the room is too chilled, the wood floor too cold to venture out from under the soothing comfort of the quilt to read a book, or make a note.

The hand wanders straight down the body, perhaps impatient for either satisfaction or sleep, and begins a gentle teasing between the thighs. Mmm, yes. For if there is joy there, then it is truly a coupling with someone loved. The eyes close. The hand picks up pace. There is a flush of heat to the chest. Fingers caress an erect nipple. The contentment inspired by this robust isolation, this wonderful, familiar touch, encourages a quick, deep arousal. And perhaps it would all be over soon if not for the sudden, startling crash of sound filling the room. Hand quick to retreat, eyes dart open. Was it a thunder of wind against the glass that made such an explosive noise? A fir bough banging against the outside walls? You listen carefully, wondering if Mr. or Mrs. Earnshaw have been awakened and are surveying the house for damage. No additional sounds. But then it is as if the window has been flung wide open as a quick cannonball of gust bursts through and funnels about the room like a dark tornado, lamp and table to the floor, your hair on end. Then stillness. Then silence.

Pleasure far away now, fear arises, because you realize that the window is completely intact, still shuttered closed. Nothing more happens. You hope to write it off to the rich food, or the mysterious state between full consciousness and sleep, or the naughtiness of pleasuring yourself in a strange bed used by others, but you are again startled, this time by the sight of two unearthly figures hovering near the ceiling: a man and a woman, translucent, completely naked. She has long flowing dark hair, thick and wild, a perfectly symmetrical face, and full breasts, capped with lovely delicate nipples. He is tall, athletic, very well formed, darkly complected, with eyes full of black fire. Although fright is the first order from this apparition, it is quickly replaced by curiosity, as the figures float down and settle comfortably in bed with you.

You are not sure of the exact state you are in. It could be a retreat to the borders of sleep, a yielding to the heat of fantasy, a search for the full passion of a sensual dream. Regardless, a certain serenity settles upon you while lying not beside, but *within* these two kindred spirits. With serenity comes vision; with vision comes full emotions, from bitter hate to intense love, from warm acceptance to cold revenge, from fiery anger to perfect joy. You must not fight, but welcome this possession at the moors. To those of a welcoming nature, all the secrets and passions of Wuthering Heights, of Heathcliff and Catherine, will be revealed...

Volume I

CHAPTER ONE

One fine summer morning—it was the beginning of harvest—Mr. Earnshaw, the old master, came down the stairs, dressed for a journey. He turned toward Hindley, his son of fourteen, and Catherine, his daughter of eight.

"I'm going to Liverpool today. What shall I bring you both? You may choose what you like, only let it be little, for I shall walk there and back, sixty miles each way."

Hindley named a fiddle and Catherine, a lass who could ride any horse in the stable, chose a whip.

It seemed a long while, the three days of his absence, and often little Catherine asked when he would be home. Mrs. Earnshaw expected him by supper time of the third evening. She put that meal off hour after hour. At just about eleven o'clock, the door latch was finally raised and in stepped the master. He threw himself into a chair, laughing and groaning, and bid them all stand off, for he was nearly killed and would not have another such walk for three kingdoms.

"At the end of it, to be frightened to death!" he said, opening his greatcoat, which he bundled up in his arms. "See here, wife, you mustn't take it as a gift from God, although it's as dark almost as if it came from the devil."

The family crowded around, and, over Miss Catherine's head,

was a peep of a dirty, ragged, black-haired child, big enough to walk and talk, with a face that looked older than Catherine's. Yet it stared blankly and repeated some gibberish that nobody could understand. Mrs. Earnshaw was ready to fling the child out the door. She did fly up, asking how could he fashion to bring that gypsy brat into the house when they had their own young ones to feed and fend for?

The master tried to explain the matter, but he was really half dead with fatigue, and all that could come across, amongst the scolding of his wife, was a tale of his seeing the young one starving, and homeless, and as good as dumb in the streets of Liverpool. Not a soul knew to whom it belonged, he said, and his money and time being both limited, he thought it better to return home with him, at once, than run into vain expenses there, because he was determined he would not leave the boy wandering the streets.

The mistress finally grumbled herself calm and the master called for Nelly, the housekeeper, a lady just eight years Hindley's senior, with fiery red hair and ample bosom, to wash it and give it clean things and let it sleep with the children.

Hindley and Cathy contented themselves with looking and listening till peace was restored, then both began searching their father's pockets for the presents he had promised them. When the former drew out what had been a fiddle, crushed to morsels in the greatcoat, he blubbered aloud. Catherine, when she learned the master had lost her whip in attending to the stranger, showed her humor by grinning and spitting at the stupid little boy, earning for her pains a sound blow from her father to teach her better manners.

The boy was christened Heathcliff, the name of a son who died in childhood, and it served as both his Christian and surname.

Despite the rough start, Miss Catherine took an immediate liking to him, but Hindley outright hated the lad, and went at him shamefully, Heathcliff's stoical response inspiring even more ill-treatment.

Old Earnshaw became furious when he discovered his son persecuting the poor, fatherless child, as he called him. He took to Heathcliff strangely, believing all he said, although it was precious little, and petting him up far above Catherine, who was too mischievous and wayward to be a favorite.

Over the next several years, the bad feeling between Hindley and Heathcliff multiplied, Mrs. Earnshaw passed, and the master, too, began to fail. He had been active and healthy, yet his strength left him suddenly. When he was confined to the chimney corner he grew monumentally irritable. The littlest thing vexed him, and suspected slights of his authority, or any ill turn directed toward Heathcliff, threw him into fits.

One morning, Catherine announced she was throwing a tea party that very afternoon and the entire household was invited. Hindley smirked. The master grumbled unintelligibly from his corner. Heathcliff asked what he could do to help.

Catherine, growing faster than her years, tested everyone's patience at least fifty times a day. From the hour she came down the stairs, till she went to bed, there seemed not to be a minute's security without her mischief. Her spirits were always at high-water mark, her tongue always wagging—singing, laughing, and plaguing everybody to do the same. But she had the bonniest eye, sweetest smile, and lightest foot in the parish. After all, she meant no harm, perhaps. Once she made you cry in good earnest, it seldom happened that she would not keep you company and offer soothing remarks until you quieted.

It was agreed by all, except perhaps the master, that Catherine was much too fond of Heathcliff. The greatest punishment she could receive was to be kept separate from him. Then her mood turned dark, her countenance sullen, and all knew it wise to leave the lass to her room. For Heathcliff, separation from his companion was about the only thing that could etch misery onto his dark brow and he would refuse to take food, or exit his room until the pair was, once again, united.

"All assemble," proclaimed the young lady on the designated afternoon. She had donned her Sunday's best and carefully arranged the house's finest china around the table, places set for five.

A new round of grumblings from the master and he refused to move.

"I'm done with such playthings, sister," said Hindley. "And you might learn from that."

"Pooh," said Catherine. "This is not a child's party. Do you see any of my pets? It is for gentlemen and ladies. Perhaps you do not count yourself among that group."

"The setting is lovely, miss," said Nelly, hoping to prevent an altercation, which would surely provoke the master into one of his coughing fits. She sat at the table.

Heathcliff arrived wearing his Sunday's best as well, but it had been many Sundays since he last attended church, ever since the parson had called him a "bastard child" and threatened to baptize him on the spot. The lad of thirteen had grown mightily in the last year and the tops of his socks were clearly visible below the hem of his trousers, his cuffs flowered from the shortness of his jacket sleeve, and all buttons looked ready to burst.

"There's your gentleman, Catherine," said Hindley, "a true squire if there ever was one, looking gift wrapped for Christmas and smelling mightily of the barn."

"Hush," said Catherine, but she could not contain her giggles and this caused Heathcliff to turn red as the fire's embers, for it was only Catherine's opinions that seemed to carry true meaning to the young lad. He sat, lowering his head toward the table.

"Look, Father," said Hindley, as he approached Heathcliff and began a forceful pinching along his arm that the lad bore without blinking or shedding a tear. "Here sits the ragamuffin you prefer so to your own flesh and blood. And perhaps he is, at least that is what Ma believed."

"'Tis a lie!" cried the old man, finding the strength to rise to his feet with the aid of his walking stick. "And you were born a heathen to repeat it." The stick came crashing down on Hindley's back, as he crouched before the blow. Tears formed in his eyes as he left the room in shame.

Heathcliff's own eyes rose from the table and he could not hide the joy in seeing his oppressor get his due. That was when Catherine slapped him boldly across the face, leaving a mark of rouge. "Do not take pleasure in my brother's misery."

Heathcliff did not lower his eyes, nor voice a complaint. He could not take his eyes from Catherine, like a puppy staring at his mistress. He knew all that was Catherine: the dainty lady, the generous riding companion, the thoughtful playmate, the wild rogue who could turn harsh as quickly as milk left to the sun. Heathcliff knew this and it still did not sway his affections.

"Children, please," said Nelly.

"I'm not a child," said Catherine.

"True," said Mr. Earnshaw, falling back into his chair, a deep wheeze escaping his chest. He looked toward the fire. "The devil."

"You've ruined my party," Catherine said plainly, then left the room, though there were no tears from this young hellion. Nelly cleared the table. Heathcliff sat on the floor, next to the old man, near the fire, and was rewarded with the master's hand resting fondly at his shoulder.

At last the curate, the one who taught the Earnshaws and the Lintons (the family north at Thrushcross Grange)—who had witnessed the elder son's many manifestations of scorn toward both his father and Heathcliff—suggested that Hindley be sent to college, and Mr. Earnshaw agreed, though with heavy spirit, for he said, "Hindley was not born to thrive at the Heights, but who knows if he will be happier to wander?"

Hindley rejoiced in this opportunity to further his education, be rid of an oppressive, ailing father, a sister who seemingly felt no love for him, and, most significantly, be banished from the presence of a gypsy knave who had brought nothing but a dark cloud over Hindley's own head since the day he arrived with the gift of a crushed fiddle.

With Hindley gone, Nelly just able to keep order at the house, the young pair aged into teen adolescence and ran like wild, rude savages. Often, even Catherine would not be seen at Sunday church. Nelly, at the request of the old master, who now rarely left the bed, would deny Catherine supper and order the stable hand, Joseph, to thrash Heathcliff until his own arm ached. The curate took on the cause, banning Heathcliff from his lessons and setting many chapters for Catherine to learn by heart. The boy bore any degradation well, unfeeling toward the beatings, happy that Catherine taught him what she learned. Young Catherine would laugh at any punishment the minute the pair were together again, at least the minute they had contrived some naughty plan of revenge: The curate found his notebook misplaced, Joseph mysteriously fell off a horse while galloping on a loosened saddle, and who could have snipped a long lock of Nelly's hair in the middle of the night?

Their chief amusement was to run away to the moors in the morning and remain there all day. That was where they discovered Black Rock Cragge.

Well hidden, the place was a perfect union of height and depth, just about centered between Thrushcross Grange and Wuthering Heights, inhabited by clutters of black rock that sharpened at the top like arrows pointing toward the sky. They provided strong shelter from the ever-present winds and offered a multitude of hiding places from any stray traveler who happened to wander this far off the road, which was rare. Below the precipice on which the rocks lay was a sixty-foot drop into a pool of black water, surrounded by more sharp rocks, the liquid surface seemingly reflecting all of its surrounding stone. It was said that in a time long past, there was volcanic activity at this site and these rocks were the last remnants. The pool itself was supposed to have had warm healing powers for all who bathed there, but now it was completely fresh cold water that funneled itself to a river serving most of the farms in the region.

On this day, dress already slightly torn, face blackened with the grime of play, while walking along the dirt road, Catherine challenged Heathcliff to a race and was off to the rocks before such challenge was accepted.

"Unfair!" shouted Heathcliff, although he knew that no protest would be favorably received, so he dashed off after her.

Being much bigger and stronger, Heathcliff could have overcome Catherine before the rocks, but he reduced his strong pace, allowing her to win, knowing this left a much better chance for her mood to stay sweet, as she was.

If Catherine knew of his yielding, she certainly gave no indication as she flopped in the tall grass by the first group of rocks. "A fine strapping lad you are," she said, "losing to a lass like me."

He dropped down beside her, breathing far less heavy than she. "No shame in losing to one as beautiful as you."

"Oh, Heathcliff." She took his hand in hers. "When I am with you, everything seems perfect."

He nodded, staring into the lovely face of his friend. There were so many words he wished to speak, ones that mouthed his gratitude for her welcoming him so warmly into the fold of Wuthering Heights; that revealed the ever-present thoughts that dwelled on her beauty; that expressed the joy he felt every time she graced him with her company. But he felt that he might fumble, say the wrong thing, or use an incorrect word, and would risk the brunt of her mockery, or, even worse, her displeasure. Pleasing her was all he wanted. He was nothing compared to her, but when he was with her, he felt a reason to live.

She brushed the wild hair from his face. They were on their sides now, faces just inches away, staring into each other's dark eyes, their breath mixing as they spoke. "Will you promise never to leave me?" she asked.

He could not meet her gaze. He turned away and formed his words carefully. "Will you promise never to forsake me?"

"I would never do such a thing."

He turned back to her. "Then I promise never to leave you."

"What would I do without you, my love?"

Her tender expression caused his heart to soar and his words to flow with greater ease. "The Heights would be hell if it were not for you, dear Catherine, even with Hindley gone. It is for you that I wake each morn."

"I, too."

There was a pause in speech as their eyes locked again, a heated moment forming where it seemed that they would press forward for their very first kiss. Instead Catherine said, "Will you swear your love for me?"

"What would such a swearing mean?" replied Heathcliff.

"It might relieve my dark dreams."

"I hear your cries at night and lay awake full of sadness."

"I feel so alone sometimes." With her mother passing, father ill, brother turned cold, Catherine was not always the free spirit upon whom Nelly doted. "In the morn, I can't wait to see your face and then it is like I am reborn." Without a mother to prepare her, the prospects of a future with a proper gentleman were slim. Only Heathcliff could bring sense to her world and make the sun shine in a sky full of heavy, dark clouds.

"Sleep is death for me until I see you," said Heathcliff.

Though she believed his words, they did not seem enough to quell her apprehension. "Then don't you see how important it is to swear our love, how important that we seal it in a way that cannot be broken?"

"Aye. Then I will swear it."

"As do I."

"But how shall we seal it?" he asked, for he did not just want their moments, he wanted their lifetime, together.

She dropped her hand from his face and turned on her back, thinking. Then finally she remarked, with hard decisiveness, "The pool."

"There is no way down from this cliff."

"We jump."

"Madness."

"It is there for us, at this place, our place," said Catherine. "It calls us."

"Who knows of its depths? Any error means doom against the rocks."

"Is death not worth a risk for true love?"

Heathcliff felt compelled to nod agreement.

"Let's," she said.

Catherine stood up, took his hand, pulled him to his feet, and led him to the edge of the precipice.

Below them lay the pool of black, a circle no more than five yards in diameter.

Hands still held, their eyes locked.

"You first or me?" asked Heathcliff.

"Together," said Catherine, knowing full well this choice made death even more imminent.

That was when Heathcliff steeled his nerves . . . for he realized that death with Catherine would be no different than life, as long as they were together.

They jumped.

And fortunately for them, their aim was true and the pool was deep.

They plunged hard, but straight, the blow of water nearly knocking them unconscious. But they surfaced together, bodies atremble from the rush of feelings.

"A true test," declared Heathcliff, spitting water from his mouth.

"I know now our love can survive anything."

With a half stroke she was closer to him. Treading water, at the center of the pool below Black Rock Cragge, they kissed, for the very first time, deeply, arms hugging tightly, bodies wrapped together, catching their breath with the help of each other's mouth, as the warmth of their sweet love stifled the chill of the water and soothed any unease in their souls.

Catherine broke away suddenly with a nervous lurch. "A snake, a serpent has brushed against my leg."

Heathcliff turned crimson with embarrassment and ducked his head underwater.

It became clear to Catherine that the serpent was the growth, the hardness of Heathcliff's uncontrolled male feelings. How thrilling it was that the touch of their lips could raise such a powerful surge through her body and inspire such a potent reaction in Heathcliff. She longed for the heat of his mouth again, and perhaps another brush with the well-formed power of the serpent. But was this what a lady should desire from a gentleman?

He resurfaced and she struck as quick as any cobra, raking her nails across Heathcliff's cheek, drawing blood.

"Godless knave!" she cried. "You have tainted the purity of our love with your base passion. Must you always be the son of a gypsy whore?"

Heathcliff remained on the surface this time, unblinking, as he met her cold gaze, a tremble within him, not from the chill of the water, but from the betrayal of his body, which had ruined the most perfect of unions.

She turned and swam toward the river. He followed.

He wanted to explain that his erect feelings had come without thinking, uncontrolled, inspired by her brave leap and warm lips, and that nothing could taint their love. But it would risk another dose of her venomous wrath, a fury he deserved after proving, once again, that she was right, that he must be the son of some gypsy whore or the unwanted bastard of a thief or a peasant; that he was impure, an animal, who had fallen in love with the most elegant and lovely of human creatures.

Proven even further—as their swim to the river turned into yet another race—because no other thoughts flooded his brain except how to obtain another sweet kiss from his beloved.

CHAPTER TWO

The leap, the cold swim, the walk back to the Heights, did Catherine in. She immediately took to her bed, where she remained for several days, feverish and weak. Nelly was the one who brought light toast and tea, a cold cloth for the forehead, but it was only Heathcliff who could bring comfort.

Moving in and out of consciousness, Heathcliff at her side, she had deeply troubled and passionate dreams where she felt close to death, but even worse, ones where she saw herself separated from her closest companion. Upon awakening in a cold sweat, seeing Heathcliff, she was immediately brought back to earth in a joyful return. She thought of sharing her ominous dreams, full of large venomous snakes, purplish and red in face, spitting and lunging, that both repelled and beckoned her at the same time. She felt compelled to run but always remained fixed, unable to resist the lure of the hypnotic swaying of the large serpent.

"It is sweet to see your face," she said to Heathcliff. She could not bring herself to reveal to him that in her dreams she understood Heathcliff completely, as she understood herself, and that she was he, and he was she. Had full strength been present, she would have expressed deep regret for scratching his face after their dramatic leap from the precipice of Black Rock Cragge, followed by the even more spectacular kiss. She wanted him to know that all things between them, whether small or large, meant the world to her because of the everlasting vow they had exchanged. In her dreams—though she was still unsure about the serpent—she longed for his strong arms enveloping her body and his soft lips pressed against hers.

"I am here, my love," he replied. "I will always be here."

Heathcliff felt pained by her illness, but welcomed this chance to be by her side and share the profound tenderness he held for her in his heart. Under this duress, she lost her brazen, mischievous side and seemed more the vulnerable girl who was in need of his love, an emotion he lived to share only with her.

"Remember your promise," she muttered, needing this assurance after a dream that had separated her from the one constant in her life.

"I will never forget," he answered, as her eyes closed and she drifted off again.

It was late October and a high wind blustered around the house and roared in the chimney. It sounded wild and stormy, yet it was not cold. The family was all together in the main room. With Joseph's help, Mr. Earnshaw had been carried to his chair by the fire. A little removed from the hearth, Nelly sat knitting. Catherine, nearly fully recovered, leaned against her father's knee, and Heathcliff was lying on the floor with his head in her lap. Her fingers caressed his cheek in the very spot where she had inflicted the scratches. The master, nearly dozing, stroked her bonny hair—it pleased him to see her so gentle—and said, "Why canst thou not always be a good lass, Catherine?"

She turned her face up to his and laughed and answered, "Why cannot you always be a good man, Father?"

But as soon as she saw him vexed again, she kissed his hand,

and said she would sing him to sleep. She began singing very low, until his fingers dropped from hers, and his head sank to his breast. Nelly told Catherine to hush, and not stir, for fear she should wake him. Everyone kept as mute as mice a full half hour, and could've gone on longer, except Catherine stood to bid her father good night, and when she put her arms around his neck the poor thing discovered her loss directly and screamed out, "He's dead, Heathcliff, he's dead!"

And they both let out a heartbreaking cry, the pain running through them like a hot brand upon their hearts. Catherine held his hand and duplicated her kisses over and over, her inner fear of abandonment rising even more strongly to the surface. Heathcliff stood and embraced Mr. Earnshaw across the shoulders. He planted a kiss on his cheek—something the master had shied away from when alive—for Heathcliff truly believed that the old man had saved his life and had shown him nothing but kindness. The pair wept bitterly.

Nelly joined her wail with theirs, loud and painful, but Joseph asked what they could be thinking of to roar in that way over a saint in heaven.

Nelly put on her cloak and ran to Gimmerton for the doctor and the parson, not sure what use either would be of, then. She went through wind and rain, and brought one, the doctor, back; the other said he would come in the morning.

She left Joseph to explain matters and went upstairs to check on the young ones. Catherine's door was ajar and Nelly peeked in. Heathcliff was there. The pair lay side by side, as they had at Black Rock Cragge, pinched tight in the small single bed, staring into each other's eyes. It was past midnight and they were calm and did not need Nelly to console them, so she retreated noiselessly to her own room. There were times when she thought their extreme closeness an aberrant twist of nature. Nevertheless, she could not help but be moved by the complete natural tenderness between them.

Catherine stirred and found a book on her shelf. She read aloud to Heathcliff:

> *Though it is not life it is not death*
> *He can see us fully make our breath*
> *An angel flying above us now*
> *He can guide and show us how*
> *To live a life towards guiding light*
> *To bring comfort this holy night*
> *And find peace that will surely grow*
> *Through birth of spring to winter snow*

She closed the book and returned to the side of her mate in sorrow.

Deeply moved by her angelic voice, the intent of her words to soothe his soul, Heathcliff rose from the bed. Withdrawing pocketknife from trousers, he took his time to carve an inscription on the wall: HEATHCLIFF & CATHERINE.

He returned to her. She smiled. Their embrace entwined them as tightly as a long braid of thick hair.

All may have stayed this perfect if not for the funeral that brought young Master Hindley back to Wuthering Heights.

Chapter Three

When Mr. Hindley came home, the thing that amazed everyone and set the neighbors gossiping right and left was that he brought a wife, Frances, with him.

What she was, and where she was born, he never informed anyone. Probably she had neither money nor name to recommend her, or he scarcely would have kept the union from his father.

Young Hindley had changed considerably in the three years of his absence. He had grown sparer, lost his color, and spoke and dressed quite differently, not quite naturally, but as if he were straining to be a gentleman. He told Joseph and Nelly that they must henceforth quarter themselves in the back kitchen and leave the house for him and his wife.

Frances expressed pleasure at finding a sister among her new acquaintances, and she prattled to Catherine, and kissed her... but never quite took to Heathcliff. A few words from her, expressing a dislike for the boy, were enough to rouse the old hatred in Hindley. He drove Heathcliff from their company and banished him to sleep permanently in the barn, deprived him of instruction from the curate once again, and insisted that he should labor out of doors, forcing him to work harder than any other lad on the farm. In Heathcliff's mind there was nothing further Hindley could do that hadn't been done in their younger days and he accepted any ill-treatment with the calm stoicism of a soldier on duty...as long as he had his Catherine.

One Sunday evening, it chanced that both Catherine and Heathcliff were banished from the sitting room for making a noise, or a light offense of the kind, and when Nelly went to call them for supper, they were nowhere to be found.

Having escaped from the washhouse to have a ramble at liberty they caught glimpse of the lights from Thrushcross Grange and decided to see whether the little Lintons passed their Sunday evenings shivering in corners, while their father and mother sat eating and drinking and singing and laughing.

So they ran from the top of the Heights to the park, without stopping.

Meanwhile, Nelly searched the house, above and below, and the yard and stables. They were invisible. Hindley, in a passion, told her to bolt the doors and swore nobody should let them in that night.

Nelly opened her window and put her head out to hearken, though it rained, determined to admit them in spite of the prohibition, should they return.

Their race was swift and Heathcliff arrived first at the Grange, hardly taxed, and soon Catherine tagged along, her spirits too high from their escape to be bothered by the defeat. They crept through a broken hedge, groped their way up a path, and planted themselves atop a flowerpot under the drawing-room window. The light poured from the inside as the Lintons had not put up the shutters, and the curtains were only half closed. They were both able to look in by clinging to the ledge.

"It's beautiful," whispered Catherine.

A splendid place carpeted with crimson and crimson-covered chairs and tables, and a pure white ceiling bordered by gold, a shower of glass drops hanging on silver chains from the center, and shimmering with tiny soft tapers. Old Mr. and Mrs. Linton were not there. Edgar, sixteen, and his sister, Isabella, now fifteen, had the entire room to themselves and should have been most happy. But Isabella lay screaming at the farther end of the room, shrieking as if witches were running hot needles into her. Edgar stood on the hearth weeping silently, most unbecoming for a boy his age. In the middle of the table sat a little dog, shaking its paws and yelping, which, from their mutual accusations, seemed to have nearly been pulled in two between them.

"Idiots," whispered Heathcliff. Each began to cry because both, after struggling to get the dog, now refused to take it. The voyeurs outside the window laughed silently at the petted things. How they did despise them! For neither would want what each other had, or seek entertainment in yelling, and sobbing, and rolling on the ground.

They stepped off the flowerpot and moved noiselessly through the garden to the other side of the house. Heathcliff said, "I'd not exchange for a thousand lives my condition at the Heights for Edgar Linton's Thrushcross Grange—not even if I had the privilege of flinging Hindley off the highest gable and painting the housefront with his blood!"

"Hush!" whispered Catherine. "Do you want to announce us found and ruin the pleasure of our naughtiness?"

Heathcliff quieted and they were soon drawn to the light from a small parlor room in the back. The window higher, Heathcliff found a wheelbarrow left by loose soil in the garden and rolled it beneath the ledge. With careful balance, the pair stepped in and peered through the glass. Not a sight either had ever seen before, and it was with much self-control that they did not let out a gasp that alarmed all of Thrushcross Grange.

For inside was Mrs. Linton, the elderly ma of Edgar and Isabella, facing the far wall, her arms up over her head, palms pressed against the painted wood for support. Her skirt was lifted up, her knickers pulled down, while her manservant, a lad in his early twenties, stood behind her, his pants dropped over his tall boots, shirtwaist pulled up, and fucked her hard and deep.

It was in complete silence that both watched from the garden, eyes as large as the evening moon. They did not know which was dirtier: that they were witnessing a coupling, that it was between a servant and his married mistress, or that they refused to budge from the window.

As they made out soft moans from within the room and could see the sturdy, spread legs of Mrs. Linton, and the fine sculpted arse of her servant, seemingly doing all of the muscular work as he pushed and pulled to the full delight of all involved, their own breathing increased in bursts, loud enough to give them away if anyone had been in the nearby garden.

Catherine took pause to glance at Heathcliff and saw his mesmerized gaze. Perhaps emboldened by the wildness of the evening and what they now witnessed, or the regret of a lost chance at the Black Rock pool, or the temptation revisited in her dreams, she reached over and, through his trousers, felt his manhood between his legs. It was a miracle that Heathcliff did not yelp loud enough so even those at Wuthering Heights could hear. He bit his lip to redness. She felt its full length with her delicate fingers, her breathing becoming even more quick and shallow.

She whispered in amazement, "A boy you may be, but that is the tool of a man."

Her touch was lightning to his body, literally bringing on a direct sensation of intense heat to his center. "A girl you may be," he sputtered back, "but that is the touch of a woman."

"Take the serpent out."

"What?"

"I want to see it."

"Nay," said Heathcliff, "I am not that common."

It took maybe a few more strokes along the trouser leg and but a few gentle kisses along his neck to show Heathcliff that indeed he was.

He unbuttoned his pants, reached in, and with an awkward bending at the waist was able to remove it through the fly hole.

With the light from the window, Catherine was able to see it fully, and with a sharp intake of breath, whispered, "'Tis a monster."

Indeed, as they both glanced back toward the window—and saw that the manservant had turned Mrs. Linton sideways and had her bend over to grab her ankles and they could now see his member going in and out with purposeful strokes—it was clear that the servant was only half the size of Heathcliff.

They watched intently, curious over every movement: the arching of Mrs. Linton's neck back toward her lover, the way he grimaced as he increased his force, the manly way he grabbed her hips as if she were the horse he tamed. Tempo increased all around and the peepers seemed right on rhythm. Catherine, led by a deep desire within, unconsciously brushed her erect nipples against the ledge of the window—inspiring a warm, wet surge between her legs—while she stroked the enormous power of Heathcliff with the fist of her hand, barely able to encircle his thick shaft, heart aflutter with the feel of this man, yes, not a boy, but a man in her palm. The vision inside was truly startling and naughty, but in the garden was where true passion was being exchanged . . . by an act more simple, but so much more ardent because it was shared by two people in love.

Heathcliff marveled at the sensations pounding rhythmically through his brain. He had the vision of a man and a woman pleasuring each other with great intensity, but his focus was mostly on the lovely touch of Catherine, how her hand seemed to reach inside and soothe his soul, call upon an inner joy within his body, something, it seemed, only her touch could provide.

The finish line surely in sight for all, one final increase in speed and the seed of both men would surely be spilled, Catherine took the moment to lean forward and kiss Heathcliff fully on the mouth, her tongue touching his for the very first time. Their passion overcame them both and there was a simultaneous spasm that caused an imbalance in their support, which moved the wheels of the barrow, and both bodies went down in a loud tumble.

All the Lintons heard the ruckus and shot like arrows to the door. Edgar and Isabella arrived first, followed by their father from upstairs. After quickly arranging her garments to the proper fit, Mrs. Linton also appeared, while her manservant exited at the back, as he buttoned up, to let loose the dogs.

"Oh Papa, oh Papa!" cried Isabella.

"Mama!" howled Edgar.

Heathcliff struggled to return his unsatisfied member to his pants and Catherine urged him to hurry, as the barking dogs seemed quite near. Then he grabbed her by the hand and they took off. But all at once, Catherine fell.

"Run, Heathcliff, run!" she shouted. "They have let the bulldog loose and he holds me!"

There was an abominable snorting and to Heathcliff it seemed as if the devil had seized her ankle. Brave Catherine did not yell out, no! She would have not likely done it even if she had been spitted on the horns of a mad cow. However, Heathcliff did shout, expelling enough vociferated curses to annihilate any fiend in Christendom. He reached for a stone and thrust it between the beast's jaws and tried with all might to cram it down his throat.

The manservant came up with a lantern and shouted, "Keep fast, Skulker, keep fast!"

He changed his tone, however, when he saw Skulker's game. The dog was throttled off, his huge purple tongue hanging half a foot out of his jaws, his pendant lips streaming with bloody slaver.

The servant took Catherine up; she was sick, not from fear, but from pain. He carried her in, followed by Heathcliff, who grumbled execrations and vengeance. Another servant took Catherine to the kitchen to help stop the flow of blood from her ankle.

"What prey is it, servant?" hallooed Mr. Linton from the entrance.

He replied, "Skulker has caught a lass, sir, and there's a lad as well." He stared hard at Heathcliff. "Who looks to be an out-and-outer. Very like the robbers who put through the window so that they might murder us at their ease. Hold your tongue, you foul-mouthed thief. You shall go to the gallows for this!"

"Come in," said Mr. Linton. "I'll furnish these two a reception. Fasten the chain. Give Skulker some water. To rob a magistrate in his stronghold, and on the Sabbath, too? Where will all their insolence stop? Oh, my dear, Mary, look here. It is but a lad, yet the villain scowls so plainly in his face, it would be a kindness to hang him at once before he shows his nature in acts as well as features."

He pulled Heathcliff under the chandelier and Mrs. Linton placed her spectacles on her nose and raised her hands in horror, not clear whether from disgust or from anxiety over what the pair might have witnessed.

"Frightful thing," said young Isabella. "Put him in the cellar,

Papa. He is probably the son of the fortune-teller who stole my tame pheasant. Isn't he, Edgar?"

Catherine was brought around and as she heard the last speech, laughed. Edgar Linton, after an inquiring stare, collected sufficient wit to recognize her, as he had seen her in church, but seldom met her elsewhere.

"That's Miss Earnshaw!" he whispered to his mother, who blushed as crimson as the chairs in the drawing room, clearly uncomfortable, looking at her manservant, who glanced away. "And look how Skulker has bitten her, how her foot bleeds."

"Miss Earnshaw? Nonsense!" cried the mistress. "Miss Earnshaw wandering the country with a gypsy! And yet, my dear, the lass is in mourning and may be lamed for life."

"What carelessness in her brother," exclaimed Mr. Linton. "I've understood from the curate that he lets her grow up in absolute heathenism. But who is this ruffian? Wait. I believe he is that strange acquisition my late neighbor made in his journey to Liverpool . . . a little wild Indian from Delhi, or an American or Spanish castaway."

"A wicked boy in any event," remarked the old lady, trying to recapture her own dignity through righteous indignation. "Quite unfit for a decent house. Did you notice his language? I'm shocked that the children should have heard this. Take him away," she ordered her manservant, who cuffed Heathcliff by the collar and dragged him out kicking and screaming, and commencing with a fresh round of curses. Heathcliff refused to go without Catherine. Out of hearing distance, the servant asked him how much he saw.

"Enough to have you ousted and shot to boot," replied Heathcliff.

Then the servant struck him hard across the jaw, with a thick fist, knocking the lad to the ground. "Open your mouth, gypsy bastard, and that breath will be your last." He kicked him in the arse and sent him on his way.

Heathcliff was unable to leave his beloved in the hands of the wretched Lintons and circled quietly, returning to their original station, the curtain still looped in one corner, determined to spy again to ascertain if Catherine wished to return. If this was so, he intended to shatter their great glass panes to a million fragments unless they let her out.

Catherine sat quietly on the sofa. Mrs. Linton took off her own cloak and wrapped it tenderly around Catherine's shoulders. It was obvious they considered Catherine a young lady and him a wretched soul, which made all the difference in treatment.

A woman servant brought a basin of water and washed her feet. Mr. Linton poured for her a tumbler of warm wine. Isabella placed a plate full of cakes onto her lap, and Edgar stood gaping at a distance. Afterward, they dried and combed her beautiful hair, gave her a pair of enormous slippers, and wheeled her to the fire. Heathcliff realized it was time to trudge home, happy his love seemed on the way to recovery. Beneath his relief was a sense of uneasiness, as Catherine seemed as merry as could be, dividing her food between the little dog and Skulker, the fiend who tried to separate her foot from body. She even pinched his nose as he ate. Catherine's presence seemed to spark a spirit in the vacant blue eyes of all of the Lintons—a dim reflection from her own enchanting face. He could see they were full of stupid admiration, as she was so immeasurably superior to them . . . and to everybody on earth.

The walk home was cold, wet, and dark for Heathcliff.

The close of the evening was warm and pleasant for Catherine, as Mrs. Linton doted on her for the rest of the night, and announced that she could have the master guest room. The young lass wasn't sure if she was getting such treatment because of an instant fondness, or because Mrs. Linton hoped to keep Catherine in good favor in case she had seen too much.

As Isabella escorted her to the proper chamber, Catherine glanced out a second-story window in the hope of seeing Heathcliff making his way home safely. But the moonless light made her blind to what lay beyond at the moors.

Isabella opened the door and Catherine was greeted by a floor covered with a wonderfully soft Persian carpet and a full, grand bed with an elegant canopy and the thickest mattress she had ever seen. Mrs. Linton had given careful instructions that no one was to disturb Catherine in the morning until she felt ready to rise for breakfast, and that a fresh new dress and shoes would be laid out by one of the servants.

It felt wonderful to be taken care of like this and Catherine knew instantly that this was a life that suited her perfectly.

Chapter Four

Nelly's patience was rewarded this arduous evening, as she heard the lifting of the latch at the gate. She threw a shawl over her head and ran to open the door before someone woke Mr. Earnshaw with a knock. Heathcliff was by himself and it gave her a start to see him return alone.

"Where is Miss Catherine?" cried Nelly. "Pray tell, no accident?"

"In the arms of the Lintons," he answered. "And I would be there, too, if they had the manners to ask me to stay."

"Oh, you will catch it!" said Nelly. "You'll never be content until Master Hindley casts you out forever. What in the world led you to Thrushcross Grange?"

"Let me remove my wet clothes and I'll tell you about it, Nelly," he replied.

She followed him to the barn adjacent to the house and bid him beware of rousing the master. Once there, he sat on the bed and began undressing. She lowered herself onto the one chair, single candle in its holder, which she held with one hand and placed on her lap.

"Through a window, we first spied the Linton children arguing over a stupid puppy..."

As Heathcliff told his story, he slowly undid the buttons of his wet shirt, then tore it off his torso and dropped it to the ground.

Nelly noticed how well young Heathcliff had filled out in the past months, perhaps because of all the extra field work Hindley had forced him to do. His shoulders had broadened nicely and the muscles of his pectorals were more pronounced, hardened into thick curves that were covered with manly black hair.

Despite the damp coolness of the barn, Nelly suddenly felt perspiration begin to bead along her forehead and under her cloak and dress.

"And then we decided to venture to the other side of the house," continued Heathcliff.

His stomach rippled with power and she had heard that he could outwork any of the other men under Hindley's employ.

She let the cloak drop from her shoulders.

"We saw a light coming from the back parlor..."

She watched his fingers graze the tip of his left nipple, as if he was smoothing the hair surrounding it, making it difficult for her to follow the details of his recounting.

Without the least bit inhibition, Heathcliff stood and dropped his pants. Though the candlelight was dim, it was more than enough to illuminate his sturdy youthful cock, surrounded by a thick mass of dark hair. Having seen it before in his younger days, at the bath, rushing to dress, she could not remember it being this large. From its size, she wondered if he was aroused, but it seemed flaccid. She chastised herself for being so disappointed he donned his nightshirt so quickly, and added a silent counsel to focus on the story.

"Lo and behold, after securing a wheelbarrow so we could stand and peer through the window, we saw Old Lady Linton pressed against the wall, holding the bottom of her dress up to her waist so she was fully exposed, taking it deeply from behind from her manservant."

Nelly eyes widened with surprise, struggling a bit to breathe normally, as her perspiration evolved into more of a sweat and her attention now completely riveted on both Heathcliff and the tale he weaved.

"Old Lady Linton sure seemed to like it," said Heathcliff. "Her servant did her good and she moaned like a bitch in heat."

A voice in Nelly's head thought she should warn her charge that such talk was not proper for a young man. Indeed he was a young man now. But the isolation of the Heights had taken its toll on her. Joseph was old and crotchety, the curate was married and fierce in look. Nary a single, desirable man inhabited these parts and Nelly was still young and prime enough to nurture full desire. She crossed her legs, shifted in the chair.

Heathcliff skipped over Catherine's request, his prominent display, her subsequent grasp of the center of his arousal, as they spied on the wayward couple and felt their own desire begin to surface. He reclined on the bed. It did not go unnoticed by his listener that his well-formed cock had begun to tent his nightshirt.

"We made an unfortunate noise and then they were onto us," continued Heathcliff.

"Wait, was the manservant the one they call Robert? I have seen him at the market with his mistress."

"I wouldn't know, but he is a mean bastard who cuffed me a good one for no reason."

"A handsome lad is he. Was against the wall the only position he *fucked* her?"

Whoa, Nelly, she thought to herself, not intending to mouth such a description, but she felt such a dizzying rush from seeing Heathcliff so exposed and hearing him describe such a wicked liaison.

Perhaps Heathcliff intuited her arousal, or simply was eager to oblige any request from his caretaker, because he embarked on the finer points of all they saw, describing the sweat they could see dripping along Robert's lower back and down his muscular, smooth arse—he said now he was sure it must be Robert—remarking on the moans escaping Mrs. Linton and how she used her sturdy legs and hips to push back on Robert's cock. When Heathcliff described the change in position from the wall, to the ankles, Nelly let out a heated gasp.

"The slut she is," said Nelly. "That old lady. I never. To bend over like that and display all for her manservant."

The tone of envy did not escape Heathcliff and he enjoyed Nelly's reaction, which brought back more sensual memories from the evening, further growing his ardor, and prompted him to embellish the story with some savory details of his own.

"Aye, Nelly, for then Robert grabbed her by the hair and pulled hard, riding old Mrs. Linton as if she had just come from the stable, his hand going around to the front, as he vigorously teased her cunt and bit her ear. A loud moan she let out, surely daring with all present at the Grange, but unable to control herself as she was getting it properly, deep and hard."

The heavy groan that escaped Nelly inadvertently blew out the candle in her hand, which she thought was for the best, her full blush now hidden, but, more significantly, he could not see her staring so improperly at Heathcliff's bulging cock, as he spun his story, and absentmindedly caressed his towering member through the nightshirt while reliving the passion of the evening.

She could not know that his arousal was not from describing the coupling of Robert and old Mrs. Linton. The sight of the old lady's body had repulsed him. The recounting brought back all the full feelings of being with his beloved: her tender kisses at his neck, her wonderful strong fingers wrapped around his cock as she stroked him with such delight and skill, the final deep kiss he had dreamed about since the afternoon at Black Rock Cragge.

But the story did not end the way Heathcliff had wanted: a perfect finish with her hand, more tender kisses, a chance to please her the way she pleased him. He sadly slipped into the final chapter: the vicious Skulker; the phony airs of superiority by everyone, even Robert; the way they fawned over Catherine and how much she seemed to like it. His last words carried a deep melancholy, and Nelly felt compelled to rise from her chair and go to his bed. She lay next to him and whispered in the dark, "It's okay, Heathcliff. You're safe now. Catherine is well and being taken care of. And so are you."

Heathcliff lay on his back, Nelly on her side. She pulled him close and he did not recoil, needy of her feminine comfort.

She held him a long while, but both were too agitated to find sleep. There was a voice that told her to behave, but the moistness between her legs inspired by the young man's words and body would not go away. The image of his fine phallic specimen straining against his nightshirt was with her as if the room were still lit. He turned once, on his side, and although there were at least nine inches that separated them, she felt the brushing of his tip against her leg.

Instinctively, she reached her hand down, slipped it under the nightshirt, and took Heathcliff in her grip. He let out a soft, boyish moan that ran counter to what she held in her palm and that brought on a moment's hesitation, but the thrusting of his hips in her direction, sliding the head and long thick shaft through her fist, was all the encouragement she needed.

Nelly delicately let her fingers ripple along the full strength of Heathcliff's cock. His moan was deeper now and he returned to his back. She pulled herself closer, close enough so her own pussy pressed against his sturdy hip. The pressure there caused her mouth to open, and a deep breath to escape, but she managed to stifle any moan, not wanting him to know how much pleasure surged through her body by being this close, by holding his exquisite manhood in her nimble fingers.

He was surely in need of comfort and she always had a great fondness for the boy who had clearly become a young man. And there was comfort that she needed: more warmth on the many cold nights along the moors, the feel of a man beside her, the secure knowledge that she was able to please him, the wonderful sensual feelings that arose from being so close to such defined masculinity. She added kisses by his ear and stroked his cock with increased vigor.

She could feel the veins swell in her palm, the surges that went up to the head of his massive member. His eyes were closed, his hips rotated slightly, up and down, to her rhythm, and this pleased her. Discreetly, she pressed herself even tighter against his hip, biting her lip from the sweet feel of his hard body rubbing against hers. The wetness sliding down her legs turned from a trickle to a steady flow. She immersed her face into the full thickness of his hair and breathed in the delicious scent: a worker, a man of open air, youthful perspiration that made her long to be young Catherine. It took all her willpower to continue stroking— urging on this relief she could provide—and not raise his nightshirt and her own dress while mounting him and riding him with a passion that would surely overshadow the loveless coupling of Robert and Mrs. Linton.

With almost the full duplication of his encounter earlier in the evening, it would have been easy for Heathcliff to imagine that Catherine lay next to him, which would inspire the full wonderful release only his beloved could provide. But no matter how much energy and imagination he applied to such cause, he could not conjure up Catherine in this bed. The scent of Nelly was not even close to the flower of Catherine, her hand far rougher from so many household chores, and truth be known, Catherine was the only one in the world he truly wanted.

Nevertheless, he was in need and had been left unfulfilled and was desperate for anything to take his mind off the dismal end at Thrushcross Grange, and, truth be told, Nelly's perfect touch and rhythm revealed her full experience, and her heavy breathing in his ear, the feel of her great desire, all congregated through his body in one great fire of lust. So when her fist opened and her palm went flat and her hand went lower, starting now at his balls heavy with cum, and continued in the same rhythm, now caressing from the bottom of his sack, up the thick tree of his shaft, grazing his large, purplish head, he felt himself about to explode, about to cry out.

That was when Nelly felt the last bits of practical thought leave and her mind and body yield fully to this massive desire to comfort Heathcliff and harvest every ounce of desire, lust, and need pounding through her. She lurched down to his waist, forcefully tugged away his nightshirt, and used her lips to take his entire cock head and much of his shaft deep into her mouth, while she thrust her free hand down between her legs to the moistness of her womanhood—so alive, so grateful after such a long drought—and their passion exploded simultaneously . . . For Nelly a final rush of pressure and friction against her clitoris, for Heathcliff an eruption of semen, every drop caught expertly in Nelly's mouth, as she greedily swallowed the full spouting of his seed. He clasped his hand over his mouth to stifle the scream that would surely wake Hindley, and she, fortunately, had most of her animal sounds stifled by the full thickness of Heathcliff's glorious manhood.

Such a charge would leave anyone speechless and motionless and they both remained so for a few tender moments. Then Nelly got up, planted a plain kiss on the forehead of Heathcliff, wished him a good night, and left the room. In the shortest of times, both were able to slip off into a deep, blissful sleep.

Chapter Five

The very next day, Mr. Linton paid a visit to Wuthering Heights, recounted the previous evening's events, and read Master Hindley such a lecture on how best to guide a family. From all points of view, Hindley was supremely embarrassed: his own flesh and blood caught trespassing and peeping like the most common of beggars and thieves, caught alongside the dirtiest mongrel cur in all of Yorkshire; then to be chastised on his own property, in front of his own servants by a man so respected and revered as Mr. Linton, was just too much. Upon his return from college, with his lovely wife at his side, the most important thing to Hindley was to make Wuthering Heights an estate that others envied, as they did with Thrushcross Grange, to have both heads of family looked upon not as farmers, but as a fine gentleman and genteel lady, as were Mr. and Mrs. Linton.

When the tale was completed, Mr. Earnshaw's face as red as a spring tomato, the master used all of his embarrassment and anger to rise to action, bidding Joseph to bring Heathcliff back from the fields. He was so grateful that Mr. Linton accepted his wife's invitation to tea. She seemed to know how to make even a difficult situation a proper one.

Tea done, Heathcliff, completely passive, yielding silently to

Joseph's grasp, allowed himself to be pressed face-first to the horse tie, his shirt removed to bare back.

Normally it was Joseph who delivered any floggings, but in the company of all of the household, and especially Mr. Linton, Hindley decided to administer the punishment himself, delivering blow after blow to Heathcliff's back. The lad grimaced with pain, but refused to let escape his mouth even a whimper of weakness. Heathcliff drew enduring strength from the thought of his beloved, how she kissed him last night, grateful she was not here to witness his humiliation. Only Nelly turned away and retreated back to the house.

Done, Mr. Linton remained unperturbed by the viciousness of the flogging administered by Hindley, for the lad was not one of them, but a bastard runaway. He seemed impressed with Hindley's clear decisiveness and force, and communicated such with a firm nod in his direction.

Mrs. Earnshaw stepped forth and said to Mr. Linton, "Kind sir, you do us great honor with your presence at the Heights and even greater honor to welcome my sister-in-law into your home." Mr. Linton nodded again, as if saying *of course*. "Could you do us one more kind service?"

"What is it, Mrs. Earnshaw?"

"Could you take care of Catherine while she is at the mend? I am sure she would benefit greatly not only from the loving care of Mrs. Linton, but also from the noble teachings of a lady so fine as your wife, one known at the church as the most proper in the county."

"Excellent idea, Mrs. Earnshaw."

"Yes, excellent idea," echoed Hindley, beaming with pride over his wife's foresight and intelligence.

"My family has taken quite a liking to young Catherine, especially Edgar. Even Skulker is inseparable from her now, despite their first unfortunate meeting. And her foot will need time to heal and I know my wife can give Catherine the same education she gives Isabella."

"It's settled then," said Hindley with delight.

As Heathcliff lay face-first in the dirt, this news caused more suffering than any lash from a whip. The thought of that whore Mrs. Linton instructing his precious Catherine turned his stomach; the idea that his beloved would prefer the elegance of Thrushcross Grange over the unrefined simplicity of Wuthering Heights pained his heart; but what really wrenched his soul was the fear Catherine might favor the well-schooled and proper Edgar Linton over the likes of someone as common and uneducated as himself.

As if sensing Heathcliff's most tender point of weakness, Hindley gave him a good kick in the side and told him the next word he spoke to Miss Catherine without permission would ensure his final banishment from the Heights.

It was five weeks that Catherine stayed with the Lintons, set to return home for Christmas. During that time she enjoyed the motherly pampering of Mrs. Linton—something she surely missed from her own ma—who seemed fully assured that either Catherine had not witnessed her indiscretion, or was becoming lady enough to know that one doesn't tattle.

If Heathcliff had been careless and uncared for before Catherine's absence, he became ten times more so since. Only Nelly did him the kindness of calling him a dirty boy, and bid him wash himself once a week. His clothes saw many weeks' service in mire and dust and his thick uncombed hair, the surface of his face and hands, were dismally beclouded. He talked to no one, with or without permission.

Often Nelly visited him in his chamber, late, quiet, only after she was sure the household was at full peace. She lay next to him and tried to comfort him. He remained passive in her arms, indifferent to her light kisses on his cheeks. The only visible spark in spirit came when she duplicated what she had administered their first night together. Though grateful for the release—as he lay perfectly still and she soothed him with her hand and mouth—when it was over he felt a certain emptiness...because it was not Catherine. He was reminded not only of their last night together at the Grange, their touch of lips in the Black Rock pool, but of everything they had shared. With her, whatever they did seemed connected to their love. And now his love resided somewhere else.

Nelly did not deceive herself that she was simply a nurse, a nightingale to a troubled young man. She knew she took her pleasure, wanted her satisfaction, welcomed her release as well, entranced by his passiveness, his muscular taut torso, oversized cock, and, at these times, even his dirtiness. The unwashed sweat from the bush of hair under his arms and around his cock added an even more titillating, musky scent to his youthful body, and as she kissed his neck, or took him into her mouth, his powerful aroma washed over her, heightening the sweet rewards he brought her with his growing response, and inspiring within her an ever-increasing sweet affection for her handsome charge.

He said nothing when she finished, gave him her ritual kiss to the forehead, and bid him good night, except one evening he whispered in the dark, "Naughty Nelly."

Catherine's return brought with her a cured ankle and much improved manners. Mrs. Linton had planned reform by trying to raise Catherine's self-esteem with fine clothes and flattery, which she took to readily. Instead of a wild, hatless little savage jumping into the house, and rushing to squeeze everyone breathless, there lighted from a handsome black pony a very dignified person, with black ringlets falling from the cover of a feathered beaver.

Hindley lifted her from her horse and exclaimed with delight, "Why, Catherine, you are quite a beauty! I should scarcely have known you. You look a lady now. Isabella Linton is not to be compared with her, is she, Frances?"

"Isabella does not have her natural advantages," replied his wife. "But she must not grow wild again here."

Nelly stepped forth and Catherine kissed her gently. Nelly helped her remove her habit and there shone beneath a grand plaid silk frock, white trousers, and burnished shoes. When the dogs came bounding up to welcome her, Catherine's eyes sparkled joyfully, but she dare not touch them, lest they should fawn upon her splendid garments. She looked around for Heathcliff. Mr. and Mrs. Earnshaw anxiously watched their meeting, thinking it would enable them to judge what hope they had in separating the two friends.

He skulked behind the barn door, unsettled by the bright, graceful damsel about to enter the house, instead of the rough-headed counterpart he expected.

"Is Heathcliff not present?" she demanded, pulling off her white gloves, displaying fingers wonderfully whitened with doing nothing but staying indoors.

"Heathcliff, you may come forward," ordered Hindley, enjoying his discomfort and gratified to see what a forbidding young blackguard he would be compelled to present himself as. "You may wish Miss Catherine welcome, like the other servants."

Catching a glimpse of her friend in concealment, Catherine flew to embrace him. She bestowed six or seven kisses on his cheek within a second, and then stopped, and drawing back, burst into a laugh, exclaiming, "How very black and cross you look...and how funny and grim! But that is probably because I am used to Edgar and Isabella. Heathcliff, have you forgotten me?"

She had reason to put forth the question, for shame and pride threw double gloom over his countenance and kept him immoveable.

"Shake hands, Heathcliff," commanded Mr. Earnshaw. Then added with much condescension, "Once, in a way that is permitted."

"Nay!" replied the lad, finding his tongue at last. "I shall not be laughed at. I shall not bear it!"

And he would have left the circle, but Miss Catherine seized him again.

"I did not mean to laugh," she said. "I could not stop myself. Heathcliff, shake hands with me at least. Why do you sulk? It was simply that you looked so odd. If you wash your face and brush your hair it will be fine. You are so dirty!"

She gazed with concern at the black fingers she held in her own, and also at her dress, which she feared would lose embellishment if contacted by his.

"You don't have to touch me!" he answered, following her eyes and snatching away his hand. "I shall be as dirty as I please. I like to be dirty. I will be dirty."

With that he dashed back into the barn, amid the merriment of the master and mistress, and to the serious disturbance of Catherine, who could not comprehend how her remarks should have produced such an exhibition of bad temper.

Nelly spent the rest of the day putting cakes in the oven, and making the house cheerful with great fires befitting Christmas Eve, for the Linton teenagers had been invited to spend the morrow at

Wuthering Heights, and the invitation had been accepted, on one condition: Mrs. Linton wanted full assurance that her darlings be kept carefully apart from that "naughty, swearing boy."

While cleaning after dinner, Nelly became misty-eyed remembering how old Earnshaw used to come in when all was tidied and call her a lively lass and slip a Christmas shilling into her hand. She went on to think of his fondness for Heathcliff and his dread that he would suffer neglect after his death and that naturally led her to consider the poor lad's situation now. She found him smoothing the glossy coat of the new pony in the stable, and feeding the other beasts, according to custom.

"Hurry, Heathcliff," she said. "The kitchen is so comfortable and the Earnshaws are upstairs; make haste. Let me dress you smart before Miss Catherine comes out and then you can sit together, with the whole hearth to yourselves, and have a long talk till bedtime like the old days."

He continued with his task and never turned his head toward her. Nelly returned to the house.

In the morning, Heathcliff rose early and carried his ill humor onto the moors, not returning to the house until the family had departed for church. Fasting and reflection seemed to have brought him a renewed spirit. He hung around with Nelly for a while as she prepared Christmas day dinner for the family and guests.

Finally, after having screwed up his courage, he exclaimed abruptly, "Nelly, make me decent. I want to be good."

"'Bout time, Heathcliff," she said. "You have so grieved Catherine she's sorry she ever came home. It seems as if you envy her because she is more thought of than you."

The idea of *envying* Catherine was incomprehensible to him, but the notion of *grieving* her he understood clearly. In the fields, he could barely concentrate on his work and had nearly slashed his leg with a scythe, as he mindlessly cut away at unwanted weeds. At night, he tossed and turned, unable to sleep, frightened that he may have lost what they had forever.

"Did she say she was grieved?" he inquired.

"She cried when I told her you were gone again this morning."

"Well, *I* cried last night," he returned, "and I had more reason to cry than she did."

This gave true insight to Nelly of the state of her friend. For she remembered him crying hardly at all as a child and although she could feel the slight cracks in his heart these weeks Catherine was gone, she felt the stoical lad was holding everything intact.

"You had reason to go to bed with a proud heart and empty stomach," said Nelly. "But if you are ashamed of your touchiness then you must ask pardon and offer to kiss her…only do it heartily and not as if you thought her converted into a stranger by her grand dress. And now, I'll take time to arrange you so that Edgar Linton shall look quite feeble beside you. You are taller and twice as broad across the shoulders, and you could knock him down in an instant."

As Nelly washed and combed, Heathcliff's face brightened, then it was overcast again, and he sighed. "Nelly, if I knock him down thirty times that wouldn't make him less handsome or me more so. I wish I had light hair, fair skin, blue eyes, and was dressed, and behaved as well, and had a chance to be as rich as he will be!"

"And cried for mama at every chance," she added, "and trembled if a country bumpkin heaved his fist at you, and sat home all day because of a shower of rain. Heathcliff, you are showing poor spirit. Wish and learn to smooth away the surly wrinkles, the vicious canine expression, and raise your lids frankly. Look to the glass and there you'll see a good heart and a bonny face. Who knows if your father was emperor of China and your mother an Indian queen, each of them able to buy up, with one week's income, Wuthering Heights and Thrushcross Grange together?"

Nelly chattered on and Heathcliff gradually lost his frown and began to look quite pleasant, when, all at once, the conversation was interrupted by a rumbling moving up the road and entering the court. He ran to the window, Nelly to the door, just in time to behold the two Lintons descend from the family carriage, smothered in cloaks and furs, and the Earnshaws dismount from their horses. Catherine took the hand of Edgar and Isabella, brought them into the house, and set them before the fire, which quickly put color in their white faces.

Nelly urged Heathcliff to hasten now and show his amiable humor; and he willingly obeyed, but ill luck would have it that as he opened the door leading from the kitchen on one side, Hindley opened it on the other. The master, irritated to see him clean and cheerful, and eager to keep his promise to Mrs. Linton, shoved him back with a sudden thrust and warned him to stay in the garret till dinner was over. "He'll be cramming his fingers in the tarts and stealing the fruit if left alone in there."

"Nay, sir," said Nelly. "He'll touch nothing, and I suppose he must have his share of the dainties."

"He'll have his share of my hand if I catch him downstairs again till dark," cried Hindley. "Be gone, vagabond! You are attempting the coxcomb, are you? If I get a hold of those elegant locks, see if I won't pull them a bit longer!"

"They are long enough already," remarked Edgar Linton, peeping from the doorway. "I'm surprised they don't make his head ache. It's like a horse's mane over his eyes."

He offered this remark without any intention to insult, but

Heathcliff's violent nature did not wish to endure the impertinence from one he hated, already, as a rival. He seized a tureen of hot applesauce and dashed it full against the speaker's face and neck—who instantly began a lament that brought Isabella and Catherine.

Hindley snatched up Heathcliff directly and conveyed him to the barn, where he administered a remedy rough enough to cool the lad's fit of passion and leave himself red and breathless . . . and unfulfilled, for it seemed that no matter how much he punished Heathcliff, the lad did and said as he pleased. But this did not stop Hindley from holding on to the anger, confident that when the time came, Heathcliff would get all that he deserved.

With a dishcloth, Nelly scrubbed Edgar's nose and mouth, telling him it served him right for meddling. His sister began weeping to return to the Grange, and Catherine stood by confounded, blushing for all.

"You should not have spoken to him," she barked at Edgar Linton. "He was with ill temper and now you've spoiled your visit and he'll be flogged. I hate him to be flogged! I can't eat my dinner. Why did you speak to him, Edgar?"

"I didn't," sobbed the youth. "I promised mama that I would not say one word to him, and I didn't!"

"Well, don't cry," replied Catherine. "You're not dead. Don't make more mischief. My brother is coming. And quiet, Isabella! Has anyone hurt *you*?"

"Now, now children, take your seats," cried Hindley. "That brute has warmed me nicely. Next time, Master Edgar, take vengeance with your own fists . . . it will give you an appetite."

The party recovered its equanimity at the sight of the delectable feast. The Lintons were hungry after their ride, and easily consoled, since no real harm had befallen them.

Mr. Earnshaw carved bountiful platefuls and the mistress brought them joy with lively talk. Nelly observed Catherine, with dry eyes and an indifferent air, cut through the wing of goose before her and smile with delight as she shared her own tales with her friends. She thought Catherine unfeeling to dismiss her old playmate's troubles so easily and did not remember her being this selfish.

Then, as if young Catherine had a window into her caretaker's thoughts, she lifted a mouthful of potato to her lips, then set it down again. Her cheeks flushed and tears gushed over them. She dropped her fork to the floor and hastily dove under the cloth to conceal her emotion. The day was purgatory and she longed for the opportunity to slip off and pay a visit to Heathcliff—who had been locked in the garret by the master—and at least bring him some food.

In the evening there was a dance and Catherine begged her brother to liberate Heathcliff, as Isabella had no dance partner.

"An ill-behaved animal deserves to be chained and so locked shall he remain," offered Hindley.

The emotions lingering from dinner threatened to burst into visible tears. But she did not want to give her brother the satisfaction. She had an urge to slap his face as well, as she had done occasionally when they were younger, knowing her father would intercede, but that would hardly be ladylike in front of Edgar and Isabella. She did not want to do anything that would prevent her from being with Heathcliff this Christmas day.

After the evening came to completion and the carriage was summoned to bring the Lintons home, and Hindley and his wife had retired, Catherine approached Nelly, who was still cleaning in the kitchen. "Does thou know where my brother has set the key for the garret?"

Reaching into her apron pocket, whispering, Nelly said, "'Tis here. I was going to bring him a plate."

"Let me take it," said Catherine.

"Aye," said Nelly. "This will awaken the lad from his slumber of sadness."

Food in hand, still in her party dress of pure white silk, Catherine mounted the stairs to the garret and called lightly for him through the door. He stubbornly declined to answer. "You have not eaten since breakfast," she entreated. Still no reply. With tender care she used the key to open the door and then locked it quietly behind her.

Heathcliff lay on the bed, unmoving.

"What are you doing, Heathcliff? Why do you lie so still? Why do you not heed my words?"

"I'm trying to decide how I shall pay Hindley back. I don't care how long it takes, if I can only do it. I hope I will not die before I do."

"For shame," said Catherine. "It is God's task to punish the wicked. We must learn to forgive."

"God won't have the satisfaction that I shall. I only wish I could decide the best way. Let me alone and I will decide. While I think of this, I don't feel the pain."

Catherine placed the plate on the table beside him. "You have been wronged, my love. It is plain to all except my ignorant brother, his fatuous wife, and the Linton brats."

"You still call me your love after welcoming so agreeably an eternity apart from me?"

"I needed time to heal. My thoughts were only of you."

"You call the Lintons brats, yet you fawn over Edgar as if he is a peacock at full plume?"

"He was very kind to me at the Grange. He has a good heart.

I do not think he meant ill with his comments." She sat next to him on the bed. "You are the only one I fawn over. You are my peacock, with plumage so fine the other birds shrink with envy." She stroked his hair.

"Are you not worried that by touching me you will soil your Christmas finery?"

After a pause, Catherine reached for the gold chain around her neck, a locket at its end. It had been a present from her late father. In it he had placed one of her sweet baby curls and told her to cherish it forever. She placed it in Heathcliff's hand. Knowing how important and personal this ornament was to Catherine, he grasped it with delicate reverence. He opened it, knowing the hair of his beloved was inside. Unfeeling to the pain, he plucked out several of his own hairs and placed them besides hers, then closed the locket.

He said, "I will cherish this almost as much as the gift of your love. And wherever I go, as long as there is breath in me, this locket will stay."

To Heathcliff's great surprise, Catherine was not done giving Christmas gifts. She stood up and carefully removed her dress. Heathcliff saw the full billow of her crinoline petticoat. She removed that as well, clad now only in her silk underthings, and Heathcliff was mesmerized by the slender beauty of his beloved, stripped to reveal the real Catherine, not a fancy doll produced by someone who pretended to be a lady, but fucked her manservant while her husband reclined upstairs.

"Will you eat now?" she asked. She did not want her companion to be denied anything on this special day. She had felt him slipping away since her return from the Grange and she missed the ease with which they had shared their love. Though she had reveled in her time with the Lintons, there were moments when she had been alone in the garden, or restless in the giant bed, when she had hungered for Heathcliff with all of her being. Their ongoing passion had been ignited in a new way outside the Lintons' window, a shared spark that had not been allowed to grow to full flame because of the unfortunate events that had followed. This was their night.

"You are all the nourishment I need," he said as he took the hand that had stroked his hair and pulled on it gently, so that his love lay by his side. They embraced, each body slipping into the other as easily as the garret key into the lock.

"Thy garments scratch me," said Catherine.

"Shall I remove them?"

"Allow me."

Catherine stood, over him. As he looked up he could see her full, womanly breasts stretched against the fabric of her undershirt, the nipples, flushed with excitement, pointing through, so clearly shaped it was as if there were no material covering them. She looked down toward his trousers and saw the beginning bulge of his manhood. "I dreamt of the serpent," she said, "each night at the Grange. Only it was no longer a fearful dream now that I had touched him and gleaned pleasure from the feel. I dreamt of it with longing, for my touch was unfulfilled."

"I, too, was unfulfilled," said Heathcliff, "because I did not get to touch your sacred place."

She ran her fingers through his thick hair again, pulling this time, perhaps hard enough to hurt, but it brought only a sound of pleasure from her friend. She traced her finger across his defined forehead, lightly across his lids as they closed, gently along his cheeks, then brushing across his lips. He opened his mouth slightly and she penetrated there with her finger and he briefly licked and sucked her flesh, drawing murmurs of approval.

He opened his eyes. She unbuttoned his shirt, slowly, staring straight into his eyes. And he stared back. Never would he have believed that an act so simple could seem so sensual. As he lifted his torso so she could remove the shirt, she began a similar tracing with her finger, marking the clearly defined lines of his pectoral muscles, circling his sturdy brown nipples buried deep in fine black hair. She leaned forward, by his armpit, and inhaled deeply the scent of his masculine fineness. "You are all man, my dear Heathcliff. Not a finer one breathes in all of England."

"And not a fairer lass inhabits this land."

She unbuttoned his trousers, needing to hold his cock down with one hand in order to slip them off. He wore no underwear, which delighted Miss Catherine. He lay below her, completely naked. She stroked his entire body with her eyes, as if they were her hands: the broad shoulders; the bold, muscular arms with bulging biceps; the narrow hips; the elegant pack of muscles at his stomach climbing from waist to chest like steps on a ladder; the thick, dark legs, fine hairs in abundance. Then, of course, the hands. These she had seen and known since their childhood. Strong hands, with thick fingers, each a tree that gripped everything with power. Often dirty and grimy, but so powerful to the touch that it thrilled her even as a child to feel her hand held by his.

He reached a hand toward her stomach, but she grabbed it, stopped him. "Don't touch...yet. Watch."

He obeyed. It was thrilling for her to understand that the sight of her tamed him, that one so powerful and explosive as he could be rendered docile and weak in her presence.

For Heathcliff, the pleasure was overwhelming, to be this close to his beloved, to be this intimate with someone he knew in every way, but this one. It was with great willpower that he resisted pulling her down beside him so they could be body to body, flesh to flesh. But, as was her bidding, he remained patient.

Ever so slowly, she inched her undershirt up, at first revealing her flat stomach, hardened from years of riding, then her glorious breasts, so full, erect, nearly pointing upward with the strength of her youth. Her areolas were a pale brown, dark only because of the whiteness of her flesh. They seemed to hover over his face and he longed to suck them. However, he heeded her warnings.

Then, with the most titillating move he had ever seen, something that made the full fucking of Robert and Mrs. Linton look as passionate as one of the curate's schoolbooks, Catherine stared him straight in the eye, pupil to pupil, and slowly, provocatively, inched her underskirt down. The gentle sway of each hip, from one side to the other, as she lowered it, made his cock grow to lengths that even he never imagined. Then before him was her womanhood, her bush thick and wild, hiding the treasure that was Catherine, so sweet, so dark it took the willpower equivalent to the strength of five men to keep him from leaning forward and kissing it, to keep from thanking his beloved for the gift, for the vision of her immaculate body.

Then, just as Heathcliff thought there could be no visual treats left, Catherine took the pins out of her hair, gave her neck a quick shake, and the full, dark curls tumbled to her shoulders.

"My love," whispered Heathcliff.

"My darling," whispered Catherine.

She allowed her hand to be taken this time and was brought to his side.

It was not by experience, but by incredible sensuous instinct that the pair continued this gentle lovemaking. Although almost everything on this night seemed like a first, they had locked inside them the wisdom of two beautiful creatures constructed for full carnal pleasure. Inspired by the feelings and tension between them that had been nurtured and grown since their childhood, their touch, their whispered expressions of love, their exchange of caresses and kisses, held more power than any lightning in a storm.

Side by side, as equals, they kissed passionately. Without thought, their tongues escaped their mouths and entered the one opposite, touching, playing, caressing, as did their hands over each other's bodies. It was as if neither had eaten, and the only meal that could satisfy this hunger was each other.

Heathcliff pushed Catherine to her back and began to lick and kiss her neck, tasting her. She arched her throat and moaned softly. He licked down while cupping her full breasts in his hands and began nuzzling and sucking her nipples. Catherine thrashed under him. "Heathcliff, my love, I missed you so much. Never leave me, please."

"Never," replied Heathcliff.

She ran her hands down the center of his back, contouring the thick muscles resting on each side of his spine. Although the room was chilled, they lay uncovered, sweating from the heat of their passion, conjoining the fluid of their perspiration, the moist-ness of their saliva when they kissed.

Heathcliff advanced his hands along her arms, caressed the in-sides of her wrists, delighted over her warm response. She ran her fingers down the crack of his ass, separated by hard muscle fleeced with dark hair and she felt him arch into her with plea-sure, his enormous cock pressing against her thigh.

He kissed along her stomach, gentle at first, then licked with long strokes, and her eyes closed and she grabbed a fistful of his hair. He licked along her inner thighs, quick flicks, then long dashes, like a painter with a brush.

As he neared her greatest source of pleasure with his mouth, she murmured, "Heathcliff, Heathcliff, Heathcliff, you are everything to me..."

With that he entered her warm pussy with his thick long tongue.

This did not take long, Catherine so energized from his touches, kisses, licks everywhere. For when he found the bump of her pleasure and took it into his mouth, held it there lightly with his teeth, and licked it unmercifully, she could do nothing but thrash and call out his name as he finished her off in a mix of explosive energy and stifled sound as she put a pillow over her mouth and came on his.

Heathcliff rose above her, looking down on her now, and Catherine was overcome with wonder that the person who could make her feel so uncontrolled, so needy, so hungry with his mouth, was the same person she had known so well for most of her life.

He kissed her deeply and she could taste the juice of her lust and this excited her even more. She felt him line his cock up at the entrance to her pussy.

"No!" she said, sharply.

She nudged him to his back and duplicated all of his acts down his chest and stomach until she got to his cock. There she paid homage to a creature she never could have imagined in her naughtiest dreams. She could never get enough of this man. Everything they shared was as natural as a walk holding hands. The fire that had been sparked at the Lintons was now at full force, roaring to the sky, her body driven to give and receive enjoyment. She kissed his balls, licked the sweat off them, spurred on by his sounds of pleasure. She licked the shaft, up and down, as if it were a tall Christmas dessert. She stroked his body, everywhere—stomach, chest, thighs—as she used her mouth vigorously, now taking the hugeness into her throat, feeling him stretch her cheeks and flatten her tongue. She sucked, up and down, worshipping this manhood with her undivided attention, her fingers fluttering under his balls.

"Nay, slow down, Catherine," mumbled Heathcliff. "I shan't be able to control myself and I want it to be inside you, touching, pleasing you."

But she ignored his entreaty. Their separation had only intensified her love and her need to lay with him, naked, vulnerable, with the person she trusted most in this world. She continued with more pace, wanting to taste everything about him, consume this man with all her passion. And Heathcliff was helpless to her desires as he poured mouthful after mouthful of sweet nectar into her mouth and she lapped, sucked, swallowed all that she could.

Then they both collapsed in a heap, side by side.

"'Tis a wonder, you are," exclaimed Heathcliff.

"As are you," she replied, barely able to catch her breath.

Then there was nothing more said, for they had shown it all. They lay still for nearly an hour, silent, awake.

Finally, Catherine spoke: "I must go."

"I don't want you to," said Heathcliff.

"And I don't want to," said Catherine, "but if my brother finds me here, there will be a hanging."

"Then let's leave this place," said Heathcliff.

"It's my home. There will be nothing out there for us until we each find a better station."

"But you will remember your promise, sealed by near death, that you would never forsake me?"

"I will always remember, long past death."

She got up from the bed and dressed. He felt the chill of her departure from his side.

She left him after one more sweet kiss upon his lips. "I'll see you in the morn."

Like that she was gone.

Whatever love he had felt before now seemed much multiplied. Yet he wondered why Catherine had stopped him from fully consummating their passion. Did she enjoy her oral pleasure so much she did not want to stop? Was it a sense of propriety, saving herself for the night of their marriage? Or was she saving her purity for the likes of someone like Edgar Linton? It was the voice of Nelly that told him to fight the dark thoughts, for his darkest of thoughts had always made trouble for him.

To calm himself, he grabbed the locket from the side table and grasped it to his heart. He would endure any beating or humiliation tendered by Hindley or any other, even endure short separations from his beloved, as long as she remained his, and he remained hers, and they could always share each other as joyously as they had done this Christmas night.

Chapter Six

During the days following Christmas, all in the household could sense something was different between Heathcliff and Catherine, even Joseph, who was known to search for spectacles that rested firmly on his nose. Everyone knew of the extreme closeness of the pair, a bond since childhood, but now it seemed as if they kept a deep and hidden secret, something in the quick glances, the sly smiles, when they happened to be in the same room, or pass in the field. Mrs. Earnshaw was the most suspicious and bent the ear of her husband. Nelly was sure she knew what had transpired, but feigned ignorance when questioned by the master.

Hindley nearly doubled Heathcliff's workload, ordering him to the fields before the sun even rose and forcing him to stay there even after the sun had set, while working every day, including the Sabbath. He took to locking Catherine in at night and whenever stirred in his sleep by the slightest sound, or to use the chamber pot, he made a check of her door. Catherine remained steadfastly furious that she was being held captive and spit fire at her jailer. "You are not my father!" she cried. "And never such a man could you be, you wretched soul!"

Ignoring her insults as if she were a wayward child, Hindley said, "Where do you need to go at night, that such a caging would make a difference?" Her words retreated, bringing an ugly, all-knowing smile to his face. "Would you go to the blackguard our father loved so much, who has brought so much shame to this house and brings shame on you as well?"

"The only shame here is you and your mousy wife."

Catherine knew that through Mrs. Earnshaw, Hindley was the most vulnerable, so she was already a step away and out of the house before the blow he launched could find a resting place.

Although it greatly limited their time together, it did not stop the young lovers from fighting desperately for their tender moments. Hindley to town, Mrs. Earnshaw in bed, sick as usual, Catherine would volunteer to bring water to the hands. Slipping off into the tall grass for their abbreviated pleasure, they would roll in the dirt, embracing, and kissing. There was never the place or time to duplicate Christmas evening—certainly no more trips to Black Rock Cragge—and on occasion Heathcliff tried once more to fully consummate their love, but Catherine continued to avoid it. Heathcliff did not mind. To hold her, to see her, to know that she was his, was joy enough.

Nelly, fully respectful of their love, stayed away from Heathcliff at night, although she found pleasure quite often, when alone in her chamber, revisiting those evenings in her mind, her hand pressed firmly between her thighs.

For the first time in a long while, the Heights settled calmly, achieved generally because Mrs. Earnshaw became pregnant, yet remained sickly, and Hindley devoted most of his energies to nursing his wife. In his heart, Hindley had room for only two idols—his wife and himself—and he doted on both, and adored one. He was cheered when the doctor told him that with proper care and attention, the baby and mother would be fine.

In her late teens now, Catherine became queen of the countryside, a rare beauty, and many young men noticed her in the village or at church. Her infancy long past, she had no peer and was turning into an even more haughty and headstrong creature, vexing Nelly quite often with her arrogance, but always affectionate in the end. Her one constancy was Heathcliff, his hold on her affections unalterable. Young Edgar Linton as well, even with all his boastful superiority, became a regular attendant. After all, with Heathcliff working all day, and she locked up all night, a girl her age needed some companionship.

When at Thrushcross Grange, Catherine had no temptation to show her rough side. Her ingenious cordiality gained the admiration of Isabella, and the heart and soul of Edgar, acquisitions that flattered her from the start, for she was full of ambition, and that led her to adopt a double character without exactly intending to deceive anyone.

At the Lintons', when she heard Heathcliff termed a "vulgar young ruffian," and "worse than a brute," she took care not to act like him. At the Heights, she had small inclination to practice politeness that would only be laughed at, and restrain an unruly nature when it would bring neither credit, nor praise.

Edgar seldom mustered courage to visit Wuthering Heights openly. He had terror of Heathcliff after their first two meetings and shrunk from encountering him. Yet he always received the best attempts at civility from Hindley, who avoided offending him at all costs—knowing why he came—and how important he could be to Catherine's future.

Edgar's appearance at the Heights seemed almost distasteful to Catherine. She was not artful, never played the coquette, and had an objection to her two friends meeting at all. For when Heathcliff expressed contempt of Edgar, in his presence, she would not agree, as she would in his absence; and when Edgar articulated disgust and antipathy to Heathcliff, she pretended that the depreciation of her friend were of scarcely any consequence to her.

The long hours and less frequent time with his love eventually took its toll on Heathcliff. At his best, a lad with glorious features and superior intellect, he contrived to create an impression of inward and outward repulsiveness. He had lost the benefit of his early education and had extinguished any curiosity he once possessed in pursuit of knowledge, and any love for books or learning. His childhood sense of superiority, instilled in him by the favor of old Mr. Earnshaw, faded away. The equality he once struggled to maintain with Catherine in her studies was yielded in poignant but silent regret. He acquired a slouching gait, and ignoble look; his naturally reserved disposition became exaggerated into an almost idiotic excess of unsociable moroseness, and he took dark pleasure in exciting aversion rather than esteem.

Catherine and he saw each other as much as they could, whenever he had a respite from his labors, but as time wore on and she spent more time with Edgar, he ceased to express his fondness for her in words and recoiled with angry suspicion from her feminine caresses, as if conscious there could be no future gratification in lavishing such marks of affection on her.

One afternoon, Hindley had gone from home and Heathcliff presumed to give himself a holiday. He came to the house and announced his intention of doing nothing, while Nelly assisted Catherine with the arranging of her dress. She had not anticipated his choice to be idle and thought she would have the whole house to herself and had managed to inform Edgar of her brother's absence, and thus was preparing to receive him.

"Are you busy this afternoon?" asked Heathcliff. "Are you going somewhere?"

"No, it's raining."

"Why do you wear the silk frock then? Nobody coming here, is there?"

"Not that I know of," stammered Catherine, "but shouldn't you be in the field now, Heathcliff? It's an hour past dinner. I thought you were gone."

"Your brother does not often free us from his accursed presence," remarked the boy. "I'll not work a lick more today, but will stay with you."

"But Joseph will tell," she offered. "You better go!"

"Joseph is loading lime on the far side of Black Rock Cragge. It will take him to dark so he'll never know."

He approached the fire and sat down. Catherine thought for a second, with knitted brows, realizing the need to smooth the way for any intrusion.

"Isabella and Edgar spoke of calling this afternoon," she said. Then, at the conclusion of a minute's silence by both, added, "As it rains, I don't expect them, but they may come, and if they do, you run the risk of being scolded for no good."

"Order Nelly to say you are engaged, Catherine," he persisted. "Don't turn me out for those pitiful, ridiculous friends of yours! I'm at the point, sometimes, of complaining that they . . . but I'll not—"

"That they what?" cried Catherine, gazing at him with a troubled expression. "Oh, Nelly!" she added petulantly, jerking her head out of caretaker's hands, "you've combed my hair quite out of curl! That's enough, please leave me alone. What are you at the point of complaining about, Heathcliff?"

"Nothing. Only look toward the wall." He pointed to the almanac, a framed sheet hanging near the window, and said, "The crosses are for the many evenings you have spent with the Lintons, the two dots are for those spent with me. Do you see how I've marked every day?"

"Yes. Foolish. As if I took notice!" replied Catherine in a peevish tone. "And what is the point in that?"

"To reveal that I *do* take notice," said Heathcliff.

"And should I always be spending time with you?" she demanded, growing more irritated. "What good is that? What do you blabber about? You might be dumb or a baby for anything you speak to amuse me, or for anything you do, either."

"You never said before that I talked too little, or that you disliked my company, Catherine!" exclaimed Heathcliff with much agitation. "Certainly not on the Christmas night . . ."

"Children," said Nelly, quick to see Catherine blush, and, yes, at this moment they did cackle like children.

"It is no company at all, when people know nothing and say nothing," muttered Catherine.

Her companion rose, but he hadn't the time to express his feelings further, for a horse's hooves were heard on the flags, and, having knocked gently, Edgar entered, his face brilliant with delight at the unexpected summons to the Heights.

Indeed, Catherine marked the difference between her friends as one came in and the other went out. The contrast was like exchanging a bleak, hilly, coal country for a beautiful fertile valley. And his voice and greeting were as opposite as his aspect, sweet and low, and his words were pronounced absent of any gruffness.

"I've not come too soon, have I?" he asked, casting a look at Nelly. She had retreated to tidy some drawers at the far end of the dresser.

"No," answered Catherine. "What are you doing there?" she asked Nelly.

"My work, miss," Nelly replied. Mr. Hindley had given her directions to make a third party in any private visits Edgar chose to make.

Catherine stepped behind her and whispered crossly, "Take yourself and your dusters out of here. When company are in the house, servants don't begin scouring and cleaning in the room where they are!"

"It's a perfect opportunity, now that the master is away," said Nelly. "He hates when I fidget over these things in his presence. I'm sure Edgar won't mind."

"I hate you to fidget in *my* presence," said Catherine imperiously, not allowing her guest time to speak. She had failed to recover her composure since her dispute with Heathcliff.

"I'm sorry, Miss Catherine" was Nelly's response. She proceeded diligently with her occupation.

Catherine, assuming Edgar could not see her, snatched the cloth from Nelly's hand, and pinched her, with a prolonged wrench, very spitefully on the arm.

Nelly had always tried to love Catherine, but she had been hurt extremely, so she started up from her knees and screamed out, "That's a nasty trick! You have no right to nip, and I'm not going to put up with it!"

"Lying creature! I did not touch you!" she cried, her fingers tingling to repeat the act, her ears red with rage. She never had the will to conceal her passion and it always set her entire complexion to blaze.

"Well, then, what's this?" retorted Nelly, showing a decidedly purple witness to refute her.

Catherine stamped her foot, wavered a moment, and then, irresistibly impelled by the naughty spirit within her, slapped Nelly on the cheek, a stinging blow causing both eyes to fill with water.

"Catherine, my love, Catherine!" interjected Edgar, greatly shocked at the double fault of falsehood and violence his idol had committed.

"Be gone, Nelly!" repeated Catherine, trembling all over.

The caretaker remained stubbornly unmoved and Catherine lifted her hand and was about to deliver another smack, when young Edgar stepped between them and implored her to behave. How astonished the young man felt, when Catherine did not withdraw the blow but continued forward and applied it over his own ear in a way that could not be mistaken for a jest.

Nelly drew back in consternation, and walked off to the kitchen, leaving the door of communication open.

The insulted visitor moved to where he had laid his hat, pale and with quivering lip.

Though she did not give it voice, Nelly remarked to herself, "That's right. Take warning and be gone! It's a blessing that you have glimpsed her true disposition."

"Where are you going?" asked Catherine, advancing to the door.

He moved aside and attempted to pass.

"You must not go!" she exclaimed with force.

"I must and I shall," he replied softly.

"No," she persisted, blocking the door. "Not yet, Edgar Linton, sit down. You shall not leave me with ill temper. I will be miserable all night and I won't be miserable for you."

"How can I stay after you struck me?" asked Edgar.

Catherine remained silent.

"You've made me afraid and ashamed of you," he added, his voice gaining power. "I'll not come here again. And I refuse to stay!"

Her eyes glistened and her lids began to twinkle.

"And you told a deliberate lie!" continued Edgar, confident now that his righteousness ruled.

"I didn't!" cried Catherine, recovering her speech. "I did nothing on purpose. Well, go, if you want...get away! And now I'll cry until I'm sick."

She dropped to her knees by a chair and set to weeping in serious earnest.

Edgar persevered in his resolution to depart and made it as far as the court. There he lingered. Nelly resolved to encourage him.

"The miss is dreadfully wayward, sir," she called out. "As bad as any marked child. You better ride home, or else she will be sick, only to grieve us."

The soft thing looked back through the window. Edgar possessed the power to depart as much as a cat possesses the power to leave a mouse half killed or a bird half eaten. Nelly realized there would be no saving him and he was doomed to his fate.

So it was. Edgar turned abruptly, hastened into the house again, and shut the door behind him. When Nelly went in after a while to inform them that Hindley had come home rabidly drunk, ready to pull the place about the ears—his ordinary frame of mind in such condition—the pair had broken the outworks of youthful timidity, and forsook the disguise of friendship to confess themselves as lovers. For they were embracing and Catherine kissed him fully upon the mouth.

After hearing her warning, the pair rose and Catherine escorted her companion to the door, but not before sneaking a look back over her shoulder toward Nelly—who watched them carefully— to deliver a short, but clear, smile of triumph.

Chapter Seven

Having received accurate intelligence of Hindley's drunken arrival, Edgar made haste to depart on his horse while Catherine retired to her chamber. Nelly hoped there was enough time to take the shot out of Hindley's fowling piece, which he was fond of playing with in his current state, to the hazard of the lives of any who provoked him, or even attracted his notice too much. But Hindley entered, spewing oaths dreadful to hear, before Nelly could complete her task.

He pulled the gun out of the glass storage cabinet, waved it about the room—causing Nelly to duck—and sang, "A hunting we shall go..."

Had the mistress not been resting, gathering all strength for the final stages of her pregnancy, she would have put a stop to such nonsense.

Edgar went to the kitchen window, flung it open, and glanced about the skies, as if looking for a bird to shoot. Unfortunately, Heathcliff came walking across the courtyard to the stables. A shot rang out. Nelly rushed to the front door, in time to see Heathcliff collapsed to the ground...although apparently unscathed. He rose to his feet, looked toward the window at Hindley, clearly aware now where the shot had come from. With a calm boldness, he walked directly toward the window, right at Hindley, and held his arms spread wide like the wings of a bird as if saying, *Here I am. Is this what you want?*, daring Hindley to take another shot. Despite the inebriation, Hindley would not have missed from such point-blank range. Perhaps there was some sense left in the master's brain, reminding him that he had a wife and would soon be a father. Or maybe it was the audacious sneer on Heathcliff's face—almost welcoming the opportunity for death—that caused Hindley to lower the gun, close the kitchen window, and retreat quietly into the main room.

The master saw Nelly staring at him transfixed, speechless over how close Heathcliff had come to expiration. Hindley, bully that he was, perhaps still humbled by Heathcliff's challenge, grabbed Nelly by the back of the neck, like a dog. "By heaven and hell," he exclaimed, "you should know better than to leave my loaded guns about." He gave Nelly a shove just before letting go. "Be careful I do not fire in your direction!"

Stumbling, but maintaining her balance—for Nelly, truly a woeful day—she looked her master straight in the eye and said, "I would rather be killed by someone like you than be touched."

Perhaps he grew weary of playing the bully in his own house—far too easy—perhaps he had no heart left to terrorize the innocent, or perhaps there was a fierceness in Nelly that exposed him as well to the coward that lay beneath his master's finery, for he let out a surly "humph" and climbed the stairs to be with his wife.

Nelly went to the kitchen. She assumed Heathcliff headed to the barn, but it turned out, afterward, that he had only flung himself on a courtyard bench by the wall.

Miss Catherine made her way down from her chambers and into the kitchen.

"Are you alone, Nelly?" she asked.

"Yes, miss."

She approached the hearth. The expression on her face seemed disturbed and anxious. Catherine's lips were half asunder as if she meant to speak. She drew breath, but it escaped in a sigh instead of a long sentence.

Nelly continued slicing the carrots.

"Where's Heathcliff?" she asked.

"About his work in the stable."

There followed another long pause, during which a tear or two dropped from Catherine's cheeks.

As was common in her youth, Nelly was sure the lass had come to apologize for her shameful conduct, always one to make amends no matter how bad the temper.

"Oh, dear!" she cried. "I'm very unhappy!"

"A pity," observed Nelly, aware of her miscalculation. Lately, Catherine felt small trouble regarding any subject, save her own concerns. "You're so hard to please, so many friends, so few cares, and you can't make yourself content."

"Will you keep a secret for me?" She knelt down besides Nelly and lifted her winsome eyes to her face with the sort of look that turns off bad temper, even when one has all the right in the world to indulge it.

"Is it worth keeping?" Nelly answered less sulkily.

"Yes, and it worries me, and I must let it free. I need to know what I should do ... Today, Edgar Linton asked me to marry him, and I've given him an answer. Now before I tell you whether it was consent or denial, you tell me which it should be."

"Really, Miss Catherine, how can I know?" replied Nelly. "Considering the exhibition you performed in his presence this afternoon, I would say it wise to refuse him. Since he asked you after that, he must either be hopelessly stupid, or a venturesome fool."

"If you talk like this, then I won't tell you any more," she replied peevishly, rising to her feet. "I accepted him, Nelly. Be quick and say whether I was wrong!"

"You accepted him? Then what good is discussing the matter? You have pledged your word and cannot retract."

"But, say whether I should have done so. Please do!" she exclaimed in an irritated tone, chafing her hands together, frowning.

"There are many things to be considered, before that question can be answered properly," said Nelly sententiously. "First and foremost, do you love Edgar?"

"Who can help it? Of course I do."

"Why do you love him, Miss Catherine?"

"I do. That's sufficient."

"By no means. You must say why."

"Well, he is handsome and pleasant to be with."

"Bad."

"And because he is young and cheerful."

"Bad, still."

"And, because he loves me."

"Indifferent, coming there."

"And he will be rich, and I shall like to be the greatest woman of the neighborhood, and I shall be proud of having such a husband."

"Worst of all! And, now, say how you love him?"

"As everybody loves. You're silly, Nelly."

"Not at all. Answer."

"I love the ground under his feet, the air over his head, and everything he touches, and every word he says. I love all his looks and all his actions and him entirely and altogether. There now!"

"And why?"

"Nay, you're making a jest of it. This is exceedingly ill-natured. It's no jest to me," said the young lady, scowling and turning her face to the fire.

"Far from jesting, Miss Catherine," replied Nelly. "You love Mr. Edgar because he is handsome and young and cheerful and rich and loves you. The last, however, accounts for nothing. You would love him without that, and with it, you wouldn't, unless he possessed the four former attractions."

"To be sure not. I would only pity him—hate him perhaps, if he were ugly, and a clown."

"But, there are several other handsome, rich young men in the world; handsomer, possibly, and richer than he is. What hinders you from loving them?"

"If there be any, they are out of my sight. I've seen none like Edgar."

"You may see some; and he won't always be handsome, and young, and he may not always be rich."

"He is now. And I have only to do with the present. I wish you would speak rationally."

"Well, that settles it, Catherine. If you only have to do with the present, marry Mr. Linton."

"I don't need your permission for that. I *shall* marry him; and yet, you have not told me whether I'm right."

"Perfectly right. If people should only marry for the present. And now, let us hear what you are unhappy about. Your brother will be pleased. The old lady and gentleman will not object, I think; you will escape from a disorderly, comfortless home into a wealthy, respectable one; and you love Edgar, and Edgar loves you. All seems smooth and easy. Where is the obstacle?"

"*Here*! And *here*!" replied Catherine, striking one hand on her forehead, and the other on her breast. "In whichever place the soul lives—in my soul and in my heart, I'm convinced I'm wrong!" She wondered if it were impossible to make Nelly understand both her deep love for Heathcliff and her overwhelming fear of never breaking free of the limitations of Wuthering Heights.

"So very strange!"

"It's my secret, but if you mock me, I'll not explain it."

She seated herself next to Nelly again. Her countenance grew sadder and graver, and her clasped hands trembled.

"Do you ever have queer dreams?" she asked, suddenly, after some minutes' reflection.

"Now and then," Nelly answered.

"And so do I. I've dreamt things that have stayed with me ever after, and changed my ideas. And this one—take care not to laugh at any part of it."

"Don't, Miss Catherine. We're dismal enough without conjuring up ghosts and visions to perplex us. Come, be merry, and like yourself!"

"I shall oblige you to listen. I've no power to be merry tonight."

"I won't hear. I won't hear it," repeated Nelly hastily.

Nelly was superstitious about dreams, and Catherine had an unusual gloom in her aspect that made Nelly dread what might fall from her lips. "If I were in heaven, Nelly," continued Catherine, "I should be extremely miserable."

"Because you are not fit to go there," she answered. "All sinners would be miserable in heaven."

"But it is not for that. I dreamt, once, that I was there."

"I tell you I won't harken to your dreams, Miss Catherine. I'm going to fetch more wood."

Catherine laughed and held her down.

"This is nothing," she cried. "I was only going to say that heaven did not seem to be my home, and I broke my heart with weeping to come back to earth, and the angels were so angry that they flung me out, on top of Black Rock Cragge, where I woke sobbing for joy. That will do to explain my secret. I've no more business marrying Edgar Linton than I have to be in heaven, and if the wicked man in there had not brought Heathcliff so low, I shouldn't have thought of it. It would degrade me to marry Heathcliff, now..."

Nelly wondered if Catherine really did understand love, understand that the heart and soul of a man was the only thing that could bring true happiness to a woman. Nelly would consider Heathcliff a fine husband even if he were the poorest lad on earth. Suddenly she became aware of Heathcliff's presence on the bench just outside the window. Having noticed a slight movement, she turned her head, saw him rise, and steal away, noiselessly. "...so he shall never know how I love him," continued Catherine. "And that, not just because he's handsome, Nelly, but because he's more myself than I am. Whatever our souls are made of, his and mine are the same, and Edgar's is as different as a moonbeam from lightning, or frost from flame. And when it comes to passion, Heathcliff is like a roaring bonfire standing tall to fullest bluster the moors have to offer, and Edgar is but a candle, flickering for a few seconds, only to be vanquished by the first breeze."

The back of the settle prevented Catherine from noticing Heathcliff's presence or departure, but Nelly started and bade her hush.

"Why?" she asked, gazing nervously around.

"Joseph is here," Nelly answered, catching, opportunely, the roll of his cartwheels up the road, "and Heathcliff will come in with him. I'm not sure whether he was at the door this moment."

"Oh, he couldn't overhear me at the door," said Catherine. "Let me know when supper is ready. I want to be convinced that Heathcliff has no notion of these things—he has not, has he? He does not know what being in love is?"

"I see no reason that he should not know," returned Nelly. "And if *you* are his choice, he'll be the most unfortunate creature that was ever born. As soon as you become Mrs. Linton, he loses friend, and love, and all! Have you considered not only how you'll bear the separation, but how quite deserted in the world he'll be? Because, Miss Catherine—"

"*He* quite deserted! *He* separated!" she exclaimed. "What was I to do with my brother working him to the bone and locking me up at night? But who can really separate us, pray? Every Linton on the face of the earth will melt into nothing before I consent to forsake Heathcliff. That's not what I intend! I shouldn't be Mrs. Linton were such a price demanded! He'll mean as much to me as he has all his lifetime. Edgar must shake off his antipathy and tolerate him. Nelly, I see now, you think me a selfish wretch, but, did it ever strike you that, if Heathcliff and I married, we should be beggars? Whereas if I marry Edgar, I can aid Heathcliff to rise, and place him out of my brother's power."

"With your husband's money, Miss Catherine? You'll find him not so pliable as you calculate upon; and though I'm hardly a judge, I think it's the worst motive you've given yet for being the wife of young Edgar."

"It is not," she retorted, "it is the best. My love for Edgar is like the foliage in the woods. Time will change it, as winter changes the trees. But my love for Heathcliff resembles the eternal rocks above the ground, a source of visible delight, and completely necessary. Nelly, he's always, always on my mind—not as a pleasure, but as my own being—so don't talk of our separation again. It is impracticable, and—"

She paused, and hid her face in the folds of Nelly's gown, but Nelly jerked it forcefully away. She was out of patience with her folly!

"If I can make any sense of your nonsense, miss," said Nelly, "it only goes to convince me that you are ignorant of the duties you undertake in marrying; or else, that you are a wicked and unprincipled girl. But, trouble me with no more secrets. I'll not promise to keep them."

"You'll keep that?" she asked eagerly.

"I shall not promise," repeated Nelly.

She was about to insist, when the entrance of Joseph finished their conversation, and Catherine moved her seat to a corner, while Nelly finished supper.

After it was cooked, Joseph and Nelly argued over who should carry some to Mr. and Mrs. Earnshaw, and didn't settle it till all was nearly cold. Then they came to an agreement that they would let them ask, if they wanted any, for they feared particularly to be in their company after Hindley's day of drinking.

Nelly slipped off to bring Heathcliff a plate, but he had barricaded himself in the barn and answered none of her calls. She left the food outside. Her worst fears seemed realized, because Heathcliff never locked himself inside the barn.

At evening's end, Hindley emerged, groggy, ill-tempered, hair wild, eyes bloodshot red. He came down to the kitchen looking for food and told Catherine to be prepared for her nightly incarceration. Nelly took the occasion to accompany her charge upstairs, where she whispered, "I brought Heathcliff some food to the barn, but he has barricaded himself inside and refused to answer. I fear he really heard a good part of what you said and quit the kitchen just as you complained about your brother's conduct toward him."

She jumped in fright and made Nelly promise to wait until the house was completely settled and then to come unlock her. She said she must reveal to Heathcliff the full nature of her plan, that she could convince him to grant her entrance, and that she had to be with her love tonight of all nights.

Nelly knew she might get her own flogging if the master discovered this aid to Catherine's cause, but she felt it was right. The brother had no right to lock up his sister and the sister must do her all to right the wrong of her words.

The house was dark and all was quiet. Nelly tiptoed from the back room and crept up the stairs in her nightgown. A moonless night, completely black in the house, Nelly only knew her way because all was imprinted in memory. This was as good a night as any to free Catherine. Hindley would surely be passed out.

But perhaps all miscalculated that evening, for maybe it was the creak of floorboard, the squeak of hinged board as Nelly lifted the wood that trapped Catherine inside, or maybe that sleep all afternoon had left Hindley awake this night. Catherine was waiting, but so was Master Hindley, who came storming out of his room to throttle them both.

"The insolence!" he cried, staring at Catherine. "The betrayal!" he shouted, glaring at Nelly. "You two must take me for a proper fool! In cahoots are you to thwart the wishes of the master of Wuthering Heights! Don't think I don't know where you're headed, sister. You shame this house with your slutty soul. It's a wonder young Master Edgar can even stand the sight of thee. And Nelly, because of this disobedience, this is your final night at the Heights. And now, as master, and lord of this household, I will teach all of you a lesson you will never forget!"

His tone so fierce, his breath so sour, it caused Catherine to retreat a step and make herself small against the door. But she took advantage of his slight pause by sputtering, "I get so fearful at night, dear brother, *locked* in such a small space. It is I that pleaded with Nelly to release me from my chamber, so that I may have a brief walk around the moors to help me sleep."

"You must take me for an even bigger imbecile if you expect me to believe that drivel."

"'Tis true," she insisted, looking at Nelly. But the caretaker remained frozen in silence, knowing her time here was over, and refusing to lie to save her neck. "If you go to the barn, you will see that Heathcliff has locked himself in and no one can penetrate."

"No one," said Hindley, with an evil stare. With that he took Catherine by the arm and flung her ahead. She tripped and tumbled down the stairs. Her wrist snapped as she reached out to break her fall. Nelly hurried after her, to give aid, and to avoid the same fate. "Don't think I don't know you have been fucking that gypsy trash since who knows when. Probably even when Father was alive, such a whore you are!"

Joseph heard the commotion and came forth from the back room as well. Mrs. Earnshaw pulled her husband's pillow over her ears and tried to drown out the noise, barely able to turn on her side she was so large with child.

Hindley ordered Joseph to fetch the ax and bring the women to the barn, while he found the whip.

Once all were at the barn, Hindley kicked aside the untouched plate of food at the entrance, and did not even bother to check if the door was indeed impassable. He commanded Joseph to break it down, and he, using the ax, made quick work, and all four were inside, Joseph illuminating the room with his lantern.

Heathcliff lay on his bed, as calm as could be, wide awake, staring straight at Catherine. Clutching her wrist, she burst into a horrible weeping.

"Master Hindley, please," said Nelly. "This error was ours and Heathcliff had no part."

"No part? Is it possible that my sister fucks herself? That tart has shamed the honor of this household and this bastard shall pay."

"NO!" screamed Catherine, lurching toward Hindley, trying to grab him with her one good hand. He cast her off and beckoned Joseph to keep both women at bay.

"Off with your shirt and on your knees by the side of the bed!" ordered Hindley.

Heathcliff immediately stood and began removing his shirt. It pleased Hindley to show Catherine what a sniveling weakling her favorite was. No protest, no fight, willing to take his punishment like the most common of slaves. But instead of turning, falling to his knees, facing away from them with his elbows on the bed, Heathcliff walked slowly around to the other side of the bed, crouched to the floor, and faced them all, which allowed him to continue his hard, cold stare at Catherine. She wept profusely as she wished death for both her and her love rather than have him receive and her witness the wrath of a man so insipid and cowardly.

Hindley did not like the deliberate way Heathcliff ventured to the other side of the bed, as if it were he who controlled the punishment. He was about to order him to crawl forth and grovel at his boots to beg for mercy, although certainly none would be given. But something about Heathcliff's unwavering stare told him that his current spot on the floor was not negotiable ... and this angered the master even more.

With grand, pompous steps, Hindley walked to other side of the bed, turned, faced Joseph, Nelly, and Catherine, along with Heathcliff's back, and proceeded to flog his flesh like a being possessed, conjuring up all the anger and pain he felt since the arrival of Heathcliff, whipping his back again and again as if trying to crush his spine like the thwarted gift of the fiddle. Even Joseph turned away. Catherine wanted to, but Heathcliff's stare held her fast. Never had she seen his eyes so black, so free of emotion.

Nelly began to weep for his pain as well. From the extra ferocity of Hindley's blows, it dawned on her that Heathcliff was suffering not because of Catherine's attempted escape, but because he had challenged Hindley publicly in the courtyard, daring Hindley to fire his gun point-blank. How humiliating it must have been for the bully Hindley to retreat after that, after not having the courage to pull the trigger again when challenged. He probably was not sleeping all afternoon, but lying in bed next to his frigid wife, plotting his revenge, building his anger, and waiting desperately for the right opportunity to unleash his righteous vengeance.

Nelly also knew that Heathcliff must have known that his actions would inspire this kind of violent retaliation, yet did so anyway. And he was big enough and strong enough to fight back, to break Hindley in two if he wanted to, whether Joseph was there to give aid or not. He could have left the house and stayed in the fields until Master Hindley cooled off. But Heathcliff clearly wanted this. He wanted to luxuriate in physical pain to block out the emotional scars underneath, but his own suffering wasn't enough. He wanted to hurt Catherine deeply and decisively because of her betrayal; he was simply incapable of doing such damage directly and welcomed Hindley to do his dirty work.

And the more Heathcliff withstood the blows without sound or remark—just that ever-present stare at his beloved—the harder Hindley tried to strike, drawing rivers of blood, until the leather of several of the straps frayed or broke off, until his arm felt like the weight of an anvil and his face looked reddish and wild enough to foreshadow an attack to his own heart, until Heathcliff's eyes closed as he drifted into unconsciousness.

"I hate you!" screamed Catherine as the four made their way

back to the house, just before she picked up a shovel by a stall and whacked her brother in the head.

It was fortunate she had but one good hand, because the anger and venom she put into the swing surely would have killed him if both hands were sturdy. She ran into the house. Hindley was too weak to follow and inflict retaliation. Besides, he was cut open like a stuffed pig and began to stagger. "Tend to me," he ordered Nelly.

"I've been relieved of my responsibilities," she said with cold bitterness, "and will depart in the morn." She left the barn on her own accord.

Joseph helped the master to the kitchen, where he applied a dry towel.

"I'll fetch the doctor in the morning," said Joseph. "You'll need a few stitches, Catherine a splint for the wrist, and young Heathcliff will surely need tending to."

He left the master at the table, alone, to ponder his own wickedness, and retired to bed.

Chapter Eight

With just a few hours of dark left, sure everyone was asleep or fully ensconced in their respective rooms, Nelly crept out of bed again. In the kitchen, she filled a basin with water and grabbed a handful of fresh towels. Careful as could be, she made her way out of the house and to the barn. With the door shattered, cold air filled the space. She found Heathcliff on the bed, on his stomach.

She pulled a stool to his bedside and, delicately, used the wet towels to clean his wounds. Heathcliff opened his eyes, looked at her. Still shaken by the brutality of what she had witnessed, she whispered nervously to help keep her mind at ease so she could nurse him properly. "A lad such as you should never allow the likes of him to rain such hurt. I know you worry about being cast out, about surviving without a penny to your name, but the life of a beggar is better than life like this." His eyelids seemed to lift just a shade wider. "I know, I know, the lass has broken your heart, but is that cause to receive such blows without defense? I know the girl loves you down deep, but the emotions that float on top, those are as flimsy as an umbrella in a windstorm."

He moved his neck so he could face the other way and she was presented with the back of his head, the wild hair flowing to his shoulders. Though his reception was cold, she was glad to see he was getting some energy back, that he had survived the beating. If ever there was a man who could bear such a flogging, it was Heathcliff.

She cleaned him tenderly, carefully, knowing the touch of cloth to his open wounds only inflicted more pain, but she wanted to reduce his chance for infection. Many of the wounds were already caked with dried blood. He remained still, silent.

Finally done, she spilled the bloody water onto the dirt of the barn and piled the soiled towels in the empty basin. She was about to leave, when Heathcliff managed to turn over on his back.

"Don't, lad," she said. "You'll open the wounds."

He ignored her, and began to unbutton his trousers. He refused her help and with effort cleared them from his legs and lay completely naked.

As troubled as her heart might be, Nelly ran her eyes over his masculine fineness. "For old times' sake," she told herself, as it was probably the last time her eyes would be treated to the likes of this. She stood, bent down to kiss his forehead good night, when she felt him grasp her hand. She looked down at her petite fingers in his monstrous palm. With just a roll of his eyes downward, she knew what he wanted.

"Nay, Heathcliff. You must regain your strength. This should be the last thing on your mind."

Nevertheless, he did not relinquish his grip.

She sat on the stool, pulled it a little closer. "A randy one you are," she said, "even in such a state." He freed her hand.

She gently stroked the underside of his cock with a flutter of her fingers. If this was something that would take his mind off the pain, then she was happy to oblige; it was a pleasure for her to oblige, as it had been a long while since she had the delight of seeing the young man naked. He let out the faintest of groans.

It thrilled her to please him, for in the entire county there was no man as handsome and well formed as Heathcliff, and to know that he welcomed her touch so eagerly caused a heat through her body and a tingle along the flesh of her legs and arms.

Quick to respond, as always, his cock soon stood on its own. With expert stroking, Nelly played the nurse who went the extra mile to soothe her patient. One hand caressed his hard stomach and chest, while the other teased the cock with light strokes. She wandered down to his legs, knowing he liked to be touched along the inside of his thighs. Her favorite spot was the soft, tender area just under his balls. Her touch there invoked the loudest approval since her arrival, and the tingle spread to her womanhood, already alerted, alive, eager for more.

At full attention, she pushed the stool aside, and got down on her knees, almost looking up at this beautiful phallic specimen. She licked around the base of the cock as she held it up straight with both hands. She could taste his sweat, a salty flavor that always aroused her sharply.

So lovely to be alone with him in this barn, to be the one he turned to for comfort. She knew nothing could sway his love for Catherine, but even he could not deny the passionate effect of her caresses and licks, his sculpted body warming to her touch.

Patient as always, she finally started with her tongue at the shaft, licking up it, down it, around it, the cock at such full attention it felt like a steel rod. At the head, well swollen with desire, she flicked back and forth, and delighted in hearing Heathcliff's groans of pleasure. Her own wetness began a slight trickle down her thigh.

Hands and fingers at work, she caressed all over his body as if he were a piano beneath her. Mouth over the top of his cock head, pulling him slowly inside her throat, she sucked his glorious instrument. Her applications, his sounds of approval, brought the familiar music of the stolen moments she had grown to cherish.

She had an overpowering urge to repeat their familiar pattern, and slide her free hand down between her legs, to caress her most tender spots and match the rhythm of her sucking. But she resisted, raising her focus even more to provide pleasure and healing for one who had been so wronged.

The time grew near—as she could feel his final surge of growth, recognize the slight arch of his hips just before he would explode into her mouth—and she quickened her sucking, relaxing her throat, to take in almost the full length of him.

Only instead of getting his usual sweet rush of semen—the taste, the hard flow, the ferocious spasming in her throat that usually intensified her own deep orgasm—instead of the familiar finish where she swallowed everything and typically fingered her own passion into a finish that filled her with both affection and gratitude—he pulled his cock out of her mouth.

She looked at him quizzically. He grabbed her by the hair and pulled her next to him, planting on her the deepest, most forceful kiss she had ever received, his tongue replacing the cock that had been in her mouth. Unable to resist, she kissed him back, until there was a slight pause for both to catch their breath and he reached a hand into her nightshirt and began to play with her left nipple.

She took that time to stand to her feet.

"Let us take this no further, Heathcliff. I am more than content to give you the pleasure you so richly deserve, but if that is not all you want then I must depart."

She turned to leave, but he grabbed her hand again, forcefully. She turned back to him. "Although you are indeed a bonny lad, you are still just that compared to me. You're the young 'un whose tears I wiped and whose body I bathed naked in the tin tub. I know it wasn't right to pleasure you the way I have, but you're a hard man to resist. But resist I must."

She tried to leave again, but his grip held firm.

"You're in no condition to lay fully, if that's what you have in mind, and from the way you touched my nipple, I'm pretty sure that's it."

There was still no relief from his pressure.

"You must think of Catherine here. I know she did you a wrong turn, but the lass loves you with the passion of a full-grown woman and I know you love her with a feeling that would make every woman in the county green with envy. I know you heard of her promise of betrothal, but I believe love conquers all... although if that were really true you would be in love with me as well," she said with a wee smile. Their eyes met, which was un- usual when they had these carnal encounters, as it made it easier for her to enjoy his manhood without seeing the face that re- minded her of the boy she had cared for. For him, he just seemed completely disconnected when accepting her ministrations. Even when their eyes made contact, it was as if he was not seeing her.

Nelly managed to surprise him by jerking her wrist out of his grip, which enabled her to make a turn to leave.

With superhuman strength, he managed to rise from the bed. She hesitated, in case he might collapse, and he took that oppor- tunity to grab her with both hands.

"Stop!" she cried, pushing her hands against his chest. He threw her to the bed and let his substantial weight fall on top of her, pinning her to the mattress.

He tugged on her hair, exposing her throat, and began licking her vigorously along her neck. She tried to turn her head away, but his mouth found hers, his tongue lashing against hers, and she felt his full, powerful presence. He tore off her nightshirt, ripping it to shreds, discarding it on the floor, and she was completely naked under him. She tried to fight him with her fists, pounding his chest, making no headway. Her hands a distraction, he finally took both wrists in his meaty right palm and held them above her head, binding her, while he sucked, licked, and bit her nipples, causing her to cry out in pain, a pain that made her nipple grow in his mouth and inspired heated surges of pleasure through her breasts.

"Stop now, Heathcliff! I will not be taken like some common whore dragged upstairs in a tavern."

The first words spoken by Heathcliff this night, spoken while not looking directly at her, were, "You are a whore!"

And then he lowered his body and his tongue went deep into her quim, as thick and long as an average man's penis, and she knew the words he spoke were true. Because a whore was helpless, and helpless she was against an attack so forceful and passionate.

Nevertheless, she did struggle and squirm and did her best to feign protest, but she could not resist the full power of his tongue, going deeper than any man had before, expertly flicking back and forth inside her walls, causing her hips to shake and spasm, her quim to yield fully to one who seemed so greedy to devour her with the savage fury of a man deeply possessed . . . which only spurred him further, as he licked her into the deepest, fullest orgasm she had ever experienced, causing her to cry out with a moan fraught with the intensity of all the wavering affection, hesitation, and desire that had coursed through her since returning to the barn.

Done using his mouth and tongue, he climbed up her body, and presented his cock. With his hand, he pressed it against her face, making her feel helpless to it, but also hungry for more of his hardness, the smooth texture and contours of the swollen veins, the delicious scent of his manhood, the wonderful masculine taste that was purely him and no other.

This aroused in her a deep, smoldering passion, to both resist the whims of a man so haunted and to abandon herself fully to this powerful, extraordinary being.

He arched his hips and lowered his arse onto her mouth, and ordered her to lick, which she did, zestfully, thrashing under him, unable to resist all that was Heathcliff, luxuriating in a taste that was so strong, yet arousing, livid that he could reduce her to one so common, so needy for the basest of actions.

"I hate you for this," she snapped.

He reached back, squeezed her right nipple between his thumb and index finger, turning it with a slight twist, causing her to cry out in discomfort and intense gratification, forcing her to increase the tempo of her tongue, licking him with even more vitality.

The deep stimulation gave him an even mightier erection and he was finally ready.

He slid down her body and rose above her, parallel, and she knew he was about to enter her. "No, Heathcliff. You go too far!"

He turned her over onto her stomach and let loose with several hard slaps along her bum cheeks. The vulnerability of being turned like a rag doll and laid bare to the force of his hand, coupled with a rush of bawdy sensation from the sharp stings of his firm blows, caused her arse to turn crimson and her own animal moans to escape from somewhere deep inside her, as she crushed her mouth against Heathcliff's pillow and took in even more scent and taste from this man attempting to own her fully.

The huge penetration by him at this angle caused her to cry

out. If she was not so moist from desire and hunger, it might have hurt. Instead it was a noble piercing, one that made her feel his presence as she had no other man.

He fucked her.

With no quarter given.

Powerful, deep infiltrations that opened her up completely, causing all the sensations within her to escalate more and more, as if being commanded by each of his forceful strokes.

She whimpered under him, angry that he was taking her this way, angry that it brought so much pleasure to her being, angry that, against her sincere wishes, her arse rose into the air as an offering, inviting even further penetration. A penetration that seemed to reach thoroughly into her inner being and brought explosive, swirling sensations that completely clouded her vision.

The force of his ingress deep inside her resembled the snap of Hindley's whip on his back.

He bit her neck and she couldn't help crying out, "Oh, Heathcliff, all man you are, though a dastardly one."

He grabbed her by the hips, as he had seen Robert do, and lifted her up even higher so he could angle even deeper. She buried her face downward, made one last monumental effort not to succumb so entirely to the mission of this man.

But Nelly did not have the force of will of one such as Heathcliff. The fury, the repetition, the deep, primal arousal that washed all through her like a storm swallowing up the shore, broke every last amount of resistance, and her body, and soul, went limp in full submission to his penetration.

And as he doubled his speed, the width and length of him expanding toward the final release, and she came in wave after wave, Nelly had no choice but to murmur in the rhythm of his thrusts, "Yes, Heathcliff, you are my master, truly, forever, I have no other, master, master, master, I love you with all my heart."

With that, Heathcliff exploded inside her, filling her with rivers of fluid, pounding her with his last few frenzied thrusts, as he screamed out one simple word upon completion...

"CATHERINE...!"

Chapter Nine

Just before the light of dawn, not long after Nelly had left his bedside, the dark figure of Heathcliff moved swiftly along the moors. He carried nothing, for he owned nothing. He wore no shirt, for the only one he possessed, a bloody mess, was left in the barn. He soon arrived at Black Rock Cragge, surveyed the surrounding landscape of the place he called home since arriving from Liverpool. To the north was Thrushcross Grange. To the south was Wuthering Heights. To the east, first light of day was about to break, but there was only a slight clearness above the horizon. The rest of the sky was a charcoal black of storm clouds.

Heathcliff stood, shirtless, at the edge of the precipice, above the pool where Catherine and he had sealed their vow, arms rising up to the heavens, palms turning outward, as he welcomed the tempest.

The storm came rattling over the moors in full fury. There was a violent wind, as well as thunder, and either one or the other split a tree across the roof of the Earnshaw house and knocked down a portion of the east chimney stack, sending a clatter of stones and soot into the kitchen fire.

Joseph thought a bolt had fallen in the middle of the family, and swung onto his knees, beseeching the Lord to remember the

patriarchs Noah and Lot, and, as in former times, spare the righteous, though he smote the ungodly.

At Thrushcross Grange, it was lightning that did strike, as the
terrible wind had blown open the gate to the dog kennel, and
the dogs ran wild and loose in fright, and a bolt came piercing
down from the sky to strike Skulker's metal-studded collar, frying
the canine into a dead crisp.

Heathcliff held his position at Black Rock Cragge as the hard
rain struck his face, as a bolt of lightning revealed a twisted smile
on his face.

He had listened to his beloved speak of the many ways she
loved another.

He had heard his darling say that to marry him would degrade
her.

He had heard his most venerated speak words that violated
their sacred vow.

He had allowed a cowardly bully to have his way with him.

He had endured the pompous and shallow Linton family separating him from his treasure as if he were trash to be tossed to
the pigs.

He knew now that he could have had his way with Catherine
at any time: in the garret on Christmas night, during their stolen
moments in the fields, if he had wanted to take her the way he
had Nelly this very eve, and that she would have been powerless
to resist the strength in his hands, the fire in his eyes, the hunger
in his mouth, the forceful strength between his legs.

Even now . . . if he wanted her.

But after all that had happened tonight he could not see one,
single, solitary way to have Catherine in the truest of forms. He
could love her as Heathcliff: falling to his knees for the chance
to place his lips upon her feet, rising each day simply to rest his

eyes upon her loveliness, baring his soul just to receive her sim-
plest of touches. But she needed more, much more. She needed
Edgar as well. And though the lad was as spineless as a worm,
he had the fair skin and blue eyes of a gentleman, the costume
and manners of a man of dignified birth, the wealth and station
of someone who could fulfill Catherine with the luxury of life at
the Grange and the noble status of being called his *wife*.

What was the point if he could not have her completely and
she would not be satisfied with all that was him?

But should they all be absent of the suffering that ripped
through his soul as the storm whipped through the firs on the
moors?

"NAY!" shouted Heathcliff to the sky, daring God to strike him
down now if he so planned.

But as bolts of lightning came and went, from sky to ground, all
around the moors, there was nary a flicker at Black Rock Cragge.

"Then a curse be on them!" cried Heathcliff. "A curse for a
thousand years and more. I place a curse on the Earnshaws and
Lintons, for all the pettiness you inspire, the meanness of spirit
you invoke, and because you would not allow two people to love
in the pure righteous way that lay buried in their hearts."

A loud, angry bolt came crashing down, but it did not strike
Heathcliff and he continued to smile.

"A curse on all those Earnshaws and Lintons living and all those
to be born! For as I stand here on the cragge, as long as I draw
breath, and even from the hell where I will surely land, I will reap
pleasure from seeing each and every one of you suffer!"

Despite the rain pounding his face, Heathcliff let out a horrific,
bone-chilling, bloodcurdling scream that paled the death cry of
any wounded animal, a scream that startled awake and went
down the spine of each Earnshaw and Linton like a razor split-

ting a soul in two—although they could not be sure it was human, animal, or just the storm they had heard—disturbing deeply every last one of them, including the baby curled inside Mrs. Earnshaw.

And then he jumped.

VOLUME II

Chapter Ten

Perhaps an hour after dawn broke, and the terrible storm had been reduced to a steady, driving rain, Joseph came stomping into the house, wet to the bone. The rest of the family was at breakfast.

"To let you know, sir," he said to Hindley. "I just went to check on young Heathcliff before riding to Gimmerton for Dr. Kenneth, but the lad is nowhere to be found."

Hindley replied, "Perhaps a blessing has fallen upon this house and the filthy urchin has made a fortuitous departure." Perhaps it was the baby that kicked, because Mrs. Earnshaw let out a sharp cry of discomfort. "Let me know if he does appear. It will be pleasure no matter what: for either he has disappeared for good, or I will have the joy of putting my boot to his arse and sending him on his way."

"No!" said Catherine, quickly jumping to her feet. With her left hand supporting the ailing wrist, she was out the door, into the rain.

"Stop!" ordered Hindley, but she paid no heed.

Nelly was at the counter. Hindley had not shunned her this morning and seemed content to allow her to prepare breakfast. She was too sore in body, and too weak in heart, to take action toward packing her things.

Catherine went first to the barn, only to be confronted by bloody sheets and Heathcliff's blood-soaked shirt upon the floor. She searched all around the estate. When she returned to rummage the house, she said to Nelly, "I wonder where he is. I wonder where he *can* be! My brother has wronged him deeply, but I pray it did not cause his final parting."

"Perhaps he's gone to Gimmerton to seek the doctor," said Nelly, feeble in voice, unable to apply true conviction. Heathcliff never asked for a doctor in his life.

Catherine could not be persuaded into any tranquility and went back out in the rain, wandered to and fro, from the gate to the door, in a state of extreme agitation, which permitted no repose, and at length made her way out to the fields, in the hope Heathcliff had taken up his usual station.

Though she couldn't see how he could work after the thrashing he had received last night.

None of the other workers had seen him.

Catherine—without shawl or bonnet, catching all the water she could with her hair and clothes, drenched for her obstinacy in refusing to take shelter—stared out at the moors. Though visibility was poor, it was still plain to see there was not a soul on the horizon. She made her way to Black Rock Cragge.

Once there, seeing no man hidden behind the rocks, she found herself at the edge of the precipice. Could it be possible that he had jumped? She could see no body below. If she had, she was sure she would leap to join him. It was still possible, however, that he had jumped to his death against the rocks, as the pool, flooded from the rain, could have carried him out to the river, whose current ran south at a strong pace, even stronger after such a rainfall. She was about to turn back to home, when she noticed her locket placed on a flat stone near the edge.

Her scream rivaled that of her beloved's: deep, loud, as true to pain as an open wound. She fell to her knees, quickly soiled by the mud the storm had created. She raised her eyes upward, the same view Heathcliff had challenged just hours earlier, beseeching the heavens for some insight, some comfort. But her emptiness remained. She lowered her eyes toward the swirling pool below, shivering with the thought that at the bottom lay clues but no answers. She covered her face with both hands, and, with full anguish, wept profusely into her palms, the heavy tears rolling past her wrists and down the length of her arms.

It was fortunate that Joseph had already brought Dr. Kenneth from Gimmerton, for Mrs. Earnshaw had gone into an early labor and her screams, also, traveled across the moors.

Hindley waited outside his chambers as the doctor tended to his wife. When Catherine arrived, pale, shaken, soaked to the bone, the locket hidden in her hand, Hindley said bitterly, "Still running after the lad as usual. A whore you are, a whore shall you remain!"

Her knees buckled and she fainted to the floor. Hindley grabbed her good wrist and felt the fire in her flesh. "She's ill, damn it," he said to Joseph. "I don't want to be troubled with more sickness here. Take her to bed."

Dr. Kenneth was a busy man that day, going back and forth from Mrs. Earnshaw to Catherine. Nelly was not much help, as she had taken to her chambers as well, claiming she also had fever.

The doctor applied a cool compress to Catherine's forehead, then noticed the bump on her wrist and quickly surmised it was broken. As he splinted it he asked Hindley how that happened, and the mouse explained it must have been from her fall after fainting.

It was Joseph who came to rouse Nelly out of bed. He told her that a fine baby boy was born to the Earnshaws, but that she must come to help nurse it, to feed it with sugar and milk, and take care of it, day and night. "The doctor said the missus must rest, and has been in consumption these many months."

"Is she very ill?" asked Nelly.

"I guess she is, yet she looks bravely," replied Joseph.

Outside of the Earnshaw chambers, Nelly encountered Hindley, and she asked, "How is the baby?"

"Nearly ready to run about," said Hindley, putting on a cheerful smile.

"And the mistress?" she ventured to inquire. "The doctor says she's—"

"Damn the doctor!" he interrupted, reddening. "Frances is quite right. She'll be perfectly well by this time next week."

Nelly entered the chambers and took the baby, who had been named Hareton, into her arms: her first bonny little nursling, his eyes as dark as night. She looked at Mrs. Earnshaw, who was clearly delirious with fever, then left to go downstairs for a feeding.

Hindley tended to his wife doggedly for the remainder of the week, furiously affirming her health improved every day. When the doctor warned him that his medicines were useless at this stage of the malady, and he needn't put him to further expense by attending her, Hindley retorted, "I know you need not. She's well. She does not want any more attendance from you! She never was in consumption. It was a fever and it's gone. Her pulse is as slow as mine now, and her cheek as cool."

He told his wife the same story, and she seemed to believe him, but one night, while leaning on his shoulder, in the act of saying she thought she should be able to get up tomorrow, a fit of coughing took her—a very slight one—he raised her in his arms; she put her two hands about his neck, her face changed, and she was dead.

It was Hindley's turn to cry out. Although pain was clearly there, he lacked the passion to match the decibels of Heathcliff's curse or his sister's anguish.

Hareton fell wholly into the care of Nelly. Nearly oblivious to the child, Hindley grew desperate; his sorrow was of that kind that would not lament. He neither wept nor prayed—he cursed and defied—execrated God and man, and gave himself up to reckless dissipation.

The other servants could not bear his tyrannical and evil conduct long. Joseph and Nelly were the only two to stay, and she did only because the infant needed tending. Even the curate stopped calling and nobody decent came near Wuthering Heights.

Catherine fell into a violent, thrashing delirium and Dr. Kenneth pronounced her dangerously ill. He bled her and told Nelly to let her live on whey, water, and gruel; and take care she did not throw herself down stairs, or out the window. While still with fever, at the times she regained consciousness, she would often cry out to whoever would listen, "Please! You must search the river! Drag it. Inquire along the way if anyone has seen my Heathcliff. You must! If he is dead I must know. If he is alive I must be with him! Curse all those who mean him ill will!"

Whether it was Hindley, who visited rarely, or Edgar—who visited only once, and left in tears either from her condition, her entreats, or both—neither heeded her pleas. Nelly comforted her and took up her cause with the master, but her requests were denied as well.

Old Mrs. Linton finally showed up, and set things to rights, and scolded and ordered everyone, and when Catherine was convalescent, she insisted on conveying her to Thrushcross Grange, for which deliverance Nelly was very grateful.

But, the poor dame had reason to repent her kindness. She and her husband both took the fever, and died within a few days of each other.

Catherine returned to the Heights, fully recovered, saucier, more passionate, and haughtier than ever, but always with the undercurrent of sadness in her dark eyes. Heathcliff still had not been heard from since the evening of the great storm.

One day Nelly had the misfortune, after Catherine had provoked her exceedingly, to lay the blame of Heathcliff's disappearance on her. From that period on, she ceased to hold any communication with her caretaker, save in the relation of a mere servant. Joseph also fell under a ban; he *would* speak his mind, and lecture her all the same as if she were a little girl; and she esteemed herself a woman, and the mistress, and thought that her recent illness gave her claim to be treated with consideration. The doctor chimed in, saying she ought to have her own way and it was nothing less than murder for any one to presume to stand up and contradict her.

From Hindley she also kept aloof. Tutored by Dr. Kenneth, and from serious threats of a fit that often attended her rages, her brother allowed whatever she pleased, and generally avoided aggravating her fiery temper. He was rather too indulgent in humoring her caprices, lost mostly in the mourning of his wife and the deterioration of his household. Not from affection, but from pride, he wished earnestly to see her bring back honor to the family in an alliance with the Lintons, and, as long as she let him alone, he gave her free rein.

Edgar Linton, as multitudes have been before, and will be after him, was infatuated; and believed himself to be the happiest man alive on the day he led Catherine to Gimmerton chapel, to be wedded in holy matrimony, just months after his parents' death.

Much against Nelly's inclination, she was persuaded to leave Wuthering Heights and accompany Catherine to Thrushcross Grange. Little Hareton was growing fast and had just begun to sit up. It made for a sad parting, but Catherine's tears were more powerful than Hareton's. When Nelly refused to go, and when Catherine found her entreaties did not move her, she went lamenting to her husband and brother. The former offered Nelly munificent wages, the latter ordered her to pack up. He looked forward to no women in the house now that there was no mistress. As to Hareton, the curate should take him in hand, by-and-by. And so, Nelly had no choice left but to do as ordered. She told the master he had gotten rid of all decent people, the most conspicuous being Heathcliff, and the result would be to ruin himself even faster. She kissed Hareton good-bye, but queer as it was, the child who had brightened every time he saw his care-taker, from feedings, to changings, to long walks on the moors, suddenly received the kiss as if she were a stranger.

As for Heathcliff, since the fateful day of half-truths and deceit, a cowardly flogging, a rough, bloody tumble in the barn, his pronouncement of a deep curse on all of the Lintons and Earnshaws, his precarious leap from the precipice of Black Rock Cragge, no one had seen hide nor hair of him, nor heard news of any appearances in other counties. All presumed he was very long gone, or dead.

Chapter Eleven

How deep a love did Edgar hold, to forgive his betrothed, on the night of their wedding, the headache she confessed to possess?

"All the wine, the rich food, the endless prattle from those I hardly know, has left thunder within my skull, dear husband," said Catherine as she settled into bed.

"Shall I fetch the doctor, my pet?" he asked, as he stroked her forehead.

"Nay, I will recover by the morn. Can we not just rest here this evening and be with each other like brother and sister?"

"Of course, my love. I completely understand. The chance simply to lie with you all night has been in my mind since our first kiss."

"I just want our first to be perfect."

"Indeed it shall."

The room dark now, they lay silent, each on their backs. Edgar inched his fingers toward Catherine and found her hand. He grasped it tightly, fully content to fall asleep with the tender feel of his wife's hand within his.

Catherine was wide awake. She had rejoiced heartily the day Edgar had taken her as his wife. She believed it would help her forget the desertion of her beloved Heathcliff... and set her straight in the life station she deserved and had always felt destined for. At the very least, it had helped her escape the chaos of Wuthering Heights and the vileness of Hindley.

Yet, this was the time she worried about, alone in bed with Edgar. For she felt for him like a brother, the brother she wished Hindley could have been. Although his kisses were tender and sincere, they did not light a fire that even a small look from Heathcliff could inspire. She often found herself staring out the window, while her husband slept soundly next to her, toward the south, imagining the pointed rocks of Black Rock Cragge. The thought of the place where Heathcliff and she had first kissed, where they had sworn their love forever, brought the only spark within her body since the day of her marriage to Edgar. On sadder nights, she looked to the same place, and wondered why he had broken his promise and departed (to another world, or to another place?) without the locket that symbolized their powerful union. Lest melancholy overcome her, she forced herself to turn away and focus on her husband; no sweeter man had ever walked the earth. She knew that her wifely duties could not be forsaken, although she would like to put it off for as long as she could, for fear of disappointing Edgar with an austere response, and, even worse, having it confirmed that her married life was doomed to be one without passion.

As time passed, Catherine grew more than fond of Edgar at Thrushcross Grange. Even to his sister, Isabella, she showed plenty of affection. Both brother and sister were very attentive to her comfort. It was not the thorn bending to the honeysuckles, but the honeysuckles embracing the thorn. There were no mutual concessions; one stood erect, and the others yielded; and who *can* be ill-natured, and bad tempered, when they encounter neither opposition nor indifference?

Despite their growing affection, Edgar was still a homebody, one who preferred to read a book by the fire, or write long letters to London acquaintances. Though enjoying the luxury of many servants at the Grange and the fine wardrobe Isabella helped her pick out, Catherine missed the days when Heathcliff and she roamed the moors like common heathens, dirty and unkempt. They had been free to race where they pleased and hold each other in deep embrace, their flesh turning even darker from the strong summer sun.

Edgar had a deep-rooted fear of ruffling Catherine's humor. He concealed it from her, but if ever he heard Nelly answer sharply, or saw any other servant grow cloudy at some imperious order of hers, he would show his trouble by a frown of displeasure that never darkened on his own account. He, many times, spoke sternly to Nelly about her pertness and averred that the stab of a knife could not inflict a worse pain than he suffered at seeing his lady vexed.

Unable to grieve a kind master, Nelly learned to be less touchy; and, at the start of the marriage, the gunpowder lay harmless as sand, because no fire came near to explode it. Catherine had seasons of gloom and silence, now and then: They were respected with sympathizing silence by her husband, who ascribed them to an alteration in her constitution, produced by her perilous illness, as she was never subject to depression of spirits before. The return of sunshine was welcomed by answering sunshine from him. Between them grew a deep and growing happiness, although one that was not complete.

One evening, Edgar put Catherine to bed, but instead of joining her immediately he brought up a bowl of warm, fragrant oil from the kitchen and placed it on her bedside table.

"What is this, husband?" asked Catherine.

"Hush, wife. Enjoy."

With that, he rolled her onto her stomach and hiked up her nightgown to midthigh.

Warm oil in abundance in both hands, he began a soothing massage along her calves and thighs.

"Pleasant indeed," said Catherine. His touch surprised her, perhaps because of the addition of warm oil. Though his kisses, his hand holding, his embraces, were not unpleasant, there was usually a cool dryness to his skin that inspired no tingle or warmth on her part. Just the feel of her hand lost in the grasp of Heathcliff made her whole body increase in temperature.

With careful pressure, he glided his fingers over the flesh he so adored, taking great satisfaction at pleasing the woman he loved. Once she seemed as warm as the oil in his hands, he was tempted to lift the nightgown even farther to see the full curve of her arse, and the flowing arch of her back, something his shy wife had denied him so far. But he was afraid of being rejected, so instead of going higher, he went lower... to her feet.

He touched the soles of her feet lightly at first, careful not to cause a start. It was Nelly who had revealed to him this secret of pleasuring a woman. "It is the window to the rest of the body," she had told her master, when he lamented the platonic nature of his relationship with his wife. "Open this window and you will be allowed to climb in to see the house."

And the window did open, wide enough to extend the most cordial of invitations. Catherine enjoyed the heated pressure of his fingers working the tenderest spots of her sole. The surges through her body relaxed her in a way that brought an inner peace, and she felt her body sink heavily into the mattress, losing her concern over disappointing Edgar, not pining for something long gone, but welcoming, finally, a touch that spoke to her not only of emotional, but physical love.

He took his time, infinitely patient, one side of him content to touch only here for the rest of the night, she seemed so pleased. He kneaded the ball of each foot deeply, pressed a full hand over the toes and down, stretching them. When he got to the tender area at her heel and pressed rhythmically and with authority, he heard his precious love let out a soft moan, like a soothing note from a string plucked.

For Catherine enjoyed his touch immensely, the pressure at her feet warming her body up through her scalp. She needed this. She missed this. How often had she serviced her own needs while revisiting her kisses with Heathcliff, the feel of him in her hand just outside these very windows, their glorious Christmas night when he licked her into a delirious fever and it took all of her willpower not to give up her womanhood with complete abandon, the stolen kisses and caresses that had seemed so difficult to obtain afterward, but perhaps more rewarding for the same reason?

"Edgar, your touch is golden," she murmured into her pillow.

This gave him courage as he finished with deep pressure on both feet then went directly to sliding her nightgown up over his treasure's shoulders and off, meeting no resistance at all, pleased by her welcomed assistance.

There she lay naked before him, a vision of godly beauty he worried he would never behold, for he had deliberately left the candle burning in the hopes he could witness this vision. Lest the absence of his touch leave her cold, or prone to second guess, he began to massage her ample buttocks, eliciting a groan of pleasure that stirred, deeply, his own loins.

Edgar need not have worried about any second-guessing. His hands at her legs and feet had served to relax her, open her for the possibility of even more intimate caresses. But his manipulations at her buttocks took him through yet another door, and she felt a deep stirring in her quim, unconsciously rotating her hips down, into the mattress, causing a pressure between her thighs that added to her excitement, moistened her desire, and had her longing for more.

Lacking the fortitude to spread her splendid cheeks and work the tender opening, he moved up to her back and shoulders.

"Edgar, my love," she said, in a tone he had not heard before. He took pause to remove his own nightshirt, and husband and wife lay naked together. He rested the full length of his entire body on top of hers and she could feel the beginning of his hardness against her buttocks. He kissed her passionately along the neck and cheeks until she turned enough so that his lips found hers. He felt abandonment in her kisses that he had not been rewarded with before and, again, would have been content to do this all night. But it was she, this time, who made a gesture, which was to roll onto her back.

The sight of her luscious full breasts nearly surged him to orgasm. She took pleasure at the lust and need in his eyes. With a sensual arch of her back, her breasts seemed to rise on their own, closer to his face. The greediness in his stare aroused her further, and she enjoyed the sense that every movement she made, from a turn of the head, to a delicate touch of her tongue to her lips, to the way she cupped her breasts now in both hands and presented them to her husband, caused him to tremble and stir and reveal his full neediness. "You may touch them," she said.

Grateful to his queen for sharing the gifts of her flesh, he warmed a new round of oil in his hands and commenced to cupping, kneading, massaging, caressing her perfect orbs, paying particular attention to her brownish nipples. Catherine's eyes closed and she encouraged him with deep sounds of pleasure. He had built within her a long-awaited opera: the opening preparing her for the events to come; the middle stripping her of all resistance and inspiring a need for more; and now she looked forward to the grand finale, eager, after all these dormant months, for her body to sing with great pleasure and chorus the erotic joy so essential for one as young and vital as Catherine. Her legs spread beneath her husband.

Courage buoyed, he began kissing her nipple with even greater ardor, more like worshipping, suckling, greedy for this pleasure from his wife. He felt her hands run through his hair.

This touch of hers, something with such intent he had not felt before, roused him to full growth, and he could feel his member pulsing with need, dripping fluid from the tip, the result of her profound effect on his entire being.

Although he would have liked to go further, to touch and explore her beautiful quim with both his hand and his mouth, he was completely ready for the consummation he had dreamed about before their marriage, and certainly hungered for since that blessed day.

He laid himself parallel to Catherine, his face directly above hers. He looked down on her, but she was so full of lust that her eyes remained closed. He kissed her passionately, their wet tongues gliding into each other's mouths. Then he entered.

The years of riding had left nothing intact down there and had it not, Heathcliff's tongue that Christmas night would surely have done the deflowering. Catherine kept her eyes closed in anticipation of this moment. Her primary reasons for delaying the inevitable had been twofold: firstly, she worried that she would imagine she was being mounted by her love, Heathcliff, and do her husband the severe disgrace of calling out the wrong name in a final fit of passion; secondly, she worried that if she did not fantasize about her beloved, Edgar would feel the dry lack of passion between her legs and suffer injury because of his failure to inspire her arousal. She wanted to be married. She wanted him to be happy. She wanted this pleasant, easy life that Thrushcross Grange provided.

She needn't had given thought to either reason, for Edgar slipped easily into her moistness, as she had been greatly inspired by his gentle, sensuous touch and the feeling brought forth in her by his deep desire; and the penetration was so quick, so shallow, she had neither time nor inclination to conjure images of Heathcliff, as she realized that what she thought upon her arse was just the beginning of Edgar's arousal was really his full passion, and that his manhood was more boyhood, not even the size of Heathcliff's tongue.

Edgar came immediately with a whimper and a tremble, so overwhelmed he was by his wife's willingness to allow him access to her most precious and honorable place.

He withdrew and spooned his body next to hers. He asked, "Did you feel equal pleasure?"

"I feel so fortunate to be your wife," she replied.

The next morning, Catherine feigned sleepiness, so she did not join her husband for breakfast. Before departing for Gimmerton, Edgar returned to her bedside—still full of the glow from their first consummation—and said, "You are my love. And always will be." He pressed forward to kiss her lips and she made a slight, startled turn, and he ended up getting her cheek.

"I love you, too," she replied.

As she remained in bed, halfway between sleep and full consciousness, Catherine saw herself lying on her stomach, reading a book, in front of the main fireplace at Wuthering Heights. Across from her, Heathcliff sat in a chair, whittling a piece of wood into a whistle, as he had often done during their childhood. She found herself staring up at him, his body more imposing and massive from her angle on the floor. She remembered how clean and delightful he smelled as they embraced in the Black Rock Pool, also conjuring the feeling of his manhood bursting from him and brushing against her leg, sending shivers through her spine. Her breathing quickened. She trailed a hand down her body, at the Heights and in her bed, and began a slow teasing around her quim. The more she rubbed, the more she rotated her finger at the bump of her pleasure, the more clearly she saw, and felt, the presence of Heathcliff. She liked that he was so available to her, that she was not locked in her room, that they were not stealing time in the fields, that this was not a clandestine visit to the garret. No one else was around and they were free to be who they wanted to be, and do what they wanted to do. She rubbed more vigorously and Heathcliff looked up from his whittling and smiled with happiness: happy to be alone with her, happy to see her begin her pleasure so freely. There was so much contentment right now within them both. They were with each other in a way that had never been possible before. Heathcliff undid the buttons of his trousers and removed his erect cock. This stirred her mightily, for she enjoyed everything about his cock: the salty taste, the musky scent, the beautiful curved vision of it. She rose to her hands and knees and crawled on all fours to Heathcliff...up close, her face soon between his legs. She took a moment to sniff his member, then she took turns alternating the brushing of each cheek along the sides of his shaft, like a cat purring for affection. She kissed his ball sack, then up along the bulging veins, around the swollen head, tenderly, before she took this glorious specimen into her mouth. Completely without thought, she sucked, fingers still gyrating against her clitoris, applying deep pressure, as Heathcliff's cock penetrated her mouth, and a passion grew within her body that she had only come close to feeling on that beautiful Christmas night. There was a temptation to quicken her pace with both her hand and mouth and give them both the pleasure they sorely needed. But this was not enough. Christmas night had not been enough. She rose to her feet, pulled her dress over her head, swiveled slightly so Heathcliff could enjoy the sight of her body as the golden flames from the fireplace reflected off it. He leaned forward and kissed her stomach. He said, "Catherine, you are the most beautiful woman to walk this earth." He started to undress, but she stopped him, gently pushed him so he rested against the back of the chair. Slowly, with great, sensual care, she undressed her man: unbuttoning his shirt so she could run her fingers through the thick garden of hair along his chest, pulling the garment from his shoulders and taking time so her fingers could linger on his broad shoulders, then down his muscular back. Her actions were so simple, yet they inspired the deepest arousal in both of them, their breathing quickening, their desire as thick as the warm air in the room. As much as Edgar had stimulated her last night, it did not compare to the feelings Catherine felt now in her bed, envisioned now in her childhood home. She slid off Heathcliff's pants, enjoying his passivity, enjoying the way his eyes couldn't help feasting on her full nakedness. She climbed into his lap and they kissed deeply, eyes open, as they stared into each other with the full power of their eternal love. His mouth tasted so sweet, like the succulent wind in the moors. The thickness of his lips enveloped her and his arms went around her, and she felt completely safe and at ease. She lifted up her hips, reached down and took hold of his manhood, then guided him slowly, tenderly, deep inside her. Oh, the rush of magnificent sensation that went through her to be penetrated by her one true lover. There was a deep exhalation of pleasure that sounded in both the master chamber of the Grange and in the great room at the Heights. It was a sound they both made together, simultaneously rejoicing in the union that now seemed perfect, as it was always intended to be. She held him still with her quim, their eyes never wavering, their kisses never stopping, and let herself get used to the immense size of him, the idea of Heathcliff entering her so extremely that it was as if his tip touched her womb. This was how they were meant to be joined. And then she began to rise and fall, repeatedly. Sometimes, when she was all the way down on him, she rested, then grinded, rotating her hips in a circular fashion so he tasted fully her riches and she could feel all the superb sensations of his cock brushing against her inner walls. She kissed his neck. He licked her ear. She said, "Heathcliff, there should be no separation between us. We were destined for this." He responded with, "There is no other time than this moment we are joined." They continued to make love. Soon she could not help but bounce upon him with the passion of a caged lioness set free. He held her steady with a hand between her shoulder blades. Although there was a temptation to close the eyes and get lost in their own personal excitement, neither did, as if the vision of the other's joy was the greatest pleasure they could receive. Now Catherine knew what it felt like to be complete. Now she knew what deep love was supposed to be. Now she knew that nothing else was important but the fulfillment, the connection of two people who could only be whole when with each other, doing this, making love in the sweetest fashion imaginable. They both so clearly wanted to make this last forever, to be connected in this way day in and day out, the only nourishment necessary was their love. Yet their obsession with each other was so overwhelming that Catherine could not stop herself from riding Heathcliff hard, with zest, with need, with the hunger of one who was starved. He, the same, thrusting up now, his hips rising off the chair, causing a penetration so deep she felt as if she could taste him in her throat. They both cried out, with the extreme pleasure of what they experienced, with the intense joy of being granted this gift of the other, with the perfect contentment inspired by a spiritual lovemaking that would make all of England blush with envy. Their final joining cemented even further as the liquid of their passion poured forth, mixed, and like their minds, hearts, bodies, and souls, became one.

Catherine opened her eyes in a start, her body a pool of exhaustion and sweat, and realized that she had, literally, just shouted her pleasure and that surely everyone in the household had heard. She did not care, although she was grateful that Edgar was on his way to Gimmerton. Then, like a sudden, unexpected bolt of lightning ripping through the air, she burst into tears, burying herself face first into her pillow, lamenting aloud, "Heathcliff, my Heathcliff, why have you abandoned me, why have you broken your promise and forsaken me? You have disappeared from the earth, yet remain so strong in my heart. I love you. I need you. I cannot live without you ..."

The happiness and warm companionship of the early years of Edgar and Catherine's marriage eventually came to a standstill, as if the bright and cheerful road they had been traveling along was suddenly inhibited by a massive mound of stone, leaving them unsure of which direction to turn. In the long run, as Catherine had once said to Nelly: In order to survive, we *must* be for ourselves, and the mild and generous are only more justly selfish than the domineering. Their bliss ended when they both began to feel that their interests were not the chief consideration in the other's thoughts.

Or perhaps it was the curse blasted by Heathcliff at the precipice of Black Rock Cragge?

Or perhaps it was simply his return?

Chapter Twelve

On a mellow evening in September, Nelly was coming from the garden with a heavy basket of apples. It was past dusk, and the moon looked over the high wall of the court, causing undefined shadows to lurk in the corners of the numerous projecting portions of the building. She set her burden on the house steps by the kitchen door, and lingered to rest, and draw in a few more breaths of the soft, sweet air. Her eyes were to the moon and her back to the entrance, when she heard a voice say, "Nelly, is that you?"

It was a deep voice, and foreign in tone; yet, there was something in the manner of pronouncing her name that made it sound familiar. She turned about to discover who spoke, fearfully, for the doors were shut, and she had seen nobody on approaching the steps.

Something stirred on the porch. Moving nearer, she distinguished a tall man dressed in dark clothes, with dark face and hair. He leaned against the side, and held his fingers to the latch, as if intending to open it for himself.

Who can it be? wondered Nelly. *Mr. Earnshaw. Oh, no. The voice has no resemblance to his.*

"I have waited for her an hour," he resumed, while she continued staring, "and the whole of that time all around has been as still as death. I dared not enter. You do not know me? Look, I'm not a stranger!"

A ray fell on his features; the cheeks were sallow, and half covered with black whiskers; the brows lowering, the eyes deep and set and singular. Nelly remembered the eyes.

"What!" she cried, uncertain whether to regard him as an apparition or a worldly visitor as she raised her hands in amazement. "What! You come back from the dead? Is it really you? Is it?"

"Dead I'm not, nor have I ever been," said Heathcliff.

Nelly, their last encounter never far from her thoughts, did not know whether to slap him or kiss him. Instead she drew forward and embraced him.

His stiffness in return left the embrace short-lived and she stepped back.

He glanced up from her to the windows that reflected a score of glittering moons, but showed no lights from within. "Are they at home—where is she? Nelly, you are not glad—you needn't be so disturbed. Is she here? Speak! I want to have one word with her—your mistress. Go, and say some person from Gimmerton desires to see her."

"How will she take it?" exclaimed Nelly. "What will she do? The surprise bewilders me—it will put her out of her head! And you *are* Heathcliff? But altered! Nay, there's no comprehending it. Have you been for a soldier?"

"Go, and carry my message," he interrupted, his impatient tone revealing the quick spark of the boy she knew so well. "I'm in hell till you do!" The spark was even harsher now that he seemed to be a full-grown man.

He lifted the latch, and Nelly entered, but when she got to the parlor where Mr. and Mrs. Linton were, she could not persuade herself to proceed, full of an uneasy feeling about this return.

At length, Nelly resolved on making an excuse to ask if they would have the candles lighted, and she opened the door.

Husband and wife sat together, in matching rocking chairs, moving back and forth in synchronized rhythm, in front of a window whose lattice lay back against the wall, and displayed beyond the garden trees and the wild green park the valley of Gimmerton, with a long line of mist winding nearly to its top. Wuthering Heights rose about this silvery vapor, but the old house was invisible, as it rather dipped down on the other side.

Both the room, and its occupants, and the scene they gazed on, looked wonderful and peaceful. Nelly shrank reluctantly from performing her errand, but then worried that if Catherine came upon Heathcliff in the garden by chance, the mistress might drop stone dead at the sight of her former love, who she felt for sure had leaped to his own expiration.

She muttered, "A person from Gimmerton wishes to see you, ma'am, and awaits in the garden."

"What does he want?" asked Mrs. Linton.

"I did not question him."

"How insolent to call at this time of the day. Send him away."

Nelly leaned very close to her mistress's ear and whispered one simple word: "Heathcliff."

It was as if she suddenly leaped again at the Black Rock pool, suspended in the air, full of fearful apprehension and joyful anticipation, then was struck with full force by the blinding jolt of icy water.

The master seemed bewildered that his love made such a hasty departure, one so forceful that her chair swayed violently back and forth.

"Who is it?" inquired Mr. Edgar.

"Someone the mistress does not expect," replied Nelly. "That

Heathcliff, you recollect him, sir, who used to live at Mr. Earnshaw's."

"What, the gypsy—the plowboy?" he cried. "Why did you not say so at first?"

"Hush! You must not call him by those names, master," said Nelly. "She'd be sadly grieved to hear you. She was nearly heartbroken when he disappeared and she feared him dead."

"My wish exactly," declared Edgar, as he began to sway with much force in his own rocker, perhaps frozen with anger, or fear of making a scene that would upset his lovely flower.

Heathcliff let Catherine see him at first, then slipped behind a group of tall hedges.

She ran to him, out of breath with excitement, and leaped into his arms, scissoring her legs around his torso, and showering him with kisses.

"You're alive! You've returned!"

The light pressure of Heathcliff's hand at her shoulder guided Catherine's return to the ground, where she landed on both feet.

"Look at you," she declared, catching her breath, for his transformation, reflected in the evening's moon, was something to behold. He had grown into an even taller, more athletic, well-formed man, beside whom her husband would seem quite slender, youthlike. His upright carriage suggested the idea of military training. His countenance was much older in expression and decision of feature than Edgar's; it looked intelligent, and retained no marks of former degradation. A half-civilized ferocity lurked yet in the depressed brows, and eyes full of black fire, but it was subdued; and his manner was even dignified, quite divested of roughness though too stern for grace.

"Take me to meet your husband," said Heathcliff.

"So soon?" she replied. "I still have not gotten used to seeing you again. Tell me what happened. Where did you go? What have you been doing?" She surveyed the fine cut of his suit, the elegant way it was tailored for his broad shoulders. "Have you made your fortune?"

"Take me now."

"I must have time to prepare Edgar. He is of sensitive nature and you appearing out of—"

With swiftness and fury Heathcliff grabbed Catherine and pulled her to him, her breasts against his belly, her neck arched so his faced hovered over hers and his dark eyes bore into her. She felt sure he was going to kiss her and in such a strong embrace felt helpless to resist, though she wanted to, especially since Edgar was so close by. She closed her eyes, anticipating the force of his passion coming down on hers and igniting the need that lay buried, surfacing only when alone enough to focus her full thoughts on the very man who held her now.

Instead, he whipped her around, then pulled her tight again. This time her bum was against his middle and she could feel the full weight, shape, and form of his cock against her arse cheeks. It had been so long, she was not sure if he was aroused, or, even in his natural state, he seemed so much bigger than Edgar.

He bowed his head and began licking the side of her neck.

"Please, don't," said Catherine. "I'm a married woman now." But her tone revealed her full enthrallment, as she felt herself melt in his strong arms. "My love, I missed you so much." His embrace, the touch of his persuasive tongue against her neck, left no room to think about Edgar.

With a great bend of knees, and to Catherine's great surprise, he reached down and pulled her dress up to just above her waist, then pulled her knickers down to her ankles. "Stop, Heathcliff!" she ordered, as she tried to grab his hand to prevent such a violation, but she was a mere gnat to his great strength. He quickly centered on her quim, with hand and fingers, fluttering through her thick hairs, resting firmly on her clitoris.

He began a slow, tantalizing teasing of her pussy and she melted once again.

Heathcliff enjoyed her resistance immensely, the way she fought to keep any sense of propriety, the way she professed deep concern for her husband and their marriage, but continued to yield with great fervor. While he made his fortune these past few years, he had also perfected the lessons learned his last night at Wuthering Heights, when Nelly had fought him hard, yet given in so completely, helpless to the power of his body, the firm caresses of his hands, the artful use of his mouth and tongue, and, most of all, the strength between his loins. If he could have stayed away, he would have, not wanting to risk another mortal rejection by the one who had permeated his thoughts every day, whether a waking hour, or a deeply troubled slumber. Until finally he had no choice but to return, understanding that the only way to exorcise this haunting Catherine had imposed upon him, the only way to find relief from the tortured feelings within his distressed soul, was to find her and be with her in every way possible. But he would not take the chance that Edgar would outshine him in any way again. He had secured some means and had plans for more, along with strategies that would put into practice the knowledge he had gained. He would not just inspire love within Catherine, for that had not been enough. He was sure that if he possessed her in every way possible, made her long for him over all others, made her tremble with rage if he even glanced at another woman, made her helpless to the forceful commands of his lust, the zealous needs of his body, she would have no choice but to abandon everything and be his forever.

Whispering now, soft, but with the sense of aggression Heathcliff was capable of, he said in her ear as he also licked and bit her lobe, "You must always do as I say. If you do not know it now then I will soon teach it to you. It was my mistake not to take what is mine, but I will atone for that mistake and have you at last."

She could not even respond, because the simple touch of his finger rubbing rhythmically on her clitoris aroused her more than anything Edgar had ever done to her, including their monthly consummation. After her marriage, these charged sensations were limited to just fantasy, and lately, so much time passing since Heathcliff and she had even shared a kiss, they were becoming a fading memory.

He rubbed and kissed and grasped her so tight she could barely breathe, and she felt so weak in the knees she thought she might faint. But fainting was not what she wanted, because that would rob her of the immense pleasure invading every pore, her body welcoming all of the intense feelings as a mistress would her long-lost lover.

"No, please, Edgar is beyond yonder window."

She must make him stop. Such a scandal this would be. She could not shame her husband on his very own property.

"As his mother the whore was when we watched," replied Heathcliff. "Are you my whore?"

"No!" she said sharply.

"You will be," he replied back, as he felt the shudder go through her body.

His kisses, his binding embrace, along with the vigorous rotation of his finger that sent charges through the swollen curve of her womanhood, soon brought her close to orgasm. Expertly, he knew what was about to happen, and after edging her to the brink, a brink where she feared she might cry out and alert Edgar to what was happening, he pulled the finger away. She groaned her huge disappointment, her quim shuddering with desperation now that his attention was gone. She struggled to turn in his arms, desperate to see into his eyes, to understand the full meaning of all he was attempting.

But then, with the very same finger, he entered her deeply and she went limp against his body.

The sensation was overwhelming. It was not just that he penetrated her body, but that he invaded her thoughts. Her forestalled her orgasm went right back on track as he masterfully fingered a quim that had ached for a touch such as this ever since Heathcliff's departure. He pressed forward against her and she felt the imposing size of his cock against her arse, a dimension that was all Heathcliff, a bulk that captured the full essence of his power.

"You will do everything I tell you," he whispered.

"No." She was not a whore and she would never be one. But her words had escaped with far less conviction.

Heathcliff clearly enjoyed seeing her fight wither, and pushed his finger even deeper inside her. If he was not holding her, she would have fallen to her knees in submissive pleasure.

"You will see me whenever I tell you to," he continued.

"No." She was Catherine, mistress of Thrushcross Grange, a rider of horses better than any man, the wife of a gentleman respected and revered by all . . .

"You will take me to see that excuse of a man you call *husband*."

. . . except maybe Heathcliff.

The penetration of his finger soon found the perfect rhythm, as the digit had upon her clitoris, and, completely against her nature, seemingly out of her control, her hips began to buck, meeting the thrusts of his wrist.

Who was this man who had returned? she wondered. It was the scent of Heathcliff, only cleaner. It was the sound of Heathcliff, only more powerful. It was the feel of Heathcliff, only more overwhelming.

"We are going to go into that house and you will introduce me properly to your husband as if I am your long lost lover who has finally returned. You can not help doing so, because I control you now, with just one finger."

Yes, one finger made her yield in a way that she never could with Edgar.

"No, Heathcliff," she said, rallying her dogged determination. "I will never give in to you in this manner you desire. For I love you too much and know you love me."

There was a hesitation, a break in his rhythm, and she felt sure that she had broken through his defenses with the mention of her love, and brought out the old Heathcliff by reminding him of how much he loved her. This pleased her, because all would be nothing without their love.

Yet he began again with renewed intensity, but instead of continuing with his straight and fast penetration, he curled his finger as if he were bringing it back out of another opening above the one he entered, and he rubbed the spot hard there, which caused her to begin a wail that would have reached the Heights itself if Heathcliff had not stuck the long finger of his other hand into her mouth and told her to suck it as if it were his cock—which she did, greedily—as she ejaculated fluid onto his hand in the complete helpless abandon of the most powerful orgasm she had ever had.

Done, he let her go, spinning her back around so she faced him.

He said, "Now take me to him and do as I ask."

Despite knowing that something in the dishevelment of her clothes and hair, the catch in her breath, or simply the scent of sex upon her body would reveal to Edgar what had just happened—how could anyone know, or she fully explain, or even understand what had just transpired?—she turned toward the house, pulled up her silk knickers, and, completely stripped of choice, bid Heathcliff to follow.

"Oh, Edgar, Edgar," panted Catherine, as she ran up to find her husband in the parlor. She flung her arms around his neck. She did not completely understand all that had occurred in the garden, but the aura of sexual fulfillment remained charged through her body, along with the unabashed joy she felt now that her lifelong companion had returned, and the void, the loneliness, might finally be over. "Oh, Edgar, darling! Heathcliff's come back—he is!" And she tightened her embrace to a squeeze.

"Well, well," cried her husband, crossly, "don't strangle me for that!" He took a step back, looked at his wife, perplexed, unsure why she suddenly seemed so unkempt and unclean. "He never struck me as such a marvelous treasure. There is no need to be frantic!"

"I know you didn't like him," she answered, repressing her intensity. "Yet for my sake, you must be friends now. Shall I tell him to come up?"

"Here," he said, "into our parlor?"

"Where else?" she asked.

He looked vexed, and suggested the kitchen as a more suitable place for him.

Catherine eyed him with a droll expression—half angry, half laughing at his fastidiousness.

"No," she added. "I cannot sit in the kitchen. I will have Nelly set two tables here. One for you and Isabella, being gentry, the other for Heathcliff and myself, being of the lower order. Will that please you, dear? Or must I have a fire lighted elsewhere? If so, give directions. I'll run down and secure my guest. I'm afraid the joy is too great to be real!"

She was about to dart off again, but Edgar arrested her.

"Let Nelly bid him step up," he said. "And, Catherine, try to be glad, without being absurd! The whole household need not witness the sight of your welcoming a runaway servant as brother."

After Catherine fixed her hair and did a quick washing, Nelly ushered Heathcliff into the presence of her master and mistress, whose flushed cheeks betrayed signs of warm talking. But Catherine's features glowed with another feeling when her friend appeared at the door. She sprang forward, took both his hands, unwashed, and led him to Edgar; and then she seized Edgar's reluctant fingers and crushed them to his.

The master seemed momentarily surprised at the elegant changes Heathcliff presented. He remained for a minute at a loss how to address the plowboy, as he had called him. Heathcliff dropped his slight hand, and stood looking at him coolly, smirking—as if far less than impressed—till Edgar chose to speak.

"Sit down, sir," he said, at length. "Mrs. Linton, recalling old times, would have me give you a cordial reception, and, of course, I am gratified when anything occurs to please her."

"And I also," answered Heathcliff, "especially if it be anything in which I have a part."

He took a seat opposite Catherine, who kept her gaze fixed on him as if she feared he would vanish. He did not raise his eyes to hers, often—a quick glance now and then sufficed—but it flashed back, each time, more confidently, the undisguised delight he drank from hers.

They were too much absorbed in their mutual joy to suffer embarrassment; not so Edgar. He grew pale with pure annoyance, a feeling that reached its climax when his lady rose—and stepping across the rug, seized Heathcliff's hands again, and laughed like one beside herself.

"I shall think it a dream tomorrow!" she cried. "I shall not be able to believe that I have seen, and touched, and spoken to you once more—and yet, cruel Heathcliff! you don't deserve this welcome. To be absent and silent for all of these years and never to think of me!"

There was a temptation to reveal his true heart, to explain that thoughts of her had never left him, not after the crash of body to water the night of the storm, not during the struggle with the rising tide of the river, not while he bit and clawed his way to find a proper place in this world, not while he formulated his plan to return to her and possess her in a way that left no chance for another rejection. But he did not want to reveal any weakness. His weaknesses were what had driven her into the arms of another.

"A little more than you have thought of me!" he answered boldly. "I heard of your marriage, Catherine, not long since, and, while waiting in the yard below, I meditated this plan—just to have a glimpse of your face—a stare of surprise, perhaps, and pretended pleasure. And also to greet the man who bested me for your heart. But nay, you'll not drive me off again—you were really sorry for me, were you? Well, there was cause. I've fought a bitter life since I last heard your voice, and you must forgive me." Against his intention, his last words lost the bold pomp and escaped with sad sincerity. "For I struggled only for you..."

She was about to reach her hand toward his face to bestow the most tender of caresses.

"Catherine, unless we are to have cold tea, please come to the table," interrupted Edgar, striving to preserve his ordinary tone, and a due measure of politeness. "For I'm sure Mr. Heathcliff must leave soon and will have a long walk, wherever he may lodge tonight."

With that, Heathcliff stood from his chair and looked at Catherine. "Your husband speaks with wisdom. The hour grows late."

He took a step toward Catherine and, for a second, both she, Nelly, and Edgar froze, because it seemed as if he were about to sweep her in his arms and kiss her fully on the mouth. Instead he reached for the locket around her neck, the very same one he had left for her at Black Rock Cragge, sure it still held the locks of their hair.

He took a very deep breath, slowing down his words, not wanting anything in his tone to expose both the joy and heartache this locket had brought to him—joy at receiving it, heartache at feeling compelled to leave it behind, and delirious pleasure to see that Catherine still wore it around her neck. It was not only a weakness he did not want to reveal, but a helpless *vulnerability* around his beloved, a sentiment he worked hard to bury, but could not dismiss. This exposure had not served him well before, and could be the ruin of his plan to win her back, and, significant as well, could cripple his intention to be the cold, cruel, full-blooded instrument of the curse he had so angrily cast on the precipice of Black Rock Cragge.

He murmured a very simple "Lovely," then let it drop against her bosom.

"But where are you going?" asked Catherine. "How will you find lodging at this late hour?"

He turned and headed down the stairs, but not before saying, "I plan to pay a call on Master Hindley, your dear brother . . ."

Chapter Thirteen

Later that evening, Nelly was awakened from her first nap by Catherine gliding into her chamber, taking a seat on the bedside, and pulling her by the hair to rouse her.

"I cannot rest, Nelly," said Catherine by way of apology. "And I want some living creature to keep me company in my happiness. Edgar is sulky, because I'm glad of a thing that does not interest him. He refuses to open his mouth, except to utter pettish, silly speeches; and he affirmed I was cruel and selfish for wishing to talk when he was so sick and sleepy. He always contrives to be sick, at the least cross. I gave a few sentences of commendation to Heathcliff, and he, either for a headache or pang of envy, began to cry. So I got up and left him."

"What use is it praising Heathcliff to him?" Nelly answered. "As lads they had aversion to each other, and Heathcliff would hate just as much to hear him praised; it's human nature. Let Master Linton alone about him, unless you would like to open quarrel between them."

"But does it not show great weakness?" pursued Catherine. "I'm not envious. I never feel hurt at the brightness of Isabella's yellow hair, and the whiteness of her skin; at her dainty elegance, and the fondness all the family exhibit for her. Even you, Nelly, if we have a dispute sometimes, you back Isabella, at once; and I yield like a foolish mother. It pleases her brother to see us cordial, and that pleases me. But, they are very much alike. They are spoiled children, and fancy the world was made for their accommodation; and, though I humor both, I think a smart chastisement might improve them, all the same."

"You're mistaken, Mrs. Linton," said Nelly. "They humor you. I know what there would be to do if they did not! You can well afford to indulge their passing whims, as long as their business is to anticipate all your desires. You may, however, fall out, at last, over something of equal consequence to both sides; and then those you term weak are very capable of being as obstinate as you."

"And then we shall fight to the death, shan't we, Nelly?" she returned, laughing. "No, I tell you. I have such faith in Edgar's love that I believe I might kill him, and he wouldn't wish to retaliate."

Nelly advised her to value him the more for his affection.

"I do," she answered, "but, he needn't resort to whining for trifles. It is childish; and instead of melting into tears, because I said that Heathcliff was now worthy of anyone's regard, he ought to have said it for me, and been delighted. Edgar must get accustomed to him, and he may as well like him. Have you noticed the changes about Heathcliff? There is something about him that is more forceful, almost arrogant."

"This is a side I have seen before," said Nelly, glumly.

"But considering how Heathcliff has reason to object to Edgar, I'm sure he behaved excellently! He is reformed in every respect, apparently, quite a Christian—off to visit my brother and offer the right hand of fellowship to his enemies all around."

"You are as innocent as a newborn," said Nelly, "if you think such a thing is true . . ."

* * *

At Wuthering Heights, the servant girl Mary was kept a busy lass trying to tend to young Hareton and put him to bed in the corner of the great room, while providing the six drunken, card-playing souls with the food and drink they called for without politeness.

"Your ma's lily-white arse!" cried Hindley, as he slapped his cards on the table and reached victoriously for the pile of coins, spittle spewing from his mouth. The others, a collection of no good blackguards if you asked Mary, threw their cards on the table in disgust.

Poor thing, Hareton remained perfectly quiet right where Mary put him, terrified of encountering either his father's wild-beast fondness, or his madman's rage—for in one he ran the chance of being squeezed or kissed to death, and in the other of being flung into the fire, or dashed against the wall.

"There, I've found it at last!" cried Hindley, after staggering into the kitchen and picking up the carving knife. "I know it's you, Mary, who has sworn to murder me."

"Aye," cried the toothless postman, who had but one coin left in front of him.

"With the help of Satan," continued Hindley, "I shall make you swallow the carving knife."

"But I don't like the carving knife, Mr. Hindley," she answered good-naturedly, knowing his jests when in this state of inebriation. "It's been cutting red herrings. I'd rather be shot if you please."

The *gentlemen* at the table gave a round of full belly laughs.

"You'd rather be damned!" said Hindley. "And so you shall. No law in England can hinder a man from keeping his house decent, and mine's abominable! Open your mouth."

He held the knife in his hand and pushed its point between her teeth, but Mary spat it out, her saliva landing on Hindley's chest, laughed, and said it tasted detestably.

"Oh!" said Hindley, releasing her, then he noticed Hareton reclining nearby, eyes wide open, staring at his papa. "I beg your pardon, Mary, it must be Hareton who has vowed to do me in." He walked toward the child. "He deserves a flaying alive for not coming to welcome me, and for screaming as if I were a goblin. Unnatural cub, come hither! I'll teach you to impose upon a good-hearted, deluded father."

He picked the boy up and exhibited him to his mates, who booed heartily. Knife still in hand, Hindley said, "Don't you think the boy would be handsomer with his ears cropped? It makes a dog fiercer, and I love something fierce."

The lads encouraged him heartily.

"Besides," continued Hindley, "it's internal affectation—devilish conceit, it is, to cherish our ears—we're arses enough without them."

"Agreed," said the postman, raising his pint of grog.

"Hush, child, hush!" exclaimed Hindley. "Well then, it is my darling! Dry thy eyes—there's joy; kiss me. What! It won't? Kiss me, Hareton! Damn thee, kiss me! By God as if I would rear such a monster! As sure as I'm living, I'll break the brat's neck."

Poor Hareton was squalling and kicking in his father's arms with all his might, and redoubled his yells when he carried him upstairs and lifted him over the banister. Mary cried out that he would frighten the child into fits, and ran to rescue him.

The commotion stopped all at once, as if suddenly all sound were forbidden, because from the door came a fierce and angry knocking.

All looked at the entrance wondering who the blazes would call at this late hour and with such bluster. Joseph ambled up from his corner chair and opened the door. Surprising, considering the shock, that a man of his age and of his disposition did not drop dead at the instant upon seeing Heathcliff.

"Step aside," said Hindley, "so we may see what the devil brings us."

Joseph obeyed his master's request.

Heathcliff stepped in. It wasn't until he proceeded to the center of the room that Hindley was able to verify that his eyes were not deceiving him, which must have caused him to loosen his grip on Hareton, who gave a sudden spring and delivered himself from the grasp that held him, and fell.

There was scarcely time to experience the thrill of horror, before Heathcliff—with the instinctive quickness of a cat, and the strength of an athlete—arrived underneath just at the critical moment. By natural impulse, he arrested his descent, and set him on his feet—the child gazing at him curiously—then looked up to discover the author of the accident.

A miser who has parted with a lucky lottery ticket for five shillings and finds next day he has lost in the bargain five thousand pounds could not show a blanker countenance than Heathcliff did on beholding the figure of Hindley above. It expressed, plainer than words could do, the intensest anguish at having made himself the instrument of thwarting his own revenge. Had it been dark, Heathcliff might have tried to remedy his mistake by smashing Hareton's skull on the steps.

Hindley descended, sobered and abashed.

"It's your fault, Mary," he said, "you should have kept Hareton out of sight; you should have taken him from me! Is he injured anywhere?"

"Injured!" she cried angrily. "If he's not killed, he'll be an idiot. Oh, I wonder his mother does not rise from her grave to see how you use him. You're worse than a heathen, treating your own flesh and blood in that manner!"

Still glancing nervously at Heathcliff, he attempted to touch the child. At the first finger his father laid on him, Hareton shrieked into louder convulsions than before.

Mary quickly conveyed the boy to her own chamber, leaving Hindley no choice but to stand face-to-face with his sworn enemy.

Trying to put on a bold front for his associates, perhaps also intimidated by the clear change in size and stature of Heathcliff, he said, "And, hark you, Heathcliff! Clear you, too, quit from my reach and hearing. How dare you appear after such long, unannounced absence in a place where you are not welcome and will never be! Lads, escort this hooligan to the door, better yet, face-first to the mud of the moors."

Heathcliff turned toward the spotty crew of drunken fiends, their clothing stained with food and drink, hair wild and disheveled. If his size and imposing demeanor weren't enough to freeze them at the card table, the fact that he drew back his great-coat and exposed both a pistol and a knife seemed to do the trick.

Flustered, but intent on not being shown up, Hindley said, "I would murder you myself tonight, if there were not so many to bear witness."

Heathcliff made a sudden reach for a pint bottle of brandy from the dresser—causing Hindley to a retreat with a momentary flinch—poured some into a tumbler, and passed it to Hindley, then said, "Perhaps this will soothe your tremble."

Embarrassed at the exposure, but unable to retort, Hindley took the drink and finished it in one quick gulp.

Heathcliff turned to the players, who stared transfixed— perhaps simply glazed from their condition—at the reunion be-

fore them, and said, with a dark chuckle that more than supported his aura of danger, "Pity Hindley cannot kill himself with
drink."

All, except Hindley, laughed nervously. Then there was another
awkward silence, during which Heathcliff stared intently at the
those seated around the table, glanced over at Joseph and nodded
toward him, receiving the like in return, until his black eyes
finally settled on Hindley again, who, although quite a rarity, was
speechless.

Heathcliff said, "Is this a night of game or not? Let me not inhibit the satisfaction of money exchanging hands. Hindley, I hear
you are the most skillful player in all of Yorkshire County. Do you
mind if I join?"

Heathcliff did not wait for an answer, as he pulled up a chair,
and patted the empty seat of the one next to him and beckoned
Hindley to come forth. Hindley sat. To the great surprise of everyone, especially Hindley, Heathcliff pulled out an ample purse of
gold coins and let it drop on the table with an authoritative thud.
Then he chafed his hands together and said, "Let's play."

None of them was a match for Heathcliff's skill, least of all
Hindley, who perhaps still hadn't recovered from the shock of
dropping his son and seeing Heathcliff catch him. But the way
the sober Heathcliff laughed and rejoiced as he summarily picked
the pockets of all the drunks who had come to play—and they,
penniless, were forced to withdraw one by one—irked Hindley
down to his core; and though he should have withdrawn from the
game long before, he responded to Heathcliff's goading and skillful play by going upstairs to his chamber, time and time again,
and returning with more coin.

For Heathcliff, it could not have been easier to snatch candy
from the small fingers of Hareton's hand. It did not take long

to figure out Hindley's *tell*. Whenever Hindley was bluffing, he would make an extreme gesture around the nose, as if picking it, scratching it, or just searching for something in there that seemed beyond his reach. If the nose was not touched, Heathcliff would quietly withdraw from the hand. If it was ransacked, Heathcliff would sucker him in for all he was worth, sometimes feigning insecurity and doubt with his *slow playing*, other times goading Hindley into betting even more as he questioned his manhood and preyed on his vanity.

A hand like this made for the last of the evening. Hindley had gone for his final storage of coins and laid it all on the line, nearly drawing blood from a nostril already quite red from the touch of his dirty fingernails. Heathcliff—like a lion hiding in the bush— knew this was time to go in for the kill. He called Hindley's last bet and raised with all the coins in front of him.

A collective gasp was heard from the others, too exhausted to go home, too intrigued to rest head to table.

Hindley stammered, "I wish to remain in the hand, but I have no coin left to match."

Heathcliff let out a glorious roar, downed a hearty gulp from his grog, then spat it onto the pile of coins at the center of the table. He said, "Don't you mean that you are bluffing and now you seek a way to amend your error in judgment?"

The weary heads turned toward their host. Humiliated, backed deeply into a corner, he put on a bold front by saying, "I would surely like to call your raise, for I know the strength of my cards humbles those that you have, but, truly, I cannot make coin appear from thin air."

"Tell you what," said Heathcliff as he leaned in real close to his neighbor, Hindley, so close his sour, alcoholic breath struck him in the face like a blow. "Put your trust in me. If you win this hand, then all the coin at the table shall be yours. If I win, I get the coin and will offer an equivalent to the value of what you would need to match my bet."

There was a hesitation by Hindley. "What is this equivalent?"

"Trust me or fold," said Heathcliff without inflection.

Hindley had lost all the money he had in the house anyway, and now he had a chance to retrieve it, and it would be a fine pleasure to best this devil at the last.

"Done," he said, turning over his cards, revealing two knaves and two threes.

All eyes swiveled to Heathcliff, who, without the fanfare the group would have expected, laid down three kings.

There was a deep stone silence by everyone. Had anyone glanced at Joseph, they would have seen him smile.

"What?" stumbled Hindley, suddenly white as a ghost. "Impossible." Then, "What...what is it that you would consider the equivalent?"

Only the black eyes revealed his full triumph, as Heathcliff pronounced, "A year's free lodging at Wuthering Heights..."

Chapter Fourteen

The news of Hindley's defeat spread quickly throughout the county. Perhaps happiest was Catherine, who had still not forgiven her brother—who she believed could not be more morally corrupt than he was—for breaking her wrist and, most significantly, administering the flogging responsible for Heathcliff's departure. She was thrilled Heathcliff would be quartered within walking distance of the Grange, as it presented more opportunity for her to see him than if he had settled in Gimmerton.

Yielding to Nelly's advice, Catherine praised Heathcliff less to Edgar and allowed her husband more frequent access to her bodily pleasures. Thinking he no longer needed to open the window, as the house was becoming his, he bypassed the warm oil and foot massages, going right for the thing he lusted for most, which was fine with Catherine as it made the entire encounter that much quicker. Nevertheless, her attitude rewarded her with much sweetness and affection, and in return, it made the house a paradise for several days; both husband and wife profiting from the perpetual sunshine.

After one such night, she suggested that she take Isabella to Wuthering Heights on the morrow, in the afternoon. Edgar seemed to have renounced the peevishness that Heathcliff's appearance aroused in him, though his spirits still seemed subdued by the exuberance Catherine had exhibited. But perhaps to keep the new sunshine intact, and because Isabella could be the perfect chaperone—to Catherine's hidden delight—he agreed.

As the two strolled toward the Heights, on a beautiful sunny afternoon, Isabella seemed quite pleased because of her sister-in-law's interest in inviting her along. She was a charming young lady; infantile in manners, though possessed of a keen wit, keen feelings, and a keen temper, too, if irritated. The prospects of worthy young men were thin in the immediate surroundings of the Grange, and she didn't make it often enough to Gimmerton. And, yes, she, too, had taken notice of Heathcliff on the night of his return: no longer the posture of a servant, blessed with a tall, commanding stature; and he no longer seemed as poor as a beggar.

Heathcliff met the ladies at the gate and suggested they all continue enjoying a blissful walk in the sunshine. They each took his arm. Catherine did not mind. She was sure she knew why Heathcliff had come back, and that he only had eyes for her.

Out deep in the moors, Catherine said to Isabella, "Sister, would it be possible for you to ramble as you please, while I walk privately with my long lost friend?"

Isabella was taken aback at this obvious dismissal and looked to Heathcliff to rescue her from this fate. He simply smiled and nodded and she slipped her hand from his arm and stormed off to the east.

It wasn't long before the naughty pair was at Black Rock Cragge and Catherine jerked Heathcliff's arm, which brought them both, well hidden, behind the first set of rocks.

"Do not play games, sir!" she exclaimed. "Tell me why you left and why you return."

"You seemed to enjoy my games."

She did not blush and play the innocent flower. Their encounter in the garden had been strangely pleasing, but it was clear that the Heathcliff who had returned was not the same one who had left. She hoped this visit to their most sacred place would soften his newfound arrogance.

She said, "You broke the promise you made me here—you left me."

He retorted, "You broke the promise you made me here and forsook me."

"You did not hear all I said that day."

"You did not understand all that was completely in my heart." This he was sure of, for if she did, then it would not have been so easy for her to seek the arms of another.

She frowned, disappointed that he used the verb "was." At her most dismal of times since her marriage to Edgar, she had tried to draw comfort that maybe, somewhere, Heathcliff was alive and thinking of her. But, in a way, this new Heathcliff was as distant and unknown as the absent one. She wanted him back, fully.

"So," she asked, with a saucy smile, "why have you returned?"

The urge certainly was there to shout his love once again at this place where they first opened their hearts completely, then take her in his arms, and bestow the sweetest of kisses. Instead, without any passion in his tone, with the discipline of a soldier at battle, he replied, "So you can suck my cock."

She recoiled, tempted to slap him hard across the face. "I warn you, sir, again, of my marital status and that I will not be treated like a tart."

Heathcliff unbuttoned his pants and let them drop to the ground. She could not help staring at him, completely without shame. Even semierect, he made Edgar, at full bloom, look like a breakfast sausage.

She looked at his eyes; they seemed cold, passionless. She had the urge to spin away in a huff, and join her sister-in-law at the moors.

Then she thought of her fantasy, the one she had fashioned alone in her bed after Edgar had departed for work, the one she had often repeated, reviewed, refined from the great room of the Heights, to the fields, to the moors, with varied positions and a grand variety of sensual exchange. How she had purred as her cheeks rubbed along his shaft, marking his body with her scent, thrilled that his stamp, too, was upon her. She could not let this chance fly by without the opportunity to make fantasy a reality. Catherine dropped to her knees—greedy to taste him again, a sweet flavor she feared these many years that she would be forever denied—and took him fully into her mouth.

She sucked with much passion. The flavor of him, the feeling of his glorious cock entering her mouth, brushing vigorously along her tongue, caused her pulse to quicken and her quim to moisten in the familiar heavy fashion that only Heathcliff could inspire. It surprised her that she did not elicit the familiar moans of pleasure that she remembered, or was that just in her fantasies? She did feel him grow to the incredible size she recalled, but lately, as memory faded, thought she must have imagined.

So much temptation for Heathcliff to close his eyes and toss his head back and rejoice at the familiar sensations brought forth by the tender mouth of his beloved. Instead, with cold fortitude, he stared straight down, lording his towering position over her humbled one, enjoying that he pierced her mouth with the timber of his passion.

She stared back up at him in defiance, refusing to submit to the rough way he thrust into her. She took his cock out of her mouth and began the tenderest of licks against his balls and the underside of the shaft, running her fingers along the insides of his thighs, knowing that in this position, it can be either person in control.

As she licked him everywhere, her face buried between his legs, she was thrilled by it all: the wonderful warmth and texture of his flesh, the masculine size of him, being alone, outdoors, with this man she could never stop thinking about. She unconsciously squeezed her own thighs together, the pressure giving her a momentary start, which fashioned itself into a soft groan, and she felt a moistness begin to flow down her legs. Heathcliff, Heathcliff, Heathcliff, this was living, truly.

"Fuck," he mouthed silently. *This glorious lass will make me come in an instant...and what a delicious tongue she possesses— what deft touch—even more arousing because she takes so much pleasure as well.*

He took a step back and ordered her to stop. His sharp tone disturbed her, but she was even more bothered to be denied further access to his magnificent body. He slowly, seductively, unbuttoned his white shirt, eyes still upon her, making her wait, and then the fabric parted and it was as if the red sea gave way and before her was the Promised Land. She could see the taut muscles of his abdomen, the almost pear-shaped, iron arc of each pectoral. As in her fantasy, she wanted to crawl forward and run her hands across his flesh, taste the droplets of perspiration beading along each muscular curve, and swallow this man whole. But he dropped to the ground, lay on his back in the tall grass, and arched his hips in her direction. "Mount it," he commanded.

The arrogance of this man, ordering her about. Though she remained on her knees, she did not budge.

"We can rejoin Isabella," said Heathcliff with a smile she had seen twice now since his return, but had never seen before.

Who knew when she would get this chance again?

She had come to worry that between Edgar's halfhearted attempts and her fading memory, her passion would become prematurely dry, as if she already were older than her years. The feelings of pity and disgust she had felt toward Edgar's mother after witnessing her base liaison had lately turned to envy, wishing she could have such a dangerous passion.

And now Heathcliff was here, not quite as she had imagined in her fantasies, but certainly available in all his regal fineness. There was an ache between her legs that longed to be soothed, a desire there for the most exquisite, forceful pressure only Heathcliff could provide, a longing for the deep entering and passionate exchange from someone she loved.

She pulled off her knickers, pulled up her skirt, straddled her longtime companion, and, for the very first time, lowered herself onto his sweet, beautiful, monstrous cock.

The joy, the nobleness of the penetration, thrilled her, inspiring her eyes to close and her mouth to elicit a momentary swoon. Damn, how she missed this man!

Fortunately, she was very moist from the sucking and the sight of him. Nevertheless, it was as if she were a virgin all over again, as Edgar had not done much to expand her from a girl to a woman.

She felt all woman now, going down on her beloved Heathcliff.

Once he was all the way inside, deep into her, she rested, then opened her eyes to look at him. He stared at her with passion. But it was a passion she could not discern. It reminded her of how he had been transfixed the Christmas she had undressed in front of him, but also how he had stared the night Hindley nearly flogged him to death.

"Do you gaze with love or hate?" she asked.

He bit his lips hard, nearly drawing blood, so he did not reveal all he felt after finally being inside the only woman on earth he truly wanted. He replied, "Fuck my cock!"

Helpless to resist the dirtiness of his commands, the surge of his mighty penetration, she obeyed.

Indeed, she rode him as if he were a horse out on the moors. He lay perfectly still, refusing even to aid her with an arch of the hip, or a hand on her arse. He just watched, seemingly feeling no desire to expedite his own orgasm, surely entranced by the passion in Catherine's face as she made love to his cock, extracting the pleasure she so desperately needed.

Despite feeling overwhelmed by the sensations, she gathered her will to open her eyes and look down at him again. His stare never wavered. Angry he could be so unfeeling, frustrated that she could not resist his efforts to make her feel so completely dirty, she spat in his face.

He used his fingers to wipe it up, then put her spit in his mouth and swallowed.

It doubled her arousal that finally she had gotten some reaction out of him, that he did not recoil from her taste, but welcomed it. And she could not deny how exhilarating it was to be this dirty: a married woman unable to control her desire to be with another man while hidden among the rocks—one who had returned with a new cruelty and anger—with her sister-in-law just yards away. All of it—along with his overwhelming cock forcing its way up inside her—made it so that she couldn't help from coming, couldn't stop from coming, as her passion welled up from somewhere deep within, screamed out of her throat, quickly mixed with the sweet wind of Black Rock Cragge, then blasted along the vastness of the moors.

Just when she thought it could not get any more intense,

she felt him gush inside her, filling her with his manly semen, although he remained perfectly still. The corporeal feeling of his most precious fluid flowing from him into her, the titillating knowledge that she had inspired this superb reaction, caused her to shout her passion again.

With a physical effort she did not know she possessed, she drove, gyrated, pounded her quim onto this man, extracting every last ounce of bliss she could find, then collapsed forward onto his chest, her head to the side. As she rained kisses on his breast, he was still deep inside her, losing none of his fullness even after orgasming.

"I still love you, Heathcliff," she said. "With all of my being."

No, it was not exactly as she had envisioned in her fantasy, and it was frustrating that Heathcliff had returned with such an aloof edge, but there was something within her body, even deeper within her heart, that felt their love was intact. Her time with Edgar had shown her how empty a passionless life could be. She knew she needed this man, but was not sure how he needed her.

He felt warmed to hear her words and ascertain that the seeds of his plan were taking hold. Yet he turned his head to the side, for fear that Catherine would see the sadness that had formed in his eyes, a sadness from not giving himself as freely as she had, as freely as he wanted. He replied, simply, "Good."

Isabella was unusually silent, as the two women finished up their afternoon sojourn, waved good-bye to Heathcliff, and headed back to the Grange.

Catherine seemed content to remain quiet, reliving in her mind every detail of her recent tryst. Not so was the case for Isabella, who finally blurted out with annoyance, "You have been most harsh, sister."

"Whatever do you mean?"

"You tell me to ramble where I please, while you saunter on with Mr. Heathcliff."

"That's your notion of harshness?" said Catherine, laughing. "It was no hint that your company was superfluous; we didn't care whether you kept with us or not; we are childhood friends and had much to catch up on."

"Oh, no," cried the young lady, suddenly weeping. "You wished me away, because you knew I liked to be there!"

"Are you sane?" asked Catherine. "I'll repeat our conversation, word for word, Isabella, and you point out any charm it could have had for you."

"I don't mind the conversation," she answered. "I wanted to be with . . ."

"Well!" said Catherine, pausing in midstep.

" . . . with him," she completed, turning to face her sister-in-law. "And I won't always be sent off." Gathering fury, she added, "You are a dog in the manger, Catherine, one in heat; and desire no one be loved but yourself!"

Catherine gave further pause, wondering how much Isabella had heard from the Cragge, then unleashed her own venom. "You are an impertinent little monkey!" she exclaimed. "But I'll not believe this idiocy! It is impossible that you can covet the admiration of Heathcliff, that you can consider him an agreeable person! I hope that I have misunderstood you, Isabella?"

"No, you have not," said the infatuated girl. "I think I can love him more than ever you loved Edgar, and he might love me if you would let him!"

"I wouldn't be you for a kingdom, then!" Catherine declared, emphatically. "You're mad! Heathcliff is an unreclaimed creature, without refinement, without cultivation, an arid wilderness of shrub and stone. I'd as soon put your canary into the park on a winter's day as recommend you to bestow your heart on him! It's deplorable ignorance of his character, child, and nothing else, which makes that dream enter your head. Pray don't imagine that he conceals depths of benevolence and affection beneath a stern exterior! He's not a rough diamond, or a pearl-containing oyster of a rustic; he's a fierce, pitiless, wolfish man. He'd crush you like a sparrow's egg, Isabella. I know he couldn't love a Linton; and yet, he'd be quite capable of marrying your fortune, and expectations. Avarice is growing within him, a besetting sin. There's my picture; and I'm his friend—so much so, that had he thought seriously to catch you, I should, perhaps, have held my tongue, and let you fall into his trap."

Isabella regarded her sister-in-law with indignation, as they finally arrived at the doors of Thrushcross Grange. "For shame! for shame!" she repeated, angrily. "You are worse than twenty foes, you poisonous friend!"

"Ah, you won't believe me, then?" said Catherine. "You think I speak from wicked selfishness?"

"I'm certain you do," retorted Isabella, "and I shudder at you!"

Then she ran into the house and up the stairs.

"Good," cried Catherine after her. "Try for yourself, if that be your spirit; I have done, and yield the argument to your saucy insolence."

Isabella burst into Nelly's chamber, copious tears streaming down her cheeks. "Must I suffer from her egotism!" she wailed, as she flung herself on the floor in front of a seated Nelly. She sobbed the rest of the story, then finished with, "All, all is against me; she has blighted my single consolation. But she uttered falsehoods, didn't she? Mr. Heathcliff is not a fiend; he is an honorable soul, a true one, or how could he remember the likes of her?"

"Banish him from your thoughts," said Nelly. "He's a bird of bad omen; no mate for you. Catherine spoke strongly, yet I can't contradict her. She is better acquainted with his heart than I, or any one besides; and she would never represent him any worse than he is. Honest people don't hide their deed. How has he been living? How has he got rich? Why is he staying at Wuthering Heights, the house of a man he abhors? They say Mr. Earnshaw is worse and worse since he came. They sit up all night continually. And Hindley has been borrowing money on his land and does nothing but play cards and drink."

Isabella stood up and made poor attempt to dry her tears. "You are leagued with the rest, Nelly!" she declared. "I'll not listen to your slanders." Before stalking out of the room she added, "What malevolence you must have to wish to convince me that there is no happiness in this world!"

Happiness? Nelly was not sure that any happiness could stem from a man so tortured as Heathcliff. Yet she understood completely how difficult it was to remain immune to his charms.

During the night was a much typical windstorm, sweeping its way across the moors, doing damage at the Heights and the Grange. The morning brought a welcoming sunshine. There was a justice meeting at the next town and Edgar was obliged to attend, and had his manservant drive the carriage, promising Catherine the lad would clean the yard and garden upon return and repair any damage the windstorm had caused.

Heathcliff, aware of his absence, took occasion to call.

Catherine and Isabella sat in the library, on hostile terms, but silent: the latter alarmed at her recent indiscretion, and the disclosure she had made of her secret feelings in a fit of passion; the former was really offended with her companion, but resisted effort to laugh at her pertness, hoping for some peace, but also wary of antagonizing her sister-in-law further and thus risking an accounting made by sister Isabella to brother Edgar.

Catherine did laugh with delight when she saw Heathcliff pass the window. Nelly swept the hearth and noticed a mischievous smile on her lips. Isabella, absorbed in her meditation, or a book, remained till the door opened, and it was too late to attempt an escape, which she gladly would have done had it been practicable.

"Come in, that's right!" exclaimed Catherine, gaily pulling a chair to the fire. "Here are two people sadly in need of a third to thaw the ice between them and you are the very one we should both of us choose. Heathcliff, I'm proud to show you, at last, somebody that dotes on you more than myself. I expect you to feel flattered—nay, it's not Nelly; don't look at her! My poor little sister-in-law is breaking her heart by mere contemplation of your physical and moral beauty. No, no, Isabella, you shan't run off," she continued, arresting, with feigned playfulness, the confounded girl, who had risen indignantly. "We were quarrelling like cats about you, Heathcliff, and I was fairly beaten in protestations of devotion and admiration, and moreover, I was informed that if I would but have the manners to stand aside, my rival would shoot a shaft into your soul that would fix you forever, and send my image into eternal oblivion!"

"Catherine," said Isabella, calling up her dignity, and disdaining to struggle with the tight grasp that held her. "I'd thank you to adhere to the truth and not slander me, even in joke! Mr. Heathcliff, be kind enough to bid this friend of yours release me. She forgets that you and I are not intimate acquaintances, and what amuses her is painful to me beyond expression."

The guest answered nothing, but took his seat, an expression of thorough indifference upon his countenance. His refusal to act nearly brought Isabella to tears, and inspired a smile of triumph upon Catherine's face. Again, Isabella turned to her tormentor and whispered an appeal for liberty.

"By no means!" cried Catherine in answer. "I won't be named a dog in the manger again. Isabella swears that the love Edgar has for me is nothing to that she entertains for you. I'm sure she made some speech of the kind, did she not, Nelly? And she has fasted ever since our walk, from sorrow and rage that I dispatched her out of your society, under the idea that it's unacceptable."

"I find her far from unacceptable," said Heathcliff, twisting his chair to face them. He looked her up and down, coldly, but with detail, as if making an appraisal to purchase a colt. "For she is a comely lass."

How it shocked Catherine to hear such praise. Even Nelly shook her head with disgust, as Catherine, from jealousy, grew white, then red in rapid succession, while Isabella, from shame at being held up like meat at the butcher's, felt tears beading her lashes. She bent the strength of her small fingers to loosen the firm clutch of Catherine, and perceiving that, as fast as she raised one finger off her arm, another closed down, and she could not remove the whole together, she began to make use of her nails, and their sharpness presently ornamented the detainer's with crescents of red.

"There's a tigress!" exclaimed Catherine, setting her free, and shaking her hand with pain. "Be gone, for God's sake, and hide your vixen face! How foolish to reveal those talons to *him*. Can't you fancy the conclusions he'll draw? Look, Heathcliff! There are instruments that will do execution. You must be aware of your eyes."

Catherine watched Isabella race for the door and slam it behind her. Nelly quickly followed to give comfort. Catherine then smiled toward her friend for a sign of approval, but was quickly vexed by his expression of great amusement. She spat, "I represented all of your failings in a plain light for the purpose of erasing her adoration. But don't notice it further. I wish to punish her sauciness, that's all. I like her too well, Heathcliff, to let you absolutely seize and devour her up."

"And I like her too ill to attempt it," he said, but then added, "except in a very ghoulish fashion. Her eyes; they detestably resemble Edgar's."

"I wish I had her angel eyes."

"She's her brother's heir, is she not?"

"I should be sorry to think so," returned his companion. "Half a dozen nephews shall erase her title, please heaven!"

"Isabella Linton may be silly," said Heathcliff, "but there would not be one man in the county who would not be most pleased to see the parting of her legs and receive her girlish smile of invitation."

"And what about my invitation?" asked Catherine, as she positioned herself behind him while he remained seated in his chair. She kissed his neck, ran her fingers through his long hair, remembering clearly the power these ministrations used to have on her beloved. "Edgar will be gone for the rest of the day. I can retire to my chamber and you can slip up the back stairs unnoticed, and have me in my marriage bed." She caressed his chest through his shirt, toying with his nipples, then worked her fingers down, along his abdomen, until she grabbed a fistful of his cock through his pants, immensely pleased to feel its hardness. She liked being in control this way, as well, and was sure that if she got Heathcliff in her bed she could erase his arrogant manner, obliterate all thoughts of Isabella, and have him at her whim. All three images, along with the feel of his hard cock, and his strong scent that re-called the pleasant air of the Heights as she buried her face in his hair, filled her with immense desire and moistened her deeply.

"The hour grows late," said Heathcliff. He got up and exited through the double-glass doors that led to the garden.

Her first urge was to call after him, to go after him, and sway his thoughts of departure, for the memory of their recent en-counter remained fresh in her mind, and simply the sight of him through the window had caused her pulse to quicken. But she thought to herself, *This knave continues to test me with his haughty manner and superior airs. He refuses to recognize my new station. I will not allow him to treat me as a plaything, like a puppy in a kennel.*

She forced herself to turn her back and retreat to the chair by the fire.

Isabella was inconsolable and Nelly left her chamber to clean the master bedroom.

While Catherine rocked vigorously before the fire and took her anger out on the chair, Nelly cleaned and longed for the sim-ple days when the old Master Earnshaw was alive and Isabella wept face-first into her pillow. Suddenly, all three heard sounds of chopping in the garden. The servants were gone and they won-dered who was making such ruckus. Nelly and Isabella went to bedroom windows, Catherine to the double-glass doors to find the answer.

Heathcliff stood alongside the fractured garden lattice that had been destroyed by the windstorm, and chopped fresh planks of wood.

Answer given, each lady could have returned to what they had been doing, but such was not the case.

For Heathcliff chopped like a man possessed and there was

nothing more titillating to these three than a man of Heathcliff's physique and angry demeanor in action. Despite the cool day, Heathcliff soon stripped himself of jacket, unbuttoned his shirt, and stood bare-chested in the garden. Rivulets of sweat, glistening like silver in the bright sun, poured down his face and chest and stomach, along the forest of dark black hair that trailed to his groin. He rested for a moment and wiped the sweat off his brow with a hand, revealing a glimpse at the full, dark thicket under his armpit, causing a quick intake of breath in the ladies.

He seemed oblivious to being watched, but such was not the case, as he knew the sounds of his work would alert the in-habitants of the house. He seemed indifferent either way. He got down on his knees, needing to curve slightly his muscled back, which caused his firm buttocks—clearly outlined against his pants, the stain of sweat making them more defined—to arch up, as he put hammer to nails, making them plunge deeply with one blow into the wood flesh.

This sensuous action, and exquisite view of his perfectly shaped arse, caused Nelly to withdraw from the master bedroom and tiptoe her way up to the privacy of the attic; Isabella to un-consciously tighten her thighs together, causing the pressure of deep arousal; and Catherine to lift up her skirt and work a hand underneath her knickers until her finger found her already slightly swollen clitoris.

Heathcliff hammered and the women watched. There was only one window at the end of each attic wall. It was oval, and just above the floor. In order for Nelly to see she had to lie down, stomach first, on the floor, and peer through the glass to the gar-den below. She cursed herself for her naughtiness, for giving in to the sight of the man who had taken her so brutally. But it was still a night she could not forget, and she often touched herself and treated her breasts forcefully, slapping them, twisting the nipples, as she imagined all that Heathcliff had done. This memory, and the sight of her lust object hard at work below, made it nearly impossible for her to keep her hand from sliding down under her stomach, and onto her pussy, to begin a rhythmic caressing.

Isabella was short of breath and felt shame to be watching so, but she could not tear her eyes away. Heathcliff stood up and began to line up the attached wood so it would stand on the base he had constructed. He let the frame structure rest and took water from the fountain and drank with gusto. He then splashed water on his face and shook his neck, shiny droplets swinging freely from his hair. That was when Isabella put her hand between her legs and pressed deeply against her quim, an action that caused her to cry out softly.

Catherine had her knickers all the way down, her dress to the floor. She remembered the feel of Heathcliff's cock deep inside her, the way she couldn't help working her body up and down, legs spread wide to snatch him, to receive him, frantic for sensation, for his presence. She pressed herself tight against the glass of the doors, desperate to feel pressure from something. She wanted this vision of Heathcliff before her to crush himself against her in all of his masculine fineness. She rubbed herself vigorously and watched his broad shoulders stretch as he raised the frame again.

Nelly wrenched pussy to fist as she lay on the dirty wood floor, spying on her prey, like the whore she was, at least around Heathcliff. She panted with desire, burning up at the sight of the man who had tamed her. Isabella, still girlish in her approach, rubbed her pussy up and down, enjoying the friction, cooing when her hand brushed her clitoris, staring at a man in a way she had never done before.

Catherine groaned like an animal. How she wanted him. The

woman that he had laid bare since his return was revealed as one of great appetite, one who wanted her man in all of his natural glory: his harsh sounds, his strong scents, his rough touch, even his brutality. For all that was Heathcliff, and he had made it so that she could not hide her hunger to be with him any way he desired. And how she wanted to go out there and straddle his face and make him lick her the way he had done that Christmas. Instead her forceful, unrestrained finger fucking—like his cock yesterday at the moors—caused the doors to rattle and it caught Heathcliff's attention, which did not inhibit her, only aroused her further, as he turned now and stared directly at her, and she pressed her luscious breasts even tighter against the glass, flattening her perfect nipples, her hips flexing toward him, fully exposing her pussy, to make it as if not only she, but her quim were calling out for him to leave his station and come through the glass and fuck her into submission.

And it drove her to madness that Isabella could be upstairs and have the opportunity to view Heathcliff in the same manner. How dare she impose herself between them in the hopes of separating a bond formed since childhood! How dare Heathcliff take notice of her beauty, one that, at times, Catherine felt outshone her own! Heathcliff was hers and she could not act the proper wife any longer!

Through the muffled sound of the glass, her lips mashed against the pane, he heard her cry out, "Heathcliff, my love, I want you so much. Come to me please!"

The boldness of her display, the desperateness of her pleas, delighted him. He scanned his eyes upward, and though the windows were shaded, he had the sense of being observed, watched, undressed by additional feminine eyes...and this also pleased him, especially since Catherine was probably aware of this as well.

But none of it compared to the full abandonment in Catherine's tone, and the completely unguarded feeling he had never quite heard her express this way. For the first time, he felt, truly, that he had the opportunity to win her back. To make sure he also had the chance to keep her, Heathcliff, with his unique willpower, showed no reaction to her pleas and simply turned back to hammer the final nails.

As the structure stood tall and Heathcliff's last rhythmic pounding continued, each woman found her closing pace. Eyes to body of this man and back to pressure at the pussy . . . wonderful. Wonderful to be a woman in secret, taking this pleasure from an object seemingly so eager to be worshipped. Though for Catherine there was also the unashamed gratification of exhibiting her womanhood, exercising the power between her legs in order to entice whom she wanted.

Each with her own rhythm, all three might have orgasmed at different times, if Heathcliff hadn't stopped suddenly, unbuttoned his fly, pulled out his stallion of a cock, and urinated all over the standing wood frame.

The sight of his outrageously massive member—golden liquid arcing in the sunlight, fully drenching the lattice—caused a simultaneous feminine shudder throughout the home at Thrushcross Grange. Such a womanly groan had not echoed in these walls before, reverberating from the ground floor, to the second, to the attic, with the same superb stamp of pleasure and splendid rush of moistness.

Catherine buckled to her knees, her orgasm deep and shattering, garnering much joy at the yielding of her body and soul to this most handsome, powerful man.

She watched Heathcliff give his tool a final shake, button up, and head back to Wuthering Heights.

Chapter Fifteen

Nelly's heart invariably leaned toward Master Edgar. He was kind, trustful, and honorable. She wanted something to happen that would free both the Heights and the Grange of Heathcliff, quietly, leaving everyone as they had been prior to his advent. His visits, in their own, although longed for by Catherine and Isabella, were a nightmare for all, including the master. His presence at the Heights was an oppression past explaining. Despite the adult cruelty of Hindley, she remembered his innocence as a child, before being corrupted by rivalry. Nelly sensed in the air, in the ground, in the house, that God had forsaken the stray sheep there to its own wicked wanderings, and an evil beast prowled between it and the fold, waiting his time to spring and destroy.

On one afternoon, she took to wandering near the Heights, in the hope of catching glimpse of Master Hindley doing well, for the news in Gimmerton was that he was very long on drink and very short on coin.

As she got close to the gates, she observed an elf-locked, brown-eyed boy setting his ruddy countenance against the bars. Further reflection suggested that it must be Hareton, *her* Hareton, not altered greatly since she left him.

"God bless thee, darling!" she cried. "Hareton, it's Nelly...thy nurse."

He retreated at arm's length, and picked up a large flint.

"I have come to see thy father, Hareton," she added.

He raised his missile to hurl it, which quickly stifled her unabashed joy at seeing her very first nursling, and prompted her to offer a soothing speech. But she could not stay his hand. The stone struck her bonnet, and then ensued, from the stammering lips of the little fellow, a string of curses that, whether he comprehended them or not, were delivered with practiced emphasis, and distorted his baby features into a shocking expression of malignity.

This grieved Nelly deeply. Fit to cry, she took an orange from her pocket, and offered it to propitiate him.

He hesitated, then snatched it from her hold, as if he fancied that she only intended to tempt and disappoint him.

She showed another, keeping it out of his reach.

"Who has taught you such common language, my child?" she inquired. "The curate?"

"Damn the curate, and thee! Give me that," he replied.

"Tell me where you got your lessons, and you shall have it. Who's your master?"

"Devil daddy," was his answer.

"And what do you learn from Daddy?"

He jumped at the fruit. She raised it higher. "What does he teach you?" she asked.

"Naught," said he, "but to keep his gait—Daddy cannot bide me, because I swear at him."

"Ah, and the devil teaches you to swear at Daddy?"

"Aye—nay," he drawled.

"Who then?"

"Heathcliff."

"Do you like Mr. Heathcliff?"

"Aye. He pays Dad back when he goes at me. He curses Daddy for cursing me. He says I can do as I want."

"And the curate does not teach you to read and write, then?" she asked.

"No, I was told the curate should have his teeth dashed down his throat, if he stepped over the threshold. Heathcliff has promised that!"

She put the orange in his hand and bade him tell his father that Nelly was waiting to speak to him, by the garden gate.

He went up the walk, and entered the house, but, instead of Hindley, Heathcliff appeared on the door stones, and she turned directly and ran down the road as hard as ever she could race, making no halt until she gained the guidepost, and feeling as scared as if she had raised a goblin.

The next time Heathcliff came by the Grange, Isabella chanced to be feeding some pigeons in the court. She and her sister-in-law had not spoken since Heathcliff's last visit, but, likewise, Catherine had dropped her fretful complaining, and the house had reached an uneasy truce.

Heathcliff, normally, had not the habit of bestowing a single unnecessary civility on Isabella. Now, as soon as he beheld her, he took a sweeping survey of the housefront, hoping Catherine was at a window. He stepped across the pavement to Isabella and said, "What a fine afternoon it is, now that I've laid eyes on your beauty."

She blushed as a pale rose and said, "Catherine is in the house. Do you wish me to fetch her?"

"Forget Catherine. Who wishes to be greeted by the stem, when one can be received by the flower?"

"Oh, Mr. Heathcliff, a flatterer you are, as well as a brute."

"Thus convicted. A brutish flatterer in the eyes of a one-woman jury." During his struggles to make his fortune, when he saw further how deeply women were attracted to his physical presence, and aloof manner, he had also discovered how powerful an effect it had when he mixed in a kind word, or a well-intentioned compliment. He took a step closer. "And what penalty shall I pay?"

"Mr. Heathcliff, you tread too close. We are unchaperoned." His proximity brought back the memory of his work in the garden and what she had shamelessly done in the privacy of her chambers—and now her blush turned crimson.

With his thumb, he traced her features: flattening the fine, silky hairs at the brow, pressing against the curve of her high cheekbones, caressing her lips. She wanted to ask him to stop, but felt helplessly weak in the knees. His glance bore down on her with those dark eyes that surely could eclipse any light. He parted her lips and entered her mouth with his thumb.

"There is no sense fighting your feelings after they have been clearly revealed. Catherine has done us both a service by allowing us to cut through the thicket and bramble of mundane courtship."

"Is that what this is . . . courtship?" she asked, raising her chin so his thumb slipped out. Whatever it was, she was certainly enjoying his full attention, finally.

He pulled her to him, grasped her glowing golden hair from behind, and kissed her deeply on the mouth, his tongue finding hers, and she was again helpless to resist the forcefulness of this most handsome gentleman. This was exactly how she had imagined it ever since his return, when alone at night in her chamber.

But then with a sudden, gruff movement from his knee, he parted her legs and pressed himself forward, the hardened muscle of his thigh fitting tightly against her quim, applying the same pressure she had done with her hand when she had watched him in the garden.

Gathering full strength of will, she broke from his grasp. "You take too many liberties, sir, and turn what could be beautiful into something wicked."

He smiled the sinful smile that seemed to make his eyes go darker, and said, "You didn't think it was so wicked when your tongue greeted mine like a familiar lover."

She turned from him and ran into the house, her eyes moistening with sorrow.

He approached the entrance to the kitchen and saw that Catherine *had* been watching. He entered the house.

"Heathcliff," she said, "what are you about, raising this stir? I said you must let Isabella alone! I beg you will, unless you are tired of being received here, and wish Edgar to draw the bolts against you!"

It stirred him to see her jealousy, her desire for him more acute after seeing him toy with another. "God forbid that Edgar should try!" answered Heathcliff harshly. "God keep him meek and patient. Every day I grow madder that he has his heaven with you."

"That you're intent upon turning into hell?" she cried. "Don't continue to vex me! Why have you disregarded my request? Did she come across you on purpose?"

"What is it to you?" he growled. "I have a right to kiss her, if she chooses, and you have no right to object. I'm not *your* husband; *you* needn't be jealous of me!"

How she detested him just then, showing favor to the sister of her husband, delighting in the touch of her golden hair, pressing his thumb upon the perfect features of her face and

entering her mouth. Did he not see the whore she was, allowing him such entrance? There was only one way to combat this
insolence.

"That's right, I have a husband, which is why I'm not jealous of
you."

She did not need words, he thought to himself; she might as
well take a knife and plunge it into his heart.

"Clear your face, you shan't scowl at me!" she added. "If you
like Isabella, you shall marry her. But, do you like her, tell the
truth, Heathcliff? There, you won't answer. I'm certain you don't!"

"And would Edgar approve of his sister marrying me?"

"Nay."

"He might spare himself the trouble," said Heathcliff. "I could
do as well without his approbation."

"You're doing this just to hurt me, aren't you? You will wound
her as well, but I'm not sure you even care enough, for my punishment is your guide."

"As long as you bring voice to such subject, Catherine, I have a
mind to speak a few of my own words, now, while we're at it."

Despite her pangs at seeing her beloved kiss another—someone
who Catherine believed might be more beautiful than she—and
despite his harsh tone, Catherine welcomed this.

"I want you to be aware," he continued, "that I know *you* have
treated me infernally . . . infernally! Do you hear? And if you flatter
yourself that I don't perceive it you are a fool—and if you think
I can be consoled by sweet words you are an idiot—and if you
fancy I'll suffer unrevenged, I'll convince you to the contrary, in a
very little while! Meantime, thank you for telling me your sister-in-
law's secret. I swear I will make the most of it." With much force,
he added, "And stand you aside!"

Though his words were hurtful, at least she was making him

see her, arousing him out of his cocksure masculine superiority and forcing him to go toe to toe.

"I've treated you infernally," exclaimed Catherine, "and you'll take revenge! How will you take it, ungrateful brute? How have I treated you infernally?"

"I seek no revenge on you," he continued. "That's not the plan. The tyrant grinds down his slaves and they don't turn against him, they crush those beneath them. You are welcome to torture me to death for your own amusement, only, allow me to amuse myself a little in the same style. If I imagined you really wished me to marry Isabella, I'd cut my throat!"

Yes, that was it. That was what Catherine wanted to hear. The more aroused he became, the less he could play his games, and the closer he came to the truth.

"Oh, the evil is that I'm *not* jealous, is it?" cried Catherine. "Your bliss lies in inflicting misery. Quarrel with Edgar if you please, Heathcliff, and deceive his sister; you'll hit on exactly the most efficient method of revenging yourself on me!"

Heathcliff understood the veracity of Catherine's words—Isabella was the most tender point within her. But how had he allowed her to control the situation? How had he allowed her to stoke his anger like a flame in the fireplace, raising his ire, arousing him from the smooth steadiness of his plan? He took a deep breath and, with casual deliberateness, underscored with clear-cut triumph, added, "It is not deception to hunger for someone as lovely as Isabella."

The chord he had struck made him more keenly aware of how beautiful Catherine was when devoured by the true light of passion, as her cheeks glowed like embers, her dark eyes widened with feeling. Such an exquisite vision made his heart tremble. Yet he could also see how deep was the pain of his words and wished instantly to retract them, felt compelled to fall to his feet, and shower kisses upon her ankles.

And he might have, if she had not slapped him hard across the face.

It was not the sting, but the audacity! By reflex, he yanked her closer by the hair and raised his hand to return equal blow.

She did not wilt, but shot lightning bolts from her eyes, daring him to retaliate.

He embraced her fiercely, with both arms, and kissed her deeply on the mouth as she bit his lip and drew blood.

When they both paused for air, she pulled back and said, "I am not Isabella who runs from the fire of your mouth, or the force of your hand. I know what lies beyond in thy heart . . . and thy soul."

This time it was Catherine who reached for him with fiery passion, then stood on her toes and kissed him fully on the mouth, her tongue forcing its way through the barrier of his lips, only to turn tender as it teased the sharp curve of his palate.

Heathcliff felt himself yield to her burning fervor; and with this yielding, he felt the *weakness* permeate his body, the divine surrender that only Catherine's kisses could inspire. This weakness would no doubt please Catherine, as it had done in the past, and lead to a profound and delightful lovemaking. But how would she react after to the *vulnerability* only she could expose, something that had made him so expendable before? She would accept him as a lover, but would that be enough to make her give up her husband and submit in every way possible? She must have no room in her heart even for the companionship of another. History would not repeat itself! Such full possession would complete his life, and, as he was already doing with Hindley, bring the full wrath of his curse down on Edgar, destroying the one who had stolen his beloved in the first place.

He shoved her to her knees, tore open his fly, dropped his pants fully, and before allowing her the pleasure of sucking his cock—fully formed from their passion—he offered it the way she had used her hand, and slapped it across her mouth.

This was just more wood upon her fire. She desperately wanted to take him into her mouth, as nothing could ever stifle her desire to taste this devil. How sweet to be on her knees, worshipping at Heathcliff's altar. How wonderful to be presented this object she had lusted so heartily after just days earlier. Now she could have it. Now she could swallow it. Now she could feel its glorious penetration anywhere she wanted.

But it could not go on like this, the way he toyed with her emotions. She gathered full heart and instead of yielding to the submissive nature of her posture, and the chalice dangling before her as an offer to quench her thirst, she caught Heathcliff by surprise and spun him around, pushed him forward so he was forced to lean toward the kitchen sink for support. Before he could protest, before he could rearrange himself, she reached through his legs and began the sweetest, gentlest caress of his cock and balls. Lest he gather willpower to fight off her ministrations and impose his body once again, as he had been doing so skillfully, she withdrew her hands and placed both upon the fine, hirsute arse cheeks of her lover, parting them, then leaned forward, paused briefly so he could feel her hot breath on this most tender of openings, then began the most gentle of seductions by kissing, licking, teasing his most vulnerable spot.

Curse this witch, thought Heathcliff, *what is she doing down there?* He remembered using his arse to make Nelly submit, as he had done with others, to punish her as the proxy for his beloved, but had derived little pleasure from it. Now it was as if he was being soothed by velvet strokes into a placid euphoria that left his body unable to move, and his hips in betrayal, as they thrust back to hasten a deeper penetration.

Nelly had been drawn to the kitchen upon hearing the loud sounds of their arguing, and had been listening by the door, but worried even more after hearing the sound of a slap, and then complete quiet. She hurried upstairs, found Edgar, and related the scene, as near as she dared.

Encouraged by Heathcliff's response, Catherine found her rhythm, obviously one very pleasing to Heathcliff. She burrowed deeper into this part of his manhood, freeing up her hands again, so that she could return to her delicate touches around his cock. He soon grew massively in her fist and she heard his soft groans of surrender.

Edgar had difficulty hearing Nelly to the close. "This is insufferable!" he exclaimed. "It is disgraceful that she should own him for a friend, and force his company on me! Call my two men out of the hall. Catherine shall linger no longer to argue with the low ruffian. I have humored her enough!"

Catherine parted the muscular buttocks of her lover even farther, which allowed her tongue to probe as deep as it could. She flicked, licked, and tickled her lover there and felt a pliancy in him that she had not seen since his return. She wanted him all for herself and would refuse to share him with anyone, especially her rival, Isabella.

One hand was on his cock now, stroking forcefully up and down; the other couldn't help reaching down to stroke herself under her dress. She was soaked, her quim never so moist, something that started during the heat of their argument and gushed fully as she used her tongue to penetrate her man and possess him once again.

Perhaps it was the dirty thrill of doing all of this while her husband rested above them, or perhaps she sensed some unforeseen danger, but she rapidly increased the tempo of her tongue thrusts in, then out, while stroking Heathcliff with greater heartiness, her other hand a blur as it dashed across herself at lightning speed, causing even more swollen moistness.

Heathcliff felt that it was important that he make a stand and not come, not allow her to see that she could control him with her sensual touches and licks, for this would go against all he had envisioned. But it was easier said than done as her fist guided his manhood and her tongue laid bare his own complete vulnerability as he allowed her all the access she desired with an even wider parting of his legs.

Heathcliff exploded mightily, letting out a loud, passionate groan as Catherine shoved herself as deep as she could inside her lover, and finished herself off as well with a frenetic finger finale and a deep, glorious moan...no, she would never let him leave again!...just as they heard Edgar by the door, bidding the servants to wait in the passage.

Catherine stood up, covered up, as quickly as she could. She grabbed a dish towel and completed a hasty clean up of Heathcliff's mess, as he managed to stow his cock with great difficulty, and close one button, just as she tossed the towel into the sink, and Edgar stormed in.

"What is this?" asked Edgar, addressing her. Their nervous expressions revealed clearly that some violation had taken place, but, fortunately, or unfortunately, he could never have imagined the true nature of what had occurred. "I need to know exactly what has transpired between you two!"

"Have you been listening at the door, Edgar?" asked Catherine, as she swept her hair back off her eyes, trying to put him on the defensive to avoid addressing his inquiries. In this passionate state, if he probed her too deeply, she might confess how wonderful it was that Heathcliff had returned, how alive he made her feel, which would surely give Edgar insight into where he came up short.

Heathcliff, who had raised his eyes at Edgar's speech, now gave a sneering laugh, drawing Edgar's attention to him.

"I have been so far forbearing with you, sir," said Edgar, the fury in his voice unmistakable. "Not that I was ignorant of your miserable, degraded character, but I felt you were only partly responsible for that; and Catherine, wishing to keep up your acquaintance, I gave in, foolishly. Your presence is a moral poison that would contaminate the most virtuous. For that cause, and to prevent worse consequences, I shall deny you, hereafter, admission into this house, and give notice, now, that I require your instant departure!"

Heathcliff measured the height and breadth of the speaker with an eye full of derision.

"Catherine, this lamb of yours threatens like a bull!" he said. "It is in danger of splitting its skull against my knuckles. By God, Mr. Linton, I'm mortally sorry that you are not worth knocking down!"

Edgar walked toward the door to fetch the men from the passage, but Catherine reached first and locked it.

"Fair means!" she said, in answer to her husband's look of angry surprise. She wanted to see what lay deep in her husband's core, if he had hidden any of the fierce will of someone such as Heathcliff. "If you have not the courage to attack him, make an apology, or allow yourself to be beaten." If he did not, then who was Edgar to impose a full separation between them and deny her the passion Heathcliff could inspire? "It will correct you of feigning more valor than you possess. No, I'll swallow the key before you shall get it!"

He tried to wrest the key from Catherine's grasp, but she flung it into the hottest part of the fire; whereupon Mr. Edgar was taken with a nervous trembling, and his countenance grew deadly pale. For his life, he could not avert that access of emotion—mingled anguish and humiliation overcame him completely. He leaned on the back of the chair and covered his face.

"Oh! Heavens! In old days this would win you a knighthood!" exclaimed Catherine. "We are vanquished! We are vanquished! Heathcliff would as soon lift a finger at you as the king would march his army against a colony of mice. Cheer up, you shan't be hurt!"

"I wish you joy of the milk-blooded coward, Catherine!" said Heathcliff. "I compliment you on your taste: the slavering, shivering thing you preferred to me! Is he weeping, or is he just going to faint from fear?"

Heathcliff approached and gave the chair on which Edgar rested a push. He'd better have kept his distance, for Edgar, to Catherine's great surprise, quickly sprang erect, and struck Heathcliff full on the throat a blow that would have leveled a slighter man.

It took his breath for a minute; and, while he choked, Edgar walked triumphantly out the back door into the yard, and from thence, to the front entrance.

Heathcliff turned more red with shame than with discomfort, allowing the sniveler to sneak in a cowardly blow in front of the woman he loved.

"There! You're done with coming here," cried Catherine. "Get away, now. He'll return with a brace of pistols, and a half dozen assistants. If he did overhear us, of course, he'd never forgive you. You've played me an ill turn, Heathcliff! But, go—make haste! I'd rather see Edgar at bay than you."

"Do you suppose I'm going with that blow burning in my gullet?" he thundered. "By hell, no! I'll crush his ribs like a rotten hazelnut, before I cross the threshold! If I don't floor him now, I shall murder him some time, so, as you value his existence, let me get at him!"

Catherine pulled him close, embracing him fully, looking up at his grizzly, handsome face, for she realized that nothing her husband could do would affect her feelings for Heathcliff. She simply could not be without this man! "If you deliver this message on Edgar's own property the law will have you and then we will be apart. Unless you bid us both make haste from here together, you better leave."

How desperately he wanted to hear these words from his beloved. How wonderful it would be to put all this behind him and run away with Catherine. How perfect it would feel to give in to the overwhelming urge he felt at this moment to sweep her in his arms, kiss her with all of his heart and soul, and sweep her out of this house and away forever.

But how soon would she come running back to her glorious estate, one she had coveted since their visit by the garden window? How soon would she want to return to her husband, the most respected magistrate in the county?

And all his objectives had not yet been completed. Waiting for Edgar's return, and thrashing him soundly, the same fate he wished for Hindley, would only be an appetizer, without promise of a full meal. All Lintons and Earnshaws must deteriorate slowly to make it the true feast he desired.

He regarded Catherine with careful study, and she seemed perplexed by his curious look. Heathcliff had discovered this afternoon that she was not as easily tamed as the other women he had been with. She had caught him by surprise with her delicate tongue at his most tender spot. During his absence from the Heights he had learned much about gaining the upper hand by exploiting the weakness of men; and, as for women, he had ascertained that not only were they drawn to his brutish side, desiring the distinct control he wielded, but they hungered most when he left them just short of being completely fulfilled. Yet Catherine seemed able to resist his full mastery. But . . . he understood now that *jealousy* was something she could not control and could be the key to possessing her in a way that would ensure their lifetime together.

Heathcliff grabbed the poker, smashed the lock from the inner door, and made his escape as Edgar and his men tramped in from the yard.

Edgar was flushed from the passion of the moment and the redemption achieved by striking a fierce blow upon the throat of his nemesis. Seeing Heathcliff gone, he dismissed his men, and stared at Catherine, who averted her eyes.

He grabbed her by the arm with a force inspired by his recently acquired authority, and escorted, no, dragged her up to their chamber.

"Unhand me!" she cried. "What gives you reason to think you can treat me like a cow to market?"

"Hush!" said Edgar. "You embarrass this household enough already."

Responsive to the fresh potency in his tone, she quieted.

Once behind chamber door, he said, without anger in his voice, but with much sorrowful despondency, "I neither want to wrangle, nor reconcile, but I wish to learn whether, after this afternoon's events, you intend to continue your intimacy with—"

"Oh, for mercy's sake," interrupted Catherine, stamping her

foot. She preferred anger over this pitiful sadness, for if she looked too closely at the grief flooding Edgar's face, she would yield to her husband and ask for his forgiveness...although she could not be sure if it was forgiveness for shaming the household, or because she was afraid he would cast her out. "Let us hear no more of it now!" she added with even more rancor.

"To get rid of me—answer my question," persevered her husband. "You *must* answer it. Will you give up Heathcliff hereafter, or will you give up me? It is impossible for you to be *my* friend and *his* at the same time. I absolutely *require* to know which you choose."

"I require to be let alone!" exclaimed Catherine, furiously, the emotions of the day, from Isabella, to Heathcliff, and now Edgar, becoming too much too bear. "I demand it! Don't you see I can scarcely stand? Edgar, you—you leave me!"

She could not answer him, because she did not know. A future here, at the Grange, with Edgar, was so clear a vision. Yet she desired so much more the chance to be with Heathcliff in any way he desired, but could not see even an idea as to where it would lead.

To summon Nelly, she rang the bell, but did not stop the rhythmic clanging till it broke with a twang. This day was too much! Why did Heathcliff not simply carry her away from all of this? Her brain fired within her skull like a tempest upon the moors. To throw herself out of the window would give more comfort than she felt right now.

Nelly entered leisurely, only to see the mistress shaking her head side to side and grinding her teeth so hard that they might be crashed to splinters.

Edgar looked at her with sudden compunction and fear. He immediately ordered Nelly to fetch some water and stilled Catherine's head by holding her face in his hands. "My love," he said. "I am so sorry for vexing you like this." She had no breath for speaking.

Nelly brought a glassfull; and, as Catherine would not drink, sprinkled some on her face. In a few seconds Catherine stretched herself out stiff, and turned up her eyes—while her cheeks, at once blanched and livid, assumed the aspect of death—and vomited into a flowerpot. She collapsed back on the couch, her eyes closing, her breathing still.

Edgar looked terrified. "I am a wretch for imposing my insecurities on one so fragile!" he lamented to Nelly. "I never should have handled her so roughly. She is but a delicate flower who has always been a good wife, the only wife I desire!"

"There is nothing in the world the matter," Nelly whispered to him suspiciously, knowing that even as a child, Catherine would feign an uncontrolled fit to deflect strong accusations and punishment. Nelly did not want Edgar to yield to her manipulations, though she could not help harboring some fear in her heart.

"She has blood on her lips!" he said, shuddering.

Perhaps overhearing Nelly, or perhaps truly overtaken with the weight her life had recently taken on, Catherine started up suddenly, her hair flying over her shoulders, her eyes flashing, the muscles of her neck and arms standing out preternaturally, then rushed from the room.

The master directed Nelly to follow. She did, to the guest chamber door, where Catherine hindered her from going farther by securing it against her.

And she would not even offer to descend to breakfast the next morning. At the door, Nelly asked whether she would have some carried up.

"No!" she replied, peremptorily.

The same question was repeated at dinner, and tea; and again on the morrow after, and received the same answer.

Edgar grew deeply despondent and spent most of his time in the library. He still chafed from Heathcliff's visit and despised this swarthy savage who had no respect for any person, or the conventions of civil living such as marriage. But of more concern was the ill turn taken by his wife. He had acted as brutish as Heathcliff, sunk to the level of such a common man, and look at the price he paid. Catherine had turned so very delicate after her serious illness just before their marriage. He knew that. He knew it best to encourage only her sunshine and stay away from her storm. He hadn't acted the proper gentleman at all! And now she would not let him to do anything to bring comfort, or apology, for his base behavior.

Edgar did, however, summon Isabella for an hour's interview. For Nelly had informed him, as well, that she had been alone with Heathcliff in the garden. He tried to elicit from her some sentiment of proper horror for Heathcliff's advances, but he could make nothing of her evasive replies, and was obliged to close the examination, unsatisfactorily. He added, however, a solemn warning: "If you are so insane as to encourage this worthless suitor, it will dissolve all bonds of relationship between you and me."

On the third day of Catherine's self-exile, it was Edgar who brought up a tray of food. He pleaded to be allowed entry. To his great joy, she acquiesced. Before eating, she told him that she was with child.

Chapter Sixteen

Upon hearing the news of his wife's pregnancy, Edgar's face beamed like a bright star on a dark night. When she finished her meal, he requested that she return to their chambers and lie down on the bed. He lay next to her, wonderfully at peace now that an heir was in the making.

He kissed her tenderly and Catherine welcomed his touch and returned it with her own affection. He held her close. She rested her head upon his stomach, still a bit weak from her lack of food and the emotional strain since Heathcliff's return.

Edgar stroked her hair with the caress she remembered the night of the oil massage, when they had fully consummated their marriage.

"I miss your touch," said Catherine.

"Selfish soul that I am, it is I who have neglected you, rushing to take my pleasure. But you seemed in accordance."

"I am in accordance with what pleases you, and you seemed happy."

In truth she missed his tender love, the way he stroked her body, caressed her breasts as if they were treasures beyond compare. True, Heathcliff aroused her passion in a way that Edgar could not, but Heathcliff's recent denial of any tender touches and feelings also left her empty.

Edgar stroked her hair and she murmured her approval. It felt wonderful to have her full attention again. The relaxed ease in which she allowed him to hold her made Heathcliff seem a more distant memory. He vowed not even to mention his name. He began to massage the scalp, mixing in some light pulls of her long, elegant, dark strands.

She cuddled even deeper into her husband. Here she felt safe. Was that not the most important thing?

She undid his pants.

"Nay, wife, you must rest. I am perfectly content."

She continued to unbutton him and, with his help, slid his pants down to his knees.

She stroked his penis with her thumb and index finger, encouraging it to grow. With Heathcliff, nothing less than a fist would suffice to cause movement to his monster, and even a fist shrunk from his thickness.

"Will you always love me, Edgar?" she asked.

"Forever and ever."

"Will you love our child?"

"More than life itself."

Responding to her touch and soothing tone, she felt him grow in her hand.

"You need this as well, don't you, Edgar?"

"Yes."

"Not just my love, but my sex?"

"Yes."

"You dream of me?"

"Always."

As if rewarding him, she undid her blouse and camisole,

exposing herself to him fully. He groaned with near-delirious pleasure. She loved his reaction to her breasts. Heathcliff, once an ardent admirer, had neglected them since his return.

Edgar became fully erect.

"Do you want my mouth on it?" she asked, something she had only done once before with Edgar, but he came too quickly, and she did not particularly care for the taste of him or his semen.

"Yes." His head was back, eyes closed, face a picture of heavenly rapture.

"Ask me for it."

"What?"

"Ask me for my mouth on your *cock*."

Hearing his angel use such a word stirred him even further.

"Please, Catherine, may I have your mouth on my cock?"

"Call me *mistress*."

"Please, mistress, may I have your mouth on my cock?"

"You may, for being such a good boy."

"I am a good boy."

"A good boy is one who trusts his wife."

"I do."

She rewarded him by taking the head of his penis in her mouth and licking it with her tongue. He groaned loudly, but she stayed slow, hoping he could last.

Withdrawing the head from her mouth, she said, "A good boy can become a good man if he does not burden his wife with silly questions, outrageous accusations, and bold ultimatums."

"I understand."

"Do you?" She took him again in her mouth and with delicate fingers played with his balls.

"Completely."

She sucked deeper. "Are you sure?"

"Yes."

"Yes, what?"

"Yes, mistress."

She easily took him all the way down her throat and he bucked, and lurched, and spoke words in a rush, in a voice that was higher than usual, almost girlish, as he said, "I will burden you with nothing, for you are my wife, with my child, and, at this moment, I am the happiest man on earth, my sweet, sweet love, I will be yours forever and no one can stand in our way..."

She felt him ready to surge, and pulled it out of her mouth, and wanked the shaft vigorously with her hand and he spilled his meager load all over his belly, as he cried out with wild abandon, a change for Edgar, who never stopped worrying about the servants and what they could hear.

"Thank you, my love," he said with the gratefulness of a sinner being given ultimate dispensation.

All felt right in their marriage again, except being with him like this exposed the empty place within her that Edgar could not fill. She couldn't help recalling how deeply Heathcliff had entered her as they lay upon the ground at Black Rock Cragge; how he had tamed her with just one finger in yonder garden; how he had turned her into an animal needing release from a glass cage as he repaired the lattice; and, finally, how sweet it had been to be the one penetrating with *her* tongue, feeling a yielding within him that deeply stirred her loins. Performing such an act on Edgar would repulse her, and he was entirely too proper to welcome it himself. But everything she did with Heathcliff aroused her deeply: gazing into his eyes; accepting his touch anywhere upon her body; tasting the moistness of his mouth; breathing in the wind-filled scent of his hair; exchanging heated words that reflected the flame of real living. Hard living, an existence that did not settle for the passive, mundane familiarity of life at the Grange, but announced that true life, deep passion, did exist, within her, and that he was the only one who could fill the emptiness and make her whole.

She got up to fix her hair. Just before leaving the room, she said, "Clean yourself up."

Edgar replied, "Yes, mistress."

The news of Catherine's pregnancy spread quickly through the household and brought a renewed cheer. Since Heathcliff's return, the multitude of odd events, hidden secrets, open arguments, and the public brawl had caused the emotions of the servants to teeter to and fro—and they had come to prefer invisibility in the shadows of any room where their master and mistress might sit, and had spoken to each other in hushed tones—as if all human feeling at Thrushcross Grange had fluctuated up and down like a seesaw, one that had not swayed randomly, but had been controlled by a strong hand.

But with the prospect of a child coming soon to bring laughter to the household, to ensure the noble Linton line, a quiet and pleasant balance returned. Even Nelly relaxed, no longer feeling as strong an urge to save her kind master by getting to the bottom of Heathcliff's plans.

Edgar treated Catherine like a queen, buying for her a new, elegant wardrobe, sized to fit her growing condition, and pearl earrings that hung like perfect, full raindrops from her delicate ears. Catherine discovered that servicing her husband with hand and mouth made him so much more calm and loyal, and that he would let loose with a particularly passionate throb or pulse when she called him a *naughty boy* or a *good boy*—depending on her mood—curling up small in the bed, or laying his head in her lap, as he whispered, "I love you, mistress."

He adored that she was his mistress, for if she was *his* mistress, then she was no one else's.

Though she assured him she was completely recovered from her feverish display, Edgar insisted that Dr. Kenneth be summoned to make sure she was cured and to check on the health of the baby. Catherine gave in, secretly delighted to be doted on fully once more. This delight, however, did not erase thoughts of the man who lived just a few miles away. She had not heard from him since his hasty departure from the kitchen, and, lately, had resorted to staying in bed later, waiting for Edgar to depart for work, so she could place a hand between her legs and revisit the recent times with her lover in an even more vivid manner. There were moments alone, when her sadness returned, because she wondered if the news that she was with child had cooled Heathcliff's ardor, or deflated his hope of being with her, and that he assumed a bond had been formed with Edgar that could not be broken. She longed to see Heathcliff again, to embrace him, to share their kisses, to explain that nothing could break the bond they shared, that her life at the Grange was simply events taking their course, but that the future of her living only existed with him.

Nelly met Dr. Kenneth at the gate and filled him in all the delirious actions Catherine had taken. He was a plain, rough man, one quickly to the point. "Nelly, I can't help fancying there's an extra cause for this. What has there been to do at the Grange? We've odd reports up here. A stout, hearty lass like Catherine does not fall ill for a trifle; and now she must also worry for another. It's hard work bringing them through the fevers, and such things. How did it begin?"

"The master will inform you," she answered, "but you are acquainted with the Earnshaws' violent dispositions, and Mrs. Linton caps them all. I must say this; it commenced in a quarrel. She was struck during a tempest of passion with a kind of fit. That's her account at least; for she flew off in the height of it, and locked herself up. Afterward, she refused to eat. But now, with full acceptance of the life of another growing within her, she seems completely recovered."

"How is Edgar handling it?" asked the doctor.

"His heart would break if anything happened to his beloved. But now they are both as if on honeymoon."

"I told him to beware," said Dr. Kenneth. "He must bide the consequences of neglecting my warning. Hasn't he been thick with Mr. Heathcliff lately?"

"Heathcliff frequently visits the Grange," answered Nelly, "though more on the strength of the mistress having known him as a boy than because the master likes his company. At present, he's discharged from the trouble of calling."

"And does Catherine turn a cold shoulder on him?"

"I'm not in her confidence," returned Nelly.

"She's a sly one," he remarked, shaking his head. "She keeps her own counsel. But she's a real little fool. I have it from good authority that during the darkness of night she is often seen walking on the plantation at the back of your house, glancing longingly toward the moors, and the direction of Wuthering Heights. My informant said that this very evening last, she met with a stable boy and pressed upon him to travel to the Heights and deliver to Mr. Heathcliff the message that she was prepared to run away with him this very night. You urge Mr. Linton to look sharp!"

The news filled Nelly with fearful dread, but her first instinct was to hold her tongue, and suffer matters to take their course.

The doctor gave Catherine a thorough examination, while

Edgar and Nelly looked on. The master did not move a muscle, barely breathing, watching every shade, and every change in Catherine's painfully expressive features as she was listened to and probed. Dr. Kenneth spoke directly to Edgar when he pronounced that her illness had had a favorable termination and all indications were that the baby was thriving.

Nelly couldn't help noticing Edgar's childlike delight. He kissed his wife and she patted him lightly on the head.

The doctor continued that it was essential that they preserve around her perfect and constant tranquility. "The threatening danger is not so much death, as permanent alienation of intellect."

Nelly hated to dampen the renewed spirit in Edgar and the household, but she realized that if she did not relay Dr. Kenneth's story the worst would occur before anything could be done to stop it.

She shared it as gracefully as she could, assuring him that the doctor's sources were not necessarily reliable and that something like this could not have occurred.

The peace that had marked his face these many days turned to aged lines. He did not know what to think or believe. He hesitated at confronting his wife with such an outrageous tale and risk the shattering of their harmony, yet he would not let her sneak off in the night with his child.

Catherine retired cheerily to bed, but it was only she in the household who found sleep. Nelly lay wide awake in her bed, thoughts fluctuating between anger and horror that Catherine would dare consider abandoning her husband for someone like Heathcliff . . . while with child as well! She also revisited his work in the garden and how she had demeaned herself by wallowing in the dirt of the attic, hand between her legs, to spy on a man with no character. The hand returned again as she reviewed these thoughts in detail, experiencing the same carnal pleasure multiple times...until she found sleep.

Sleep was not something Edgar found that night, as he stared at his beloved, watched her tremble and talk in her sleep, curl to her side, even execute snores that he thought endearing. She would not leave on his watch.

By early morn he realized he had been dozing and forced his eyelids open in a start. There she was: his beloved, Catherine...sleeping as soundly as a cherub. How foolish to listen to the gossip of servants!

At breakfast, after serving porridge and fruit to Catherine and Edgar, Nelly went upstairs to see what was keeping Isabella, only to discover that she, along with most of her clothes, were gone.

Chapter Seventeen

Word came to Edgar that last night Isabella and Heathcliff had been spotted at a blacksmith's shop, two miles out of Gimmerton—to have a horse's shoe fastened—not very long after midnight, by the blacksmith's lass, who had gotten up to spy on who they were. She knew them both directly. And she noticed the man—Heathcliff, she was certain, nobody could mistake him—put a sovereign in her father's hand for payment. The lady had a cloak about her face, but having desired a sip of water, while she drank, it had fallen back, and she saw her very plain. Heathcliff held both bridles as they rode on, and they set their faces from the village, and went as fast as the rough roads would let them. The lass had said nothing to her father, but she had told it all over Gimmerton this morning.

"Are we to try any measures for overtaking and bringing her back?" inquired Nelly. "How should we do it?"

"She went of her own accord," answered the master, his voice a mixture of anger and relief. "She had a right to go if she pleased. Trouble me no more about her. Hereafter she is only my sister in name; not because I disown her, but because she has disowned me."

And that was all he said on the subject. He did not make a single inquiry further, or mention her in any way, except to direct

Nelly to send what property she had left in the house to her fresh home, wherever it was, when Nelly knew it.

Catherine was in the downstairs parlor when she heard the news and she fainted straight away. Edgar carried her to their chamber and left Nelly to nurse her as she thrashed in a feverish delirium once again. He was heartbroken over her dramatic reaction, but relieved that his rival had gone off with another, although he wished, with all his heart, that it had not been with his sister.

Whenever Catherine would regain full consciousness, she would immediately long for the troubled peace of a blackout, for when fully awake, all the pain and misery of her beloved choosing another over her would knife her heart and shred her soul into so many pieces there seemed to be no way for them ever again to form a whole. How could he forsake her like this? How could he toss her aside and choose the sister of her husband, her rival since childhood? More so, how could she do without the flesh and bone of her true mate by her side? There was no reason to live. She tried to take comfort in knowing she had a child within her, but then rambling thoughts would tumble through her mind, as she struggled with the highest fever yet, that perhaps this baby was what had separated her from the man who completed her. Worst of all, she now understood the full anguish she had caused Heathcliff by accepting Edgar's proposal in marriage. She understood that such an extreme ache could cause one to do anything to find relief. She could not stop the weeping, despite the swelling it caused in her eyes, the wrenching she felt in her lungs, and the misery that coursed through her heart. Oh, Heathcliff!

There was one time before Isabella had sent her secret message to Heathcliff that she had met with him late at night. The clandestine nature of their rendezvous, the romance of being alone with him in the dark, the thrill of being held in his strong arms, had prompted Isabella to give herself more freely. What propriety was left after sneaking off and disobeying her brother's wishes? But though he had tried, she had not allowed a full deflowering. She had promised herself to save such consummation for her wedding night. He was so convincing while he held her, turned her toward the moon over the moors, clasped her from behind, and rubbed her seductively between the legs as he painted a beautiful picture of the marital bliss that could be theirs . . . whispering about how much she craved him inside her, how much she needed to escape the shadow of her brother. At the end of the evening, as he had walked her back to the house, he told her he did not want her like this, and that he would not visit again, unless she was willing to accept his marriage proposal. So many tortured nights she could not sleep, wandering the plantation, dreaming of their night on the moors, fantasizing about how incredible it would feel to be with this man, in his bed, in his life, every day for the rest of her life. And so she had accepted! Her brother might burn with bitter anger at first, but even he would have to realize that she had saved his marriage. And Catherine, her rival, well, there was little optimism that the hurt this union would cause could be mended. Isabella hoped that one day Catherine would realize that she had started a family with Edgar, and the Grange was where she was destined to remain. At her more devilish moments, Isabella wished she had been present when Catherine had received the news.

There had been a promise of at least a small church wedding and a luxurious honeymoon in London. But along the way, Heathcliff insisted they share a bed. So in order to keep her virtue intact—she had held on to it this long—Isabella agreed to a quick marriage by the justice of the peace in a village just fifty miles from Gimmerton.

She was nervous, but eager to be with the man she had lusted after since his return. Out in the dark of their plantation the night they met to escape, she had exhibited some last-minute hesitation, knowing what Edgar's strong reaction would be. But Heathcliff had spoken of love, had spoken of her as the only woman capable of making him forget Catherine. And when he had kissed her, it was not only as if he had taken her breath away, but as if he were able to reach inside and caress her heart. It was then that Isabella knew why Catherine was so obsessed with Heathcliff, his handsomeness, his masculine charm, for there was no other like him. To change her mind would risk losing him, and, even worse, seeing him in the arms of Catherine once again.

He escorted her up the stairs of a small, dirty inn. "Surely, even a town of this size must have more worthy accommodations," said Isabella. Heathcliff insisted he was tired from all of the riding and that one bed was as good as any other.

Once in the room, he gave her a moment to freshen up and change into her nightgown. Her hands trembled with excitement: finally, to be with the man who had inspired an awakening within her that she never thought she was capable of. She shook with nervousness as well, for she had seen his manhood and could not figure out how she would be able to manage the full bloom of his instrument.

Isabella floated from the powder room into the bedroom that held her beloved. Her hair was done up in a perfect set of curls, hands powdered white, body carefully scented in all of the right places. He was right, where there was love, there was luxury, and her love helped her block out the dreary dirtiness of their *honeymoon* suite.

"You move like a noble lady," said Heathcliff. "You make this room your palace and I your servant."

"Nay, you are my husband."

She moved to embrace him, but he held her steady with a raised hand. Slowly, he began to undress. "Watch," he said. "It is something you're good at."

Isabella could not help but blush, wondering if he knew she had been at the window while he had repaired the lattice, and, even worse, what she had done while drinking him in with her eyes, as if she'd been blistered with thirst and he an oasis.

Seductively, he pulled back his shirt and revealed again the full manliness of his chiseled torso. He shook his long black hair out of his eyes and it was with great willpower that she did not give in to this sensuous action and rush to his arms. He enjoyed her reaction to even his slightest of movements, enjoyed the power each part of his body held over her eyes as they remained transfixed.

He unbuttoned his pants, but hesitated. She realized she had been staring, frozen, at the bulge between his legs, and did not look up until he laughed, causing renewed blush at her eagerness to feast her eyes on this grand rooster.

"Do not toy with me, husband. I long to feel you in my arms with abandon, release the emotions you have inspired but I would not set free until you called me wife."

He let the pants drop, causing a hard intake of breath. She was not sure if he was fully aroused, but he had the equipment to rival any stallion.

He beckoned her to come forth. A side of her would have preferred he had a bath first, to wash away the muck of the road, yet something about the scent of Heathcliff, even when dirty, aroused her immeasurably.

She went to his arms, about to kiss him, when he turned her

toward the large mirror over the dresser. With the weight of his body, he nudged her closer to the glass.

His powerful arms crisscrossed across her chest, as he stood behind her.

"Look at yourself, Isabella. You see a noble lady, powdered and puffed in full grandeur. You see yourself such, as Edgar sees himself a nobleman, as all of your family perceives themselves, nearly royal in stature."

He ripped her nightgown apart with one complete sweep and let it drop to the floor, exposing her full bosom and delicately trimmed private parts.

"But I will peel away all the perceptions that are false, and show that underneath lies the sordidness of the most common scoundrel, and the base feelings of the lowest soul."

Isabella turned to protest, to make effort to break away and confront his words with her own sharp tongue. But he put both her nipples between each thumb and index finger and teased them with a gentle caress, instantly calming her ire.

She moaned her approval.

His slow caress turned to a sudden twist, causing her to cry out in discomfort.

"Please, Heathcliff. More gentle."

"You will learn to enjoy the pain."

He delicately cupped her full breasts, sensually kneading them with his strong hands, and she closed her eyes and swooned slightly. He licked along her earlobe, letting his hot breath brush against her neck. "Yes, my love," she whispered.

Thumb and finger at the nipples again, hard, turning, and she cried out once more, but this time her exclamations revealed more of the throbbing pleasure that joined intensely with the sting.

"That's it, Isabella. Don't fight it. Give in to your body and more gratification than you ever dreamed of will be yours."

The cupping of his hands at her breasts turned rougher, and she could feel her chest swell with desire. Her nipples seemed to leap to his fingers, whether he teased or twisted.

From his sensuous licking at her ear, he went to her neck, and she arched her head back and let her weight fall against his. His tongue was like a wand that marked spells along her flesh. He went back to her earlobe, grabbing it with his teeth, caressing lightly, with love it seemed, until he bit a little more sharply.

"Heathcliff!" She struggled again to break free of his arms, but was helpless in his mighty grip.

"Look in the mirror now. Not so noble. I see the coarse desire that existed before you yourself were aware."

She was about to voice further protest, but then he slid his hand down her stomach and rested it firmly between her thighs. With one finger he began a circular caress at her most vulnerable spot.

Who was this man? she wondered, a tremble forming in her body. He seemed keen on not addressing any of their love tonight, only reducing her to the most prurient of creatures.

Yet this already familiar touch caused her to melt once again.

Heathcliff missed the aggressive resistance, the more forceful protest of Catherine, even Nelly, wanting to feel an even greater stirring within himself. He took a finger from his free hand and began teasing Isabella lightly along the lips, then they parted and he entered her mouth. Obediently, instinctively, she began to lick the shaft of his finger, enjoying the salty grime after such long travels on a horse.

"You lick like the slut you are, a whore who encourages her patron for more."

She wished to spit the finger out and voice further objection to such a crude metaphor, but she did feel base, as if uncontrollably shaped by his confident control over her body and emotions. And, strangely, this aroused her even more.

"Suck it, like the dirty tart you are."

Suck it she did, with much enthusiasm. If his finger aroused her this much, she could barely imagine how sweet it would be to taste his . . .

"Imagine it's my cock," he said suddenly. Not only could he read every nuance of her body's needs, but he could see into her mind as well!

He moved his finger in and out, as she continued sucking, and she relished this feeling.

"Nay, a finger this size could never be my cock," he added. "Imagine it's Edgar's feeble member."

This time she did discharge the finger, then drove her elbows into his stomach and spat, "I'll not have it!"

There you go, Isabella, he said to himself with much enjoyment, as his own pulse quickened and his cock strained harder against her buttocks.

"Oh, you will," he answered, with a wry smile.

For the first time, his finger penetrated her quim, causing a sharp intake of breath and a deep stirring within.

She was beginning to understand who this man was, her husband. And this both frightened and thrilled her.

He moved his finger in and out, as he had done in her mouth, expanding her walls, providing full pressure that released the heavy moistness of her desire.

She felt overwhelmed by the massive strength of his arms, the shoulders that pressed against her back, immobilizing her. But perhaps the deep sensations he ignited in her quim did the most to quell any resistance.

He whispered, "Your plentiful wetness reveals the real Isabella."

To deny after such a yielding would be hollow. She could only part her thighs and allow him deeper entry. Perhaps this *was* her true nature and it took a man like Heathcliff to expose her so clearly? She relaxed completely, as he repeated his finger thrusts forward, then backward to recharge for another forceful return deep into her sacred opening, all of it gathering the moist tide within, which carried her forward, launched her almost airborne, toward the climactic waterfall that awaited her, so sweet, so welcoming, as she closed her eyes and recalled the muscular vision of him in the garden, while crying out, "Yes, Heathcliff!"

But, just at the brink, he withdrew his finger, halting her progress, causing a disorienting balance within her that would have dropped Isabella to her knees if he was not holding her so tightly. She moaned in anguish, as a starving animal might after having been presented a feast, only to have it suddenly wrenched away.

She hoped, no, she prayed, that this was all part of some game to please her, that he perceived she fancied this rough treatment, this incessant teasing, and that they would laugh about it in the morning. He was obviously so much more experienced than she was. And perhaps, simply, this was also the manner which gave him the most pleasure?

Either way, her insides quivered in anticipation of the larger penetration she hoped would come soon, joining husband and wife, sealing their union in both a physical and spiritual way.

He raised his left arm across her chest and neck again, making it difficult for her to breathe. He brought his right index finger, soaked with the deep need and passion he had inspired within her quim, around to the entrance of her bum, and began a gently caress.

"Heathcliff, no, this is not a place for love."

"Precisely," he answered.

He caressed the delicate flesh by the opening, teasing her with just a bit of entry, and there, too, she began to feel fire.

This was surely no ordinary man, but one built for the needs of the flesh, one designed to probe the innermost feelings of women—he went in even deeper—and exploit them.

He worked the finger, massaged her nipples, licked her neck, and she felt herself drifting toward a pool of submissive need. His presence in her arse made her feel him everywhere, as he manipulated her body, peeled away at the surface of her desires, and, as he had prophesied, discarded every notion of propriety she had held sacred.

"Take it, my hot little bitch," he whispered huskily into her ear, his voice like thunder now, every sensation heightened. And despite the roughness of his actions, the foulness of his words, no, perhaps because of both, she felt an even deeper arousal within her.

He, too, must have felt equal pleasure, because he withdrew his finger and pressed his hugely swollen cock against her arse. This heightened her fever, able to feel how much he wanted her by the vast weight and size against her bum, but she also trembled with dread that he would replace his finger with his cock, and turn their honeymoon into a night of buggering, something already proven, several times this evening, she would probably be helpless to resist.

In a plea to retain some honor and dignity, she whimpered, "No, Heathcliff, not there. Please, I beg you."

Her tone of helplessness brought another surge to his considerably engorged member. "Beg you will, for everything, for even the slightest reward or kindness."

Maybe it was her pleading, maybe it was some sort of kindness on his part, or maybe he never intended such a salacious violation, because he penetrated not her arse, but her quim from behind, very slowly, helped considerably by the pool he had inspired, letting her get used to his size, obliterating her virgin width, and, once fully inside, causing her to feel as if she truly were possessed by this man.

"My, love," she cried out. "You are magnificent!"

This penetration of Isabella, this taking from behind, this owning of her, released within Heathcliff his full intent and desire, for after the kind moment of making a slow and cautious entry, after going all the way up her so that she felt almost as if he were lifting her off her feet, he began what could only be described as *fucking*...hard...with a clear-cut intensity that Isabella had difficulty completely discerning, so overwhelmed was she by the booming presence of his hands back at her nipples and breasts, his mouth lathering her neck with rough, titillating licks, his cock going deeper and deeper, in and out, with full devilish force.

She braced her arms against the dresser to support her body against his powerful, repetitive thrusts, still helpless to resist, yielding also to the rhythmic derision of his words, as he barked...

"You are mine, completely. You will lick my feet as well as my boots. You will bathe me when I ask, take pleasure in servicing my every need. For you are my whore, a mere receptacle, not worthy of beholding my presence without permission."

Startled, she looked up at the mirror and saw the twisted look of pleasure and hate in his face. He saw her stare and slapped her hard across her arse cheeks, causing an instant reddening, but inspiring an even deeper surge where his cock entered. "Don't look at me! Don't ever look me! Unless I give you permission."

Obediently, she lowered her head, staring at the scratches in the cheap dresser wood.

He grabbed her hair in his hand and pulled, causing her to look up.

"No! Do not look down either. Look at yourself. Look at what noble and grand Isabella has become. Imprint it in your memory and do not forget it."

She did watch, for she did feel as if she had to do whatever he said, and saw nothing noble.

His forceful pounding, the penetration of him was so deep and masterful that, indeed, he was touching her soul with all that was dark.

With a deep breath, and dogged determination—like a colt who bucked fiercely when mounted by her first rider—she gathered herself one more time to struggle to break free, managing to twist her body and rake her nails along his neck, claws that drew blood.

He laughed at her struggles and seemed inspired by the wound she inflicted to double his effort, to go faster and deeper, as he rode her back hard, without pity, overpowering her completely in every way, the colt still, settled, completely passive, as she finally discerned the full intent of this man, yet knew there was nothing she could do to combat the force of her rider and that the only choice now was to surrender completely to her fate and accept being fully tamed.

Together, husband and wife exploded into an orgasm that darkened her brain as well as her soul and produced flashes behind her eyes, a climax that caused his head to rear back, his toes to curl, and the hair on his arms to stand on end, all of it inspiring a deep, primal, simultaneous scream of sordid satisfaction that roused a mighty laugh, some perverse grins, and another round of drinks for the patrons below who relished in the sounds of two newlyweds on their honeymoon.

Done, Heathcliff withdrew. Isabella surely would have collapsed to the floor if he hadn't lifted her up, almost a baby in his strong arms, and carried her to bed. He lay next to her, each on their side, facing each other. She kept her eyes averted down in submissive respect to her husband. Finally, she felt his hand at the back of her head, pushing her toward him. He brought her face to his chest. Instinctively, she opened her mouth, and he adjusted so she could fasten on his erect nipple.

She began a suckling at his breast, enjoying the warm comfort of her master in her mouth. He stroked her hair gently. "That's a good lass," he said. "Today you learned to enjoy it. Soon you will learn to crave it."

Eyes closed, as she continued to suck covetously, so very grateful for this kindness, she knew her husband to be right.

He let her fall asleep this way, feeling almost jealous of her contentment. As well as he knew the amorous needs of a woman, he also understood their needs afterward. For after the complete vulnerability of lovemaking, especially such intense intercourse as this, there was always a hole, an emptiness, as if part of the soul had been opened up and leaked out. When one was in love, this hole would be filled immediately upon the first postcoital embrace and produce a moment even greater, so much sweeter, than the strongest physical or emotional passion from the act itself.

Heathcliff knew all this because he believed that, in this instance, women and men were the same. No matter how much he enjoyed any sexual encounter, he always felt complete emptiness when it was over if there was no one next to him who he loved, no one there who could complete his soul. It was only Catherine, the true love of his life, who had been able to fill the emptiness with a euphoric feeling of wholeness, as she had done in their youth without them even attempting the fullest consummation.

But now, ever since his return—as he replaced some of his love with sensual strategies to win Catherine back fully; incorporated Isabella as a means to inspire his beloved's unrestrained jealousy; and trained his new wife to be a pawn in the unleashing of his satanic curse—all he felt at these endgame moments was a deep, painful, lonely ache in his heart.

Chapter Eighteen

"I'm dying! I'm on the brink of the grave!" cried Catherine, as she thrashed in her bed, and her rising fever increased her despair. "My God! Does he know how I'm altered?"

Nelly put a cold, moist compress on Catherine's forehead, which caused her mistress to open her eyes. Nelly did not know if the *he* was Heathcliff or Edgar, but she did not want to ask.

Perhaps Catherine perceived her disapproval, because she continued her lament with "I've been tormented. I've been haunted! But I begin to fancy you don't like me. How strange. I thought, though everybody hated and despised each other, they could not avoid loving me—and now they have all turned to enemies, especially Heathcliff who has forsaken me again, and Isabella, the traitor, who has run off with my beloved just to strike a dagger in my chest!"

Tossing about, Catherine increased her feverish bewilderment to madness, and tore the pillow with her teeth, then raised herself up all burning and desired that Nelly would open the window. They were in the middle of winter, the wind blew strong from the northeast, and she refused.

"Give over with that baby work!" cried Nelly, dragging the pillow away, and turning the holes toward the mattress, for Catherine was removing its contents by handfuls. "Lie down, you're wandering. There's a mess. The down is flying about like snow!"

A succession of shudders convulsed Catherine's frame and Nelly took her by the hand. Catherine's free hand clutched at her bedclothes and pulled them over her eyes.

"Why, what *is* the matter?" cried Nelly, sternly. "Wake up!"

Trembling and bewildered, she held Nelly fast, then opened her eyes in a start. The horror gradually passed from her countenance; its paleness gave place to a glow of shame.

"Oh, dear! I thought I was at home," she sighed. "I thought I was lying in my chamber at Wuthering Heights. Because I'm weak, my brain got confused, and I screamed unconsciously. Don't say anything, but stay with me. I dread sleeping, my dreams appall me."

"A sound sleep will do you good, ma'am," said Nelly.

"Oh, if I were but in my own bed in the old house!" she went on bitterly, wringing her hands. "And that wind sounding in the firs by the lattice. Do let me feel it—it comes straight down the moor—do let me have one breath!"

To pacify her, Nelly held the casement ajar, a few seconds. A cold blast rushed through, she closed it, and returned to her post.

Catherine lay still, now: her faced bathed in tears. Exhaustion of body had entirely subdued her spirit. She muttered, "I imagined I was in my youth; my father was just buried, and my misery arose from the separation that Hindley had ordered between me and Heathcliff. I laid alone, Heathcliff banished from the house, and spent the night weeping. Oh, I'm burning! I wish I were out of doors—I wish I was a girl again, half savage and hardy, and free . . . and laughing at injuries, not maddening under them. Pray, open the window again, wide, fasten it open! Quick, why don't you move?"

"Because I won't give you your death of cold," answered Nelly. "You won't give me a chance of life, you mean," she said sullenly. "However I'm not helpless yet, I'll open it myself!"

And sliding from the bed before Nelly could hinder her, she crossed the room, walking very uncertainly, threw the window back, and bent out, careless of the frosty air that cut about her shoulders as keen as a blade.

Nelly entreated and finally attempted to force her to retire, fearful the icy wind would cause her fever to spike to a temperature that could prove fatal. But she soon found her delirious strength much surpassed hers. And Nelly became convinced Catherine *was* delirious, as there was no moon, and everything beneath lay in misty darkness; not a light gleamed from any house, far or near; and those at Wuthering Heights were never visible, but Catherine cried, "Look! that's my room, with the candle in it, and the trees swaying before it . . . and the other candle is Joseph's garret . . . He's waiting till I come home to lock the gate . . . Well, he'll wait a while yet. It's a rough journey, and a sad heart to travel it; and we must pass by Gimmerton Church to go that journey! We've braved its ghosts often together, and dared each other to stand among the graves and ask them to come . . . But, Heathcliff, if I dare you now, will you forsake Isabella and venture there? If you do, I'll keep you. I'll not lie there by myself; they may bury me twelve feet deep, and throw the church down over me; but I won't rest till you are with me . . . I never will!"

Perceiving it in vain to argue with her insanity, Nellie wrapped a shawl around Catherine, gently closed the window, and led her back to bed. Catherine should be grateful that Heathcliff ran off with Isabella; it gave her the one chance for a happy life with Edgar, though Nelly fretted deeply about the sister of her master, knowing she was ill equipped to handle the twisted appetites and motivations, no matter how thrilling, of one as driven as Heath-cliff.

There was a rattle at the door handle and Edgar entered to check on Catherine.

"It's deathly cold in here, Nelly. Fetch my wife another blanket."

Ever since Catherine had relapsed to her bed and the doctor had pronounced that she had encountered a brain fever, no mother could have nursed an only child more devotedly than Edgar had tended her. Day and night he was watching, and patiently enduring all the annoyance that irritable nerves and a shaken reason could inflict. Hour after hour, he would sit beside her, praying for the gradual return of bodily health, and flattering his too sanguine hopes with the illusion that her mind would settle back to its right balance also, and she would soon be entirely her former self.

The haggardness of Catherine's appearance smote him speechless, and he could only glance from her to Nelly in sad astonishment as Nelly wrapped her in another blanket.

"She's been fretting," said Nelly, "and eating scarcely anything, but never complaining."

At first Catherine gave him no glance of recognition . . . he was invisible to her abstracted glaze. The delirium was not fixed, however; having weaned her eyes from contemplating the outer darkness, by degrees, she centered her attention on him, and discovered who it was that held her.

"Ah, you are come, are you, Edgar Linton?" she said with angry animation. "You are one of those things that are ever found when least wanted, and when you are wanted, never!"

"Rest, my love." He sat next to her on the bed. "Can I get you some water, perhaps some dry toast?" He touched her stomach gently and felt the round, popped bulge of her pregnancy.

"I'm not sure your child will appear before destiny brings me to my narrow dwelling beneath the dirt."

"Hush."

"Promise me, Edgar, that my final resting place will not be among the Lintons, under the chapel roof; but in the open air, at Black Rock Cragge, with a headstone, nearer to my true home, and you may please yourself, whether you go to them, or come to me!"

"Catherine, what are you saying?" He stood from the bed. "I will not make that promise! You are Catherine *Linton*! Am I nothing to you anymore? The news of Heathcliff married to another attacks your heart and makes you speak of death. Do you love that wretch more than—"

"Quiet!" cried Catherine. "This moment! You mention that name again and I end the matter, instantly, by a spring from the window!" Somewhere in her heart she knew it was Heathcliff she should be cursing, for torturing her by escaping with Isabella. But, at this confused moment, her anger focused wholly on Edgar. His presence made every encounter since Heathcliff's return fall short of what it could have been. She was on her way to reclaiming him fully in the kitchen when she had to rush because of Edgar's presence at the door. And it was Edgar who had impregnated her, the last nail in the coffin that drove her beloved into the arms of another. With eyes filmed so thick she could barely see, chest so congested she could barely talk, she sputtered, "What you touch at present, you may have; but my soul will be on that hilltop before you lay hands on me again."

"Her mind wanders, sir," interjected Nelly. "She has been talking nonsense the whole evening, but let her have quiet and she'll rally. As Dr. Kenneth said, we must be cautious not to vex her."

"I desire no further advice from you!" said Edgar, sharply, the toll of Catherine's words, his fear for his heir, rousing him from his usual soft demeanor. He stormed out through the door, but careful to close it gently, so as not to disturb his wife.

Some six weeks after her departure, Isabella sent a short note to her brother announcing her marriage with Heathcliff. It appeared dry and cold, but at the bottom was, dotted in with pencil, an obscure apology, and entreaty for kind remembrance, and reconciliation, if her proceeding had offended him, asserting that she could not help it then, and being done, she had now no power to repeal it.

Edgar did not reply to this. A fortnight later, Nelly received her own letter:

Dear Nelly,

I came last night to Wuthering Heights, a place sorely lacking in external comforts, and heard that Catherine has been, and is yet, very ill. I must not write to her, I suppose, and my brother is either too angry or too distressed to answer what I send to him.

Please inform Edgar that I'd give the world to see his face again—that my heart returned to Thrushcross Grange in twenty-fours after I left it, and that I am full of warm feelings for him . . . and Catherine!

I want to ask you two questions: the first is,

How did you contrive to preserve the common sympathies of human nature when you resided here? I cannot recognize any sentiment which those around share with me.

The second question; it is this,

Is Mr. Heathcliff a man? If so, he is mad? And if not, he is the devil? I shan't tell you my reasons for making this in-

quiry, but, I beseech you to explain, if you can, what I have married. Don't write, but call, very soon, and bring me something from Edgar.

Now, you shall hear how I have been received in my new home. When I first entered the kitchen—a dingy, untidy hole—by the fire stood a ruffianly child, strong in limb, dirty in garb, with the look of Catherine in his eyes, and about his mouth. Realizing it was Edgar's legal nephew, I approached to shake hands and kiss him. I said, "How do you do, my dear?"

He replied in a street jargon surely reserved for common urchins and I did not comprehend.

"Shall you and I be friends, Hareton?"

An oath, and a threat to set Throttler on me if I did not fuck off. *Did you know that Throttler is the offspring of my own dear, deceased Skulker?*

I walked around the yard in search of Heathcliff, and through a wicket, to another door, at which I took the liberty of knocking, in hopes a servant might show himself.

It was opened by a tall, gaunt man, without neckerchief, and otherwise extremely slovenly; his ghostly eyes were lost in masses of shaggy hair that hung on his shoulders.

"What's your business?" he demanded.

"My name was Isabella Linton. I'm lately married to Mr. Heathcliff, and he has brought me here, but left me by the kitchen door."

"Is he come back, then?" asked the servant. "Well then be sure to turn your lock and draw your bolt."

"But why?"

"Look here!" he replied, pulling from his waistcoat a large pistol. "I cannot resist going up with this, every night, and trying his door. If once I find it open, he's done for!"

"Hush!" I said, "or I will report you to your master!"

"My master! I have no master. I am Hindley Earnshaw!"

Such a notion I would never have perceived. He was unrecognizable from my childhood memories. "The owner of Wuthering Heights?"

"No longer!" he cried. "I've lost it all to that scoundrel. Oh, damnation! I will have it back; and I'll have his gold, too; and then his blood; and hell shall have his soul!"

Nelly, at this point, I must tell you, I am still at this wretched place less than one hour before all of this occurred. But the worst is yet to come.

I finally met a servant named Joseph who kindly fixed me dinner, horrible that it was, my new husband still nowhere to be found.

At bedtime, I retreated up the stairs to the master chamber, when I heard Hindley's tread in the passage, the bulge of the pistol visible in his pants. I pressed to the wall and stole into the nearest doorway. He passed on, entered his chamber, and shut the door.

I realized I was in Hareton's room, who was fast asleep. Too scared to venture out, I found comfort in a chair and soon dozed uneasily, only to be awakened in the middle of the night by Mr. Heathcliff. He demanded to know what I was doing there.

I told him my fear of Hindley coming in with his pistol to our room.

He laughed uproariously at the notion Hindley was any threat, then turned sour once again, as if I had said something of mortal offense. He swore the room was not, nor ever should be mine. I'll not repeat his language, nor describe his habitual conduct; he is ingenious and unresting in seeking to gain my abhorrence! I assure you, a tiger, or a venomous serpent, could not rouse terror in me equal to that which he awakens. He told me of Catherine's illness, how she is restricted to bed in agony, and how this causes him to suffer so ... how he suffers? ... then accused my brother of being behind it all; promising that I should be Edgar's proxy in torment, till he could get a hold of him.

I do hate him, Nelly. I am wretched. I have been a fool! I shall expect you every day—don't disappoint me!

And please warn everyone at the Grange to be wary of this man—my husband—with only the one name ... Heathcliff.

ISABELLA

Chapter Nineteen

After receiving Isabella's epistle, Nelly went to the master, and informed him that his sister had arrived at the Heights, and had sent her a letter expressing her sorrow for Catherine's situation, and her ardent desire to see him; with a wish that he would transmit through Nelly, as early as possible, some token of forgiveness.

"Forgiveness?" said Edgar. "I have nothing to forgive her, Nelly. You may call at Wuthering Heights, if you like, and say that I am not *angry*, but I'm *sorry* to have lost her, especially as I can never think she'll be happy. It is out of the question my going to see her, however; we are eternally divided. And should she really wish to oblige me, let her persuade the villain she has married to leave the country."

"And you won't write her a little note, sir?" she asked imploringly.

"No," he answered. "It is needless. My communication with Heathcliff's family shall be as sparing as his with mine. It shall not exist!"

Mr. Edgar's coldness depressed Nelly exceedingly, as did Heathcliff's marriage to Isabella. Heathcliff had to know the deep effect it would have on Catherine, though no one could have anticipated such a debilitating illness. He loved her too much to punish her, but also loved her so much he would do almost anything to win her back. Pity poor Isabella if this was true.

As she walked from the Grange to the Heights, she puzzled her brains how to put more heart into what Edgar had said, when she repeated it; and how to soften his refusal of even a few lines to console Isabella.

Isabella had been on watch for Nelly every morning, and saw her through the lattice, as she came up through the garden causeway. Nelly nodded to her, but she drew back, as if afraid of being observed.

Nelly entered without knocking. There never was such a dreary, dismal scene as the formerly cheerful house presented. If Nelly had been in the young lady's place, she would, at least, have swept the hearth, and wiped the tables with a duster. But she already partook of the pervading spirit of neglect that encompassed her. Her pretty face was wan and listless, her hair uncurled, some locks hanging lankly down, and some carelessly twisted around her head. Probably she had not touched her dress since yester evening.

Hindley was not there. Mr. Heathcliff sat at a table, turning over some papers in a pocket book, but he rose when Nelly appeared, asked how she was doing, quite friendly, and offered her a chair.

He was the only thing there that seemed decent, and Nelly thought he never looked better. So much had circumstances altered their positions, that he would certainly have struck a stranger as a born-and-bred gentleman, and his wife a thorough little slattern.

Isabella came forward eagerly to greet Nelly and held out one hand to take the expected letter.

Nelly shook her head. Isabella wouldn't understand the hint, but followed Nelly to a sideboard, where she went to lay her bonnet, and importuned her in a whisper to give her directly what she had brought.

Heathcliff guessed the meaning of her maneuvers, and said, "If you have got anything for Isabella, as no doubt you have, give it to her. You needn't make a secret of it; we have no secrets between us."

"I have nothing," replied Nelly. "My master bid me tell his sister that she must not expect either a letter or a visit from him at present. He sends his love, ma'am, and his wishes for your happiness, and his pardon for the grief you have occasioned, but he thinks that after this time, his household, and the household here, should drop intercommunication, as nothing good could come of keeping it up."

Isabella's lip quivered slightly, and she returned to her seat in the window. Her husband took his stand on the hearthstone, near Nelly, and began to put questions concerning Catherine.

"Mrs. Linton is now just recovering," said Nelly. "She'll never be like she was, but her life was spared, and if you really have regard for her, you'll shun crossing her way again. Nay, you'll move out of this country entirely. I'll inform you Catherine Linton is as different now from your old friend Catherine Earnshaw as that young lady is different from me! Her appearance is changed greatly, her character much more so."

"That is quite possible," remarked Heathcliff, forcing himself to seem calm and not lunge forward to grab the shoulders of Nelly and give them a good, hard shake. His beloved never to be like she was! How dare Nelly surmise that Catherine Earnshaw was only a memory. He had felt the recent passion of her lips against his, the feel of her body embraced in his arms. There was nothing Linton about her! But Heathcliff knew he must not put off Nelly, as he was in deep need of her help. "Before you leave this house,

I must exact a promise from you, that you'll get me an interview with her—consent or refuse, I *will* see her! What do you say?"

"I say, Mr. Heathcliff, you must not—you never shall through my means. Another encounter between you and the master would kill her altogether!"

"With your aid that may be avoided!" he declared sharply, his facade of calm starting to fade. "And should there be danger of such an event—should Edgar be the cause of adding a single trouble more to her existence—why, I think, I shall be justified in going to extremes! I wish you had sincerity enough to tell me whether Catherine would suffer greatly from his loss. The fear that she would restrains me; and there you see the distinction between our feelings. Had he been in my place, and I in his, though I hated him with a hatred that turned my life to gall, I never would have raised a hand against him. You may look incredulous if you please. I never would have banished him from her society, as long as she desired his. The moment her regard ceased, I would have torn his heart out, and drank his blood! But, till then, I would have died by inches before I touched a single hair on his head."

"And yet," interrupted Nelly, "you have no scruples in completely ruining all hopes of her perfect restoration, by thrusting yourself into her remembrance, now, when she has nearly forgotten you, and involving her in a new tumult of discord and distress."

"You suppose she has nearly forgotten me!" he snorted, his fist pounding the wood of the table for emphasis. "You know as well as I do that for every thought she spends on Edgar, she spends a thousand on me! At a most miserable period of my life, I had a notion of the kind, it haunted me on my return to the neighborhood, but only her assurance could make me admit the horrible idea again. And then, Edgar would be nothing, nor Hindley, or all the dreams that ever I dreamt. Two words would comprehend my future—'death' and 'hell'—existence, after losing her, would be hell."

Isabella stood from her chair.

"Yet I was a fool to fancy for a moment that she valued Edgar's attachment more than mine," continued Heathcliff. "If he loved with all the powers of his puny being, he couldn't love as much in eighty years, as I could in a day. And he is scarcely a degree dearer to her than her dog, or her horse. It is not in him to be loved like me, how can she love in him what he has not?"

"Catherine and Edgar are as fond of each other as any two people can be!" cried Isabella with sudden vivacity. "No one has a right to talk in that manner, and I won't hear my brother depreciated in silence!"

Isabella deserved more than a shake of the shoulders, and it took much willpower not to grab her forcefully by the arm. He had not asked for her opinion, and certainly not one in defense of her brother. She should have learned by now not to express her thoughts without permission. But he must not let this get out of hand. He had one purpose here and one only, though he couldn't let such insolence go ignored.

"Your brother is wondrous fond of you, too, isn't he?" observed Heathcliff with a scornful laugh. "He turns you adrift on the world with surprising alacrity."

Hitting her sore point, she returned to the chair. "He is not aware of what I suffer," she replied meekly. "I didn't tell him that."

"You have been telling him something, then—you have written, have you?"

"To say that I was married, I did write—you saw the note."

"And nothing since?"

"No."

"My young lady is looking sadly the worse for her change in condition," remarked Nelly. "Somebody's love comes short in her case, obviously—whose may I guess, but perhaps I shouldn't say."

"I should guess it was her own," said Heathcliff. "She has degenerated into a mere slut! She is tired of trying to please me, uncommonly early. You'd hardly credit it, but the very morrow of our wedding, she was weeping to go home. However, she'll suit this house so much the better for not being over nice, and I'll take care she does not disgrace me by rambling abroad."

"Well, sir," returned Nelly, "I hope you'll consider that Isabella is accustomed to being looked after, and waited on, and that she has been brought up like an only daughter whom everyone was ready to serve. You must let her have a maid to keep things tidy about her, and you must treat her kindly. Whatever your notion of Mr. Edgar, you cannot doubt that she has a capacity for strong attachments, or she wouldn't have abandoned the elegancies, and comforts, and friend of her former home, to fix contentedly, in such a wilderness as this, with you."

"She abandoned them under delusion," he answered, "picturing in me a hero of romance, and expecting unlimited indulgences from my chivalrous devotion. But, at last, I think she begins to know me. It was marvelous to discover that I did not love her. I believe, at one time, no lesson could teach her that! And yet it is poorly learnt, for this morning she announced that I had actually succeeded in making her hate me! Can I trust your assertion, Isabella, are you sure you hate me?"

He moved closer to her and she recoiled, nearly slipping from her chair.

"If I left you alone for half a day, won't you come sighing and wheedling to me again?" He touched her neck with his hands. She flinched at first, but he began to massage her shoulders and then she relaxed. He slipped his hands down to her breasts, cupped them fully, then, as on their honeymoon, twisted the nipples sharply with his fingers. Her face revealed an anguish to cry out, but instead her eyes closed and she moaned, almost against her will.

Nelly recognized Heathcliff's spell on Isabella, the same that had been cast upon her. She was instantly sad for her charge, knowing the self-loathing and confusion that could come from a relationship like this. But she was also jealous, her having a man who could probe so deeply into a woman and pull out a stranger, one who was soon revealed as one's own twin.

"I dare say," continued Heathcliff, as he released her nipples and she turned her head in shame, "she would rather I seemed all tenderness before you; it wounds her vanity to have the truth of her taming exposed. No brutality disgusts her. I suppose she has an innate admiration of it. Now, was it not the depth of absurdity—of genuine idiocy—for this painful, slavish, mean-minded bitch to dream that I could love her?" He pushed the bulge of his cock by her face, and without saying a word, she turned her head toward his pants and, with much contentment, breathed deeply.

"Tell your master, Nelly, that I never, in all my life, met with such an abject thing as she is. She even disgraces the name of Linton." The more he pressed himself against her, the quicker her breathing, the more pronounced her arousal. "I've sometimes relented, from pure lack of invention, in my experiments on what she could endure, and she still creeps shamefully back. I have even offered full right for her to claim a separation—if she desired to go she might—but still you see her here." He kissed her full on the mouth and she reached up, tenderly, to touch his face. Done, she left her mouth open and he spit in it. She swallowed greedily. "The more I torture this greedy, selfish whore, the more she professes her love for me."

"Mr. Heathcliff," said Nelly, perspiring herself, finding difficulty in blocking out the memory of their unholy tryst, just yards from here, in yonder barn. "This is the talk of a madman, and your wife, most likely, is convinced you are mad, and, for that reason, she has borne with you hitherto. But now that you say she may go, she'll doubtless avail herself of the permission. You are not so bewitched, ma'am, are you, as to remain with him of your own accord?"

"Take care, Nelly!" answered Isabella, her eyes sparkling with both hate and lust. There was no misdoubting by their expression the full success of her partner's endeavors to make himself both detested and worshipped. "Don't put faith in a single word he speaks. He's a lying fiend, a monster, and not a human being! Oh, Nelly, promise you'll not mention a syllable of this infamous conversation to my brother or Catherine—whatever he may pretend, he wishes to provoke Edgar to desperation—he says he has married me on purpose to obtain power over him, and he shan't obtain it—I'll die first! I just hope, I pray that he may forget his diabolical prudence, and kill me! The single pleasure I can imagine is to die, or to see him dead!"

"That will do for the present," said Heathcliff. "Go upstairs until called upon. I have something to say to Nelly."

She quieted, stood, lowered her head, and walked obediently up the stairs.

Nelly immediately stood up and hastened to resume her bonnet. "Do you understand what the word 'pity' means?" she asked. "Did you ever feel a touch of it in your life?"

"You are not going yet!" he interrupted. "Come here now, Nelly. I must either persuade or compel you to aid me in fulfilling my determination to see Catherine, and that without delay—I swear that I mean no harm. I don't desire to cause any disturbance, or to exasperate, or insult Edgar. I only wish to hear from herself how she is, and why she has been ill, and to ask if anything that I could do would be of use to her."

"Are you blind to all you have done?" retorted Nelly. "Your return has built a wall between husband and wife. Your toying with Catherine's emotions has left her bedridden with serious infirmity!"

He took a step toward her, his unrestrained passion surfacing in his tone. "I constructed no wall, but lifted the fog so all obstacles could be seen clearly! I no more toyed with Catherine than she has toyed with me. She fully desired to be re-awakened, to breathe life again with all of its vitality. Her only problem now is the sight of Edgar, whose very presence makes clear the passionless life she leads and the dismal prospects for her future. She did not become ill in my company, only his! I was wrong to leave her, and now my only desire is to make amends!"

Nelly lowered her eyes from Heathcliff's fervent stare. She was not sure she could ever match the full depth of his ardent feelings. To be loved this way must be incredibly thrilling, yet so very dangerous. "You must leave her be," mumbled Nelly. "Her husband must shoulder the task of making her well."

"Do you not understand that I will not be denied!" thundered Heathcliff. "Last night, I was at the Grange garden six hours, and I'll return there tonight and every night I'll haunt the place, and every day, till I find an opportunity of entering. If Edgar meets me, I shall not hesitate to knock him down, and give him enough to ensure his quiescence while I stay. If his servants oppose me, I shall threaten them off with these pistols. But wouldn't it be better to prevent my coming in contact with them, or their master? And you could do it so easily! I'd warn you when I came, and then you might let me in unobserved, as soon as she was alone, and watch till I departed—your conscience quite calm, you would be hindering mischief."

"I'll not play that treacherous part in my employer's house!" She did not know what was completely right in this situation. But the one thing she was sure of was that the night Heathcliff had deserted Wuthering Heights, during the extreme turmoil of the storm, she had felt a heaviness in her heart and a foreboding in her soul for all who inhabited both the Grange and the Heights. That feeling had been lingering ever since Heathcliff had returned, and now it felt stronger than ever.

She turned to exit. He grabbed her arm roughly. "Don't persist, sir! or else I shall be obliged to inform my master of your designs, and he'll take measures to secure his house and its inmates from any such unwarrantable intrusions!"

"In that case, I'll take measures to secure that you do as I ask, woman!"

Despite her firm resistance, he dragged her to the back of the house, and down the dark, moldy stairs of the cellar he had turned into his own personal dungeon.

Chapter Twenty

After tossing Nelly into his cellar-dungeon, Heathcliff lit a solitary candle then bolted the door behind him. Nelly witnessed an abundance of props that took her breath away. On a table were wooden clothespins, rope, assorted paddles, leather collars, a collar with a round ball attached to it, several phallic-shaped objects, a blindfold, and a small whip. Suspended from the ceiling was a hammock-like swing, which had a leather seat and backrest for support.

"You're not only in league with the devil," said Nelly, "but he has lent you his toolshed."

Heathcliff laughed darkly. "If these are the tools of the devil, then my wife must call him her dear friend."

"I'll not stand for it."

"Then arrange a meeting with Catherine."

"Never."

"Then undress."

"Nay."

"Would you rather I tore off your clothes and had you walk home holding on to the shreds?"

Nelly undressed. As she slipped out of her underthings, she noticed, on the ground, a hair ribbon the rose color Isabella usually wore.

Heathcliff circled her, his eyes glossing over her body. She was bigger boned than both Catherine and Isabella, but well shaped, and with fuller bosom. He remembered with affection the nights she came to him in the barn and soothed his loneliness with her delicate touch and kind mouth, giving him brief moments when he could forget his despair.

He stopped in front of her. Nelly looked up at his commanding presence. The emotions she had tried desperately to stifle all these years, knowing how tied his heart was to Catherine, flowed freely, and she stared into his eyes with deep tenderness and need. He seemed to understand her look, and the driven, brutal man that had dragged her here in the first place seemed to retreat, and she saw full sensual desire within him as well. He leaned forward and kissed her gently on the lips.

How she welcomed this. How great was the urge to clasp her arms around his neck and express her own deep feelings for this striking specimen.

But as quickly as the tenderness had appeared, it seemed to vanish, as he pulled away and began circling her again, this time with a cold, evaluative stare, as if she were a horse he wished to race and he was estimating how fast she would be able to run. She lowered her head in shame, her trepidation returning.

"It has been a while since I had view of your nakedness," said Heathcliff. He must stay focused, he told himself. He would find the dark place—and the surges within him that came with such a discovery—but, most importantly, he must secure Nelly's aid to make it possible to be with his beloved once again and right the wrongs that had occurred since his return. "It's been a while since I heard you profess your love and call me master."

"Edgar is my only master."

"We'll soon see."

He stopped his circling. Still fully clothed he pressed himself against her from behind. She felt his hot breath against her neck as he spoke. He worked a hand down her body, caressing her breasts, teasing her belly, until he got to her quim. With a finger, he touched her opening and entered just a bit. Smiling, he stepped away and held the finger in the candlelight, the shiny reflection of her moistness clearly visible at the finger's tip.

"Your words say one thing," offered Heathcliff, "your body another."

Damn your soul, thought Nelly, and damn her own for betraying her.

"I miss your fire," said Heathcliff, "the red flame between your legs that matches the hair on your head and welcomed me so willingly."

"Unbolt the door, sir, and I'll show you how willing I am."

"I remember your resistance well. It stirred me to new heights. Isabella exhibited that at first, but now she is completely my lamb, and quite boring." He was right in front of her now, so close she could smell his strong breath, which somehow aroused her, perhaps reminding her of the scent she had breathed in as he took her so unmercifully long ago. "Sit in the sling."

She looked behind her. "This contraption?"

"Aye."

"Nay."

He grabbed her so forcefully her instinct to fight back surged without thinking. He caught her fists as she raised them to strike. She tried to knee him, but his catlike quickness helped him avoid such a blow. He shoved her into the seat, quickly raised her arms so they were parallel to her shoulders. With forearms bent, her hands grasped the chains that tethered the sling from the ceiling as a child would grab the supports of a swing. He quickly bound her wrists to the chains with ropes from the table. She kicked out her feet again. She persisted and he grinned, stepping between her legs, parting them, a strong hand glued around each of her ankles, as he held her still. She struggled, but the strength of his arms was too much for the force of her legs. When she calmed, he bent her legs at the knee, then fitted, then tied the feet into separate leather stirrups that also hung from the ceiling.

"What hate you must have in your heart," said Nelly.

"Sometimes hate and love are not so different."

Silently she agreed.

He pulled on a rope suspended from a pulley and it caused the sling to raise her even farther in the air. He secured the rope. She lay seated: dangling, floating, completely immobilized, helpless to this man. To further stoke her vulnerability, he tied a blindfold around her eyes.

Complete black before her, bound and perched in the air with a man who had great passion for everything, including brutality, made her tremble.

She knew she could lie to Heathcliff and swear she would arrange a meeting, only to scramble home to safety, while making sure he never stepped foot on the Grange again, and she was never in his presence as long as she lived. But she felt helpless to do anything right now, both physically tied and emotionally bound to the needs of this man.

She felt the cold bite of the clothespins clamping down on her nipples and she yelped.

"Patience, Nelly, and full pleasure will be yours."

"I feel only pain," she mouthed.

"An excellent start."

She felt the blood rushing to her nipples as they swelled instantly.

He must have been on his knees, because first she felt his warm breath on her thighs, then his tongue. Absent was the rush of the attack with his mouth she remembered in the barn. He was all patience, as if he had all night to do his business. She felt him lick and caress her inner thighs with the tip of his tongue. As cruel as he could be, the sweetness this man exhibited sometimes surprised her. He made her wait for his touch on her pussy lips, and her body twitched slightly in his direction.

She had not been with a man since the night with Heathcliff in the barn. She had only fantasized about him since, doing some of the very same things, though she had never seen nor heard of a sling. If given choice, she would have dashed for safety. But right now, she realized she had no choice and that made her even wetter.

She felt his fingers part her lips and he blew hot air on her exposed clitoris, which made her shiver, made it ache for touch.

"Am I your master?" he asked.

She refused to answer.

He made her wait. Unconsciously, she shifted her weight, which caused the sling to swing fully toward his mouth, and she felt some moist pressure against her quim, which caused her to cry out.

Encouraged, he pressed his mouth deeper, and as delicately as a bird feeding on the nectar of a flower, he started licking her there. Up and down, slowly.

"My God, Heathcliff, you are a master."

"Your master?" she heard his voice inquire.

She did not answer.

His licks increased with speed and intensity and then it was like she was lost in a pool of her own need, lust, desire, hanging in midair, bound, blinded, surges of swollen pain and pleasure flooding her nipples, making her feel completely helpless to his mouth.

He found her perfect rhythm and was carrying her to the place she so desperately needed to go and he stopped only briefly to ask her once more, "Will you say it?"

She refused, simply focused on the volcano of an orgasm that was about to erupt but just as she was there, she felt him pull away and heard him stand.

"My God, Heathcliff! No! Please! Don't stop!"

"You will learn to do everything I say...or suffer the consequences."

With that, he was soon behind her again. He reached for a wood paddle and addressed her bum cheeks firmly with it, smacks that caused her arse to tighten, and her nipples to pulse with even more desire from the sting. His force swung her forward, which meant she swung back as well, meeting each blow with the momentum of her own body weight suspended in the sling.

The pain was not the same sensation she might feel if all of this were being done under different circumstances, by some other person, or simply to punish. In her aroused condition, each infringement by this man—focused so completely on her—powered an erotic force upon her body and her mind, which produced the sting of hurt, but greatly contributed to a whirlwind of sharp pleasure sweeping through her.

Her eyes, under the blindfold, soon grew moist from the discomfort, yet, when she felt his hand turn her face, and place the head of his enormous cock at her lips, she opened her mouth willingly.

She sucked him with vigor, welcoming his cock like an old friend, one she had thought of often. But it had never tasted this sweet, and the surge of his head bursting through her lips, followed by the long, thick shaft that bulged her cheeks, made her more needy for it than she had ever been, and so aroused by this very simple act of sucking her dominator, that her body shook all over.

She was sure that no other person could ever make her feel this way, and though she would welcome more of his tender kisses to open her heart, she could not help, right now, opening her mind and body in a way she had never done before, in a way she was not sure she could do without.

Even the blindfold, the bindings, the suspension, seemed to intensify everything by blocking off all extraneous stimuli. Like a blind person who developed acute hearing, all of her senses, except sight, seemed heightened to extremes from what Heathcliff was doing to her physically and mentally. This helpless, completely-focused-on-one-man feeling made everything stratospheric in her brain: the feel of his tongue inside her, the clamps at her nipples, the red burning on her bum cheeks, and now his cock sliding into her mouth. The taste, scent, and feel of him were completely overwhelming and she felt powerless to every extreme sensation streaming through her veins.

Her hearing also became heightened, and when he spoke to her with words she would normally despise, they ended up being spurs in her sides, making her pussy soaked with extra sensation.

"You are my hot, needy tart...You exist for nothing but fulfilling my every need...You can't help touching your aching pussy when you think of me...Only a slut would stay so still and allow me to take her with such force...Bite down if you hate me so much. Punish me as I punish you...No, you won't do that, because it would mean the end of my cock in your mouth and right now you need this more than anything in the world."

If she could speak, she would agree.

He placed his fingers on the back of her head and held firmly, so the force of his thrust going one way met the force of his push from the other.

She felt him grow. She felt, no, she was *absorbed* by everything: the feeling of his thick member going in and out; his rough hands on her head; the manly scent of him that crushed her and then receded with each thrust; the bristle of his pubic hair; his controlling voice directing every emotion surging through her.

"Take it! You belong to me. No one else. You are my dirty, needy concubine who lives for this and would die for it!"

Indeed she would. This was her man and she was his woman, completely. And though he used her to gain advantage for his love of another, she didn't care, just for this chance to be with him . . . any way he wanted.

Maybe it was because of the acute sensations at her nipples; maybe it was the dark she was immersed in; maybe it was the smarting of her arse cheeks; the memory of his tongue on her clitoris; the rhythm of his degrading words that at this very moment seemed true; the joy in feeling him grow larger and larger, pulsing, and throbbing in her mouth because of her lips and tongue; the great surge of semen that poured into her seemingly not with hate, but with love and gratefulness as he had done in his youth . . . or the hot wax that he dripped from the candle onto her already burning nipples, BUT . . .

She came without an ounce of pressure or friction on her pussy, as she thrashed and swallowed and swung aimlessly in the sling, her cries stifled in her throat as he continued to spurt. Her orgasm was not just centered at her quim, but every fiber of her being seemed to share in the extreme heat of it. And when he finally withdrew, and she had swallowed every drop as a good servant should, she cried out, "Yes, you are my master, my one and only true master, and I will love you forever..."

Heathcliff let her rest, let her catch her breath. "It brings me pleasure to hear that," he said sincerely. Even more softly he asked, "Will you arrange now a meeting with my beloved?"

"Never," whispered Nelly.

She heard him chuckle, lightly, and this scared her. He seemed so sure, almost as if he anticipated her response and knew her better than she knew herself, almost as if he enjoyed this last shred of resistance, because it gave him reason to continue in his own forceful manner.

She heard the door open and a bell ringing.

Shortly, she heard the door bolt again.

She felt a tongue at her pussy, licking her delicately, but with passion. It was clearly not Heathcliff's.

She felt hands cupping her breasts, creating new surges. They were clearly not Heathcliff's.

She felt long hair fall against her thighs as the tongue probed deeper. Heathcliff's hair was never this long.

As if knowing her desire for final confirmation, Heathcliff removed her blindfold and before her, on her knees, was Isabella, completely naked.

"'Tis not necessary, my child," she said.

Isabella paused and looked up at *her* master as well. He held his cock in front of her face. "Look at it."

That was all she did, clearly hypnotized, as if it were a gold medallion hanging from a chain, swaying back and forth before her eyes.

"You cannot resist it. My cock controls you."

She nodded obediently.

"Isabella, lick Nelly's pussy."

Isabella lowered her face and started again, first with tender kisses at the opening. Nelly tightened this time, now fully aware that not only was a woman pressed against her most delicate parts, but that woman was Isabella. Had Nelly not been restrained, she might have pulled away, but nothing was as it would normally be. All Heathcliff had done created a burning need within her that had just flamed brightly, then receded with the fulfillment of her release, but now sparked again, from the delicate touch of Isabella.

This woman's tongue entered her. It lacked the force of Heathcliff's, but made up for that with its graceful sliding at both her opening and at the hooded source of her pleasure, all of it creating superior sensations in Nelly's quim and throughout her body. Unable to help herself, Nelly stroked Isabella's golden hair with great affection, unconsciously nudging her forward so she would go even deeper.

Heathcliff stood by Nelly's face now, his cock, still semierect, dangling by her lips. He did not need to say a word. She could not tear her eyes away, as she, too, was under its hypnotic spell.

"Stare at me as Isabella makes you come."

She did, and it caused renewed surges at all the places that had been stimulated this afternoon.

Isabella quickened her pace, letting out girlish squeals of delight.

Heathcliff stroked his own cock so very near to Nelly's lips that she longed to taste him once more. It did not surprise her that this bear of a man was getting hard again so soon.

But then suddenly he lifted Isabella up by the hair, just as Nelly edged toward another release, and, to her great disappointment, she could not complete her fulfillment from Isabella's tongue.

He came around to Nelly's front. Isabella stood between them, facing Nelly, her back to Heathcliff. With one arm, he lifted the dainty Isabella in the air and pushed her body forward with his chest. Instinctively, she spread her legs and straddled Nelly's face. Heathcliff held fast, so she would not bend Nelly's neck uncomfortably.

Then, with his member swollen to mammoth proportions once again, he entered Nelly's quim.

As Nelly was about to cry out, Heathcliff lowered Isabella's pussy onto her mouth.

His fucking was forceful and with purpose. Nelly needed no instruction or orders, intuitively knowing what to do. She extended her tongue, and, to Isabella's great delight, began her own licking. Although a connection such as this had never entered even her wildest fantasies, the dark symphony Heathcliff orchestrated made every carnal act performed in this cold, damp dungeon burn with the music of heightened erotic pleasure. And thus the sweet taste of Isabella's quim found perfect rhythm with the force of Heathcliff's penetration and Nelly felt herself slip away into another intensely sensual spin.

As Heathcliff moved in and out of her with his usual vigorous energy, Nelly began to understand the full value of the sling. She had thought it merely a way to bind her and make her feel helpless. But, in the sling, with each thrust of Heathcliff's weapon, her whole body collapsed, legs forced upward, torso forced downward, making the enormous pressure of him even more authoritative and deep. In addition, it compressed her vaginal canal, creating more tightness, and made Heathcliff seem even bigger, as large as a lighthouse as he beamed his pleasure through her entire body, causing her to lick Isabella's pussy with even more speed and relish.

Isabella seemed to enjoy as well how the force of Heathcliff's penetrations made Nelly's face and tongue go even deeper into her pussy.

Heathcliff increased both his speed and intensity. He had them both, one held in his arm, the other firmly at the end of his cock. Nothing here was about love, but all of it was about satisfaction. These women hungered for his control and he longed to satisfy them and fulfill all of his needs as well... which meant one more grand release, but, most significantly, the final yielding to his plan... which would lead to the glorious fulfillment that would come once he feasted his eyes on the beautiful woman that was Catherine, his one and only true love, a magnificent vision that made even those in heaven weep with envy.

Heathcliff snapped at Nelly, "Promise you will help me see her!"

She avoided responding, trying to occupy her energy with pleasing Isabella.

"Swear or I will take you to the edge again then pull my wife away from you and not only will I never fuck you again, but I will never let you see my cock again."

Her body tightened into a rigid panic as his words sunk in and Heathcliff concentrated on a final rush. She knew him to speak the truth, for he had proven already he could tell exactly when she would come, and Nelly did not think she could handle these extreme feelings and deep emotions becoming aborted, yet again... nor the prospect of not being with him anymore, or not feasting her adoring eyes on his perfect manhood. Without any control on her part, Nelly's orgasm started.

All the sensations overpowered her body once more, now with the added taste and scent of Isabella's delicate flower, as her spasm pulsed and waved and arced through her over and over in an unrestrained frenzy, as Heathcliff spilled even more semen inside her, as Isabella cried out like the girl she was with her own pleasure from Nelly's tongue at her clitoris and Heathcliff's arm tightening against her breasts, as Nelly mouthed into that sweet pussy, "With all of my heart, Heathcliff, I will do all of your bidding..."

With a mighty, tigerlike roar of triumph, Heathcliff finished, then withdrew, lifting Isabella off Nelly and placing her at his feet, where she lay passively. They all took a moment to recover. Then he removed the clothespins and untied Nelly, who joined her companion on the ground.

He leaned down and gave them each a soft kiss on the lips, which they welcomed eagerly. Then he stood over them, his cock dangling just inches from their faces, as they stared up at him. Nelly and Isabella returned a kiss along his thick shaft, enjoying the strong, soaked flavor of Nelly's passion mixed with the elegant taste of Heathcliff's soft skin. As they had experienced the day he repaired the lattice in the garden, a feeling of extreme gratefulness warmed through them from being inspired by all that was so masculine about him, causing them both to whisper, in unison,

"Thank you, master."

Chapter Twenty-One

The Gimmerton chapel bells rang and the full, mellow, Sunday flow that called in the valley came soothingly on the ear, a sweet substitute for the warmth of spring that should have arrived, but remained absent.

The family had gone to church and, aside from Catherine and Nelly, only a manservant remained. Nelly sent him to the village to purchase oranges for the mistress, then went upstairs.

Catherine sat in a loose, white dress—a shawl over her shoulders that covered her large and protruding belly—in the recess of the open window, as usual. Her thick, long hair had been partly removed at the beginning of her illness and now, she wore it simply combed in its natural tresses over her temples and neck. Her appearance was altered, as Nelly had told Heathcliff, but when she was calm, there seemed unearthly beauty in the change.

The flash of her eyes had been succeeded by a dreamy and melancholy softness: They no longer gave the impression of looking at objects around her; they appeared always to gaze beyond, and far beyond, almost out of this world. Then, the paleness of her face, its haggard aspect, and the peculiar expression that arose from her mental state, clearly refuted any tangible proofs of convalescence and stamped her as one doomed to decay.

A book laid spread on the sill before her, and the brisk moor wind fluttered its pages at intervals. Edgar had placed it there, for Catherine never endeavored to divert herself with reading, or occupation of any kind, and he would spend many an hour in trying to entice her attention to some subject that had formerly been her amusement.

She was conscious of his aim, and in her better moods, endured his efforts placidly; only showing their uselessness by now and then suppressing a wearied sigh, and checking him at last, with the saddest of smiles and kisses. At other times, she would turn petulantly away, and hide her face in her hands, or even push him off angrily, and then he took care to let her alone, certain he was doing no good.

Nelly approached Catherine. There was, of course, still the practical perspective that Nelly had all along: It would be best if Heathcliff remained banished from the Grange, thus allowing Edgar and Catherine some chance to find ongoing happiness. Nevertheless, her complete submission at Heathcliff's dungeon still permeated her being. Never had she yielded so deeply. Never had she felt so empty of any force of will. Her body felt as if it had been thrust out deep into the ocean, and she had been forced to struggle and swim against the tide, ducked under, thrown back, until all strength had been sapped. Then a strong hand had lifted her out of the waves and cast her upon the shore, exhausted, bruised by the ordeal, but filled with a nearly unfathomable elation caused by the intense sensation of having been submerged into the deep and then brought to the surface as one even more fully alive. Her promise had been skillfully extracted by her master, and there was no way she could refuse him.

She whispered softly, "Mrs. Linton, Heathcliff wishes to see you."

There was a start, and a troubled gleam of recollection. Nelly looked skyward, wishing she was in church at this moment to receive some divine guidance as to whether her yielding to Heathcliff would produce blessing or sin.

"He's in the garden," continued Nelly, "and impatient to know if you will receive him."

Catherine bent forward, and listened breathlessly for any sounds from below. The clouds in her eyes began a recession. With straining eagerness, she gazed toward the entrance of the chamber.

There Heathcliff stood, tall and imposing. For a moment, it was as if all were frozen in time, as the two lovers beheld each other after such a long absence. Even Nelly was immobilized by the mixture of joy and anguish in their faces. The moment melted when Heathcliff, in just two frenzied strides, rushed to her side, and grasped her in his arms. Nelly retreated downstairs.

He neither spoke, nor loosened his hold, for some five minutes, during which period he bestowed more kisses than ever he gave in his life before. Yet Catherine, with what feeble strength she possessed, had kissed him first! She pressed her face forward, raining an equal number of endearments upon his chest, fingers clinging to his jacket for support. He could hardly bear, from downright agony, to look into her face.

"Oh, Catherine! Oh, my life! How can I bear it?" was the first sentence he uttered, in a tone that did not disguise his despair from seeing the true seriousness of her illness.

And now he stared at her so earnestly that the intensity of his gaze would surely bring tears into his eyes, but although they burned with anguish, they did not melt, for fear his expression would be a mirror to her and reflect the full gravity of her distressed condition.

"What now?" asked Catherine, leaning back, and returning his look with a suddenly clouded brow. "You and Edgar have broken my heart, Heathcliff. And you both come to bewail the deed to me, as if you were the people to be pitied! I shall not pity you, not I. You have killed me—and thriven on it, I think. How strong you are. How many years do you mean to live after I am gone?"

Heathcliff had knelt on one knee to embrace her; he attempted to rise, but she seized his hair, and kept him down.

"I wish I could hold you," she continued bitterly, "till we were both dead! I shouldn't care what you suffered. I care nothing for your sufferings. Why shouldn't you suffer? I do! Will you forget me—will you be happy when I am in the earth? Will you say twenty years hence, 'That's the grave of Catherine Earnshaw. I loved her long ago, and was wretched to lose her; but it is past. I've loved many others since—my children are dearer to me than she was, and, at death, I shall not rejoice that I am going to her, I shall be sorry that I must leave them!' Will you say so, Heathcliff?"

"Don't torture me till I'm as mad as yourself!" he cried, wrenching his head free and grinding his teeth.

The two made a strange and fearful picture. Her present countenance had a wild vindictiveness in its white cheek, and a bloodless lip and a scintillating eye, and she retained in her closed fingers a portion of Heathcliff's locks she had been grasping. While raising himself with one hand, he had taken her arm with the other; and so inadequate was his stock of gentleness to the requirements of her condition, that on his letting go, he left four distinct impressions of blue in the colorless skin.

"Are you possessed with a devil," he pursued savagely, "to talk in that manner to me, when you may be dying? Do you reflect that all those words will be branded in my memory, and eating deeper eternally, after you have left me? You know that I could as soon forget you as my existence! Is it not sufficient for your infernal selfishness, that while you are at peace I shall writhe in the torments of hell?" He took a step back from her. "For you see, Catherine, I know it is *my* fault. Upon my departure from Wuthering Heights, I placed a damnable curse on every Earnshaw and Linton at the precipice of Black Rock Cragge."

"Then there will be no peace for anyone...," moaned Catherine, recalled to a sense of physical weakness by the violent, unequal throbbing of her heart, which beat visibly and audibly under this excess of agitation.

She said nothing further till the paroxysm was over; then she continued, more kindly—

"I'm not wishing you greater torment than I have, Heathcliff! I only wish us never to be parted—and should a word of mine distress you hereafter, think I feel the same distress underground, and for my own sake, forgive me! For I never should have spoken words that hollowed our sacred vow. I foolishly considered life station over the purity of our love." She beckoned him. "Come here and kneel down again. You have never harmed me in your life and I know would never wish harm on me. Nay, if you nurse anger that will be worse to remember than my harsh words! Won't you come here again? Do!"

Instead, Heathcliff went to the back of the chair, and leaned over, but not so far as to let her see his face, which was livid with emotion over hearing these words of self-blame only now, as she was dying.

"Oh, I see!" proclaimed Catherine. "You would not relent a moment to keep me out of the grave! *That* is how I'm loved! Well, never mind! That is not *my* Heathcliff. I shall love mine yet and take him with me—he's in my soul. And," she added musingly, "the thing that irks me the most is this shattered prison, after all. I'm tired, tired of being enclosed here. I'm wearying to escape into that glorious world, and to be always there—not seeing it dimly through tears, and yearning for it through the walls of an aching heart—but really with it, and in it."

In her eagerness she rose, and supported herself on the arm of the chair. He turned to her, looking absolutely desperate . . . his eyes wide and wet, at last.

Seeing the tears of her stoical lover caused Catherine suddenly to make a spring toward him, and he caught her, and they were locked in an embrace so tight it seemed that not even death could separate them. She put her hand up to clasp the back of his neck, and bring her cheek to his, as he held her. She whispered, "Bring me to the bed."

He lifted her gently and laid her to rest on top of her quilt, stood over her, and said, "You teach me now how cruel you've been, cruel and false. *Why* did you despise me? *Why* did you betray your own heart, Catherine? I have not one word of comfort— you deserve this. You have killed yourself. You loved me—then what *right* had you to leave me? For the poor fancy you felt for Edgar? Because misery, and degradation, and death, and nothing that God or Satan could inflict would have parted us—*you*, of your own will, did it. I have not broken your heart—*you* have broken it, and in breaking it, you have broken mine!"

"Let me alone. Let me alone," sobbed Catherine, her body in a shiver. "It is you who has forsaken me with the sister of my husband! It is you who is the instrument of your devil curse that poisons us all! If I've done wrong, I'm dying for it. It is enough! You left me, too! I forgive you. Forgive me!" She held arms up to him again. "Come! I am trembling from the ice of misdeeds and only the heat of our love can warm me. Cast off your clothes, as I do mine and let us be joined in our misery and our love."

Both weeping copious tears, they tore off their clothes as if their garments were the cause of all the pain, nearly shredding them because of their haste. Then Heathcliff joined his beloved in her bed, their limbs going around each other like ropes that bound two bodies. They kissed deeply, lovingly. As prophesied, only the heat of his powerful, warm body, the eternal flame of his love, could warm her chill and calm her tremble. And only the incredible feel of his true love's body against his could rid his heart, at least at that moment, of the hate that poisoned it.

In between kisses, he moaned, "I do forgive you, my love, with all of my heart."

With her hands, she traced the many tracks of raised scars lacing Heathcliff's back, like thick, braided, leather straps embedded in his flesh, and realized this was the aftermath of his final flogging, and that he had hid them behind his shirt since his return. "Oh, darling," cried Catherine. "How you have suffered."

He could feel the frailty of her body as he embraced her, careful to avoid too much force, lest he snap her bones. "My sweet Catherine. It is I who made you suffer, by betraying you with Isabella, by toying with your body and emotions, when I could have relieved all suffering with the full exchange of my love."

"Then give it now," she said, as they kissed deeply again and she reached down to stroke the sword of his love...and Heathcliff melted to her touch.

As it became unsheathed, her energy grew with her excitement, for only her true love could tear her away from the closeness she felt to death's bed and return her to full life. Heathcliff felt his heart hammering against his chest with such force he feared it might explode, so powerful was his joy from being with Catherine, the only woman who could unearth this deepest of feeling with the simple grace of her presence. And they both understood...*finally*! Finally, she would not hold back and save herself for anyone else. Finally, he would give all of his emotions freely without any secret intention, or wicked game. Finally, as Heathcliff rested over her and aligned himself in position to enter, they would have this exquisite opportunity, just as Catherine had so blissfully foreshadowed in this very bed, to express their true love and share it in the fullest, most intimate, and most loving way.

"Edgar's here!" exclaimed Nelly as she burst into the room. "For heaven's sake, hurry down! You'll not meet anyone on the front stairs. Stay among the trees till he is fairly in."

"I must go, Catherine," said Heathcliff, seeking to extricate himself from his companion's arms. "But, if I live, I'll see you again before you are asleep and we will complete what we have started. I won't stray five yards from your window."

He stood up and began dressing.

"You must not go!" she answered, holding one arm as firmly as her strength allowed. "You shall not, I tell you."

"For one hour," he pleaded earnestly, releasing his arm to complete his task.

"Not for one minute," she replied.

Nelly moved to cover her nakedness with the quilt.

"I *must*. Edgar will be up immediately."

Pants on, he grabbed the remainder of his clothes and was about to dash.

"No!" she shrieked. "Oh, don't, don't go! Edgar will not hurt us."

"Damn the fool. There he is," cried Heathcliff, hearing Edgar mounting the stairs. He sank into his seat and said, "Hush, my darling! Hush, hush, Catherine! I'll stay. If he shot me so, I'd expire with a blessing on my lips."

"Are you going to listen to her ravings?" asked Nelly passionately. "She does not know what she says. Will you ruin her, because she has not wit to help herself? Get up! You could be free instantly. That is the most diabolical deed that ever you did."

Nelly cried out when Edgar appeared at the door.

Catherine's arm fell limp over the bed, her head relaxed to the side, and she fainted.

Edgar sprang toward his unbidden guest, blanched with astonishment and rage. Heathcliff lurched to his feet, and stood towering over his nemesis. What Edgar meant to do was not clear—perhaps he did not remember how tall Heathcliff actually was—but he stopped all further demonstrations, at once, after noticing Catherine's still form.

He sat on the bed and lifted her torso into his arms.

"Look here," he snapped at Heathcliff, "fiend that you are you still must vanish now from this house and let me tend to my wife! We will have our words later."

Heathcliff remained in place, gravely disappointed that Edgar had stopped short of accosting him, for what immense satisfaction it would be to have the opportunity to crush Edgar to the ground and whisk Catherine away.

But *wife* she was, as Edgar had stated, and they would soon be hunted down and separated forever, and no doubt Edgar would gain much pleasure to have him thrown in prison to languish.

But Heathcliff still would not leave her in this condition. He made no ill comment, or invitation that could incite a more physical display, and walked a few steps away to the parlor and sat down, allowing Edgar to focus his full attention on Catherine, for all that mattered now was the revival of his beloved, and if that weakling could accomplish such a feat, it would give Edgar this small moment of reprieve from the full wrath Heathcliff wanted to inflict.

Nelly and Edgar, with great difficulty, and after resorting to many means, managed to restore her sensation, and her eyes blinked open, but she was all bewildered. She sighed, and moaned, and knew nobody. Edgar, in his anxiety for her, forgot her hated friend. Nelly did not. She went, at the earliest opportunity, and besought Heathcliff to depart, affirming that Catherine was better, and promising he would hear from her in the morning, how she passed the night

"I shall stay in the garden," he answered, "fully awake every minute awaiting your word. And, Nelly, mind you keep your promise! I shall be under those larch trees, and if I do not receive your visit by first light of day, I will pay another visit, and pity poor Edgar if he stands in my way, for no one this time will prevent me from being with the woman I love!"

He sent a rapid glance through the half-open door of the chamber, and ascertaining that Nelly's appraisal was true, delivered the house from his presence.

About twelve o'clock that night was born to Catherine a puny, seven months' child; and two hours after, the mother died, having never recovered sufficient consciousness to miss Heathcliff, or know Edgar.

Volume III

Chapter Twenty-Two

Edgar Linton had his head on the pillow, his deceased wife by his side, his eyes shut. His young and fair features were almost death-like, *hers* of perfect peace. His cheeks were sunken and hollow, his forehead jagged with lines of deep bereavement. Her brow was smooth, her lids closed, her lips wearing the expression of bliss. No living soul could look more close to expiration than Edgar did. No angel in heaven could be more beautiful than she appeared.

What an unwelcomed infant it was those first few hours. Edgar had asked that Nelly remove it from the room before he lay down. Not only had he lost a wife, but he had not gained an heir. As written in his father's will, if no son was born to Edgar, then the estate would pass to Isabella, and then her male offspring, upon Edgar's death. The infant was female, soon to be christened Catherine and known only as Cathy.

Nelly wished yet feared to find Heathcliff. The terrible news must be told, and she longed to get it over with, but *how* to do it she did not know.

She found him a few yards deep in the park, leaning against an old ash tree, his hat off, and his hair soaked with the dew that had gathered on the budded branches. He seemed stiff and im-mobile, as if he had been standing a long time in that position.

Nelly needn't have worried about how to reveal this tragedy. He lifted up his eyes, took one look at her expression, and let out a howl not like a man, but like a savage beast getting goaded to death with knives and spears. All present at the Grange and the Heights on the night Heathcliff had let out his unearthly scream before jumping at the Cragge and who heard his demonic wail now felt the same splitting of their souls, the same confusion as to the nature of the sound, and the same eerily familiar sensation of dread. He dashed his head repeatedly against the knotted trunk, splashing blood about the bark of the tree and on his face. His sounds that fateful night had echoed his own pain and the anger he felt toward those who had caused it. This morning it reflected the same deep anger, coupled with the excruciating regret of all the pain he had caused his beloved.

Nelly wept as much for him as her, for she pitied creatures that have none of the feeling either for themselves or others.

"Oh, God! It is unutterable!" he cried, with frightful vehemence, stamping his foot, and groaning in a sudden paroxysm of ungovernable passion. "I cannot live without my life! I *cannot* live without my soul!"

He glared at Nelly, blood running down his face like tracks of tears. "I must see her."

"Impossible. In fact you must go. I am sure that Edgar has heard your howl and will dispatch his men to harm you. Flee at once!"

"It's my fault! I never should have left her! When we embraced, she had shown a renewed spirit, a spark toward living rather than dying."

"Make haste, Heathcliff. They will surely be armed!"

"It's his fault!" he rambled. "As soon as Edgar appeared, she faded instantly! I will not rest until I see him destroyed!" The pain in his eyes was greater than any wound to his head. "Oh, where is she? Not *there*—not in heaven—not perished—where? I must find her!"

The sound of many heavy boots upon the flag was heard and Heathcliff let out another bloody shout and darted through the break in the hedge.

Catherine's funeral was appointed to take place on the Friday following her decease and till then her coffin remained uncovered, and strewn with flowers and scented leaves, in the great drawing room. Edgar spent his days and nights there, a sleepless guardian. He requisitioned additional armed men to stand guard at the house, with orders to shoot the trespasser Heathcliff on sight. Concealed from all, Heathcliff still managed to spend his nights in the garden, under the cover of darkness, as well a stranger to repose.

Hindley was, of course, invited to attend the remains of his sister to the grave and he sent no excuse, but he never came. Isabella was not asked.

Against Catherine's wishes, Edgar buried her at the Gimmerton Church graveyard, under the Linton carved monument, a vacant place reserved for him, by her side. Heathcliff was banned from the burial, but it did not mean he missed it, hidden well under leafy cover at the top of an old oak tree, just thirty yards from the grave site.

He waited until all were gone, including the caretaker, and climbed down silently, on this black, moonless night, and fell to his knees in the dirt next to the grave of his beloved, in the spot reserved for Edgar.

Although it was late spring, the wind blew as bleak as winter. All around was solitary. He did not fear that her fool of a husband would wander up the den so late—and no one else had business to bring them here.

Being alone, and conscious two yards of loose earth was the only barrier between them, he said aloud, "I will have what was denied to me by your husband and feel you in my arms again. If you be cold, I'll think it is the north wind that chills me, and if you be motionless, it is sleep."

He got a spade from the tool house, and began to delve with all his might—it scraped wood; he fell to work with his hands. Coffin exposed, he undid the screws about the lid. He said, "I wished they had shoveled in the dirt above us both."

He took a deep breath and opened the coffin. Perhaps it was his imagination, because it was so dark, but he felt sure he was able to make out the beautiful features of his beloved . . . and that she was smiling. Her hands were clasped across her belly, flat now, and, as he ran his fingers along her face and neck, he felt the locket against her bosom.

He lowered himself inside the coffin and lay next to her, pressed a kiss against her cheek.

He said, "Catherine Earnshaw, may you not rest, as long as I am living! You said I killed you—haunt me then! The murdered *do* haunt their murderers. Be with me always—take any form—drive me mad! Only *do* not leave me in this abyss, where I cannot find you!"

At once, Heathcliff thought he heard a sigh, close at ear, the warm breath of it momentarily displacing the cold wind. He knew no living thing in flesh and blood was by. But as certainly as one could perceive the approach of some substantial body in the dark, Heathcliff felt a presence, not next to him, but on the earth.

A sudden sense of relief flowed through every limb, and he felt the warm aura of Catherine's love as a glow within. But, as suddenly as it had appeared, the sensation vanished, and he felt only the chill of the wind, and the frustration of feeling completely alone once again.

Nevertheless, as he rose from the grave, he now felt sure that Gimmerton Church, under the monument of the Lintons, was not where Catherine wanted her final rest.

Before he screwed tight the lid to the coffin, he got down on his knees and reached inside it one more time. With one hand, he tilted her neck up, with the other, he removed the locket and placed it around his own neck and tucked it hidden under his shirt. Then he crept quietly to the back of the tool house and found the cart used for transporting the dead. He hitched his own horse to it, and led the mare back to the grave. Inspired by the strength of his purpose, he managed to lift the coffin out of the dirt, elevating half of it onto the lip of the grass, then getting into the dirt and pushing the rest out. He repeated the maneuver to load the coffin into the cart. With much intensity, he filled the hole with the spade and smoothed the dirt so it looked untouched, using a heavy-leafed tree branch to spread soil to cover his footprints. He tossed the spade into the cart, mounted his horse, and urged her on toward Black Rock Cragge, knowing first light was soon coming.

At the Cragge, he found the spot where he and Catherine both lay and made their vow. It was below a large, pointed, arrowlike rock that was hidden from the road by another group of stones. He dug away like a madman, eyes blazing, clothes covered in dirt, hands blackened, nails grimy to the cuticles. With much gentleness and strain, he reversed his grave site maneuvers and was able to lower the wooden box into the fresh hole. He covered the coffin with dirt and smoothed it out to make it look as natural as possible. Just as first light struck the Cragge he used the spade to carve into the rock protruding just above the head of the grave, behind a thicket of grass, the initials CE.

On his knees, he hunched over the grave, exhausted, the pain of overexertion firing through every muscle in his body. He bent down and kissed the dirt covering her, tears dripping from his face, splattering the dirt. Then he stood and faced the east openly, without a blink, letting the strong rising sun strike his eyes, blinding him. Then he, horse, and cart headed back to Wuthering Heights, where he would dismantle the cart and use it as firewood, where he would carefully decide on his next plan of action to avenge her death, his loss, and the theft of their love on all the remaining, cursed Earnshaws and Lintons.

Chapter Twenty-Three

Upon entering the house at Wuthering Heights, Heathcliff ordered Isabella to prepare him a bath. She did so, gladly, warming huge pots of water and filling the metal tub. He stripped himself of his clothes, much dirt and dust falling to the ground. She did not take notice, as she was sitting on the ground and held her eyes downward. He stood over her and said, "You may look."

She raised her eyes and look she did. He towered above her, a giant of a man. From this angle he looked all of ten feet. She saw the thick flow of his dark hair along his legs, the full bush surrounding his balls, the furry trail going up from his stomach onto his fine, masculine chest, crowned with brownish nipples. The whiskers on his face had grown thick and stubbly. He had not had a bath or tended to himself since Catherine's death.

"You may bathe me," said Heathcliff.

He got into the tub and with cloth and soap she cleaned her man, tenderly, carefully. He sunk low and allowed his head to rest on the edge and closed his eyes, weary from the emotional evening with her coffin, from the stormy emotions of his last visit with Catherine. How close they had come to consummating their true love, to having their two souls joined as one; this chance now lost forever, she lost forever. Though he was sure he had felt her presence last night, if only for an instant.

"Do you believe in spirits?" he asked Isabella.

Perhaps it was from surprise that he had spoken to her with a sincere question, as he usually stayed within their roles once a connection was started, or maybe she was simply distracted by her complete focus on his defined torso, but she did not answer right away... until she saw him staring at her.

"Nay. I believe either you go up to heaven, or *down to hell.*" She looked at him coldly as she mouthed the last part of her response, then she added, "Nothing in between." Distracted from her task, Isabella took notice of how muddy his pile of clothes was on the floor. She didn't need to see that to know he had been to Catherine's grave. Although she was sure he would end up in hell, no doubt Heathcliff loved in a heavenly fashion. Last night she had shed her own private tears for the sister she had lost... as she had done even before Catherine's death, after Isabella had run off with the object of her rival's deepest love. Yet Isabella would always envy Catherine. Although Catherine was deep in the ground and Isabella was the wife of Heathcliff, there was no question who was the victor.

"I have a strong faith in ghosts," said Heathcliff. "I have a conviction that they can, and do, exist, among us, and whether destined for heaven or hell, can resist the call."

She continued the bathing. Better to focus on the pleasing feel of his flesh against her hands, than revisit, as Heathcliff so often did, old misery.

When she was done, he said, "Shave me."

She was thrilled to have this time with her master: calm, and without the rush and harshness of their sex, as just being able to serve him inspired plentiful arousal.

He sat in a chair and she lathered his face and exposed the straight razor. He closed his eyes and leaned back in the chair.

She started at his throat. How often, at first, had she wanted to use this time to end it all, slice straight through and be done with him. She could claim self-defense and surely those in the house-hold would testify to the sadistic way she was treated.

But it was never going to happen. She realized, in her own, distorted way, she loved him. She loved him for the incredible emotions he inspired in her, and for the gratefulness she felt when he allowed her access to his presence like this, a time where he was passive, but aloof, where she was subservient and fully fo-cused on her master.

Done, she delicately dried his massive body, a portion at a time, with a towel. When she finished her task, he stood in front of her. "Take off your clothes."

She obeyed and removed her tattered, soiled garments, slowly, seductively, the way he liked.

"Always the tart, I love that about you," he said.

She warmed to his words, as she believed that, in his own way, he loved her. Why else would he give her so much attention?

Both naked, he pulled her to him and wrapped his arms around her body. He did not kiss Isabella, but thrilled her by al-lowing his massive, clean presence to bless her petite, dirty one.

For him, there was no thrill. He had no desire to kiss Isabella, especially after having been in the arms of Catherine so recently. He had no desire to *make love*... anymore. Whatever spotty kind-ness he had showed Isabella in the past seemed nowhere to be found. She was the sister of the man who not only stole the woman he loved, but, with his shallow and unyielding pres-ence, had hastened her demise. She was a Linton! The anguish of Catherine's death filled him with more motivation than ever to see his curse come to full bloom. There was no escaping this pain, only diversion from it to the dark place that helped him momentarily forget, and the meager satisfaction from seeing the Earnshaws and Lintons feel even a little of what tortured his soul.

He said, "From now on, at all meals, you will not rise unless given permission, and will wear your collar at all times. Fetch it for me now from the dungeon."

She started to dress.

"Now!"

"But the servants are in the yard!"

He tugged sharply on her hair with his fist. "Have you not learned yet not to question your master?"

He released her and she left, naked, to complete her task, trembling, and wet with tears. How she hated this man!

When Heathcliff entered the dining area, Isabella, fully dressed, followed a few paces behind, head lowered, leather collar used formerly by the canine, Throttler, strapped around her neck. Joseph immediately stopped serving and said to Heathcliff, "It is blasphemy enough how you do your hellish business, but do you have to bring it in here?"

He stormed out of the house. Hareton, much taller now as he approached his preadolescence, had already eaten and was in the stable, grooming his pony. Hindley clearly noticed the collar, as he sat at the table eating his stew, but made no comment, nor revealed any reaction. Over the years he had filled himself with drink well beyond irrationality and would mutter not a syllable as he stared and rocked for hours. His hair, still wild and unkempt, had turned completely white, although he was still a relatively young man. His teeth had gone bad from neglect, and two in the front were missing, leaving ugly black gaps in his smile—which rarely happened now anyway—and the rest were yellow and decayed.

Heathcliff ordered Isabella to sit, which she did, next to him, head still lowered. Heathcliff devoured his stew; he had not eaten in over twenty-four hours. She waited patiently. Though she felt humiliated sitting at the table, wearing Throttler's collar, waiting as a servant would for her master to finish, she could not help feeling tingles course through her body. She knew that whenever their time together started, all the efforts he made to be cruel, even the efforts to ignore, meant he was still thinking of her, focused on opening her up and making her experience the depraved thoughts and frenzied sensations only he could inspire, and, as he had predicted the night of their honeymoon, she now fully craved.

When Heathcliff was done with his meal, he shoveled the scraps from his plate onto Isabella's, then placed her utensils out of her reach. Her fingers scooped what food she could into her mouth, but this was not the nourishment she desired.

Intuiting her needs, as he always did, Heathcliff unbuttoned his pants and removed his cock, half swollen with the wicked pleasure he was already feeling. She knew he meant for her to look at it, which she did, staring at the fully shaped stalk, the dark, purple head pointing so clearly in her direction. Heathcliff nodded. Isabella guided her hand down her body, her eyes never wavering from his manhood. Hindley continued to eat, emotionless, impassive, as if he had no awareness of what was happening.

She hiked her dress up, and with a finger, began a rhythmic caressing at her quim as she continued to stare at his member, which grew larger from the excitement stirred by her humiliation. And shame she did feel, as always, and it was intensified knowing Hindley was present, but, as a dutiful student of Heathcliff's training, it all served to grow her passion in a way that was as deep as it was dirty.

She did her best not to cry out, but this, too, was beyond her control, as she moaned and writhed, the collar tightening around her neck, on her way to a grand climax at the dinner table—which caused Hindley, finally, to raise his eyes and stare—as she collapsed against the back of the chair in an exhausting, ignominious, deliriously arousing finale.

With difficulty, Heathcliff tucked his full member back into his pants, then left the table to return his horse to the barn. As soon as he shut the front door behind him, Hindley turned directly to Isabella, suddenly filled with spastic animation, his eyes gleaming with burning hate as they looked to hers to make a sympathetic return. He said, "You and I have a great debt to settle with the man out yonder! If we were neither of us cowards, we might combine to discharge it. Are you as soft as your brother? Are you willing to endure to the last, and not once attempt a repayment?"

"I'm weary of enduring now," she replied, "and I'd be glad of retaliation that wouldn't recoil on myself, but treachery, and violence, are spears pointed at both ends—they wound those who resort to them, worse than their enemies."

"Treachery and violence are a just return for treachery and violence!" cried Hindley. "Mrs. Heathcliff, I'll ask you to do nothing but heed me this time by putting the key in the lock and drawing the bolts of your chamber this evening after your master falls asleep, and then simply sit still, and be dumb, and I will do the rest with my pistol, avenging the loss of my estate, while making you a free woman!"

"You mustn't touch him," she said. "The door will remain shut—be quiet!"

Heathcliff reappeared and Hindley went silent.

Heathcliff nodded. Isabella stood. She followed behind him to the dungeon.

It was there—she, tied to the sling—that he bequeathed to

Isabella her full recompense for so dutifully following all his commands, those spoken aloud and those not. He reddened her arse with the cat-o'-nine, not so hard as to hurt her, but hard enough for her to yield fully to his dominant presence, which inspired deep, throaty moans mixed with discomfort and delight. This reddened the glow of her embers as well, and, coupled with the desires and surges inspired by the bath, the shave, the collar, the subservient meal, and dutiful performance, she was more than ready to welcome him from the throne he had placed her upon.

Heathcliff needed no touch from her, not a lick or a suck. He shed his clothes and presented his cock at full attention, letting her study it one more time, so she knew every inch that would soon be inside her fully. The darkness of the place she helped take him to clouded everything but the surging clarity of his illicit desire.

He entered her, then immediately thrust deeply and with much strength, causing the sling to collapse her body down from above, up from below, and her to cry out with the pleasure of this most distinct penetration.

"Heathcliff! Heathcliff! Heathcliff!" echoed from the cellar to the house, mixed with the hard grunts of the dominator taking his gratification, imposing his will.

Hindley lowered his head to the kitchen table and covered his ears. "Madness!" he exclaimed. "This is madness that my house must hear this, that Heathcliff be not only master, but lord over all who dwell here!"

He jumped up with more energy than he had shown in months. Crazed, speaking aloud again, spittle flying from his mouth, he said, "I must avenge the death of my own sister!" He went to the cabinet and loaded his pistol. On the way to the cellar, he grabbed a sharp knife from the kitchen.

Heathcliff never needed to bolt the dungeon entrance when Isabella was inside, as there was no chance she would leave on her own. The wood door flung open and Hindley appeared, brandishing both knife and pistol, eyes wild, laughing like a loon as he shouted, "Curse you and my father, gypsy urchin, for the day you arrived at this house!"

Isabella screamed.

Had Hindley just entered and fired, he might have accomplished his task of seeing his longtime enemy dead to the floor. But, taking advantage of the verbal pause, Heathcliff removed himself from Isabella and sprung athletically toward Hindley, grasping both arms and thrusting them upward, just as the charge exploded and fired toward the ceiling. Heathcliff pulled the knife away with full force, accidentally slitting up the flesh of Hindley's arm as he secured the blade and tossed it on the ground, out of reach. He knocked Hindley to the floor as well and trampled on him, kicking his ribs. Hindley fell senseless from the excessive pain and the flow of blood that gushed from his arm. Isabella begged Heathcliff to stop.

He exerted preterhuman self-denial in abstaining from finishing him, completely; but he finally desisted and dragged the inanimate body to the settle in the far corner of the cellar.

"It is not because of your entreats that I spare him," mouthed Heathcliff. "It is far too soon to end his torment with the reward of death."

He tore off the sleeve of Hindley's coat, and bound up the wound with brutal roughness.

Then, still erect, he returned his attentions to Isabella, and entered her once more. As he pushed in and out with great gusto, her moans filled the dungeon once again, and he bellowed, "A much better day I have not had in a month, both an Earnshaw and a Linton getting it proper!"

Chapter Twenty-Four

That evening, Heathcliff made his way to Black Rock Cragge. The night still moonless, he could have walked it blindfolded. A spirit of energy drove him to Catherine's resting place, as it had driven him to her garden, outside her window so many nights since his return, hoping she might walk to him in her sleep, or that he could capture a glimpse of her lovely features through her chamber window. The energy within him was also mixed with a trembling exhaustion, the melding of feelings only insomniacs share: a frustrating sense that cessation from an active brain is not an option, joined with a supreme wish that the eyes would close and somehow inspire the mind to find peace.

He was soon at her hidden grave site, sitting next to her, his back against the rocks.

Aloud, he asked her for some kind of sign, some kind of guidance, but all he heard was the wind along the moors. He felt more content out here than in the garden. This was their place, and she was next to him.

His eyelids began to flutter. Although he owned Wuthering Heights, it never felt like his home without Catherine there. This place felt more like their dwelling, a view of the moors, always a face full of turbulent air to make the location known, whether the eyes were closed or not. They felt as if they would close, but were startled open as he heard the same soft sigh as last night, and felt the identical warm breath upon his cheek, with a softness and temperature that could not be mistaken for the wind.

"Catherine?" he said aloud.

He heard nothing in response.

He looked skyward. Although he could see nothing, he felt as if something were hovering over him, translucent, with shape, but he could not be sure.

He felt the presence lower, closer, closer. He reached up his arms and felt only the wind.

But then it was as if he were being entered, not physically entered, but there was a sudden heat, an aura within his body.

He imagined that the angels had beckoned for Catherine to come to them, but she had resisted. And they finally relented, as they came to understand her pain and perceive the purity of her love.

He told her he longed to be with her any way possible and that if she would give him some sign, he would be happy to dash his brains against the rocks so they could be reunited.

The wind picked up and he felt a chill.

He knew then that to perform such an act in the state of hate that he was in, while his curse still existed, would banish him to a hell no mortal could envision and would separate them for all of eternity.

"I hereby retract my curse," he said aloud, "and wish nothing but good thoughts for all Earnshaws and Lintons!"

Was that her laugh?

He was sure that words meant nothing to the being above who knows all and sees into everyone's heart.

How could he extract this hate from his heart without her help?

There was still so much that was unfinished. Edgar, the purloiner of Heathcliff's passion, one who tried to claim it for his own and thus killed the object of their love, was still alive, still flourishing at his estate, a baby with the name—and surely some resemblance to the mother—to give him comfort.

Perhaps she sensed his agitation, because he felt the aura spread wider within him, and provide a soothing heat.

They had laid a richer foundation for true love. She had confessed mistakes she deeply regretted, and he had revealed how he avoided the honesty of his most pure emotion, in favor of the lust for dominance to control her. But she could not be controlled. She was not Nelly, nor Isabella. She was Catherine. He should not want to control her and she should not want to control him.

How was it possible that they could accomplish so much and fall so short?

It took Catherine's death to prove to both of them that their love transcended all their feverish byplays, all life stations, all monetary means, and was strong enough to survive anything.

Except death.

Now it was too late.

Now all he had were the remaining members of the Lintons and Earnshaws who littered his soul with their very existence...and his diabolical plans that brought diversion but not decency, and certainly no peace of mind. Now all he had were the memories of his most cherished, but how could that be enough? Suddenly, he felt the warmth expand even farther through his body, felt more inhabited by his much-loved counterpart, felt a surge and feeling as if she were really within him. His heart soared and his spirits rose. He glanced up at the heavens and wondered, somehow, if it was not too late.

"My love, Catherine, have you returned?" he asked out loud. "Is there still a chance for our union to become eternal?"

These thoughts floated through his mind, like the heat through his body, warming him in spots, frigid in others. The feeling that she might be with him, along with the frustration at not knowing the complete answers to his questions, caused tears of joy, of sadness, to flow freely throughout the night, until the sun struck his face . . . and then he opened his eyes.

The refreshing surge he felt in his body led him to realize that he had been asleep for most, if not all, of the night.

He got up, stretched his body out toward the sun.

He wondered if indeed it was her spirit that had raised the questions and given him some answers, or simply the dream of her, the sense of her next to him, within him—in all her regal beauty—that had helped him find peaceful sleep.

As he walked from the Cragge to the Heights, the thought that ghosts could inhabit mortals, and that her ghost had inhabited him and made her presence felt both physically and mentally, put a spring to his steps.

Yet he wanted more: not just a sense of her, not just the memory of her, but the feel of her against him and within him. He changed his direction and headed toward Gimmerton.

Heathcliff returned to the Heights at dinnertime, and stored his packages in the master chamber. In a good mood, he allowed Isabella to use her utensils while she ate at the table. Hindley had remained in his bed all day, deadly sick, even more gaunt and ghastly, and Joseph brought him food he barely touched.

After dinner, Heathcliff instructed Isabella to bathe and prepare herself with the powder and perfumes he had bought in town.

Although this was not a usual request, Isabella did as told without question. Though his games were harsh, she found him as creative as any artist and her body simmered with anticipation.

Naked, except for her collar, she entered his chamber after completing her tasks, and saw her master lying flat on one side of the bed. What she saw on the other caused a quick intake of breath, as she pressed her open palm to her mouth in shock.

Laid out next to his body was a new white dress. At the top of the dress, where the head would be, was a long, thick, flowing black wig. Placed on the bosom of the dress was the locket she had seen Catherine wear.

"Put it all on," ordered Heathcliff.

She had thought the scent of the powders and perfumes were familiar, and now she realized they were the same that Catherine had regularly used.

At Gimmerton, Heathcliff had sniffed everything at several shops until he found the scents of the only woman he adored.

Still in shock, but knowing better than to speak, Isabella did as she was asked. Her back to him, she placed the locket on the dresser, then pulled the dress on over head, and donned the wig, adjusting it in the mirror. Heathcliff rose from the bed and stood behind her. He studied her reflection.

Their features, although both fair, were never similar in nature. Catherine was strong and sturdy in cheek bones, with full lips and dark eyes. Isabella had a paler complexion, with a more petite facial structure, and thin lips and blue eyes. The wig hid all of her light hair, and the thick curls covered much of her face. Both were thin and well shaped, Catherine with ample full bosom, with bold nipples, Isabella with pert but smallish breasts, tiny nipples barely two dots upon her chest.

Heathcliff gently removed the collar from around her throat, then reached for the locket on the dresser. He delicately lowered the chain over Isabella's head, until the end of it rested elegantly upon her chest.

Heathcliff looked at her reflection in the mirror one more time, as if he was memorizing, imprinting it into his brain. He did not seem to look at her eyes, or the shape of her mouth, rather he took her in as a whole, the woman in the dress, with the flowing black hair, and gold locket around her neck.

Heathcliff blew out the one candle that illuminated the room, and his chamber went dark. Heathcliff undressed, then returned to the bed.

"My love," he said, in a soft tone Isabella had never heard directed at her. "Come to me."

With the windows shuttered, the room was pitch black and Isabella had to feel her way forward with her hands. Once she made contact with the bed, she was able to grope her way to his side and lay next to him.

Heathcliff reached out to embrace her and pulled her body close and kissed her deeply on the mouth with his full lips.

He kept his eyes closed at all times. Behind his lids he saw himself at Black Rock, lying in the dirt, his beloved rising from the ground to be with him. The embrace he just made in the bed was the embrace he had made at their spot, his arms going forward, reaching for Catherine and pulling her into him. He rejoiced at being able to feel the warmth and softness of her body. He ran his hands through her hair and entered her mouth with the fire of his tongue. Her hands went to his back and touched the scars as she had done in her own bed. He cupped her breasts, recoiled, then moved his hand to the locket resting on her chest, blindly running his fingertips along the etched design, knowing every raised curl by heart.

He rolled on top of her, letting his weight overpower her body, as his width covered her completely and made her feel small. He kissed along her neck.

"Speak to me," he said, "as softly as you can. Tell me how much you love and need me."

"Heathcliff," she whispered. "I love you so much. I need you so much. I can't live without you. You are everything to me. The sun and the moon. You complete my heart and my soul. You are reason to wake in the morn and return to bed in the night. You are my only true love. There is no other. I am yours forever."

His abrupt kiss to the mouth quelled her words.

Then he said, "I love you forever and ever; my heart will always be yours."

From her mouth, he moved his face down her body, bypassing her breasts this time, then lifted her dress and gently flicked his tongue along her belly. He ran his thick hands up and down her legs, from the calves to the thighs, his fingers nearly able to go completely around the latter. He kissed her quim, gently, licking it, slowly. Finally, he entered with his tongue and tasted her, then withdrew and moved his body up, once again parallel.

She reached down to touch his cock and was surprised to feel that it was nearly flaccid.

No matter how hard he concentrated, no matter how much he willed himself to see them both at the Cragge, his vision was blurred. No matter how much he cried in his heart for her to return to him, to inhabit this form that lay beneath him so that they might be together in purity at last, he did not feel it happening.

Her voice did not sound like Catherine's.

Her lips did not feel like Catherine's.

Her taste did not have flavor like Catherine's.

Her quim was as far away from the delicate scent of Catherine's as a fish was from a rose.

As he kissed her neck again, almost absentmindedly, he prayed

that, somehow, Catherine would give him some sign that she was
with him.

How much would Isabella have welcomed this lovemaking on
the night of their wedding?

How often had she imagined these tender kisses during their
brief courtship?

How many nights had she wished she could feel some softness
in this man, those hands caressing her legs as had just done, instead of the harsh brutality his mouth, tongue, hands, fingers, and
cock always administered?

How delighted would she have been to be encouraged to express her love in these affectionate, endearing words?

How sweet would it have been to hear him return the same?

But now, she felt nothing.

It was not the humiliation of being asked to be someone else,
her dead rival, his true love. She was used to his degradation and
would probably have welcomed this scenario with passion had it
been presented that way.

But these days since their honeymoon, he had ruined her, both
inside and out.

She was completely dry; normally just a dirty look from him
would fill her with desire.

Her heart fluttered at calm pace, when usually it raced at the
feel of his body.

She tried imagining that his words of love were truly meant for
her, but inside she wished that he cursed her, twisted her nipples,
spanked her arse, showered on her the dirty epitaphs she now
thought suited her perfectly.

When was the last time he even touched her in this bed?

Just the dirt against her bare feet, the stale smell of the dungeon, caused her to tremble with feverish excitement.

Too much comfort. Too much *pleasant* sensation.

For Heathcliff, his thoughts became cloudy and confused from the stiffness and unfamiliarity he felt inside and underneath him. From his lips escaped a low anguished cry. He had been so sure he could draw at least some comfort from this, that Catherine would understand and do something to make Isabella feel like the vessel for his true love.

He felt as helpless as he had after discerning Catherine's death upon Nelly's face.

Which caused something to happen that had never happened before . . . his cock actually retreated to a size he could only remember as a young boy.

In a last final effort to find some comfort, he got up from the bed, and faced the wall, offering her his arse.

She would have preferred a harsh command, but, nevertheless, she jumped at the opportunity. Regardless of the tone of this evening, this very simple act could inspire the nastiness she desired.

She licked it roughly, tasting, thrusting, and she felt him stir. His scent there, no matter how clean, was always overpowering. She reached through his legs and caressed his manhood, rejoicing at feeling his full power return.

"Yes, Catherine. Lovely. I need this."

He did. For in this position, he did not have to feel her body, inhale her scent, listen to a voice that was not the one he wanted to hear. In this very same position, with these very same feelings, he could remember fully, their furtive, rushed, taboo time together at the kitchen sink, when she had claimed him while Edgar had lounged upstairs.

His erection was massive. "I love you, Catherine," he cried as he felt her tongue go in and out with brute force.

He could have let the emotions sweep him away, as they had done that day, but he did not simply want some variation of a wet dream at Black Rock Cragge. He wanted to be inside his beloved, enter her completely in every way, and feel as one with her.

He turned, lifted her up off the ground, and placed her gently on the bed. He hovered over her, his hands on either side of her torso, pushing his body away, so he did not have to take in her scent, or feel the difference in her breasts. He entered her slowly, deliberately, with tenderness, calling on all the love he possessed.

She was moist now from being on her knees behind her man—inhaling and tasting his strongest scent and flavor—and it went in deeply, smoothly.

Only once he felt Isabella's insides fully—so different from that of his beloved's—any vision, any sense, any imagined fantasy with Catherine completely vanished.

All authority went out of his cock and it instantly withered and slipped out.

Without love, without hate, he was incapable of performing.

He rolled onto his back and wept uncontrollably, whispering her name in between his deep sobs.

For the first time, Isabella saw the deep vulnerability and humanness in her husband.

It caused her to say, "A fine, strapping man you are, shriveling like a nipper at first touch. Joseph, even Hindley, in his sad, sorry state, can do more to please a woman than you."

It gave her pleasure to hurt him in the same way he had hurt her.

He lay unmoving, continuing to sob. If this was the path Catherine's ghost was going to lead him down, then it was best she kept away. He could not stand feeling as if she had been reborn and died once again.

For Isabella, it seemed as if another presence in the room had suddenly relit the candle, and she was able to see him for the ugly brute he was: sour breath, snoring at night like a windstorm, cruel to every human he came in contact with, except one. And that one he had killed.

Heathcliff fell into an uneasy, deeply troubled sleep.

Isabella, just before dawn, packed a few things in a satchel and left Wuthering Heights.

In the morning, Heathcliff saw the wig and dress on the floor, at the foot of the bed, lifeless. He found Isabella's note on the kitchen table, the locket placed upon it. He returned the locket to its place around his neck and read:

Dear Heathcliff,

I am gone, forever, from this wretched place and your sorrowful soul; for your spell over me has been broken. Pity is all I feel for you now. I leave you to wallow deeply in your own debased passions and morbid thoughts, the only companions you are truly worthy of having.

ISABELLA

P.S. I am with child.

Chapter Twenty-Five

Isabella walked the road toward Thrushcross Grange and felt the exhilaration a prisoner must feel when let out of jail. How had she remained so long at Wuthering Heights, while allowing herself to be treated that way? She knew the answer lay in the power of her jailer. When she awoke before dawn, she knew that if she didn't take advantage of her current state of mind, he would soon have her under his spell again, and she would be doomed for her remaining years to the hell that was their marriage...and under the same roof as Heathcliff was no place to raise a child.

She knocked on the door at Thrushcross Grange and was delighted that it was Nelly who answered. Nelly seemed equally as pleased, although there was a brief moment of awkwardness as Isabella stepped inside, both remembering the last time they had met.

The house hadn't changed much, although Isabella could sense the quiet despair that permeated the property. None of the dogs had come to greet her. There were usually delightful aromas cascading from the kitchen. She guessed that her dear brother had little concern for food.

Nelly served her tea and they sat in the parlor.

"Hindley is ill and recovering from a wound sustained from an attack on Heathcliff," said Isabella.

"And who is tending to him?"

"Joseph."

"Not very encouraging."

"I'm pregnant."

"That's wonderful."

"I've left Heathcliff."

"Equally as wonderful."

"How is Edgar?"

"Grief and his deep aversion to seeing Heathcliff has transformed him into a complete hermit," said Nelly. "He has thrown up his office of magistrate, ceases to attend church, avoids the village on all occasions, and spends a life of entire seclusion within the limits of his park and grounds; only varied by solitary rambles at the moors, and visits to the grave of his wife."

"That's dreadful," replied Isabella. "I so wish he would allow me to bring him comfort."

"I wish so as well. But I do believe that time will bring resignation and a melancholy sweeter than joy. He will recall you with fondness and her memory with ardent, tender love, and take comfort that she has aspired to a better world."

"I hope you're right. And my niece?"

"A sweetheart."

"May I see her?"

Nelly cocked her head to the side to ascertain if she could hear Edgar. She signaled Isabella to be quiet and they tiptoed to the nursery. Cathy lay awake in the crib and stared at them both with curiosity.

Isabella smiled from ear to ear, and as she was about to pick her up, she heard Edgar say, "What is the meaning of this intrusion?"

She turned to face her brother. The pain in his face triggered the release of the ache in her heart, and she ran toward him with embrace and joyfully kissed his cheeks several times.

He remained impassive and she pulled away, her elation visibly ebbing from her countenance.

"What can melt the coldness of your heart that you feel so compelled to present to me?" she asked.

"Nothing," he replied. "My heart did not turn cold. It merely witnessed your chilly self-destruction."

"Am I not human? I expressed regret for my error of judgment almost immediately after my wedding. Do you not understand the weakness we all possess?"

That he did, but the greatest weakness within him had just died, and with her went some of his spirit. Without this spirit, there was little warmth left for anything.

"I have the most pleasing news," she said with delight. "I have left Heathcliff and I'm pregnant."

Emotion did ripple through Edgar's face, but more so because he remembered the complications of his father's will; he continued to remain stoical. "I don't know if a decision so late can lend repair to your error, but I wish you only optimism for the future."

"I feel that the best chance for all would be my return to the Grange, where everyone can flourish and my child will be with a cousin and feel the full love of family."

"I'm afraid that will be impossible," said Edgar. "You have forged your own path and now you must follow it." He started for the door, but turned back before exiting, and finally met fully his sister's gaze. He said, kindly, "You may take Fanny with you wherever you choose to go. She will feel much joy at recovering her former mistress."

He left the room.

Isabella fought back the tears. She had left Heathcliff. She had to draw courage and solace from that.

"Where will you go?" asked Nelly.

"London, perhaps. A good place to begin a new life. I will always cherish you."

The women embraced and both pairs of eyes moistened.

"Stay at least another hour," said Nelly.

"What use would that be?"

"Well, then I will summon Fanny and a carriage and a horseman."

"Thank you." She leaned down to kiss Cathy, but the infant turned away.

Before departing the house, Isabella stopped before portraits of both Edgar and Catherine in the front hall. She stood on a chair and kissed them both, then bestowed a similar salute on Nelly. Accompanied by Fanny, she was driven away, never to revisit this neighborhood again.

It was several days before Nelly received a respite from work and could make a visit to the Heights, but she felt that it was important to see how Hindley was doing. She donned her favorite dress, boldly leaving the top button open, and took time to place her red hair in full curl. She secretly added a dab of perfume behind each ear from one of Catherine's bottles left in the master chamber. Edgar had bid that nothing be moved or touched.

At the Heights, she, again, entered without knocking, and called out, but no one answered. She looked about the place and it looked no more cheerful than a morgue. Dust coated everything like a first frost. Dirty dishes overran the sink. There was a smell of stale garbage.

She climbed the stairs to Hindley's chamber, as she had done on that tragic night to free Catherine from her room, unable to keep her mind from revisiting those sad memories. She opened his door. Like a corpse, Hindley lay flat on his bed, staring up at the ceiling. She had thought he looked awful the last time she saw him, but he was even more miserable now. She saw a fresh bandage on the wounded arm and knew it was the work of Dr. Kenneth, but what else could he do to save this wretched soul? Nelly would have thought Hindley dead, if not for his loud snores rumbling through the room like the growls of a displeased dog. She stood by his bedside and leaned over slightly, recoiled instantly from the blast of alcohol on his breath.

"Paying your last respects?" asked Heathcliff from the doorway.

Startled, Nelly jumped back from the bed.

"I don't believe he's long for this life," said Nelly.

"Pity," Heathcliff replied.

Nelly remembered how fine Heathcliff looked the last time she visited the Heights, when he had introduced her to his dungeon. But the death of Catherine, and perhaps the departure of Isabella, had taken its toll.

His oily, unclean hair was matted in clumps and she could see the remaining scabs and scars from when he battered his head against the tree. It must have been weeks since he had shaved, and a long, scraggly beard rested upon his chin. His eyes were red around the edges and bloodshot lines veined his pupils, either from lack of sleeping, chronic weeping, or both. His appearance as a whole gave portrait to a man deeply depressed.

She was tempted to rush to him, to neaten the hair off his eyes, to reach her arms around him and comfort him with kisses. He had never been far from her thoughts, and now her feelings had become more unchecked with the departure of Catherine and Isabella. But his demeanor seemed a barrier to all contact. She remarked, "Hindley's not the only one who needs tending."

He walked past her to the bed; Hindley had gone suddenly quiet. Nelly approached at the other side. Heathcliff leaned forward, turned his head sideways, to see if breath still flowed from Hindley's gap-toothed mouth.

Abruptly, Hindley reached his good arm forward and grasped Heathcliff by the shirt. He tugged harshly and said, "Not dead yet, you bastard! But as the flames of hell beckon, I know it will not be long before you join me!"

Heathcliff ventured to pull his body back, but Hindley held fast with the strength of a last gasp. Finally, Heathcliff violently tugged Hindley's arm downward, which caused his own shirt to rip open as he freed himself.

He stood up.

Hindley moaned and passed out once again.

Nelly stared directly at Heathcliff, her eyes widening in horror. For around his neck, she saw Catherine's locket.

He saw where her eyes were drawn and knew the meaning of her reaction.

"Sir!" said Nelly. "That is the locket Catherine was buried with. I saw so with my own eyes. How is this possible?"

Heathcliff smiled that dangerous smile of his and replied, "Edgar had no right to deny me visit of Catherine as her coffin lay open. This locket was a present to me from her. I left it for Catherine when I departed this place to make my fortune and now it has been returned to its rightful place, as has she."

Still dumbfounded, Nelly sputtered, "But, I don't understand, what, how? How did you come by it again?"

He answered with arrogance. "Though all believe that Catherine is buried under the monument of the Lintons, such is not the case. She has been returned to her true place, Black Rock Cragge, with a view of the Heights, at an elevated spot ripe for full blasts of wind off the moors."

"You're mad!" cried Nelly. She quickly hurried to the door. "My master will be heartbroken when I tell him of such sacrilege!"

Before she could depart the room, Heathcliff was on her, and had Nelly in his arms, staring down at her face. He could not allow this to happen. He could not allow Edgar to assert his right as husband and place Catherine where she did not want to be. He struck her with both breath and words. "Your master? Do you need reminder of who your true master is?"

He scooped her into his arms, ignoring her sorrowful pleas, and carried her to the dungeon.

Once inside the dark, dank room, Nelly knew it was useless to resist, and sat helplessly on the floor, watching his every move. Heathcliff adjusted the height of the sling using the chain hanging from the ceiling. Nelly's chest began to heave with trepidation and excitement, her heart racing at an uneasy beat, her body tingling with anticipation. His strong hands went under her arms and he lifted her easily to her feet. She felt ready to swoon, having him so near once again. He stepped even closer and was about to place her in the sling when his mind became flooded with the sweet familiarity of Catherine's perfume. He froze in his spot. He looked at Nelly, sad, bewildered. A sharp pain rushed mightily to his temples. A moistness gathered in his eyes.

There was a sudden urge within Heathcliff to get on his horse and just ride somewhere far away to wallow in a sadness that could not be stifled, but would be less agonizing away from all the reminders of the graceful presence of his angel.

But he could not be separated from his beloved, even if she lay in death, and he lay in a life that felt like death.

He reached to the ground and scooped up bits of dirt in his hands, then rubbed the muck on the sides of Nelly's neck where she had dabbed Catherine's perfume. Then he led her out of the dungeon and through the yard.

The moistness around his eyes seemed about to overflow with tears.

Nelly realized she had been foolish to use Catherine's fragrance. She could never be her former mistress. He could never love her as he loved Catherine. She could never inspire such unwavering devotion and need in him.

At the entrance gate he said, "If you choose to tell Edgar about Catherine's grave, I will fight him to the death to make sure he does not claim her once again."

He kissed her lightly on the cheek and bid her farewell.

No, she would not inform Edgar about the transference of Catherine's coffin. Why inspire more bloody rancor between the two foes? Catherine was in the place where she wanted to rest anyway. Heathcliff did not deserve any more anguish.

As she walked home, as her own tears formed, she felt much regret from the parting. She wondered if she had acted the tattler in the hopes he would repeat his unearthly, sacrilegious ceremony in his unholy chapel. She was sure, from the look in his eyes, that she would never be *with* him again.

When Heathcliff returned to the house, Joseph informed him that Hindley had passed.

Heathcliff sat alone in a chair in front of the fire, remembering the kindly elder Mr. Earnshaw, at a time when life seemed much simpler. He felt no true pleasure, but definitely great satisfaction, from fully avenging Hindley's ill treatment of him that was catalyst to his separation from Catherine.

His thoughts returned to Nelly and the dungeon as he poked at the fire with an iron; so halfhearted was his parry that the flames nearly expired. There didn't seem to be any reason left to wield his manhood on the women in his life, like the mighty hammer of Thor, and impose his dominance to produce full submission to his sordid search for relief... when there was no relief in sight. He was sure that only love could relieve his tortured soul, and that love lay beneath the ground.

He stood, took a step closer to the fire, stirred the embers again, stabbing forcefully with the iron this time, inspiring renewed spark and rising flame.

There was still his curse and his plan.

There was still Edgar to crush, and Thrushcross Grange to own.

He prayed that Isabella's child would be a son.

Chapter Twenty-Six

The years passed, and as young Cathy grew into her teens, she was, indeed, the most winning thing that ever brought sunshine into a desolate house—a real beauty in face—with the Earnshaws' handsome dark eyes, but the Lintons' fair skin, and small features, and yellow curling hair. Her spirit was high, though not rough, and qualified by a heart, sensitive and lively to excess in its affections. The capacity for intense attachments reminded everyone of her mother; though she still did not resemble her, for she could be soft and mild as a dove, and she had a gentle voice, and pensive expression. Her anger was never furious, her love never fierce; it was deep and tender.

However, she had faults to foil her gifts. A propensity to be saucy was one and a perverse will that indulged children invariably acquire, whether they be good tempered or cross. If a servant chanced to vex her, it was always, "I shall tell Papa!" And if her father reproved her, even by a look, it would seem a heartbreaking business, although he never spoke a harsh word to her.

After burying Hindley, Heathcliff had declared to Hareton, "Now, my bonny lad, you are *mine*! And we'll see if one tree won't grow as crooked as another, with the same wind to twist it!"

The unsuspecting thing had been pleased at this speech, as yet unaware that this man who was once a guest had thoroughly outmaneuvered his father to become the master. In that manner, Hareton, who had been destined to be the first gentleman of the neighborhood, was reduced to a state of complete dependence on his father's inveterate enemy and lived in his own house as a servant deprived of the advantage of wages, and quite unable to right himself, because of his friendlessness, and his ignorance that he had been wronged.

And now, bordering on manhood, Hareton had grown physically tall and strong, with a fearless nature, which perhaps had discouraged Heathcliff from treating him physically ill. But Heathcliff bent his malevolence by making him a brute: He was never taught to read or write; never rebuked for any bad habit which did not annoy his keeper; never led a single step toward virtue or guarded by a single precept against vice.

Heathcliff's prayers answered, Isabella had given birth to a son—just a half year younger than the boy's cousin, Cathy—and gave him the first name of Linton. Her brother's rejection had stayed with her all the years she had raised the child in London, and she never quite recovered, always a sad woman and mother, who tried to love her son as best she could.

Whether from this heartbreak, or from extreme loneliness, or just from a general trend toward illness, Isabella passed when Linton turned fifteen. Edgar sent Nelly to recover him and she begged that he be allowed to live at the Grange and stay in her care, but the master would have none of it, heart frozen in time at the point of his sister's ultimate rejection. He ordered that the boy be brought to the Heights, to be raised by the father, perhaps the final punishment he could bestow on his dead sister.

Nelly was greeted by a pale, delicate, effeminate boy, who might have been taken for Edgar's younger brother, so strong was the resemblance.

"What is my father like?" he asked as they journeyed to the Heights.

"Black hair and eyes," said Nelly. "Stern, tall, big. He'll not seem to you so gentle and kind at first, perhaps, because, it is not his way."

"Black hair and eyes!" mused Linton. "Then I am not much like him, am I?"

"Not much," she answered, surveying with regret the white complexion, and slim frame, and his large languid eyes . . . his mother's eyes, without the vestige of her sparkling spirit.

Nelly had not been to the Heights since the day she had seen Heathcliff with Catherine's locket, although she still thought about him, especially alone at night in her cold bed. She had seen him occasionally in Gimmerton, and he was kind enough to wave or nod, although he never spoke.

The pain and despair that had been at the forefront of his countenance after Catherine's death had receded into a fixed hardness. He did not look unhealthy, nor did he look particularly unhappy, but the hurt was there, still, around the eyes, many lines webbing the corners of his lids, his beard remaining, but blossoming with flecks of gray. If sorrow was there, he seemed intent on not showing it to any human.

"God! What a lovely, charming thing!" Heathcliff exclaimed, as the pair descended from the carriage. "Damn my soul, Nelly, but that's worse than I expected—and the devil knows I was not sanguine!"

Linton trembled and seemed as bewildered as a child, as he stared at his grim, sneering father, and clung to Nelly with growing trepidation.

"Thou art thy mother's child entirely," said Heathcliff. "Where is my share in thee?"

Linton hid his face on Nelly's shoulder and wept.

"None of that nonsense," said Heathcliff. "We're not going to hurt thee."

"I hope you will be kind to the boy," said Nelly.

"I'll be *very* kind to him," he said, laughing. "My son is prospective owner of your place, and I should not wish him to die till I was certain of being his successor. And thus I have a room upstairs, furnished for him in handsome style; I've engaged a tutor; and I've ordered Hareton to obey him. I've arranged everything with a view to preserve the superior and gentleman in him, above his associates. I do regret, however, that he so little deserves the trouble. If I wished any blessing in the world, it was to find him a worthy object of pride, and I'm bitterly disappointed with the whey-faced whining wretch!"

When Cathy turned seventeen, the household, as usual on her birthday, never manifested any signs of rejoicing, because it was, also, the anniversary of her mother's death. Edgar invariably spent that day alone in the library and walked, at dusk, as far as the Gimmerton Church graveyard, where he would frequently prolong his stay beyond midnight.

Cathy persuaded Nelly to go for a ride on horseback to the edge of the moors, where a colony of game was settled, to see if they had made their nests yet.

It wasn't long before Cathy galloped ahead, inspired by the beautiful spring day. Nelly relished seeing Cathy's delight, her golden ringlets flying loose behind, and her bright cheeks, as soft and pure in its bloom as a wild rose, and her eyes radiant with untainted pleasure. She was a happy creature, an angel. It was a pity that the direction she headed toward would cloud this contentment.

Nelly lightly kicked her horse to catch up, after realizing Cathy was headed in the direction of Wuthering Heights. In the distance, she beheld that a couple of persons on horseback had already detained her, one of whom was clearly Heathcliff himself, and, after closer approach, she ascertained that the other was Hareton. Nelly spurred her horse to go faster.

Cathy had been caught in the act of plundering, or, at least, hunting out the nests of the grouse. The Heights were Heathcliff's land, and he was reproving the poacher.

"I've neither taken any eggs, nor found any," she said. "But Papa told me there were quantities up here, and I simply wished to see them."

"And who is this *Papa*?" demanded Heathcliff, mimicking her tone.

"I thought you did not know me," she replied boldly, "or you wouldn't have spoken to me that way."

Something about the sauciness of her tone, and the bold tilt upward of her chin, made Heathcliff wonder if it could possibly be his beloved's daughter. Then it was confirmed absolutely, like a sudden clap of thunder, when his gaze wandered up from her chin and rested on the flashing dark eyes of Catherine.

Nelly galloped up to them, fully out of breath, just as Cathy added proudly, "My papa is Mr. Linton of Thrushcross Grange."

If only the eyes were there to look at, thought Heathcliff, without the fair skin of Edgar and the yellow hair of Isabella, he might have a brief moment of joy.

"You suppose your papa is highly esteemed and respected then?" he asked, sarcastically.

"And what are you?" inquired Cathy, while gazing curiously at the man standing behind him, admiring the younger lad's strength and bulk, although he appeared rough and awkward. "Is that your son?"

"No, that man is not my son," answered Heathcliff. "But I have one, and if you accompany us to my house, you will be able to meet him and have proper rest before your return home."

"Miss Cathy," interjected Nelly. "We really must get back."

"Why?" asked Cathy. "I'm tired of riding."

"Hold your tongue, Nelly," said Heathcliff. "It will be a treat for her to look in on us. Hareton, go forward with the lass. You can ride with me, Nelly."

Cathy, delighted, instantly complied and joined Hareton.

"Heathcliff, it's very wrong," said Nelly as they took up the rear. "You know you mean no good. And there she'll meet Linton, and all will be told to Edgar, as soon as we return, and I shall have the blame."

"I want her to see Linton," he answered. "He's looking less sickly these days; it's not often he's fit to be seen. And we'll soon persuade her to keep the visit a secret—where is the harm of it?"

"The harm of it is that her father would hate me if he found out and I am convinced you have a bad design."

"My design is as honest as possible. I'll inform you of its whole scope: that the two cousins may fall in love, and get married. I'm acting generously towards your master. Cathy would be provided for, at once, as joint successor with Linton."

"If Linton died," answered Nelly, "and I know he is often sickly, then Cathy would be the heir."

"There is no clause in the will to secure it so," said Heathcliff. "His property would go to me."

"You're diabolical!" returned Nelly. "I'm resolved she shall never approach your house with me again!" They reached the gate.

After Cathy and Hareton dismounted, the young lass held her

reins out to Hareton. "Secure my horse," she said, as if he was one of the stable boys at the Grange.

Hareton stood with his hands in his pockets, too awkward to speak, though he looked as if he did not relish the request.

"Did you not hear me?" she said. "Shall I tell your master?"

Hareton grew black as a thundercloud, but turned away, as he could not stand such a steady gaze from her eyes.

Heathcliff looked on with amusement. Cathy turned to Nelly and said, "Mustn't this wicked creature do as I ask him?"

"I'll see thee damned, before I be *thy* servant!" growled the lad.

"You'll see me *what?*" asked Cathy in surprise.

"Damned—thou saucy witch!" he replied, then stalked off to secure his own horse.

Tears of indignation sprung to Cathy's eyes. Nelly rested a comforting hand upon her shoulder and said, "Though Mr. Hareton, there, be not the master's son, he's your cousin and is not here to serve you."

"*He* my cousin!" cried Cathy. "Nelly, don't say such a thing, that I bear relationship with someone so vulgar and crass."

Heathcliff directed the pair into the house and said, "He's the son of your mother's brother."

Linton stood on the hearth. He had grown taller since Nelly had seen him last. His features were pretty yet, and his eye and complexion brighter.

"Now who is that, Cathy?" asked Heathcliff. "Can you tell?"

"Is he my cousin Linton?" she cried, immediately drawn to the resemblance to her father. She stepped forward and kissed him fervently, and they gazed at each other with wonder.

Cathy had reached her full height; her figure was both plump and slender, sturdy as steel, and her whole aspect sparkling with health and spirits. Linton's looks and movements were very languid, and his form exceedingly slight; but there was a grace in his manner that mitigated these defects, and rendered him not un-pleasing.

After exchanging numerous remarks of fondness with Linton, Cathy went to Heathcliff, who lingered by the door, pretending to observe objects outside, when his main concern were the objects that lay within.

"So you are my uncle, then!" she cried, reaching up to salute him. "I thought I liked you, though you were cross, at first. Why don't you visit at the Grange with Linton? To live all these years such close neighbors, and never see us, is odd."

"Mr. Linton has a prejudice against me," answered Heathcliff. "We quarreled at one time of our lives, with unchristian ferocity. Therefore, you should not mention coming here, or he'll put a veto on your visits altogether."

"Why did you quarrel?" asked Cathy, considerably crestfallen.

"He thought me too poor to wed his sister," answered Heath-cliff.

Nelly shot him a most peevish look.

"That's wrong!" said Cathy. "But Linton and I have no share in your quarrel. I'll not come here, then, he shall come to the Grange."

"It will be too far for me," murmured Linton, "to walk four miles would kill me."

Heathcliff launched toward his son a glance of bitter contempt.

"I'm sure my plan has its faults," he whispered to Nelly, as they stepped aside. "Cathy will soon discover Linton's value and send him to the devil. Now, if it had been Hareton, he could walk twenty miles and back without any preponderance of perspiration. I'd have loved the lad had he been someone else. But he's surely safe from *her* love."

Linton became absorbed in stoking the fire and Cathy seemed bored.

"Confound the vapid thing, he never looks at her—Linton!"

"Yes, Father."

"Have you nothing to show your cousin, not even a rabbit or a weasel's nest? Take her into the garden."

"Wouldn't you rather sit here?" asked Linton, addressing Cathy with fatigue.

"I don't know," she replied, casting a longing look to the door, eager to be active.

Heathcliff went to the kitchen window and called for Hareton, who was in the yard.

Hareton entered the house. The young man had been washing himself, as was visible by the glow on his cheeks, and his wetted hair.

"Is he not a handsome lad?" said Heathcliff.

Cathy didn't answer. She agreed he was, but was still smarting from his recent outburst.

"Here, Hareton! Go with her around the farm. And behave like a gentleman, mind! Don't use any bad words, and don't stare when the young lady is not looking at you, and be ready to hide your face when she is. And, when you speak, say your words slowly, and keep your hands out of your pockets."

The pair walked out the door. Cathy took a sly look at Hareton, expressing some admiration. Hareton kept his eyes to the ground, though he longed to examine her more fully.

"I've tied his tongue," observed Heathcliff. "He'll not venture a single syllable. Nelly, you recollect me at his age—nay, some years younger—did I ever look so stupid, so naïve?"

"Worse," she replied, "with even more sullenness."

"I've pleasure in him, though!" he continued. "But it is merely the beginning of what he shall suffer, as he'll never be able to emerge from his coarseness and ignorance. I've taught him to scorn everything beyond the physical as silly and weak. Don't you think Hindley would be proud of his son as I am of mine? But there's this difference: One is gold put to the use of paving stones; and the other is tin polished to ape the service of silver. And the best of it is, Hareton is damnably fond of me! You'll own that I've outmatched Hindley. If the dead villain should rise from the grave to abuse me for his offspring's wrongs, I should have the fun of seeing the said offspring fight him back!"

Heathcliff chuckled a fiendish laugh. Nelly remained silent, sad for all the pain that had been exchanged by those who had lived under this roof.

Heathcliff looked at Linton. "Get up, you idle boy!" he exclaimed. "Away after them. Make sure her attentions fall on the proper cousin."

Linton gathered his energies and left the hearth.

He caught up to Hareton and Cathy at the gates of Wuthering Heights. He heard Cathy inquiring from her unsociable attendant, what was that inscription carved into the frame?

Hareton stared up, and scratched his head like a true clown.

"It's some damnable writing," he answered. "I cannot read it."

"Can't read it?" cried Cathy. "I can read it . . . it's English . . . but I want to know why it is there."

Linton giggled; the first appearance of mirth he had exhibited.

"He does not know his letters," he said to his cousin. "Could you believe in the existence of such a colossal dunce?"

"Is he simple . . . not right?" asked Cathy. "I've questioned him twice now, and each time he looked so stupid I think he does not understand me; I can hardly understand *him*!"

Linton laughed again, and glanced at Hareton tauntingly, enjoying this even more after hearing his father's praise for someone not his son.

"There's nothing the matter, but laziness, is there, Earnshaw?" Linton asked. "My cousin fancies you an idiot... There you experience the consequences of scorning 'book-larning,' as you would say in your frightful Yorkshire pronunciation."

Cathy and Linton broke into a noisy fit of merriment.

"If you weren't more of a lass than a lad," thundered Hareton, "I'd fell thee this minute, you pitiful weakling!"

His face burned with mingling rage and mortification as he retreated from the gates and left the couple alone.

Heathcliff, having stepped into the yard to overhear the conversation, smiled when he saw Hareton go, and rejoiced over the flippant pair's continued chatter and giggles, taking special notice that their hands intertwined as they strolled about the property.

He let his fine spirits carry him through to dinner, served not too long after Cathy and Nelly had returned to the Grange. Both Linton and Hareton looked at each other with a wary bewilderment over Heathcliff's suddenly hearty chatter, and raucous laughter as he recounted pleasant stories of his childhood, while Hareton's grandfather was alive, and his father was in college. He held on to this mood as long as he could; it had been a while since he had felt this good. For the children were finally of age to consider marriage, and the seeds of his plan had been firmly planted this afternoon, with hope of quick germination after extracting a promise from Cathy that she would visit Linton again tomorrow. It would send Edgar instantly to the grave to see Cathy married to Heathcliff's own son. And he would surely turn over in that very same resting place, if the sickly Linton didn't last and Thrushcross Grange passed into his full possession.

However, Heathcliff's joyful spirits didn't last very long. He couldn't help spending another restless night, this one full of haunting dreams of times *after* Old Earnshaw's death, when Hindley had returned to ridicule and beat him, and Catherine had knifed him with bitter rejection by embracing the noble gentleman Edgar and his upper-class manners...dreams so chillingly familiar to what he had witnessed today.

Chapter Twenty-Seven

"Papa!" exclaimed Cathy, the very next day, and to Nelly's great chagrin. "Guess whom I saw yesterday, during my ride on the moors?"

Edgar bestowed a glance of darts and arrows on Nelly, who quickly left the room.

Cathy gave a faithful account of her excursion and its consequences, finishing up with "Why did you conceal that my lovely cousin, Linton, was so near the neighborhood?...Because you dislike Mr. Heathcliff I discovered."

"Then you believe I care more for my own feelings than yours, Cathy?" he said. "No, it was not because I disliked Mr. Heathcliff, but because Mr. Heathcliff dislikes me and is a most diabolical man, delighting to wrong and ruin those he hates. An acquaintance with your cousin will surely lead to disaster...I meant to explain this, sometime, as you grew older, and I'm sorry I delayed it!"

"But Mr. Heathcliff was quite cordial, Papa," observed Cathy. "And *he* didn't object to the cousins seeing each other. Why will you not forgive him for marrying Aunt Isabella?"

"It's far more than that, my sweet daughter."

Edgar gave a hasty sketch of Heathcliff's evil conduct toward Isabella, and the manner in which Wuthering Heights became his property. He could not bear to discourse long on the additional topic of Cathy's mother, for though he spoke little of her, he still felt the same horror, and detestation of his ancient enemy, that had occupied his heart ever since Catherine's death. He did conclude with "Your mother might have been living yet, if it had not been for him! Heathcliff is a murderer!"

Edgar's eyes swelled with tears and Cathy rose and kissed her father, but he seemed inconsolable.

That night in bed, Cathy cried herself to sleep. She was shocked at this new view of human nature she had been presented with. Having been used to slight acts of disobedience that could be repented on the day they were committed, she was amazed at the blackness of spirit that could brood on, and cover revenge for years, and deliberately prosecute its plans without a visitation to remorse. She was also sad that she would not visit Linton tomorrow and he expected to see her again, and he would be so disappointed, and would wait for her, but she would not appear.

It was weeks before Cathy got up the nerve to take a ride by herself, without Nelly or a servant. She knew she shouldn't, but she headed to the southwest, toward the moors, telling herself that she just wanted some fresh air, and perhaps a view of the Heights.

And of course she ventured too close and a rider soon came to meet her and cried in his deep voice, "Ho, Miss Linton. I'm so glad to meet you. I have wandered these moors the many weeks since you visited, wondering why you didn't keep your promise to return, and hoping to compel you to appear once more at our doorstep."

"I shan't speak to you, Mr. Heathcliff!" answered Cathy. "Papa says you are a wicked man, and you hate both him and me; Nelly says the same."

"That is nothing to the purpose," said Heathcliff. "I don't hate my son, I suppose, and it is concerning him that I demand your attention. He has grown deeply despondent and sickly, expecting a visit from you, sworn, but not fulfilled. He is in earnest—in love—really. As true as I live he's dying for you—breaking his heart at your fickleness, not figuratively, but actually."

"How can you lie so glaringly!" responded Cathy.

"I swear Linton is bedridden by grief and disappointment. Follow me and you will see for yourself."

He accompanied her to the house and let her enter on her own, as he secured the horses.

"Is that you, Cathy?" said Linton, raising his head from the arm of the great chair in which he reclined. "No—don't kiss me. It takes my breath—dear me! Papa assured me you would call, but it has been so long I feared he spoke not the truth. Will you shut the door, if you please? It's so cold!"

Linton had a tiresome cough, and looked feverish and ill, so she did not rebuke his tone, rather she immediately closed the door, stirred the ashes to raise the fire, and brought him a tumbler of water.

"Are you glad to see me?" she asked, and was pleased to detect his smile.

"Yes, I am. It's something to hear a voice like yours. I've had to endure that brute Hareton laughing at me—Father as well—I hate them both—they are odious beings." He drank the water. "But I *have* been vexed you wouldn't come. Papa said it was because you despised me."

"Despise you?" responded Cathy. "Next to Papa and Nelly, I love you better than anybody living. Though I don't love Mr. Heathcliff." She stroked Linton's long, soft hair. "If I could only get Papa's consent, I'd spend half my time with you—pretty Linton! I wish you were my brother!"

"And then you would like me as well as your father?" observed Linton, cheerfully. "But Papa says you would love me better than him, and all the world, if you were really my wife—so I'd rather that!"

"I should never love anybody better than Papa," she returned gravely. "And people hate their wives, sometimes, but not their sisters and brothers."

Linton denied that people ever hate their wives, but Cathy affirmed they did, and instanced his own father's aversion to her aunt. She could not stop her tongue and soon all that she knew from her talk with her father was out.

Linton, much irritated, asserted her relation was false.

"Papa told me and Papa does not tell falsehoods!" she answered pertly.

"*My* papa scorns yours!" cried Linton. "He calls him a sneaking fool!"

"Yours is a wicked man," retorted Cathy, "and you are very naughty to repeat what he says. He must be wicked, to have made Aunt Isabella leave him as she did!"

"She didn't leave him," said Linton. "You shan't contradict me!"

"She did!"

"Well, your mother hated your father," exclaimed Linton, "and loved mine!"

"You little liar! I hate you now," she panted, and her face grew red with passion.

"She did! She did!" sang Linton.

Cathy, beside herself, gave the chair a violent push, and caused him to fall against one arm. He was immediately seized by a suffocating cough that soon ended his triumph.

It lasted so long that it frightened Cathy, aghast at the mischief she had done.

"I'm so sorry I hurt you, Linton!" she said at length. "But *I* couldn't have been hurt by that little push and I had no idea that you could, either—you're not much, are you, Linton? Don't let me go home thinking I've done you harm! Answer, speak to me."

"You struck me!"

"I did not!"

"You've hurt me so," he murmured, "that I shall lie awake all night, choking with this cough! Leave me to my agony!"

Near tears, Cathy rose, but she could not bear to see him suffer. She went to him, he in recline, she on her knees by his face.

"Must I go?" asked Cathy dolefully, bending over him. "Do you want me to go, Linton?"

"You can't alter what you've done," he replied pettishly, shrinking from her, "unless you alter it for the worse by teasing me into a fever!"

She leaned even closer, looking into his eyes. He did not look away. She kissed him gently on the cheek, then again, then again; then she kissed him on the mouth, for both their very first romantic kiss. But Cathy seemed to have the precocious instinct of her mother, as she whispered, "I think there are ways to tease you into a fever that you will enjoy." She kissed him fully and felt his mouth open to hers, and their tongues touch.

When she broke away, he moaned, "Oh, I do love you, Cathy. You are all I have. I feel no love here."

She stood. "Then can I visit again?"

"Tomorrow, please."

"I'll see when I can get away. I must depart now. Nelly will be suspicious."

She kissed him one more time. She said, "I love you, too."

She took a moment to fix her hair and put on her riding boots. She was a little out of breath. So much had happened these past few weeks, from meeting two cousins, and feeling so strongly connected to one of them. With the other, she didn't know what to feel. They seemed to have absolutely nothing in common, yet she could not prevent a certain curiosity about him. All of it made her feel as if childish feelings were in the past, and before her awaited the pleasures and emotions of a young woman.

She was surprised when she exited the house that her horse was ready for her, tied near the door. She looked around the yard, but did not see anyone. She rode home.

Heathcliff arose from the shadows, quite pleased with the pleasantries that had been exchanged in the house. He walked to the servants' quarters and came upon Hareton, who was pressed against a window, still looking into the room where Linton and Cathy had kissed.

Startled, Hareton pulled back. Heathcliff saw a darkness upon his countenance, which was not unusual, but, what jolted him like a goring from a bull was the look in Hareton's eyes, moist and pink for the very first time, a look he had never seen before.

Hareton was not quite as tall as Heathcliff, but he rose to his full height so they could almost stare face-to-face. Before departing to the barn, Hareton spit fully onto the ground between them, hitting both the stone and Heathcliff's boot.

That night, after all the household was deep asleep, Heathcliff got out of bed. Not a moment of sleep had visited him as he lay restless with eyes wide open. He ventured to the attic floor, where there was a large window that overlooked the moors. He pulled back the shutters, opened the window wide, inhaled a hearty taste of the wind. Though not quite full, there was enough sliver of moon to illuminate the way to Black Rock Cragge. He had not visited there since the night he spent at his beloved's grave site. He spoke aloud, his voice just barely a whisper.

"Please forgive me, Catherine, for it has been too many years since I've ventured to our place. Since the last, I have taken so little interest in my daily life. I hardly remember to eat or drink. And now these objects have come together at once and I feel a sense of purpose again, a purpose I know you would not approve of, but one that arouses my passion and brings me back to life. Should not all of life's passions be fulfilled? What else is there for me? Any sense of your presence invokes only maddening sensations that seem impossible to fulfill. If I cannot discharge the passions that will join me with you in heaven, then I must fulfill those that will bring me to hell! And I will take pleasure in it, mind! As I have done these days seeing my child and yours move closer to an unholy union that will surely destroy Edgar and add the precious Thrushcross Grange to my holdings. And see me true, I am immovable from this path. But just today, young Hareton, the son of your brother that I have reared in my image, showed me the other image he does possess. In his eyes, I saw the ghost of you, my immortal love, the spitting likeness of you and your pain. And that look challenged my right, my degradation, my pride, and my anguish. Well, I am here to tell you tonight that I will not be swayed! If our separation is indeed eternal, then I must find my earthly pleasures where I can. With my hard constitution, I am sure I shall remain above ground till there is scarcely a black hair on my head. Allow me my revenge! For miserable revenge is more life than misery alone!"

Heathcliff shuttered the window tight, returned to his chamber, relaxed easily upon his bed. He had witnessed the further blossoming of a love between Cathy and Linton, one that needed less of his heavy hand than he had thought. But why should he be surprised? Linton possessed the cultured charm of his uncle, and damn if he didn't resemble him so greatly, it was hard, sometimes, to look the lad square in the face. And Cathy, grown and nurtured under the wing of the Lintons, surely retained their shallow interest in the properness of the exterior, without concern for what lay deep in the soul. How poetic and perfect that the blood of those cursed by him would lead to an even more permanent damnation of the two families.

On this night Heathcliff had no restless dreams, but he fell into a deep, peaceful slumber.

Chapter Twenty-Eight

Cathy looked forward to the chance to visit the Heights again. She delicately sidestepped Nelly's inquiries, and her papa seemed preoccupied as usual with morose thoughts and his weak disposition.

A new horse named Minny had arrived at the Grange, just days after her last visit, and it was a perfect opportunity for Cathy, who offered to give the mare her daily exercise. She headed straight to the Heights.

She trotted up to their garden, did not see anyone, so turned around to the back. There she was met by Hareton, who greeted her kindly and offered to take the bridle.

"Not so concerned are you now," said Cathy, "about being displayed as the servant?"

"I offer assistance as your cousin."

He patted Minny's neck and said she was a bonny beast.

She admired his ease with the animal and the way the mare took to him. But the sting of her last meeting with this ruffian had not departed.

"Leave my horse alone," she said, "or else she will kick you."

"It wouldn't much hurt if it did." He surveyed its legs with a smile.

Cathy had half a mind to make the horse try.

Hareton moved off to open the door, and, as he raised the latch, he looked up at the inscription above, and said, with a mix of awkwardness and pride:

"Miss Cathy! I can read this now."

"Wonderful," she exclaimed. "Pray let us hear you—you are grown clever!"

He spelled and drawled over by syllables, the name—

"Hareton Earnshaw."

"And the figures?"

"I cannot tell them yet."

"Oh, you dunce!" she said, laughing heartily at his failure.

He stared, a scowl gathering over his eyes. He had promised himself to make an effort this time to be sociable, like Linton, but this lass rode around with a permanent stick up her arse. He turned to go toward the stables.

She watched him walk, appreciative of his broad shoulders, and narrow waist, the muscular flex in the seat of his pants as he strode like an athlete. His health, vigor, physical presence, and strong features were so much more pleasing than Linton's.

"I've come to see my cousin," she called after him.

He turned, looked at her defiantly. She averted her eyes. "My cousin Linton."

"The mouse is asleep in his chamber. It's a wonder even when he wakes up to eat."

Hareton turned away again.

"I'm a bit tired from my ride, do you think you might escort me inside so I could rest...Perhaps Linton will wake up." She smiled as brightly as she could, hoping to make amends.

He reluctantly returned, helped secure Minny, and took her inside to the parlor. Cathy sat in a chair. Hareton sat in another one that was a distance from hers. He remained silent. He didn't know which Cathy had come into the house: the saucy witch with a sharp, unforgiving tongue, or the one who had just smiled at him like a sun breaking through storm clouds?

Their silence was awkward and finally Cathy got up to look upon a shelf of books and peruse their titles. While holding her frock, she stretched to reach one, but it was too high up. Her cousin, after watching her endeavors awhile, at last summoned the courage to help her, reaching for the book she desired.

She thanked him politely and returned to her seat. She began to read silently, but had difficulty concentrating with his eyes so heavily upon her.

Finally, Hareton said, "Do you think you might read to me aloud?"

She nodded.

He eagerly pulled his chair next to hers.

She read to him, a history of early wars. She could have been reading recipes from a cookbook for all he cared; the melodic tone of her voice, the careful way she formed her words, completely enchanted him. He had not anticipated such pleasures from hearing a lass read aloud. He had not anticipated what he felt since Cathy had first crossed his path: shame from her scorn and hope for her approval.

"Do you think?" he muttered, eyes cast down.

She stopped her reading, looked at him, but he could not complete his thoughts. "Yes, I think," she said sarcastically.

He turned away in his chair. He said, "You know it is easy for the likes of you to lord your airs and language over me. I am an uneducated brute. But I can tell you, were we riding together on the moors, or farming together in the fields, I would not make you feel so stupid, though I am expert in both."

She choked her first instinct to respond sharply.

"Do I think what?" she asked, kindly.

He turned back to her. "Do you think you could teach me to read?"

"I suppose." He brightened. "If there was time. If there was time there are many things I would like to do. But it's not easy. I can't just snap my fingers and make a scholar of you."

"I'm the hardest worker you'll ever come across."

She smiled. "I'll consider it."

She continued with her reading and he continued to be mesmerized, perhaps too much so, for as his attention became completely centered by all degrees on the beauty of her voice and words, he also couldn't help focusing on her thick, silky curls. And, perhaps, not quite awake to what he did, but attracted like a child to a candle, at last, he proceeded from staring to touching. He put out his hand and stroked one curl, as gently as if she were a bird. He might have stuck a knife into her neck, she started around in such a taking.

"Get away, this moment! How dare you touch me!" she cried, in a tone of disgust. "I can't endure you. I'll go upstairs and fetch Linton if you dare touch me again!"

Hareton recoiled, looking as foolish as he could. Although his feelings were mostly uncultivated, his sensitivity was not. It bewildered him that after being immune to so many years of abuse from Heathcliff, he let everything this little wretch did wound him like a bird shot in flight. A physical argument was the only mode he had of balancing the account and repaying its effects to the inflicter.

He tore the book from her hand and tossed it into the fire, causing an instinctive cower from his abrupt action. Still unsatisfied, he took a handful of the books off the shelf and bid them join their companion in flame with one violent toss.

"Yes, that's all the good such a creature as you can get from them!" cried Cathy, regaining her courage, watching the conflagration with indignant eyes.

"How foolish was I to ask for the kindness of reading and education!" he exclaimed. "But you'd *better* hold your tongue, now," he added fiercely, "before I remove it!"

Although fearful, she did not wish to show cowardice to this scoundrel who was so much beneath her. She stood, trembling, and said, "I curse your abject soul!"

It was as if she had raised a hand and struck a blow across his face. He did not know whether it was his illiteracy, or the force of her verbal slap that left him unable to find the words to parry her off-putting passion, yet he remained thoroughly indignant that this lass would curse him in his own home, and stepped forward, eager to strike this devil to the floor.

Instead an alternative instinct overtook him and he pulled her close with all the strength of his powerful arms. The crush of her body against his chest took her breath away, and her eyes widened with emotion while he stared down at her. He leaned forward and kissed her hard on the mouth.

Sometime during the exchange of loud threats rising from the first floor, Linton had been crudely awakened from his slumber. He struggled to gain full consciousness, hearing only silence now, wondering whether he had conjured this forceful argument in his dreams, and was soon overcome with the chronic cough that had plagued him since childhood.

Cathy fought Hareton with her fists. She kicked him with her feet. But his kiss would not abate. This was the thrill Hareton had so enviously observed through the window as Cathy and Linton had kissed. It made the air sing around him. It conjured elegant words in his mind that he wanted to shout to express his joy. He never wanted this to stop!

So overcome with feeling from his passion, the fire in his lips, the sensation of being swept up by power she felt helpless against, she yielded, at first reluctantly, then ever so willingly. Her arms couldn't help reaching around his strong back, which increased the intensity of his embrace. The feel of his broad shoulders sent shivers through her body. She opened her mouth and delighted him with the touch of her tongue.

With difficulty, Linton got out of his bed and stumbled toward the door, still trying to clear the cobwebs from his brain.

The couple's passion continued, and Cathy found cause to caress his back and moan his name, but their lips were never long parted. Hearing this beautiful lass call out to him inspired an uncontrolled frenzy, and he pulled her as tight as his strength would allow, and she felt the full and authoritative pressure of his well-endowed manhood against her belly.

Linton stood at the banister, for a moment speechless at the incongruous sight below him.

With tremendous force of will, Cathy broke free, and—partly because of this coarseness he had exhibited, partly because she needed something to break the spell and curtail the raw emotions streaming through her body—she slapped him hard across the face. She ran quickly out the door before he had a chance to grasp her again and render her helpless to one as fine as he.

"You ignorant ape!" shouted Linton as he rushed down the stairs. "How dare you force yourself on the woman I love!" He approached Hareton as if prepared to wield a blow, but once eye level with the older fellow's imposing chest, he muttered, "If she did not need my comfort, I would exact her revenge." He hurried through the door after her.

It was certainly not the pain of the slap, but the force of Hareton's confusion that rendered him speechless and moistened his eyes, something he could not ever remember happening before witnessing the recent intimacy between Cathy and Linton. The stupid words spouting from Linton's lips were of no consequence and a weasel such as he was not worth the effort of retaliation. But how could such a wee lass have so much power over his feelings? What did he do that caused her to go from love to hate so quickly? He retreated to his room in back of the kitchen, promising himself he would not let the moistness form full tears.

Out in the yard, in between coughs, Linton called out to Cathy as she prepared her horse to depart. Seeing her in distress now, witnessing her in the arms of someone as common as Hareton, made him realize how much he cared for Cathy, and how much she needed him to stay steady on a proper life path. She stopped abruptly when she heard him, and they ran to each other and embraced.

"My love," cooed Linton. "I saw what transpired in the parlor." The news brought an instant blush to Cathy's cheeks. "This cousin of yours is but a beast, imposing his crudeness on one so fragile, so much nobler, so reluctant even to be near a man with the heart of a servant and the intelligence of a stone." Cathy felt tempted to come to Hareton's defense, but was afraid she might reveal the role she played in such bewildering events, a role Linton was clearly oblivious to.

And what role had she played? She remembered reluctance, but she also remembered the exquisite yielding to the sweet embrace and tender kisses of Hareton, and all the confusion that went with it. But what fire he did inspire! Not only had no one ever kissed her that way, but no one had ever looked at her in such a manner, as if she were the only star in a perfect universe. How intimidating to inspire such a physical reaction in Hareton as well. A lady should not be exposed to such primitiveness. Yet all his touches remained powerfully vivid in her mind, his arms securing her against him, the soothing heat of his lips, even his defined presence against her belly.

She took Linton by the hand. They walked. In his presence she felt comforted, for she understood everything about him, and all seemed familiar and safe. She enjoyed his kisses, and there was nothing confusing about them. Something about Hareton made her feel older than she saw herself . . . and this was both exhilarating and alarming.

Hareton watched the couple from his window. Seeing them stroll, seeing Cathy take Linton by the hand, brought forth his full complement of tears. Heathcliff was right. He had hammered into Hareton since he was little that he was an urchin, someone coarse and brutal . . . and Hareton had proved it once again. Yet he could not forget the passion Cathy had inspired, her kisses breaking down the last barriers and forcing him to admit that he possessed a fully formed love for her. When she had called out his name, his heart had soared, and along with his love, he had felt hope. But even now, as he recalled their moment, and watched Cathy in the yard, his ardor surfaced once again. What betrayal his body had imposed upon him . . . just another illustration of why he did not deserve someone as beautiful and regal as Cathy Linton.

The pair outside the window stopped suddenly and faced each other. Linton leaned down to plant a kiss on Cathy. Hareton did not notice the slight turn of her face that caused the kiss to press against her cheek instead of her lips. He was too blinded by a misery that left him emptier than he had ever felt before.

Chapter Twenty-Nine

Cathy rode with full gallop all the way back to the Grange, as her emotions continued to pound her thoughts, like Minny's hooves against the dirt. Her mind had been so much occupied with Linton, and now Hareton had wedged himself in, becoming the uninvited guest at a private gathering. She had never even dreamed that one could be kissed like that. Yet...he had made her feel so dirty. Was not Hareton the type of person, both inside and out, who could never be completely clean, no matter how hard a scrubbing he received?

As she entered the house, both her father and Nelly were there to greet her, not warmly. Nelly could not hide her frown. Papa looked pale and desolate as he sat near the fire, in his rocking chair, blanket covering his legs. Their looks of reproach were so strong, she was convinced they knew of her clandestine visits, and felt no benefit could be had from denying that she had been disobedient.

She lowered her eyes in shame, her affection for her father still the chief sentiment in her heart.

Edgar spoke without anger; he spoke in the deep tenderness of one who feared leaving his treasure amid perils and foes, and that he was, perhaps, too weak to stop her, but could only offer the strength of his words to guide his daughter.

"Tell me, sincerely, what you think of Linton," he requested. "Is he changed for the better, or is there a prospect for improvement, as he grows a man?"

"He's very delicate," said Cathy, "but he does not resemble his father in any way. As a fact, he is near spitting image of you."

Incredulous, Edgar looked at Nelly, who nodded her concurrence.

"Do you love him?" he asked.

"I know I do, but I cannot tell what kind of love it is."

"If Miss Cathy had the misfortune to marry him," said Nelly, "he would not be beyond her control, unless she were extremely and foolishly indulgent. However, if you open your doors, and your heart, you will have plenty of time to get acquainted with him, and see whether he would suit her."

Edgar sighed. With difficulty he stood and walked toward the window. Cathy rushed to his side and he welcomed her assistance. He looked out toward the Gimmerton Church graveyard. It was a misty afternoon, but the sun shone dimly, and they could just distinguish the two fir trees in the yard, and the sparely scattered gravestones.

"I've prayed often," said Edgar, "for the approach of what is coming and now I begin to shrink, and fear it."

"Hush, Father," said Cathy, "you are just prone to a fever now and then. With the warmth of spring coming, we will soon be riding together."

"I had started to think that the memory of the hour I came down that glen a bridegroom would be less sweet than the anticipation that I would soon be laid in its hollow."

This time Nelly was about to voice protest, when Edgar added, "But I've been very happy with you, my little Cathy. Through winter nights and summer days you have been a hope at my side.

But I've been as happy musing by myself among those stones, under that old church—lying, through the long June evenings, on the green mound of your mother's grave, and wishing, yearning, for the time when I might lie beneath it."

He began to wheeze. Cathy and Nelly helped him back to the chair, where he sat heavily.

"What can I do for you, Cathy?" he asked. "I do not want to leave you unattended. I do not care one moment for Linton being Heathcliff's son, nor for your cousin taking you from me, if he could console you after I'm gone. I'd not care that Heathcliff gained his ends, and triumphed in robbing me of my last blessing. But if Linton is unworthy—only a feeble tool to his father—then I will not abandon you to him!"

Cathy was full of such emotion she could not speak.

"You will be here to guide her," said Nelly. "And if we should lose you—which may God forbid—under his providence, I'll stand her friend and counselor to the last. Miss Cathy is a good girl; I don't fear that she will go willfully wrong and people who do their duty are always finally rewarded."

Cathy showered his face with kisses and murmured deep words of love. It seemed to give him strength and he rose again. He grasped her arm this time and led her for a walk about the grounds, experiencing the joy of nature he had shared so often with her mother. For a moment, there was deep regret over allowing his obsession with Catherine to deny full attention to Cathy. Yet the lass seemed to love him fully and that filled him with great comfort.

To Cathy's inexperienced notions, this look about her father was a sign of convalescence and she grasped his arm even tighter with much girlish delight and then his cheek flushed and his eyes brightened even more, and she felt sure of his recovery.

EMILY Brontë and I. J. Miller

Not so Nelly, who wiped away a tear from her eye, as she watched father and daughter stroll among bud-filled bushes that had not yet bloomed to flowers.

The next morning, Cathy mounted Minny and made the now familiar ride to the Heights. She was pleased that her father was willing to meet Linton and she was glad to deliver the invitation personally. She thought for sure, that once Papa saw Linton for the fine, educated gentleman he was, he would be comforted if a union was, indeed, formed.

Cathy couldn't imagine what Papa would think of Hareton— one who, in his own distorted vanity, imagined himself to be as accomplished as Linton because he could spell his own name! And was marvelously discomfited that she didn't think the same.

She hoped she did not meet Hareton, but at the same time she did, if only to prove that the brief hold he had over her was simply the imagination of a girl set free, without the proper refinement and perspective of a mature young woman.

A stable hand secured her horse. Cathy asked him who was about. He told her that Hareton and Linton were on the grounds, and that the master was in the fields and would be back this afternoon. Cathy was pleased she would not see Heathcliff. She worried that after the stories she had heard from Papa and Nelly that she would fall ill just from the sight of him.

She entered the house. Hareton was in the kitchen. Linton was on the great armchair, half asleep. Once Harcton saw her, he quit the room directly. Rude beast, thought Cathy, glad for the privacy.

Linton took her in fully and she smiled down on him, brightening his face.

"You are so much happier than I am," said Linton. "Before

departing this morn, Papa talked incessantly about my defects, my inability to express my feelings fully towards you. He shows enough scorn of me to make it natural I should doubt myself. And then I feel so cross and bitter. I *am* worthless!"

"You are not what you believe, nor what he tells you," said Cathy. "You have a good heart and a true soul."

"Oh, Cathy, if I might be as sweet, and as kind, and as good as you are, I would be as happy and healthy. I believe that your kindness has made me love you deeper, though I don't deserve your love."

Cathy took notice of his renewed paleness and the feeble way he had tried to lift his arm as he spoke. "Are you feeling worse?" she asked. "Has the doctor been here and given you the most unfortunate news?"

"No—better—I'm feeling better," he panted, "so much more so now that you have come." He trembled and retained her hand as if he needed its support, while his large blue eyes wandered timidly over her.

"Well then, I have wonderful news that will cheer you even more. Papa has consented to have you visit. He will be delighted to meet his nephew."

This proposal, unexpectedly, aroused Linton from his lethargy, and threw him into a strange state of agitation.

"I'm so tired," he proclaimed. "It's too hot for walking and I have no strength to ride."

"*Why* won't you be candid?" cried Cathy, her patience not sufficient to endure his enigmatic behavior. "Why cannot you say at once, you don't want me?"

Linton shivered, and glanced at her, half supplicating, half ashamed.

"My father is ill," she said, "yet he finds the strength to walk with me, and possesses the will to greet you at our home as a love of mine. Come! I desire an explanation."

"I am a worthless, cowardly wretch—I can't be scorned enough!"

"Nonsense!" cried Catherine, still in a passion. "Foolish, silly boy! Just speak what's on your mind or I shall return home."

With streaming face and an expression of agony, Linton threw his nerveless frame along the ground; he seemed convulsed with exquisite terror.

"Oh!" he sobbed. "I cannot bear it! Cathy, Cathy, I'm a traitor, too, and I dare not tell you why. But leave me and I shall be killed! You have said you loved me. You'll not go, then? Kind, sweet, good Cathy! And perhaps you *will* consent—and he'll let me die with you!"

On witnessing his intense anguish, Cathy stooped to raise him. The old feeling of indulgent tenderness overcame her vexation, and she grew thoroughly moved and alarmed.

"Consent to what?" she asked. "You wouldn't injure me, Linton, would you? You wouldn't let any enemy hurt me, if you could prevent it? Be calm and frank, and confess at once all that weighs on your heart."

"Consent to be my wife." Yes, this was what he wanted. He knew he loved her and she acknowledged loving him. It would save him from dying at his father's own hands. It would allow him to be the true *gentleman* he was destined to be, the *man* he was supposed to be. He knew that Cathy would never kiss her other cousin so willingly, but yet Hareton was so much more . . . *healthy* than he was. Such strength, such a physically imposing presence!

Moved by his passion, Cathy embraced him fully. "I do love you. And I do feel that we can have a proper life." She kissed him thoroughly, over and over on the face and neck. "I need Papa's approval and I need time to understand what is in my heart. I love you as a brother and I'm sure I can love you as a husband."

Her magnanimity provoked his tears; he wept wildly, kissing her face as well.

The front door burst open and Hareton stormed into the room. He advanced directly toward the couple, seized Linton by the arm, and swung him away.

"Get thee to thy own room!" he said in a voice almost inarticulate with passion, as his face swelled with fury. "Thou art a wolf who hides as a sheep."

A brute they all thought he was, then a brute he would be, for Hareton had witnessed firsthand the arm twisting and unrelenting manipulation Heathcliff had thrust upon Linton with so much intensity that the weakling preferred staying in bed over being in his father's company. Cathy might never want Hareton for more than entertainment, but he was convinced that a union between the two cousins would spell the same doom that had permeated their households as long as Hareton could remember.

Hareton looked toward Cathy. She could not tell whether he was going to strike, or sweep her into his arms. He grabbed her by the hand and directed her out of the house, locking the door after she departed.

He turned back to Linton, who was white and trembling, and gave such a look, that Linton scurried up the stairs like a mouse running from a hungry cat, and locked himself in his room.

Cathy banged on the front door and shrieked, "I hate you, Hareton! Harm my love and I'll kill you! Devil! Devil! Devil!"

She listened and heard nothing. She grasped the handle of the door, and shook it; it was still fastened inside. If Hareton was hurting Linton there would surely be high-pitched screams of agony.

Sick with anger from feeling so helpless, she found her horse and headed toward the Grange.

Some hundred yards off the premises, Hareton caught up to her on horseback, checked Minny, and took hold of the bridle.

"Miss Cathy, I'm ill-grieved," he began, lowering his eyes, fighting the urge to commence a full blubbering. "I do not wish to harm you. I was only protecting you from the lies and deceit of your cousin, his words designed to manipulate you in the same manner Heathcliff manipulates him."

She gave him a cut of her whip across his cheek, drawing blood. "Swine! Do not speak to me about my beloved!"

Their horses circled and trembled, sensing the anxious emotion in their riders.

Still gripping her bridle, Hareton quietly dismounted his own stallion, who scurried to the side of the road, and pulled her from Minny. Cathy trembled with anxiety, more fearful of his calm than his temper. He held her before him, both hands grasping her shoulders with strength. He said, "So, it is truth you utter, that I am not even worthy of speaking to you?"

"Any man who only spits hateful violence is not worth talking to."

"Do you think that is all I mutter?"

"Witness what you have just accomplished."

"Can you tell the difference between love and hate?"

"Not always."

"Neither can I."

He stared at her in the same manner as when he kissed her yesterday, in a way no boy or man ever had, certainly not in a way Linton had ever done. There was power in his eyes, as strong as the grip of his hands, maybe stronger. She felt herself yield to his gaze and his grasp. She wished with all of her being that he would kiss her again, as he had done last time, so she might understand whether the feelings he invoked were fact or folly. Nay, the feelings were true and in her heart, she admitted; she simply longed to revisit them.

Hareton crushed his mouth upon her and, literally, took her breath away. Then, as intense as the pressure of lips was at first, they turned completely tender, causing her to melt in his strong arms as she greeted him with equal passion. He ran his hand through her hair as he kissed her. She stroked her fingers down the deep, defined, muscular curve that centered his back. There was nothing else around them, not the Grange or the Heights, not Heathcliff or Linton, not Minny or Hareton's stallion. It was just them surrendering to a force of nature that neither could control.

But then as suddenly as Hareton had kissed her, he pulled back. She looked at him, great confusion upon her countenance, as his eyes bore down on her once again.

She knew not whether the fire in his gaze expressed love or hate, nevertheless his look burned through her, touching her heart as deeply as any of his kisses.

Their hands remained clasped as they looked at each other.

Cathy did not know how she could live without passion such as this, yet she wanted nothing to sway her from Linton. Linton had the intelligence, the delicateness, to please both her, and her father, with how *appropriate* a match he would be. Yet she could not hide her longing as her eyes met Hareton's, and she felt the same moistness between her thighs that she had experienced yesterday, but had tried so desperately to ignore.

Hareton knew in his own heart that he would probably die before he could find someone who made the ground beneath his feet tremble the way Cathy did, and he both loved her and hated her for it. He knew that he could not match the perfect symmetry of Cathy and Linton, as they had been bred to form a match, whether doomed or not. And he did not want to settle for being simply a pleasure for this perfect creature. He wanted a lifetime of sharing her heart and soul. He released her hands, mounted his horse, and headed in the complete opposite direction from the Grange, back toward the Heights. Had he looked back, or if he had been riding toward her, both would have seen the tears that trailed down the other's face, revealing full and equal heartache.

At Wuthering Heights, after securing his horse, and walking through the yard to the front door, Hareton came upon Heathcliff, scowling like a man who had been robbed of his life savings. Behind him stood the sniveling Linton, almost too scared to gloat, but there was, in the eyes, a twinkle of revenge.

Heathcliff struck Hareton with a mighty blow across the face, knocking him to the ground. He jerked him to his feet by the shoulders and dragged him to the barn. Linton stood frozen with fear.

Hareton was big enough to resist, but he remained passive. Heathcliff was his caretaker and always made him feel that scorn was something he well deserved.

Heathcliff pushed Hareton to his knees and tore off his shirt. He fetched the whip from the nail on the wall where it hung. He began a flogging.

A man with the strength and anger of Heathcliff could administer a flogging to bring a man to expiration. But that was not the strength he used. He flayed the back and shouted, "You must honor my plan. This is my house and you are cared for here by my own goodwill. You would be lost away from here, but I will banish you if you try to thwart me again. She is meant for Linton!"

"But I love her!" he cried, moved even more deeply by hearing his true feelings spoken out loud.

Heathcliff paused, then mouthed, "Oh, you poor thing." Then, confirming Hareton's deepest fears, he added, "You do not understand the nature of those at the Grange. She may use you for the man you are, but never accept you."

He commenced with more lashings, but ones tempered with sadness for the boy, someone who could help himself no more than Heathcliff had been able to at his age. No blood was drawn, only a small configuration of red marks. And as Heathcliff was about to deliver the final blow, the final exclamation point that reinforced that *his* plan must be followed, *his* revenge must be complete, a voice from the entrance of the barn cried out, "Please stop, *Father!*"

This rarely used term froze Heathcliff in midstrike, his arm, the whip, reared back, now immobilized in the air.

Both Heathcliff and Hareton turned toward Linton, who wept a torrent of tears over Hareton's punishment and the guilt from his role in making it come about.

Linton rushed to Hareton's side, hurt when Hareton refused his comfort.

Linton might call him *father*, but he bore the Linton name and blood, and reminded him of Edgar at every turn. And although Hareton was unquestionably another man's son, Heathcliff couldn't help but be reminded of his own relationship with Mr. Earnshaw. There was no doubt that the old master had loved him, and he harbored a similar love for Hareton, seeing so much of himself in this young man. He flogged Hareton as much to punish him for trying to thwart his plans, as to sway him from a path that would only lead to deeper despair.

Heathcliff let the whip drop from his hand.

Hareton easily could have stood, for he had received floggings far worse than this one, but the pain he felt within kept him at his knees, and Linton, also, remained kneeled, by his side.

"Why did you make me so coarse?" asked Hareton. "What did I ever do to you?"

"It is not what you have done, but what others have done."

"Why do you make us both suffer so?"

Heathcliff walked over to them, towering above their prostrate forms. Hareton looked up. Linton was too scared to raise his eyes and meet what he was sure would be a displeased stare, as more than anything he wanted his father's approval.

But Heathcliff simply turned around, and tore off his shirt, letting it drop to the ground. Neither had ever seen him shirtless. They both glanced up in horror at the thick, leathery scars striping his back at various ugly angles.

"This is suffering," he said.

Before walking away and leaving them to each other, he added, "If you could look into my heart you would see the same patchwork—for there I suffer even more."

Chapter Thirty

The next morning, at breakfast, while Edgar remained in bed, Cathy proposed her plan to Nelly.

"Linton is too weak to visit here on foot or horseback. Father would never set foot at the Heights, nor risk being in the company of Heathcliff. I bid you accompany me today to the Heights in the carriage and we bring Linton back here. He can surely recline and enjoy the short ride. I need you to help quell any resistance from Heathcliff." She added, blushing with the memory, "And Hareton."

Nelly's first instinct was to veto the plan, hoping Edgar would rebound, or perhaps Linton would recover enough strength to make it to the Grange on his own, for nothing good could come of Cathy at the Heights. But her father had expressed an interest in meeting Linton, and perhaps, in case he did not recover fully, a meeting should be arranged sooner rather than later. It was also best that she was along to keep an eye on her precious Cathy.

They departed after breakfast, Nelly at the reins, Cathy sitting beside her, and arrived at Wuthering Heights by midmorning.

Heathcliff greeted them warmly at the front door, but Cathy could not look him in the eye, and refused to shake his hand. Nelly took his hand, if only to remember his touch.

"Linton is still in his chamber, in bed," said Heathcliff. "Were it true that sleep could bring beauty, he would be the most comely lad in England." He laughed heartily, then looked at Cathy. "You may go to his room and wake him."

Cathy was glad to slip past him to climb the stairs, but was pleased in a way that he was here, and thus Hareton's interference could be avoided, though she did wonder if the lad was nearby.

As Nelly followed Heathcliff into the house, he said, "So how is everything at the Grange?" In a lower tone he added, "The rumor goes that Edgar is on his deathbed—perhaps they exaggerate his illness?"

"My master...*Edgar* is dying," replied Nelly, with brief blush. "A sad thing it will be for us all, but a blessing for him!"

"How long will he last, do you think?" he asked.

"I don't know," she responded curtly.

He bid her sit by the fire, while he checked on the young ones.

Upon entering the chamber, as he gazed upon Linton's face, it appeared that his son could not venture to stir, or raise his head; and Cathy, who sat on a chair by his side, did not move, on his account.

"Hallo!" said Heathcliff. "Has the whelp been playing this game for long? I *did* give him lessons about sniveling. Get up!" he shouted. Linton made several efforts to obey, but his little strength was annihilated, for the time, and he fell back with a moan.

Heathcliff advanced, and lifted him up against the headboard.

"Leave him be!" sparked Cathy. "It is the doctor you should be fetching. I've never seen him this bad."

"Nonsense," he said with curbed ferocity. "Linton, if you don't command that paltry spirit of yours—damn you! Get up directly!"

"I will, Father!" he panted. "Only, let me alone, or I shall faint! I've done as you wished—I'm sure. Cathy will tell you that she has offered her love and would consider me as husband."

Heathcliff looked at Cathy. She returned his cold glare, which became more kindly after returning her gaze to Linton. "I do love him and have come to fetch him to meet my father."

"For his approval?"

Cathy nodded.

"Stand on your feet, Linton!" said Heathcliff, with great delight. "There now—she'll lend you an arm...that's right, look at *her*. You would imagine I was the devil himself, Cathy, to excite such horror."

"Let him rest," said Cathy. "With renewed strength, the journey will be a more pleasant one."

Linton slid back down the bed, rested his head on the pillow, closed his eyes, let loose with a deep, raspy wheeze.

"Fine," said Heathcliff. "I have business now in Gimmerton. I'll return by the afternoon, when I hope to see you both gone, or I will throw the lad in the back of your carriage by myself!"

Heathcliff left the room, lighter in step, knowing that Edgar would surely approve of Linton and a hasty marriage made, considering his health...and Linton's as well.

Cathy stayed with Linton for a while, even though he soon drifted off to sleep. She liked being at his side. She liked that she could brush the hair from his eyes, and wipe the sweat from his brow: her very own little soothing thing to pet. And he was handsome, as handsome as Father. She could see herself living a very comfortable life with him. She was curious to see what her father would say, but how could he not like Linton? They were so much alike. Nevertheless, she worried about them both being so young. How could one be sure with such little life experience? She had barely strayed beyond Gimmerton. More so, she fretted that she had not seen, nor heard, of one happy marriage...and she was old enough to know that happiness was of extreme importance.

She backed slowly out of the room, careful not to disturb Linton, after hearing the snore of deepest slumber.

Cathy descended the stairs and pulled a chair next to Nelly, who sat by the fire, drinking a cup of tea. Nelly did not give Cathy much attention and the young girl wondered what she was staring at. Then, following the line of her vision, Cathy saw the same thing: Hareton sitting at the kitchen table, his hair combed neatly back, wearing what surely must have been his Sunday church outfit, however ill the fit . . . dark pants and jacket, white shirt showing more than the cuffs at the sleeve.

As if that wasn't motivation enough for a burst of hysterics, she saw his face poring over a book, his lips moving, forming language, as if he was reading aloud.

"Oh, Nelly," whispered Cathy, "did you ever see such a sorry sight?"

"Hush."

Nelly was not amused at all, for though their eyes saw the same thing, they did not perceive it the same way. Nelly absorbed before her a young man trying to be respectably dressed, seated at a table, drawing pleasure from his attempts at reading. His handsome features glowed with pleasure, as his eyes kept impatiently wandering from one page to the next. In Cathy, Nelly saw the glow of the fire reflected in her shining ringlets, her dainty nose, and beautiful profile. Was this lass too young, or too snobbish, to understand the love the lad was feeling, the lengths he would go to win her heart?

Nelly sighed deeply. When it came to love, she felt sure there was a curse upon both the Grange and the Heights.

Though she had displayed a haughty air, Cathy's eyes did not wander from Hareton. If he had been reading like this at a corner table in a tavern at Gimmerton, and she did not know who he was, and could not see the awkward fit of his clothes, her stare would be no more intense than it was now, for while watching his lips form their words, she remembered their heat against her own. Indeed, he also gave the *appearance* of one who was most serious, and had great thoughts, and would have much to say when questioned in a lively manner.

Nelly hid her smile, as Cathy stood suddenly, and walked to the kitchen.

She bent over behind Hareton and looked at the pages of the book; it was one graced with poetry.

There was a melding of Cathy's curls and his brown locks as she leaned over. It was not necessary for her to incline so far, but the closer she was, the more the immersed she became in the sweet scent of this young man who spent so much time dashing on horseback through the wind of the moors, not locked in a room convalescing on a bed.

Hareton could scarcely breathe, so acute was the feeling of her so close to him, her warm breath nearly bathing his cheek.

She asked, "Do you know your letters?"

He continued to stare at the page. "Yes."

"What is this?" challenged Cathy, pointing to the page.

"C and that's a T. Joseph has been teaching me."

"Good. Do you know your words?"

"I'm learning."

"This one?"

"Don't know."

"'Contrary.' Can you say it?"

"Con-*trary*," he mimicked.

"Excellent," she said, with real pride.

She sat next to him.

Nelly felt soothed and comforted to watch them, and they did not notice, they were so absorbed with the lesson. They both appeared in a measure, her children. She had been proud of one since birth and now, was sure the other could be a source of equal satisfaction. His honest, warm, and intelligent nature shook off rapidly the clouds of ignorance and degradation in which it had been bred; and Cathy's sincere commendations acted as a spur to him. His blossoming mind brightened his features, and added spirit and nobility to their aspect. The red firelight reached their faces, animated with the eager interest of children. The lesson continued through the afternoon, which was, perhaps, a mistake.

Nelly was dozing when she heard Cathy say, "Stop! You must listen to me! I can't speak with those clouds in your face!"

"Will you go to the devil!" he exclaimed ferociously. "And let me be!"

"No," she persisted, "I won't. I can't tell what to do to make you understand that when I call you stupid, I don't mean anything. I don't mean that I despise you. Come, do not look away. Hareton, you are my *cousin*."

Perhaps by physical awareness, or by instinctual sense, they lifted their eyes together. Heathcliff had come upon them unexpectedly, entering the front way, and had a full view of the pair at work.

And both Heathcliff and Nelly saw it. The cousins' eyes were precisely similar, and were those of Catherine Earnshaw.

Furious that Hareton had not heeded his warning backed up so forcefully with the flogging out in the barn, Heathcliff's arm rose to strike, to finish the job, and Hareton cowered in his chair. Cathy cried out, "Don't you hit him!"

Heathcliff held himself still for a moment, desperate to get control and unwilling to upset Cathy and the wheels of his plan, so he dropped his arm and walked to the hearth in evident agitation. With a deep breath, it quickly subsided.

"Well, then, let's load Linton up and you three can be on your way."

Hareton looked at Cathy with a pained expression, but she was already headed up the stairs, followed by Heathcliff and Nelly.

In the bed, Linton thrashed from side to side, eyes half open, in a feverish delirium. Nelly rushed to fetch cool water and a towel. She wet his face and whispered soothing words. He stilled. He opened his eyes. He looked at Nelly. "Thank you." He added, "I dreamt I saw Mama, and she was trying to pull me from the bed, but I was strangely bound."

"The fever is broken," said Heathcliff.

"The lad is in no condition to travel," said Nelly. "We will fetch the doctor."

Cathy and Nelly descended the stairs.

Before they could put on their bonnets, Heathcliff said, "It's late. I will fetch the doctor in the morning. Stay the night. I'm sure by the morrow the lad will be well enough to travel."

"Impossible," said Nelly. "It's best he see Dr. Kenneth this evening and we must return home to tend to Mr. Edgar."

Before they could exit, Heathcliff locked the front door and pulled the key from the lock. He held it up for them to see, then closed it tightly in his massive fist. This was his true chance to put the final pieces in place and he would not allow it to be wasted. He flashed his dark smile. It was so vigorous to feel his blood surging again!

"You shall have dinner before you go!" he commanded. "The servants are dismissed. Nelly, prepare the meal."

She knew better than to provoke Heathcliff when he was in this state, but Cathy was not so well educated to his demeanor. "Are you mad?" the lass exclaimed.

Perhaps so, thought Nelly, but if so, it was a madness peculiar to him that she knew too well, for he was one who took pleasure at invoking his physical presence to achieve his ultimate goal, which, as always, was having his way.

"How do the two cousins stare?" said Heathcliff. Hareton turned away. "It's odd what a savage feeling I have to anything that seems afraid of me!"

He drew in his breath, struck the table, and swore, "By hell! I hate them."

"I'm not afraid of you!" exclaimed Cathy.

She stepped up close, her black eyes flashing with passion and resolution.

"Give me that key—I will have it!" she said. "I wouldn't eat or drink here, if I were starving."

Heathcliff was seized with surprise at her boldness, or, possibly, reminded by her voice and glance, of the person from whom she inherited it.

She snatched at the instrument, and half succeeded in prying his fingers, when he shoved her to the floor.

Hareton got up and rushed toward him, only to be felled to the ground by a shower of terrific slaps to both sides of his head. He dared not get up.

Nelly rushed on him furiously.

"You villain!" she cried. "You villain! I curse the day the true master of this house brought you here!"

The mention of the elder Earnshaw took the venom out of the treacherous snake. For a moment, Heathcliff looked out of breath and befuddled. He retreated to the hearth and sat on a chair. He was not sure what to do, but he knew one thing: He could not let Cathy leave. She would not return again, Edgar could fail any day, and who knew how long his own son had? His revenge must be complete!

Linton, with much effort, made his way down the stairs.

Cathy trembled like a reed, and leaned against the table perfectly bewildered.

Hareton stood, and thought first to put an arm around Cathy to comfort her, but thought better not to incite further wrath.

Nelly stood near the young ones, prepared to act as shield against further violence.

"Go to Linton, now," said Heathcliff to Cathy, "and cry at your ease. I will wait no longer to see my plan fully realized. I shall fetch the justice in the morning and tomorrow I shall be your father." He added with great triumph, "All the father you will have in a few days!"

The more angry they all made him, the more he felt the presence of the old Heathcliff, the one who had returned after making his fortune with confidence and a plan, along with a swagger that went along with his cold manipulations. He would soon be master over everyone and everything!

Linton shrunk into a corner of the settle, as quiet as a mouse, though his eyes seemed clearer, and absent of full fever. He was joined by Cathy.

Hareton went to the far corner, seriously grieved.

Nelly moved quickly around the familiar kitchen and prepared their dinner. Heathcliff felt so confident in his designs, so in control, he sat in a chair by the fire and was soon dozing. Nelly tried the kitchen door, but it was fastened from the outside. She studied the windows; they were too narrow for even Cathy's little figure. Damn him, she thought. She went back to her preparations.

"Won't you have me?" whispered Linton to Cathy. "And save me—and save us both? Oh, darling, Cathy, you mustn't go, and leave me, after all. You *must* obey my father, you *must*!"

"I must obey my own," she replied, "and relieve him of this cruel suspense. The whole night! What would he think? He'll be distressed already. I'll either break or burn a way out of the house. Be quiet! You're in no danger, unless you hinder me. Linton, I love Papa better than you!"

Awakened by her strong words, Heathcliff stood, then walked over to them. Linton shrunk from him, but Cathy did not.

Heathcliff scowled and muttered, "Oh, you are not afraid of me?"

"I *am* afraid now," she replied, "because if I stay, Papa will be miserable and how can I endure making him miserable—when he—when he—Mr. Heathcliff, let me go home! I promise to marry Linton—Papa would like me to, and I love him—and why should you wish to force me to do what I'll willingly do myself?"

"To the devil with your clamor!" cried Heathcliff. "I don't want you to speak. Miss Linton, I shall enjoy myself remarkably in thinking your father will be miserable; so much so I shall not sleep. But you might as well find comfort here, for you shall not quit the place till your promise to marry Linton is fulfilled."

Nelly noticed a look on Hareton's face of such extreme distress, it appeared that if he threw himself in the fire, he would suffer less.

"I'll not retract my word," said Cathy, near tears picturing her father even more fully distressed with worry over her long absence. "I'll marry him, within this hour, if I may go to Thrushcross Grange afterward. Mr. Heathcliff, you're a cruel man, but you're not a fiend and you won't from mere malice destroy all my happiness. If Papa thought I had left him, on purpose, and if he died before I returned, could I bear to live? No! I don't hate you. Have you ever loved *anybody*, in all of your life, Uncle?"

She moved to place a hand on his sleeve.

"Keep your fingers off, or I'll kick you!" cried Heathcliff, not knowing if his anger erupted so forcefully because of the ire created by Cathy referencing love in his life, or if it was the simple touch upon his sleeve that had such an eerie familiarity. "How the devil can you dream of fawning on me? I *detest* you!"

"I know your son loves me," said Cathy, "and for that reason I love him. But, Mr. Heathcliff, *you* have *nobody* to love you and, however miserable you make us, we shall still have the revenge of thinking that your cruelty rises from your greater misery! You *are* miserable, are you not? Lonely, like the devil, and envious like him?" She cried, "Nobody loves you—*nobody* will cry for you, when you die!"

He was about to lift a hand to strike her; this creature was ruining his good mood! But then they all heard the sound of voices at the garden gate. The hour was growing late for visitors. Heathcliff hurried out, then returned in three minutes.

"It was two servants sent to see you from the Grange," said Heathcliff. "I told them you had left hours ago, and that they might check the marsh, as perhaps your wagon got stuck."

Nelly and Cathy both exhaled sounds of grief.

Heathcliff grinned maniacally, and exacted further revenge on a foolish girl who seemed intent upon getting under his skin, by saying, "You should have opened the lattice, and called out. Perhaps you really do want to stay and fulfill my wishes?"

Full grief finally turned to tears in young Cathy, as she realized she had missed her chance.

What a miserable and silent dinner it was. Everyone gathered around the kitchen table except Cathy, who refused to take nourishment, whether solid or liquid.

The hour grew late and Cathy said she wished to retire. Heathcliff had Linton show Cathy to her room.

Before departing to his chamber, Linton said to her, "Rest comfortably, my love. There could be worse things that could happen. He is so much more tolerable when he gets his way."

His docile yielding to his father made him seem so much more a boy than a man. They all bent to Heathcliff's will as if he were the mighty wind of the moors...even Nelly, who was known at the Grange to have more of the fire of a mistress than a servant. How she wished Hareton would rise up and teach Heathcliff the lesson he deserved.

She responded quietly with "I spoke truth when I promised to give him his way, if it meant I could see Papa again as one still breathing."

He approached to kiss her good night and she offered her forehead.

Downstairs, Nelly and Heathcliff sat facing each other in front of the fire. Both were so deep in troubled thought that they did not notice Hareton slip upstairs with food and a book in his hand.

He entered the room as quietly as he could, nearly tiptoeing. Cathy, her back to him, studying something on the wall, was startled anyway.

"Shhh," said Hareton. "I've brought you some food. There is no sense in you starving. It only pleases him more."

"Look at this," she said, pointing to the wall.

He placed the food and book on a table, and held the candle up to where she glanced. He ran his fingers across the carving. "I have seen this before, but never knew what it meant. Only now I know the letters."

"It says, 'Catherine and Heathcliff.'"

"I know not who this Catherine is."

She looked at him. "My mother." She sat on the bed, deeply confused, and picked at the meat and potatoes. "How foolish she must have been."

"To love him, or leave him?" asked Hareton. "For I know the dark cloud of love lost has always hung over him."

Cathy did not answer. She lay down on the bed and finished the plate.

"Would you like me to leave?" asked Hareton.

"Nay. I feel so odd in here. This must have been her room growing up. I have not stopped trembling since Heathcliff returned this afternoon."

He longed to lay next to her and hold her close to ease the tremble, but he did not want to risk upsetting her further.

She looked at the book beside the plate.

"I did not think you would be able to sleep," said Hareton. "I thought this volume could bring you comfort."

"You are very sweet," she said. "For a brute."

His smile turned to a frown. She said, "You must learn to understand when I tease you."

"It seems easier to decipher a cold trail than read a woman."

Cathy laughed. Though it pleased him to see laughter lighten her eyes, Hareton told her to be quiet. Both knew that if the wrong cousin was discovered here, there would be more hell to pay.

She picked up the book, slid over to make room for him on the bed, and he reclined next to her. She read aloud in a soft whisper,

The sun will shine, he knew not how
That it would soothe his troubled brow

Did it inspire, I long to know
One sweet dream he hoped to show
That hope and happiness would not fade
And foolish thoughts would not shade
Love fulfilled in all its glory
Two hearts as one the final story

She turned the pages and read on. His black eyes could not wander from watching her mouth form the beautiful words, with such musical sounds. Several locks of her hair rested on top of his hand, which he dare not move. She could feel his touch there, but said nothing this time, and remained still, his closeness causing her heart to beat at the pace of a hummingbird scooping for nectar.

Downstairs, as the fire burned low and the hour grew even later, Nelly looked at Heathcliff. She noticed an *unnatural* appearance of joy under his black brow, crinkled into a bloodless hue; his teeth visible in kind of a smile; his frame shivering, not as one shivers from cold or weakness, but as a tight-stretched cord vibrates.

"You are very wicked, Heathcliff," she said, his brutality today making her feel that if he would just give her the key, she would grab Cathy and flee, content never to see him again.

"Wicked? What is wicked is that I am under the same roof with Hareton and Cathy, whose own features mock me with dreadful resemblance, who bear such startling likeness to her that their simple appearance causes me agony. I earnestly wish them both to be gone or invisible."

"Can you not void your heart of its hate?"

"Easy to say, Nelly. You are conversing with one who has to remind himself to breathe—almost to remind my heart to beat. It is by compulsion that I do the slightest act, not prompted by one thought, and by compulsion that I notice anything alive or dead, which is not associated with one universal idea of an eternal re-union that I have no power to attain."

He stood and began to pace.

"But rest assured I shall be a great deal more comfortable now," he continued, "and you'll have a better chance of keeping me un-derground when my time comes. Catherine has disturbed me all of these years—incessantly—remorselessly, since I last visited her grave and felt her presence. Yet I am more tranquil now, knowing the last stages of my curse will be fulfilled, and the seeds to keep it alive for many generations are being planted. Yet, in a heart-beat, if I knew I could be fully joined with her again, I would wish for instant death at this very moment, to be beneath the dirt next to my beloved at Black Rock."

He collapsed back into the chair, let out a deep, morose sigh, and closed his eyes.

His inner sadness revealed the profound vulnerability of this man. She knew it existed, remembered it so well when he was a child, so susceptible to the sway of Catherine's needs and moods. She had seen it again, rising up from the ground to the sky like an epic windstorm, after he had received the news of Catherine's passing. And even after he had been his most cruel to her, she saw in his regret that much of what he did came from weakness, not strength. It inspired nothing but the love she had always held for him in her heart. She longed to rise from her chair and cover him with passionate kisses, bury herself deep into his lap, take care of this man, assure him there was a way for everything to be all right. Though she believed this to be true, she did not believe it was within her power to make it come about.

Had there been a moon out tonight, it would have peaked already, and begun its setting descent. The house was completely quiet. Linton fell into a troubled, fitful sleep, tossing and thrashing throughout the night. Nelly napped by the fire, as did Heathcliff, although the fist that held the key to the door never unclenched.

Both Hareton and Cathy had drifted to slumber; candle out, book facedown on her lap, he lay beside her. In her dreams she heard a soft, quiet, feminine sigh, which caused her eyes to open in a start. At her cheek, on the opposite side from where Hareton slept, she felt the lightest breath of air, which almost seemed to turn her head sideways toward Hareton. She was surprised he was there, but as she awakened, their long night of reading was revisited. She realized she would not have been able to fall asleep in this wretched place, if not for the comfort of Hareton at her side.

She leaned over him, propping her elbow against the mattress for support, and was about to nudge him awake, lest Heathcliff or Linton look in on them and discover his presence. But she remained immobile, staring at his handsomely formed features, the strong cheekbones, perfectly shaped mouth with full lips, the wide shoulders and broad chest that rested on the bed. She placed a fingertip upon his cheek, simply to feel the texture of his skin. So light was her touch that she did not disturb him, as she reveled in this time to take him in fully, without the overwhelming rush of his powerful embrace or torrid kisses. The flesh was rough from the years working out in the winds, but, as she had seen while he had worked on his reading, she knew that within him was a soft patience that helped him learn quickly.

Without thinking, she lowered her mouth to his, kissing him deeply, the taste of him warm and sweet, so different from the prim stiffness of Linton's thin lips. Such an action brought him to life. He opened his eyes and beheld her, perhaps at first not realizing whether it was dream or actuality. When she kissed him again, with even greater passion, he knew exactly where he was and what he was doing.

Instinctively, he reached his hand up to touch her golden hair, to stroke its soft texture with his fingers, as he pressed his lips against hers. Simultaneously, their mouths opened, their tongues extended, sliding over each other in a deep, romantic dance. Hareton wondered if this was what love *felt* like. He buried his hand deeper into her silky strands and heard her soft moans. She continued to glide her fingertips over his cheek. Their joining seemed as natural as sunshine upon the moors. Hareton would have been perfectly content to kiss her, like this, for the rest of the night, so deep was his pleasure, so fearful he was that he would do something too rough and risk destroying the moment.

But it was she who leaned even farther over him, dropping to her side the arm that had given her support, and rested the full length of her body over his, like a sensual blanket delicately lowered over his muscled form. His arms went around her, she slid the same under his back, and they spooned against each other in deep embrace. She turned her head to the side, sighed with deep contentment. He stroked her hair again, pulling on it slightly, which garnered more moans. Again, he would have remained this way forever, if she hadn't freed her one hand from behind his back, and, gently, slowly, work a deep caress from his firm chest, down to his rippled belly, to the hard cock bulging through his pants.

She stroked the full length and was assured that her memory had not deceived her and that, indeed, it was of the same sturdy size she remembered against her belly.

With this encouragement, something unleashed in Hareton.

When he felt comfortable, as he was on a horse, or behind a plow in the field, he was a young man with much talent and skill.

He gently rolled Cathy onto her back, and let his weight rest upon her, though not heavily. His passion turned to kisses around her face, throat, and ears, as he inhaled deeply. Her natural scent was all the perfume he needed. He licked her neck with long graceful glides of his tongue and she whimpered softly in his ear. He ran his fingers through her hair again and tilted her head back to expose more of her throat.

If he had been thinking about propriety, or what Cathy's reaction might be, he might have hesitated. But neither was doing much thinking now.

Hastily, they removed each other's clothes in between their hot kisses and caresses. When they embraced in full flesh, the feeling was cataclysmic.

"Cathy, you are the most beautiful creature to grace this earth," he whispered.

"And you the handsomest man," she cooed back.

He thrust her arms out the side and massaged his thumbs into the center of her palms, their bodies never parting, as if any full separation would cause overwhelming heartache. She felt helpless to his touches. He licked her beautiful, full breasts, the most delicate of brownish pink nipples, with hearty relish. As they enlarged to full buds, he sucked them, at first lovingly, then with added vigor, as she encouraged him with her soft groans. He cupped one breast, making it burst forth, only to be swallowed into his mouth, his pressure at her palm doubling her sensations.

He licked down her entire body, his tongue quivering for her taste, and paused at the feet. He sat up on his knees at the end of the bed, and lifted her foot into the air.

He sucked her toes, not just with his mouth, but with magic.

He devoted time to each one, letting it rest on his tongue, as he pressed his lips together and caressed the toe upward with slow erotic movements, bathing her with the hot moisture of his mouth. When he added a slight grazing with his teeth, her fingers tore at the mattress, curling full balls of the sheet into her palms.

What made it even more overwhelming was the way he looked into her eyes as he did this, as if saying: I know how much you like this, how much you want this, and I am the only one who can make you feel this way.

"Yes," cried Cathy, a little too loudly.

They paused, listened, but heard no stirring.

She took this opportunity to push Hareton onto his back. She circled his nipples with her tongue and took pleasure from his murmured cries. She liked that his chest was hairless and she could taste only his flesh as she sucked the full bump of his nipple into her mouth. She licked his belly, sliding in and out of each packet of hard muscle, causing her head to bob, every so slightly, up then down, and he turned and tossed from excitement but refused to separate. She caressed his heavy ball sack with her slim, dainty fingers and she felt that in her hand she had harnessed the whole power of this man.

She did not know how she knew what to do, but by some very natural instinct, the way she licked his thick shaft, flicked her tongue along its length, drove him wild. She adored the salty, sweaty taste of his cock and rejoiced at its wonderful curves and contours, the veins inside seeming about to burst.

Cathy ran her hands all over his luxurious body. No, she was not going to lie passively no matter how good it felt to have him devour her. This was equal pleasure to taste and breathe in the scent of this lovely man, body completely smooth, except for the thick bush of hair under his arms and around his cock.

Sensing he was about to spurt the juice of his lust, his love—yes, it did feel like love should—he nudged her mouth off him and with much easy strength placed her on her back again.

What a beautifully shaped specimen Cathy was, an hourglass marking the time, golden hair cascading to her shoulders, the lovely nest-shaped quim that drew him to her like a bee to the hive.

"Oh, Hareton!" she whispered. "How could I have been so blind to all of the gifts you are blessed with?"

He licked her, passionately, vigorously, relishing this taste of her as if enjoying the most exquisite morsel. He entered her deeply with his tongue, her inner quim velvet with moist desire, and she pulled so hard on his hair she came close to tearing away a fistful. She squirmed and turned, guiding his mouth to all the best places with the gyration of her hips. He tongued her. He drank from her. He possessed her. He lathered her with the overpowering wetness from his mouth and the fluid pleasure that transplanted them far away from their jail.

Which is why Cathy finally cried out uncontrollably—unable to exercise the willpower Hareton had exhibited—from a stunning, deep, never-ending orgasm.

That finally ended when Heathcliff burst into the room.

Cathy screamed. Hareton shouted. Heathcliff bellowed, "You did not heed my warnings, you river rats! Like your fathers, you try to thwart me to the last!"

He threw the young man against the wall and commenced to pummel him with repeated angry blows. Hareton curled into a ball and held his arms up as a shield, but otherwise did not resist.

Oblivious to her nakedness, Cathy jumped on his back and tried to grab his arms. He tossed her to the floor and turned, cocked his foot, and was about to give her a horrible kick.

That was when Hareton leaped to his feet and tackled his caretaker.

Hareton let loose mighty swings inspired by his youth and vigor that connected and bloodied Heathcliff's nose.

Recovering from the shock of Hareton fighting back, Heathcliff fired off some of his own jabs, ones that would soon darken Hareton's right eye.

With a mighty roar of passion to protect the one he loved, Hareton swung wildly and connected dead-on with his fist to Heathcliff's throat.

The impact caused immediate loss of breath and the room filled with Heathcliff's choking sounds. He collapsed to the floor, unconsciously reaching both open hands to his neck.

That was when the couple heard the key drop to the floor from his unclenched fist. Hareton picked up the key. Needing not even wordless directions, Cathy grabbed their clothes and they were out the door.

At the bottom of the stairs they were met by Nelly, who said, "Run, children, run, get thee to the Grange! I will stay to tend Linton and bring him as soon as he is able."

Cathy pulled the frock down over her body, Hareton tugged up his pants, and they were out the door, sprinting toward the moors.

It was Linton who helped his father sit upright, which took some of the pressure off his throat, and allowed him to breathe better. He brought him a tumbler of cool water, which Heathcliff swallowed with difficulty. With a cloth, Linton cleaned the blood around Heathcliff's nose. He adored this passivity exhibited by his father, his injuries opening the door for Linton to soothe in a way that was so different from simply yielding to his forceful requests. And as much as he did not want to lose Cathy, he preferred that his father not leave, but continue to allow his son to comfort.

Heathcliff's breathing returned almost to normal. For an instant, he gazed upon his son, about to thank him for his help, but all that was returned to his vision had the look of either Isabella or Edgar.

He pushed Linton aside and bolted down the stairs.

"Let them go!" cried Nelly.

But Heathcliff was a man possessed, doubly, by vengeance and anger.

He ran to the barn, grabbed the whip, then took off into the night to find Cathy and Hareton.

It was too dark to go by horseback, although the sun would be up soon. He knew where they were headed. If it was just Hareton alone, he would not be able to catch him before the Grange, but with Cathy at his side, Heathcliff felt as if he had a very good chance. Either way, the boy would get the flogging of his life and he would drag the girl back to the Heights to finalize the marriage. With Edgar fading fast, Cathy inheriting the property, Linton probably not long to live, the Grange would become his and he would see Edgar buried deep into the ground.

When all of this was done, thought Heathcliff, when Hareton, too, was saved from the misery that would be ahead of him, there would not be peace in his heart, just complacency. The knowledge that his revenge was finally complete would make it so much easier to welcome his sentence to the eternal hell and damnation that surely awaited him for tormenting so many and inflicting such a demonic curse.

Heathcliff had not been to the Grange, nor traveled in this direction, since the night he spent at Catherine's Black Rock grave site so long ago.

His breathing was labored from the blow to his throat, but he pushed himself without mercy, his footsteps thundering in his ears like heavy beats of the heart.

Perhaps it was lack of oxygen caused by damage from the blow. Perhaps it was that he could not pass this place without being drawn to the one who dwelled there. Perhaps there was an unseen hand that guided him.

Either way, Heathcliff found himself straying from the road, to take his rest at the burial place of his beloved at Black Rock Cragge.

He knew that he could give Hareton his flogging any time. And, even if the pair made it back to the Grange, Heathcliff could storm the house and return Cathy to the place where she had made her vow.

Despite the darkness, he could always locate their spot. He sat heavily on the ground, his back against the arrow rock. Breathing with difficulty, he felt along the thick grass until his fingers felt the rough carving of CE, which gave him comfort.

No matter how much he fought it, he found himself back at her side again. It was good that he visited this last time, for his final resting place would certainly be far below where his angel dwelled.

He felt no breath, heard no sigh, could not see any strange shape or form. Nevertheless, he felt that his love could hear what was in his heart.

He had hoped for some sign, tried for some way, to be with her. But the curse was too heavy. Was that the obstacle, or was he just too evil? Hindley had always made him feel as if he was ... dirty, unworthy of any love, of any contact, except whip to back.

There was a sudden change in the direction of the wind and it brought the sound of soft voices to his ears. Heathcliff crept along the ground on his hands and knees and peeked around the corner of a group of rocks. With first light close to breaking, he made out the shapes of two familiar figures in complete embrace. As the sun's rays splayed along the moors, it became immensely obvious that everything about Hareton and Cathy was so clearly Heathcliff and Catherine, and that he should rush forward and seize them both, something they should welcome, because no matter how much hate he held in his heart, he would not wish such torture on the worst of his enemies. Nevertheless, it was as if a forceful hand restrained him, and he remained frozen behind the rocks, watching, listening.

Hareton ran his strong hands along Cathy's arms to still her shivering. They kissed deeply. She was exhausted. They both were. They were sure, even if Heathcliff tracked their escape, that he could not find them in a place so secluded.

"Do you think?" asked Cathy, then paused.

Hareton smiled and said, with a complete mimic of her once-used tone, "Yes, I think."

They laughed, kissed.

"Do you think," continued Cathy, "that you could love me?"

"I already do," he responded without hesitation. "It is within you that I question whether this emotion exists or can grow."

"I think I do love you."

"*Think?*"

"I do. I have never felt this way before."

"Not even for Linton?"

"No, after being with you I understand the difference between love for a brother and love for a companion."

"But these feelings arise within you during fits of passion. All we did was probably heightened by the danger of what lurked beneath us, made more powerful by the little time we knew we had."

"Perhaps," replied Cathy. "But when you kiss me, I know positively that it will be the same tomorrow, the day after, and years to come."

"But what happens when you, and your father, see your two cousins side by side, and you see the smile that grows from the sight of Linton, one so much more refined and intelligent than I am?"

"I cannot speak for my father. I can only speak what is in my heart."

"Which is?"

"That right now I want to be with you forever and never leave you and never have you leave me."

"*Right now?*" repeated Hareton.

"Are you gifted enough so that you can see into the future?"

"No, just doubtful enough to worry about it."

"Then I will prove my love for you."

"How?"

The early rays of dawn rose enough to strike the rocks with force, and below them, they could see the pool.

"Let us both jump," said Cathy. "Let us both risk death to prove to each other that our love is true and everlasting."

They rose to their feet, held hands, and ventured forward to the precipice. They looked over at the great distance, into such a narrow pool, surrounded by large sharp rocks.

Hareton took a deep breath, and said, "That's the most preposterous thing I've ever heard!"

She looked intently at the man who came so close this past night to being her first lover.

He added, "I would risk life or limb to protect you and be with you. Why should I risk death to prove something I already know, true, deep in my heart, which makes it already proven? I want to *live* with you, not *die* with you."

She looked at her companion and understood the wisdom he possessed.

He finished with "In truth, it does not matter what we say. What really matters is how we are with each other. If how we are is good and pure, time will allow the trust to grow that will inspire a lifetime, perhaps an eternity, together."

They kissed, as deep as the pool below them.

How she loved this man.

Heathcliff suddenly drew forth from the shadows and walked toward them. Instinctively, Cathy inhaled a sharp breath and Hareton stepped in front to shield her body as soon as he noticed the whip in his hand.

Together, they took notice of a transformation in a man they had both learned to despise.

A storm of tears amassed around his eyes and drained along his face like rain shimmering down a glass pane.

He said, "Hareton, I have done you wrong and I have paid for it, and probably will for all eternity. Despite putting every ounce of my evilness into making you an ignorant, unfeeling monster, you have shown yourself to be more man than I ever was. I have hurt you, too, Cathy, by disparaging your father and forcing you on someone you were not destined for. I have hurt many. And you have inspired deep regret. For you have made me see that all of my troubles are not because of what others have done to me, but because of what I have failed to do for myself and the one I love."

The couple, standing side by side, clasped hands.

"It is too late for me to have love in this life," continued Heathcliff, "but not too late for you both. Let your hearts guide you and let nothing else interfere."

He stepped even closer and there was still an instinctive flinch in them both. With one shove, they would surely fall to instant death.

Heathcliff reached into the top of his shirt and pulled out the locket, then removed the chain from around his neck.

"Peace cannot exist with hate, only love," he said. "This you have shown me." He placed the cherished object around Hareton's neck. "This is for the one you will truly love, forever."

He dropped the whip from his hand, said, "I am finally at peace," then stepped toward the precipice, and jumped.

As always, his aim was true.

He landed hard, the tautness of his body going instantly limp, as his lifeless form melded instantly with the rocks below.

Chapter Thirty-One

After witnessing Heathcliff's leap, Hareton and Cathy let out a deep and mortal cry that was heard at both the Grange and the Heights. Edgar paused in midwalk and sensed a feeling in his soul, familiar, but different, not so much that his soul felt divided, but that it had been joined. At the Heights, Nelly was stirred in her chair by the fire. She knew that something awful had happened, yet she sensed an atmosphere of lightness around her.

There began a light morning rain.

After feeling confident that Cathy could make it home of her own accord, Hareton rushed back to the Heights. He relayed the news of Heathcliff's death instantly and was surprised to see Nelly express both remorse and relief. Linton called on what strength he had, sat on the hearth, and commenced a mighty blubbering.

Hareton was about to gather some men, horses, and the carriage to fetch Heathcliff back to the Heights. Nelly told him that it would just be the two of them and to bring one horse with a carriage for her, and a horse for Hareton, and a shovel. He thought this curious, but obeyed. They took the long way around and found a spot where they could descend to the pool. They stood over the motionless body on the rocks.

They did not think him dead!

No blood trickled from any broken skin. His face and throat

had been washed clean from the rain. His eyes met theirs so keen and fierce, that they started; and then, he seemed to smile.

Nelly brushed his long black hair from his forehead. She tried to close his eyes—to extinguish, if possible, that frightful, lifelike gaze of exultation. They would not shut—they seemed to sneer at her attempts, and his parted lips, and sharp, white teeth sneered, too!

She looked at his face one more time. Though he was the dark angel at the moments he had thrust himself upon her, she was not naïve, nor innocent enough to forget how much she had enjoyed the devil in him. Yet that was not all she had enjoyed. He had touched her in ways no one else could, not only by imposing his mind and body, but by allowing her to witness the vision of a love for another so deep, so passionate that nothing could destroy it. For this she would be eternally grateful.

She kissed him gently above the eyes and whispered, "It's up to Providence now to decide if your final resting place is above or below."

She retreated. Hareton struggled to keep rein on his emotions and focus on the task at hand. Nelly helped him load the body into the cart. Then she mounted his horse and said she was going to the Grange to check on Edgar. She told him to return the way they came, but then to bring the body back to the top of Black Rock Cragge. She shared the details of Heathcliff's relocation of Catherine's grave, the only woman he had truly loved. "Look around, sharply," she told him. "I am sure you will find the spot to lay him to rest at her side."

She turned abruptly, mounted the horse, and headed toward the Grange, her own tears of sadness over what was, and what could have been, flowing freely against her face, like the wind.

Hareton did as told and eventually made his way up to the location where he had last parted from his beloved. He searched carefully the grounds, looking closely behind each set of rocks, until he came upon an area where the grass was depressed, as if someone had been sitting. He got on his knees and felt along the grass, his fingers moving some long blades aside, until he saw Catherine's initials against the rocks.

He dug a deep hole alongside her, lowered Heathcliff inside, then filled it carefully, lovingly. Done, he rested a moment on the ground, beside his caretaker and aunt, exhausted from all the trials and tribulations the last day and a half had produced.

With respite from task, his emotions burst forth. Hareton, perhaps the one most wronged, suffered much. He wept in bitter earnest. He kissed the ground above Heathcliff, and bemoaned him with that strong grief that springs naturally from a generous heart, though it be tough as tempered steel. Hareton believed that he had the capacity to love and learn, and that, in some part, Heathcliff must have had influence in this regard.

Before departing, he used the sharp point of the shovel against the rock. Next to the CE, above the head of Heathcliff's grave, Hareton carved a large H.

After departing from Black Rock, Hareton stopped in Gimmerton to fetch Dr. Kenneth. At the Heights, the doctor checked in on Linton, while Hareton scrubbed himself clean. He told Hareton that the young man was resting comfortably, but he would not have long to live. Hareton peeked in and saw that Linton was asleep. He quietly made his way to the bedside, leaned over, and kissed him on the forehead, then departed the chamber. Linton opened his eyes, smiled beatifically.

Hareton longed for his bed, a chance to rest his weary bones, a chance to close his eyes and forget the evil from recent hours and remember only the good. Instead, he donned his white shirt, absent the jacket that had not grown with him, and his best black pants. He mounted his horse and headed to the Grange.

He was met by Cathy as soon as he entered the front door. They embraced and kissed deeply.

"Is your papa alive?" asked Hareton with concern.

"Yes, I have told him about us and he wants to see you!"

She clasped his hand and led him upstairs to the master chamber, where Nelly tended him, as he reclined on the bed. She stepped aside. The couple approached.

Though Edgar's face was pale, and his body fragile, his eyes were strong.

"Papa," said Cathy, with much delight. "This is Hareton."

Hareton's first instinct was to lower his eyes from her father's stare, but he forced himself to look straight on.

Edgar observed a tall and healthy young man, whose pants were too short and whose eye was blackened from what was probably an unruly brawl.

Then he looked at Cathy, whose own eyes were ablaze with a love that seemed to glow physically from her entire body.

He felt great comfort from her happiness and smiled approvingly.

"Oh, Papa!" she cried, leaning over instantly to kiss his forehead. He returned a kiss to her cheek and murmured, "I depart with elation in my heart from seeing you so joyful and cared for, and because I will soon be underground next to my beloved at the Gimmerton Church graveyard."

At this last remark, Hareton and Nelly looked just once at each other, then she left the room. His faint smile went undetected. As Heathcliff had spoken, it is what's felt in the heart that counts.

Edgar never stirred or spoke again, but continued that rapt, radiant gaze, till his pulse imperceptibly stopped, his eyes closed blissfully, and his soul departed. None could have noticed the exact minute of his death, it was so entirely without struggle.

Whether Cathy had spent her tears, or whether the grief was too weighty to let them flow, she sat there dry-eyed—holding hands with Hareton, who remained joined at her side—long past sunset.

Anyone walking upon the moors that night would have noticed a strange, shimmering illumination, a glow even more mysterious since it was another moonless evening.

From the top of Black Rock Cragge, there rose two lights, together, hovering above the landscape in perfect symmetry. As the radiance took on strength, it began to shape itself into the blurry, transparent outline of a man and a woman.

"My love!" cried Heathcliff, as he reached out for Catherine.

The shapes of light moved toward each other until they formed one strong, fiery ellipse, which floated back down to the ground and rested on the graves. Once earthbound, their bodies, although still translucent, were more clearly defined. They lay next to each other, naked as the time of their birth, and entwined tightly, as only familiar lovers can.

"I have waited for you all of this time, refusing my place above," said Catherine, as she kissed him deeply.

"Though I searched my heart and soul every waking hour, I could not think of a way to make this possible."

"But you did! Had you jumped to your death at any other time, we would have been doomed to separation for the rest of time."

They could not stop kissing and caressing each other as they spoke.

"For you see," she continued, "you showed that true repentance is when the inner soul recognizes the path to redemption and acts accordingly. Until this happens, the person will be blind to all opportunities." She reached her hands up, pressed her palms against his cheeks, and brought him as close as possible to her face. "When you abandoned your wicked plan with sincerity; opened your mind to understanding that only love can heal; and blessed the love shared by Hareton and Cathy, your heart was cleansed, the curse lifted, and you entered a state of grace that allowed us to be together . . . my love."

And together they were.

The sensations they felt from their kisses and caresses were not the same as when they were in full earthly form. Like the first evening Heathcliff had spent at the grave site, the feeling was a heat, an aura, a sensation reaching through them from head to toe, only now it was a thousand times more intense, growing from a mere flicker of a candle, to a brilliant, blazing sun.

Their hands were everywhere, but their lips stayed together, almost as if they worried separation would cause this moment to end. There was no need to put mouth anywhere else. The sensations easily prepared Catherine to welcome her long-lost love, and Heathcliff felt a growing strength within him that was mightier than Zeus at Olympus.

Neither was on top. They were side by side when Heathcliff entered Catherine, and Catherine received him.

It was as if not a moment had passed, as they recaptured the rhythm of their love when it was the most pure, before the corruption of doubt, anger, and insecure feelings.

Heathcliff and Catherine made beautiful love. It was a love of light that broke through the dark. It was a love of passion that lasted the test of time, hate, and vengeance. It was a love that they both had never stopped envisioning. They could not forget each other, nor would they ever. She kissed him passionately, her tongue fully entering his mouth. He entered her deeply, withdrew slowly, only to have her pull him in again, urging him to press forward, to penetrate and connect his manhood and her womanhood as one true heart and soul of two people only meant for each other, who could find no satisfaction or completion with anyone else on this earth, or above, or below.

This heavenly connection of spirit, this great, intertwining physical passion continued throughout the night, until another glorious sunrise kissed the moors, and they finally rested. There was a moment of deep openness, deep vulnerability in each of their souls, this delicate time that can be so painfully empty when true love is absent. But as Heathcliff and Catherine listened to the soft wind breathing through the grass, continued their neverending embrace, all the beautiful emotions they possessed and had shared throughout the evening did not abate

only grew stronger.

Epilogue

You awake in the morning, as fresh and as rested as you have ever been. You feel your own contentment glow within your body... not a sensation that has the soft, pleasant, onanistic finality of self-stimulation, but one that has the deep, continual satisfaction from a night overflowing with a myriad of passionate emotions, shared completely with a lover, that ends with the inner peace of full, ecstatic love.

You rise vigorously from the bed to dress. Strangely, the lamp and table that had been knocked down by the mysterious wind are in proper place, fully upright, as when you first entered the HeathCath suite.

You smell breakfast in the air and you smile with anticipation, for this long and electrifying night has worked up your appetite.

As promised, you dine on fried eggs with bangers and mash, relaying your compliments to Mrs. Earnshaw, the chef. She and her husband dine at your side.

Stomach full, heart content, you dab your mouth clean with a cloth napkin and rise. As you turn from the table, you notice a small oil painting hanging from the wall, something you missed the night before. You examine it closely and see a handsome couple, standing side by side, smiling warmly, his arm across her shoulders, hers around his waist—the man with dark hair, the woman with gold ringlets—surrounded by a brood of happy children. You realize they are standing under the entrance gates of Wuthering Heights. You read the engraving carved on a plate attached to the bottom of the gilded wood frame:

HARETON AND CATHY EARNSHAW AND FAMILY, 1812.

With closer examination, you see a familiar locket pressed against Cathy's bosom.

You turn to thank Mr. and Mrs. Earnshaw for their wonderful hospitality and delicious food. Before you speak, you can't help noticing the identical locket, still shiny and clean, around Mrs. Earnshaw's neck.

They walk you to the door.

You thank them profusely.

They smile identical smiles, and the same mischievous twinkle seems fashioned in both pairs of eyes, as they simultaneously mouth a request that they seem certain will be obliged:

"Come again."

Acknowledgments

Thank you to my own Kathryn, the guiding light in my life, who read the new pages every day on the bus to work and shared her insightful thoughts with me each evening.

Thank you to my literary agent, Meg Ruley, who kindly reached out to me with a phone call and turned my summer into a perpetual July Fourth celebration.

Thank you to my editor, Michele Bidelspach, whose insights and hard work helped me layer the characters with even deeper emotions.

At lastly, of course, I am deeply indebted to Emily Brontë herself. Thank you for hovering over my desk and allowing me to inhabit such well-drawn, passionate characters, and retell, erotically, your great and timeless story.

About the Author

I. J. MILLER is the author of four distinct literary erotic works of fiction: *Seesaw* was translated into two languages, with over 130,000 copies in print; *Whipped* appeared in both English and German; *Sex and Love*, a collection of short stories, made its debut in the summer of 2011; *Climbing the Stairs*, a novella, was released just a year later. Miller has a master of fine arts from the American Film Institute and has taught creative writing and screenwriting at the university level.

Visit I.J. at http://www.ijmiller.com.